**Deanne Anders** was reading romance while her friends were still reading Nancy Drew, and she knew she'd hit the jackpot when she found a shelf of Harlequin Presents in her local library. Years later she discovered the fun of writing her own. Deanne lives in Florida, with her husband and their spoiled Pomeranian. During the day she works as a nursing supervisor. With her love of everything medical and romance, writing for Mills & Boon Medical Romance is a dream come true.

Once at home in sunny Brazil, **Luana DaRosa** has since lived on three different continents, though her favourite romantic locations remain the tropical places of Latin America. When not typing away at her latest romance novel, or reading about love, Luana is either crocheting, buying yarn she doesn't need, or chasing her bunnies around her house. She lives with her partner in the north-east of England.

D1322666

**Also by Deanne Anders**

*Stolen Kiss with the Single Mum*
*Sarah and the Single Dad*
*The Neurosurgeon's Unexpected Family*
*December Reunion in Central Park*

*Falling for Her Off-Limits Boss*
is **Luana DaRosa**'s debut title

Look out for more books from Luana DaRosa

Coming soon!

Discover more at millsandboon.co.uk.

# FLORIDA FLING WITH THE SINGLE DAD

DEANNE ANDERS

# FALLING FOR HER OFF-LIMITS BOSS

LUANA DaROSA

**MILLS & BOON**

First Published in Great Britain 2022
by Mills & Boon, an imprint of HarperCollins*Publishers* Ltd,
1 London Bridge Street, London, SE1 9GF

www.harpercollins.co.uk

HarperCollins*Publishers*
1st Floor, Watermarque Building,
Ringsend Road, Dublin 4, Ireland

ISBN: 978-0-263-30118-2

02/22

MIX
Paper from
responsible sources
FSC™ C007454

# FLORIDA FLING WITH THE SINGLE DAD

DEANNE ANDERS

**MILLS & BOON**

This book is dedicated to all the courageous
first responders, including our helicopter crews,
who put themselves in danger daily
as they work to save the lives of strangers.

# CHAPTER ONE

KATIE MCGEE STARED at the sign reading Flight Crew as she knocked on the door of the small modular building located beside a large helipad that contained a blue-and-gold medevac helicopter. Was she ready for this? Absolutely not. Did she have a choice? The answer to that was exactly the same. But she'd promised Alex that she would help him out and she always kept her promises.

Oh, she could have turned him down, and at first she had started to because she'd assumed it was just another of his ploys to get her to come to Key West, but he had sounded so stressed when he'd called that she had known immediately something was up and he really did need her.

So after four days of driving she was finally on the island her friend now called home. And after everything that had happened in the last six months, she was lucky she'd been given this opportunity to help her friend out. She could still be in the hospital recuperating from her injury. Or she could even be dead.

But she'd survived. And now, even though there were a lot of her coworkers who had insinuated she might not be ready to get back out on the job of flight nurse, she'd proven to both them and her family that she was just as capable now as she had been before the shooting.

So why did she feel so nervous? Maybe because it was the first time in her life that she was all alone this far away from home?

Giving up on someone coming to the door, she opened it. The smell of burnt popcorn filled her nose. It seemed at least one person was awake and moving around in the quiet building.

Stepping through the door, she noticed the oversize gray couch and the big screen TV hanging on the back wall of the large open room. It was the same in all of Heli-Care operations: the bigger the TV, the happier the crew.

She wasn't surprised to see that the room was empty. Most flight crew shifts were twenty-four hours long, so it wouldn't be unusual for the crew to be catching a nap in their rooms. If she was lucky, the assistant manager would be available to set up the required new location orientation this morning and she could be on her way. After the drive from New York, she just wanted to get moved into the rental Alex had procured for the next two months, unpack her bags and take a long, cool shower.

Letting her offended nose lead her, she walked through an open doorway and entered a small galley kitchen. A tall man stood at a trash can, emptying out a burnt paper bag that was obviously the source of the smell now overwhelming the small room. Seeing a window over the sink, she hurried over to open it. It didn't budge. Two strong hands joined hers and together they pushed up the heavy window. Light green eyes with flecks of gold met hers. Unable to look away, she stood frozen in place within the circle of this man's arms.

"Hello," the man said, "you must be Katie."

His face close to hers, she studied the chiseled cheekbones and square jaw with just enough growth that there was no doubt it was intentional. His light brown curly hair framed a face that was meant for the magazines. But it was the eyes that mesmerized her. They seemed to look deep inside her.

And then it happened. The heat of his body behind her. The knowledge that she didn't know this man. A sense of danger that she couldn't control. A shiver ran up her body and breathing became more difficult.

When would this feeling of fear stop? She was safe now. This man clearly wasn't a threat.

Or was he? Those mesmerizing green eyes seemed to see deep inside her and she couldn't help but fear what he might find if he looked too close. And that flutter of attraction that had run through her right before her survival instincts kicked in and took control.

Yeah, this man could most definitely be a threat to the peace she hoped to find here on this tiny island.

As if realizing that they were standing too close, he moved back allowing her to take a deep breath. Squaring her shoulders, she forced her breathing to slow. This was not the first impression she wanted to make on someone who would be one of her new co-workers. *Never show your weaknesses*, her father had always said.

"Sorry, I didn't mean to interrupt you. Yes, I'm Katie McGee. I'm here to set up my orientation." She tried to smile as she turned toward the man, but it was all she could do to keep herself upright. She just needed a couple more minutes for her body to realize it was safe. She'd been through this so often now that she could almost time how long it took for her heart rate to return to normal and her stomach to settle. The fact that she was recovering from these little spells of hers faster than she was only a month ago had to mean that her total recovery was getting closer. Hopefully, a couple of months in more laid-back surroundings than New York City would help her get over this anxiety that came whenever she was in a situation that she didn't feel she could control.

"Oh, sorry," the man said as he grabbed a dish towel, wiped his hands and then held one out. "Dylan. Dylan Maddox. Flight paramedic, assistant manager and, as of four days ago, acting supervisor of the Key West flight crew. Sorry about the smell. I keep forgetting to set the timer."

Katie backed away from the window and looked around the room. She wished Alex had told her more about the man he had left in charge and who would be her boss until he returned. He'd been so rushed the day he'd called and asked for her help that she'd only had time to ask just the most elementary of questions concerning the operation of the local Key West office.

Realizing he still held his hand out to her, she extended her own hand. Warm fingers grasped hers in a firm grip then released.

"It's nice to meet you, Dylan. I still can't believe Alex left the way he did. Is everything okay?" she asked.

"I don't really know. He seemed pretty shook up."

"It's not like him to leave like this. He's always been

so dependable." A trait they had in common. But it had been over a year since she had seen him. Maybe the slower pace of the island life had changed him.

"Let's go to the office. He left your paperwork with me." He led her down a short hall off the kitchen, giving her a tour of the building as they walked.

"We have four bedrooms. They're small, but no one has to share," he said as they passed several closed doors, "There are two Jack-and-Jill bathrooms between the rooms. And of course you've already seen the kitchen and our lounge."

He opened the door at the end of the hall where a small desk sat with a tall bookcase behind it. "Alex wanted me to tell you how much he appreciated you coming to help. With me taking over some of the office responsibilities and other members of the crews taking summer vacations we need the extra help."

"He's always been a good friend to me. Besides, I'm getting eight weeks in sunny Florida. My New York flight crew was jealous that I was offered the assignment." And it couldn't have come at a better time. With her family pressuring her to get back to living her life, this job gave her the distance she needed right now. "I just wish I knew he was okay."

Alex's only family as far as she knew was his mother, a well-known Broadway actress, but that wasn't something that he shared with many people. She felt sure she would have heard something if his mother was ill. With her popularity as an actress on the Broadway circuit, the media would quickly have a story out if something had happened to her.

"He didn't really share what the emergency was, but he did say he'd call when he could. And he left all the information you would need with me," Dylan said as he started going through a file on his desk. "It looks like all the paperwork for your Florida nursing license is here along with all your education requirements. I see you've got quite a collection of certifications here too."

"I take my job and my qualifications very seriously," she said. She'd go head-to-head with any of the crew here as far as skills were concerned.

"I can see that," he said as he leaned back in the chair across from her.

She felt like a small ant under a microscope while he studied her. She started to make a comment, but decided she wasn't in the position to get on the wrong side of the man who would be in charge of her till Alex returned. What was it about this man that rattled her so?

She took a moment to study the man herself. He was of average height, but his muscular built was anything but average. His light brown hair was interwoven with blond highlights that no doubt came from time spent in the Florida sun. The man could have made a million bucks as a model in New York. Not that she'd tell him that. Men with looks like his got more attention than was good for them already. She knew that from her own experience. She'd grown up with four very handsome brothers.

She straightened in the chair when he got up and closed the door behind her.

"Look, Katie," he said, sitting back down in his chair, "I'm going to be honest with you. When Alex spoke to me about bringing someone new down here, I had my misgivings. Our flight team is very tight. We work well together because we've been doing it so long. I know each one of the crew's strengths and weaknesses, and they know mine. We have each other's backs every time we go out on a flight together. Not knowing how someone is going to handle themselves out there can put us all at risk."

Was this supposed to be the welcoming speech? Because so far, she was feeling everything but welcomed. Instead, she was thinking that maybe she needed to load back into her brother's old Jeep that she'd borrowed for the trip and head back up north. But she wouldn't. She needed this time alone to get herself together. Just a little bit of time to deal with what she'd been through in the last few months. Her jaw tightened and her chin tipped up. McGees didn't run home when things got tough. McGees stayed till the job was done.

"But looking at this folder, I understand why Alex wanted you here. And it shows how much your friends mean to you that you'd leave your home to come all the way down here to help Alex out. I think that's something we can work with," Dylan said as he leaned back in the chair again.

"Alex told you about the shooting?" she asked. It wasn't as if the incident in New York hadn't made the national news. There had to be cable news stations even this far into the swamps.

"He did. He was very happy that you recovered so quickly. Something like what happened to you can change a person for life," he said.

"And the rest of the team? Do they know?" she asked. She knew as the new kid on the crew there'd be a lot of curiosity about her even if they didn't know about the shooting.

"If they do, they didn't hear it from me. I do know that they'll be happy to have some extra help. We help cover our second local office in Marathon and their staff covers ours when needed."

"I'm happy to be of use wherever you need me. I can start tomorrow," she said, hoping she didn't sound as anxious as she felt. Work had become her security blanket. It was something she was good at. It felt normal, right, when everything else felt off.

An alarm, long and shrill, sounded on a phone. Standing, he pulled his phone from his belt. She heard the doors open down the hall before he opened the door.

"Be safe," Dylan called as she watched the back of three dark blue flight suits rush down the hall.

"Always," one of the crew shouted back at him.

"What's the flight?" she asked as she joined Dylan in the doorway, her heart beating wildly with the adrenaline from the sound of the dispatcher she could hear over the crew's radios as they headed off.

"Pedestrian versus scooter in the historical district. It's too tight an area to land in, but the EMTs called it out as a head injury so we'll meet them at the airport and fly the patient into Miami where there's a neurosurgeon available."

She'd done some studying of the area's available health care before she'd started the trip down and had learned that some specialties weren't provided by the local hospital, which was why it was so important for a helicopter crew to be available in the Keys.

"Like I was saying, I can start tomorrow," she said.

The phone rang on the desk and he walked back over to answer it then put the caller on hold before handing her a large envelope on the table. "Let's discuss when you start after you get settled. The code to the keypad of your rental and a map to its location are in here. I'll get in contact with you later today and we'll set up your orientation then."

He picked up his phone and punched something into it. Her phone immediately dinged and she pulled it out of her pocket.

"My number in case you need to get lost or need anything," Dylan said.

"Thanks." She stood.

She took the envelope, then left the office and found her way back to the front entrance. The humidity that had greeted her the moment she'd driven into Miami enveloped her as she stepped outside and she remembered the promise she'd made to herself of a long shower the minute she got settled into her new place. She took out the map and studied it, surprised to find that it had been hand drawn in bright colored crayons with illustrations that appeared to be fancy stick people and squares that represented buildings. Fortunately, someone had written over the roads in ink with street names and numbers and had also labeled some of the buildings. But it was the words written in bright red crayons that made her smile. Welcome to Key West was printed in large letters across the top of the paper. Not wanting to take any chances, though, she entered the address into her phone. She'd have to ask Alex when he returned for the name of the artist responsible for such a unique map. She just hoped he didn't say it was him.

"Is she nice?" Violet asked as they climbed the steps to the little cottage that was rented out to Katie.

"She seems very nice, but that doesn't mean you can ask her a bunch of questions. She's had a long trip to get here from New York, so she's probably too tired to feel like talking right now. How about we give her a few days to settle in before you give her the Violet inquisition?" Dylan said as he adjusted the basket of fruit and cheese in his arms so that he could hug his daughter to his side.

It amazed him to think of this perfect little eight-year-old as his. Not having known about her until a year ago, he was still new to fatherhood. Some days were harder than others, but they were making it work. His only fear was that her mother would show up one day and undo everything he'd done to make Violet feel like she had a stable home here with him. The idea of her mother taking her back out on the road with her, never knowing exactly where his daughter was...that was something that he couldn't let himself dwell on.

"How many are a few? Two?" she asked.

"Honey, if you make it to two days without driving this poor woman crazy with your questions, it will be a miracle." The door opened and the woman they'd been discussing stood in front of him. Her dark blond hair was down now and it fell past her shoulders and she was wearing an old Mets T-shirt and a pair of torn shorts. She looked much different from the every-hair-perfectly-in-place woman he had met earlier that day. Now she was a woman he could picture himself spending time with.

And where had that thought come from? He didn't have time or any interest in spending time with anyone besides his daughter.

"Ah, hello," Katie said as she blinked her eyes against the sunlight.

Her hair was a bit mussed up and her feet were bare.

Did they wake her up from a nap? He should have taken his own advice and let her settle in before he came over, but he was worried he'd been rude this morning. He wanted to make sure she felt welcome in the community. Even if she was only here temporarily.

What Alex had somehow forgotten to mention was that the big-city girl from New York was also a looker. And right then it was taking all his concentration and the fact that his daughter stood beside him to keep his eyes from a pair of long legs that brought out a very unwanted reaction from him.

"Sorry, we should have waited until tomorrow, but Violet wanted to meet you." He smiled down at the little girl, who was studying the newcomer seriously. "We won't disturb you. I'll just give you this—" he pushed the basket he'd bought at the grocery store into her arms "—and now we'll let you get back to it. I mean get back to resting or whatever."

As he tripped over the words coming out of his mouth, he tried to understand what was happening to him. Yes, this woman with her sleepy emerald bedroom eyes was damn sexy right then, but he didn't even know her. She was a temporary coworker. That was all she could be.

Setting down the basket, she bent down to his daughter and held out her hand. "Hello, Violet. My name is Katie. I'm so glad to meet you."

"I'm glad to meet you too, but I'm not allowed to ask you any questions for at least two days," his daughter said with a smile that could charm even the most hardened heart.

"Really? And why is that?" Katie asked.

"My daddy says you've had a long trip and are too

tired. Are you too tired?" Violet asked, the determined glint in her eyes telling him that there would be no stopping his daughter now.

Katie looked up at him and smiled before turning back to Violet. "I think I could handle a few questions. Would you like to come in?"

"Can we, Daddy?" Violet asked, her eyes begging him to let her have her way. If she ever realized just how hard it was for him to say no to her he'd be in big trouble.

"Are you sure?" he asked. They did need to discuss a few things before the next day.

"Of course. I've still got a few bags to unpack, but most everything is out of the way." She bent to pick the basket up, but he beat her to it.

"I've got this. Do you like the place?" he asked. It would be a little awkward if she started complaining about the cottage.

"I love it! When Alex said he had the perfect place for me to stay, I didn't expect anything like this," she said as they headed inside. For someone who had been half-asleep just seconds before, her face was now animated with a pleasure that for some inexplicable reason pleased him to no end. "You need to see the view in the back. And there's a path that leads down to the water. It's amazing."

Violet giggled from behind the two of them as Katie led them to the large sliding doors at the back of the cottage.

"We think it's the perfect view too," he said. Turning back to his daughter, he winked.

"You do?" Katie asked as she faced them. "You've been here before?"

"My friend Janna lived here for a few weeks, but she had to go home with her parents," Violet said, her tone leaving no room for doubt that she was not happy with her friend's parents.

"Oh, is that how Alex heard about the property?" Katie asked Dylan.

"Sort of. He asked me about a rental and I told him this place was open. I've only had it on the rental market for a couple months."

"You've only had it on the rental market for a couple months?" Katie said, repeating his words. "You own the cottage? You're my landlord?"

"Yes. I assumed Alex would have mentioned my name and the fact that I owned the rental." But there seemed to be a lot that Alex had forgotten to mention. Like how long it would be before he would return and let Dylan get back to his own responsibilities.

"And we're neighbors too," Violet said as she pushed past her father. "Come see."

Violet walked over to the sliding doors and slid one open. "That's our place next door. Isn't it pretty?"

They walked out to the small deck that he had built onto the back of the cottage, so that Katie could see the slightly larger cottage only a few yards away.

"It is very pretty. I love that color of green," Katie said before looking over at him. "You didn't think you should tell me this morning that we would be living next door or that you were my new landlord?"

"I really did think that Alex had told you. It's not like him to forget something like that." Which had him wondering even more what exactly was going on in Alex's life?

"Dylan… I mean Daddy…let me help with all the

colors," Violet said. "And he bought me my own tool belt just like his…but it's pink. Do you like pink?"

"I do like pink," Katie told his daughter before turning back to him. "Did you build this yourself?"

"We both did," Violet answered before he could speak. "It's our investment property. Daddy says we need it so that we can pay for our house before he's gray and wrinkled."

"Violet, why don't you run down to the water and see if there are any shells for Katie? I bet she'd like to collect a few to take back to New York," Dylan said. He waited until his daughter was out of earshot before continuing their conversation. "Sorry, she gets a little excited when she meets new people."

"She's adorable. I just wish I had some of her energy," Katie said. She pushed her hair away from her face, but the soft gulf breeze blew it right back. "Would you like some water? I'm afraid that's all I have right now. I should have stopped at the store on the way here, but I was so tired of driving. I don't think I, or the Jeep, could have gone any further."

"No, we're good," he said. "I was surprised when Alex said you were driving down. That's a trip not too many people would be willing to make."

"It seemed like a good time for a road trip. You know, get some fresh air. Clear the mind. I am glad, though, that I don't have to think about that return trip for a few weeks. I was surprised with how tired you can get just sitting in a seat for twelve hours."

"I'm sorry we got interrupted this morning. And I admit even though I thought Alex had mentioned my owning the cottage, I should have discussed it with you this morning." He'd known the minute he'd gotten off the phone call from the regional office that he should have made some comment about being her landlord instead of just throwing a map and key code at her as she walked out the door.

He had a lot to learn about being a landlord.

"It was a little crazy this morning. How did the flight go?" she asked, taking a seat on one of the wicker chairs he'd purchased for the deck. It was strange seeing this big-city woman in an old ratty shirt and shorts appearing so at home on the deck of his little cottage. He'd only known her for a day, even less, but something about her intrigued him.

Or was it just his need to take care of everyone? He'd learned from Alex and her employee file that Katie had been through some difficult times and he knew they weren't over yet. No one went through what she had without coming out scarred.

And he couldn't help but think that the last time a woman had interested him this much, it hadn't ended well. Except for Violet. Violet made all the heartache her mother had caused him worth it.

"He had an open-head injury, but the prognosis was good when the crew dropped him off at the Miami trauma unit. We'll check back with the hospital tomorrow and see how he's doing," he said as he took a matching chair across from her.

"Do you get many of those? Pedestrian versus vehicles injuries? Most everyone I saw on my way to the cottage was on a bike or walking in this area."

"There are more than a few tourists that decide getting on a bicycle after drinking or driving a scooter when they haven't been on one for years is a good idea. Fortunately, most only end up with skinned knees or broken arms that can be treated in the local hospital. But there are enough of the serious injuries to keep us busy flying back and forth to the mainland. Of course, we have our share of boating accidents and drownings too."

"It sounds much different from what I'm use to in New York," Katie said. She was looking into the thin line of trees that separated the cottage from the water, but he could tell her mind was somewhere else. Was it back to the night of the shooting? Alex had told him enough about the incident that he knew she'd required several weeks in the hospital.

"About what I said this morning, about me having doubts about you coming here at first, I don't want you to think we aren't glad to have you. You will find that our small crew works well together and I have no doubts that they'll be happy you are here to help. And with Alex speaking so highly of you, I do think this is a good place for you." Hearing his daughter coming up the path, he stood to go.

"I understand. The New York office was concerned about me coming back after the shooting, but I proved myself to them."

"I know. Alex told me they were impressed." He didn't tell her that Alex himself had mentioned some concerns after talking to her, though his boss hadn't been able to pinpoint what was wrong. "How about we start with your orientation tomorrow morning?"

"Look what I found for you, Katie," Violet said as she climbed the step up to the deck as she held out two shells for Katie to examine.

"They're very pretty. I'll have to get something to

keep them in so I can take them back to New York with me." Katie took the shells from his daughter.

"We have a bunch at our house if you want to come see them," his daughter offered.

"Why don't we let her get settled first," Dylan said as they walked back through the cottage to the front door.

"But…" Violet started to protest.

"What have I told you about our neighbors?" Dylan asked his daughter, brushing his hand over her curls. It was the only thing she'd gotten from him. Her slim build and baby blue eyes were a replica of her mother.

"They're not here for our entertainment. We have to respect their privacy." Violet repeated to him in a sad singsong voice.

"What time do you want me at the office?" Katie asked as they reached the door.

"Shift change is seven. If there isn't a call we'll take a ride over the islands so you can get your bearings. Then we'll get your schedule set up."

"Sounds great. I'll see you then. And, Violet," she said, calling out to his daughter who was skipping up and down the sidewalk, "maybe you can come back to help me gather some shells another day?"

His daughter jumped with joy and he listened all the way home to the description of all the shells that she hoped to collect for her new friend, Katie.

# CHAPTER TWO

THEY LIFTED OFF the ground and as the helicopter skids rose, so did Katie's spirit. She'd missed this when she'd been injured and unable to fly. She'd missed all of it. The tight quarters, the equipment bags, the speed as they climbed higher and then shot through the air. There had been no way for her to accept that her job as a flight nurse was over. This was as much a part of her life as breathing. It wasn't just what she did. It was who she was. It was why she had worked so hard to get back in the air as fast as possible.

Then she looked down and caught her breath. While Key West was larger than she had first assumed, from the air, with its small landmass surrounded by an unending view of blue water, it was like looking down on a small neighborhood in New York City. And the trees. Everywhere she looked there were colorful flowering trees that based on their size had to be hundreds of years old. That was something she didn't see much of in the city.

"Roy, can you take us south and then north up Highway One?" Dylan said over the headset.

"That's the highway I came in on. The only way in or out, right?" she said, speaking into the headset.

"It's the only road access, but we have a lot of boat traffic. We get called out for boating accident victims a few times a month. We also have a port where the cruise ships stop." He pointed over to where a large ship sat. "Occasionally there's a passenger that needs to be flown out to Miami, but most of the time their passengers end up in the local hospital for minor problems. Most of what we see is traumas or transfers from the hospital to a higher level of care."

"And this is what is known as the southernmost tip of the island," Roy said as they passed over a small area of rocks and water before they turned and headed north.

They quickly crossed the rest of the island and were following the path of the highway that would take them all the way up the coast and back to the mainland when both Dylan's and Roy's radios went off. She listened as the county dispatcher gave out coordinates of a motor vehicle crashand the channel on their radio where they would receive info on their landing location.

"Ten-four. We're in the air and responding to call. ETA under five minutes," Roy answered back to the dispatcher as they continued heading north.

"We're taking the call?" Katie said as she opened a drawer labeled IV Supplies and began to prepare a bag of fluids. Fortunately, all the Heli-Care copters were stocked the same, with their drawers labeled for quick access. "I thought this was an orientation flight."

"The Marathon crew the dispatcher was talking about is our sister crew. They're already on the scene and have requested backup. There must be more than two injured needing to be flown out to Miami. You said you were ready. Is there a problem?" Dylan said as he began checking their bags for supplies that could be needed if an intubation was required.

"No, of course not," she said as the adrenaline began to pump through her. If only she didn't feel like an trainee that was about to perform for their preceptor. She'd done these calls hundreds of times. Why was she second-guessing herself? This was just what she was wanting a few minutes ago.

"Switching to channel three for landing zone instructions," Roy said.

She listened over the headphones as Roy contacted the local fire department, which had secured the landing zone on the highway. As they got closer, she could see where traffic was backed up for at least a mile headed both north and south. Bringing traffic to a standstill on the only road in and out of the islands had to put more pressure on the first responders.

"This is Heli-Care Key West awaiting instructions for landing," Roy announced over the radio.

She saw another helicopter lift off into the sky and head north, freeing up the area for their own landing.

As the helicopter lifted, a voice came over the channel "This is local Conch Key fire and rescue. Is that you, Roy?"

"Yeah, Jones. What's happening down there? All we got from dispatch was MVC. Is the landing zone secured?" Roy asked.

"Zone secured, but it's a mess down here. Camper jackknifed into oncoming lane. Driver and passenger of second vehicle are headed to Miami for trauma. They're working on a passenger in the vehicle pulling the camper right now," the firefighter said. "The sooner you get down here the better."

Katie's stomach clinched as they started into their final approach. She forced herself to take a deep breath, and then glanced over to see that Dylan was watching her. "I'm fine. Just a few nerves. New place and everything."

Her confidence might have taken a beating, but except for a few bruises she was fit and ready to work. She just had to remind herself of that sometimes.

The skids touched down, and the two of them quickly unloaded their stretcher and scene bag as they stayed below the rotors.

Following the man she assumed was Jones, they hurried toward the scene. What was once a small travel trailer was now in pieces scattered across the middle of the road with a small compact car crushed beside it. There was no doubt that the driver and any passengers in the vehicle would be in critical condition.

Crossing a small medium, she saw a pickup truck on its side against a tree with several firefighters surrounding it. An ambulance crew was stationed beside the truck, but it was easy to see that their patient was still trapped inside the vehicle.

"What's the holdup?" Dylan asked as they approached the EMTs.

"The door crushed in on impact and they needed to use their rescue equipment on the victims in the car first. They were both unresponsive on arrival. They said this guy was talking when they arrived."

She followed Dylan as he moved to where the first responders worked. From the language of the firefighters that were operating the Jaws of Life, things weren't going well.

"How's our patient?" he asked as he moved to look

inside the crushed front end of the truck. "You couldn't get him out through the window?"

"The way the top folded in on it, it was faster to go in this way," a man closest to the wrecked truck said. "When the trailer jackknifed, it hit the side rail before hitting the tree. The whole truck was crushed."

"We're in," a firefighter said, and then moved back as Dylan moved to the opening.

Leaving the stretcher, Katie grabbed their bag. An older man, she estimated to be in his fifties, was still attached by his seat belt in the driver's seat.

"I thought they said he was talking," she said, opening their scene bag and pulling out a collar to secure the man's neck.

"He was until about two minutes ago," a fireman said as he joined them.

"Can you bring the backboard and stretcher over here," she asked the him as she watched Dylan check the man's pulse.

"He's got a pulse, but his respiration is shallow. He needs intubating but there's no way to do it without moving him first. Let's get him out and secured." Dylan took the cervical collar from her and secured it before moving back to let the firefighters transfer him to the stretcher.

She grabbed an endotracheal tube and laryngoscope and readied them for intubation. Handing them off to Dylan as soon as the man had been strapped to the backboard, she pulled out an IV kit and started working on getting access. Going for a big bore site, she cleaned the man's antecubital vein. As she inserted the needle, she suddenly became aware of a group of men crowding her back.

A bunch of nosy first responders was the last thing she needed to deal with right now.

She flushed the line and hung the bag of fluid she'd prepared earlier. Turning around, she gave the crowd of firefighters and EMTs a look that would have had her older brothers shaking in their NYPD-issued boots. Of course this group of adrenaline junkies didn't have the good sense to give her some space.

"Problem?" Dylan asked as he slid the tube into their patient's trachea.

"No. I've got this," she said as she applied the patches and hooked the man to the portable monitor. His heart rate was elevated, in the one-twenties. The men behind her pressed in even closer.

"The whole bunch of you need to take a step back." When they didn't move, she raised her voice. *"Now."*

As she turned back to her patient, she heard some of the men laugh while others complained. As she and Dylan began to rush their patient back to the helicopter, she overheard one of the men say that she must be a rookie.

They'd been on-site just over ten minutes and part of that time had been waiting for their patient to be cleared from the wreckage. The two of them had worked together as if they had for years. There was no one she had ever worked with that could have done things any better.

"Ignore them," Dylan said as she climbed into the helicopter. "They're just curious about a newcomer. It's one of the problems with living on a small island. It won't last long."

"I handled it," she said, then put the comments she'd heard behind her. There were more important things here than whether a bunch of first responders liked her. She wasn't there to be liked. She was there to keep this guy alive till they could hand him off to the closest trauma unit.

She had begun her assessment before the skids even left the ground, calling out her findings to Dylan as he radioed report to the receiving hospital in Miami.

"I'm only getting breath sounds on the right side and his oxygen sats are in the mideighties," she told him after he signed off the radio.

"Pneumo?" Dylan asked. "Or tube placement?"

Was this a test? With the extent of the man's injuries it could easily be a pneumothorax, but without an X-ray to verify placement or determine if there was a pneumo, the first thing she would normally do was replace the tube. Of course, telling her boss that his tube might not be correctly placed could be awkward, but if they were going to work together they would need honesty. That was something her father had drilled into all his children. If you couldn't trust your partner, who could you trust?

"My instincts say it's a pneumo, but we have another thirty minutes of flight time so we should replace the tube first," she said.

"Should?" he asked. One eyebrow rose above those amazing eyes that were bearing down on her.

"I'm going to replace the endotracheal tube in case there's a problem with placement," she said with more confidence than she felt. If she'd been back on her own home turf she would have told her partner what she was about to do and unless they'd had any objections she'd have moved on.

Not waiting for Dylan's consent, she pulled out the proper ET tube and supplies. After removing the tube placed by Dylan, she placed the new tube in seconds. Checking placement with her stethoscope she listened to both sides of the man's chest. She shook her head. "Still no sound on the left side."

"His sats are still holding in the high eighties and his blood pressure is stable right now. I think we can hold off and let the trauma center put in the chest tube. You agree?" Dylan asked.

"I do. The best thing for this guy is to get him to a surgeon. He's holding his pressure right now, but his stomach's tight. He's bleeding somewhere internally," she said as she was adjusting the IV fluids to give the patient a bolus to help replace the blood she knew he was losing. She reached into the man's pants pocket, checking one and then the other and finally locating a billfold. She handed it to Dylan. "The hospital will want this. His phone must still be in the truck. Maybe one of the officers will find it and can notify his family."

"Fifteen-minute ETA," Roy said over the head-phones. "Heli-Care Marathon should be cleared out by the time we arrive. Then it's back home for us, right, boss? I think Katie's pretty much got a good lay of the land by now, don't you?"

"Ten-four, Roy. I think we can head home as soon as we unload. Time to get back to the surf and sand." Dylan turned toward her with a smile that sent her heartbeat racing. This man could be a real charmer when he wanted to be.

"Whatever you say, boss," she said as she smiled back, "whatever you say."

* * *

"How did the newbie do, boss? I heard you got dispatched together." Katie heard a male voice ask. Stopping before she entered the office, she tried to remember if this was one of the two men she'd met that morning. Feeling self-conscious, and a little bit curious, she waited to hear Dylan's answer.

"She's not a newbie; she has as many years as you do in flying. And stop calling me 'boss.'"

Okay, he hadn't sung her praises, but he had let the man know she was an experienced flight nurse.

"I heard she let the guys shake her up like a newbie," the man, who was really starting to get on her nerves said. What was his name? Casey? No, that was the flight nurse going off shift.

"You know we need someone we can count on, not some big-city nurse who doesn't understand how we do things around here," the man continued.

"I heard she had a bad scene in New York and took a bullet for her patient," a female voice said, "that sounds like someone you can count on to me."

If she wasn't mistaken it was Summer's voice that she heard defending her now. It had to be since she was the only woman on the shift till tomorrow morning. She'd known she was going to like the petite blonde the moment she'd met her. Though, she did wish everyone didn't know the story of her being injured at a scene. It seemed nothing traveled faster than a juicy story. Or maybe Alex told Summer before he'd left? She'd asked Katie several questions that morning about where Alex could have taken off to. As if Katie had any more information than the rest of them. If anyone was to know where Alex was, it should have been Dylan.

Alex had always been so vague about his family. It couldn't have been easy having the paparazzi hounding him and his mother when he was growing up. And he'd never mentioned anything about his father.

"I also heard she choked the first time she went out on a flight in New York after the shooting," the man answered Summer back. "That's not cool. You know we all rely on each other here. I'm sure we're just a bunch of beach bums to her, but we can't go around insulting our firefighters and EMTs without ruffling some feathers. We depend on those guys for our safety."

"It seems to me you've all been spending too much time listening to gossip that doesn't have anything to do with you or your job. I hear what you're saying, Max. I don't know exactly what happened when she went back to work, but I can assure you she was fully cleared to work before she left New York and she did a great job on the scene today. I'd be happy to fly with her anytime. And yes, Katie's new here so maybe the guys at the scene should have given her some room."

As the door started to swing open, Katie turned and rushed toward the kitchen. The only thing that would be more embarrassing than overhearing her coworkers' objections to her working there would be for her to get caught.

An older man came into the kitchen and gave her a weak smile before heading off to the lounge where she heard the television volume increase. When Summer didn't follow him, Katie figured she'd gone to her quarters to rest.

The smart thing to do was to just pretend that she hadn't heard the conversation, but was that really the right thing to do? If she was already having problems with the staff not trusting her, what future did she have here?

But that was just her lack of confidence talking. Alex said himself that he'd be willing to fly with her. She couldn't ask for anything more than that as his vote of confidence in her.

All she had ever wanted to be was a flight nurse since the first time she'd seen a helicopter take off of the roof on the hospital where she had first started as a new nurse. She'd made that her focus for three years, taking classes and getting certifications and experience in the intensive care units so she could meet the necessary qualifications. Her father had bragged to all his buddies on the police force that his daughter was now flying the skies of New York saving lives. She'd used her father's pride in her as motivation at rehab so she could get back the physical stamina she needed to return to work.

Alex knew all this about her. He knew that she would never let anything stand in the way of her doing her job. But Dylan? He didn't know her at all.

"Hey," Dylan said, startling her as he stepped into the kitchen, "I thought you were going to come finish your paperwork."

"Sorry, I just stopped to get a bottle of water." She held up the bottle before following him back to the office.

"How much did you hear?" he asked as he shut the door behind them.

She should have known Dylan was an everything-up-front kind of guy. He had known she was headed to the office right behind the two flight crew members and while he could have pretended that she hadn't overheard them, he wasn't going to do it.

"Enough," she said. Enough to know she was already starting off on the wrong foot. He'd told her that this was a good crew that worked closely together. Her plan had been to keep her head down and work hard for the next two months, but on her first flight she'd managed to bring too much unwanted attention to herself.

"You want to talk about it?" he asked as he leaned back on the corner of the desk.

"Not really," she replied. What could she say? That all of this was because of the simple fact she couldn't handle that feeling of defenselessness she felt whenever someone came up behind her? Didn't that just sound like a strong, capable nurse you would want on your team?

"And why is that, Katie? Afraid someone might see a kink in that armor you're wearing? We've all got our issues. Take Max. He can't handle a puking patient so he carries an emesis bag with him at all times. It's how he handles it." His eyes searched hers.

Was it possible that this man could see the fear she barely kept hidden? Would he see how broken she was? She'd been able to keep her anxiety to herself, even hiding it from her family of hard-core police officers. How could this man see inside her so easily? She'd thought she was safe because Alex wasn't there. It seemed she was wrong. Dylan saw too much.

"Look, I've been through a lot the last few months, but one thing I know for sure is that nothing that happened has affected my caring for my patients." Like her father had told her when she'd come out of surgery, she couldn't lie in bed feeling sorry for herself. If she wanted to show the coward that had shot her that he hadn't won, she had to get up and get back to work.

And that was what she had done. Only it hadn't been as easy as her father had made it sound. She'd healed on the outside, but there was still something on the inside that wasn't ready to move on. But that wasn't something she was going to admit to Dylan.

"Alex told me everything he knew about your injuries. I know you were shot by some punk who didn't care who he hurt while he was trying to finish off his first victim. I know you placed yourself in front of your patient and took a bullet. I know that your patient died with you lying injured over him. And while Alex seemed to think that you were back a hundred percent, I find that a little hard to believe," Dylan said, his eyes still locked with hers.

"What do you mean? I've done everything my doctors have asked. I worked my butt off in rehab." She broke contact with him, afraid to see the pity she'd seen so much of when her coworkers had come to visit her in the hospital.

"I'm not questioning that you're up to the job here. I have no complaints about your performance today." He ran his hands through the curls that were working their way down into his eyes. "Look, Katie, I know it's hard to admit that you need help. It's hard for everyone. I just want you to know that if you want to talk to someone I'm here."

"What, like you want to be my new counselor? You have to know I've already gone through all the counseling sessions that are required after a traumatic injury. It has to be there in my employment record somewhere." The vulnerability from having this stranger know so much about her made her want to strike out. What did he really know? What did anyone know about her life now?

"Have you ever had to do it? Sat down in some office and bare all your personal feelings and failings?" she asked, knowing what his answer would be. There was no way this tough guy would ever admit that he had some type of weakness.

"Yes, actually I have. It was only once, but after a particularly bad scene when I was first starting off I was having problems sleeping. I have a friend who went into psychology who has an office in Islamorada so I went to talk to him," Dylan said as he leaned back in his chair.

"Did it help?" she asked, "Did it make any difference?"

"I can't say it was an instant fix-all, but it felt like just admitting to someone and sharing that I was having a problem with what I had seen, and having him say that it was okay, even expected, for me to have the reaction I was having helped. Soon after that, we started doing debriefing after our flights. I think that's helped us all."

"But that's different. Your friend wasn't in a position to decide if you were able to work or not. Your future wasn't being determined by him." And that didn't sound a bit paranoid, did it?

"I'm just saying if you need someone to talk to, I'm here for you just as I'd be there for any of the crew. Or I could see about getting you set up with my friend here if you think that would work better for you. He's a good man." Dylan stood and handed her a folder. "Here's the paperwork that you need to finish. You can bring it by the cottage if you want. I'll email you a copy of the schedule I'm reworking before I leave today."

"Thanks," she said as she took the folder and turned to leave. She knew she should say more. He was only trying to do his job. She should be grateful that he cared about her. After all, she was only there for the next two months. All he really had to care about was whether she showed up for her shifts or not. But that didn't make it any easier to take.

"And, Katie," Dylan said from behind her, "don't worry about Max. He can be a little grumpy, but put him out on a scene and he'll have your back."

She turned around and met Dylan's eyes as he added, "We'll *all* have your back."

# CHAPTER THREE

KATIE'S PHONE RANG as soon as she opened the door to her cottage. After her talk with Dylan, she was sure it was her counselor calling again. The woman was a nice person. It wasn't her fault that she had been assigned to Katie's case, which required her to check on her once a month. If only the woman didn't ask so many questions.

Seeing that instead it was her younger brother, she answered the call. "Hey, Mikey."

"Sis, why haven't you called anyone? Matt's been going crazy wondering if his Jeep is okay," her brother said.

"I'm glad to hear that it wasn't me he was worried about," she teased. Laying down the folder of paperwork she had to fill out onto the small dining table, she moved over to the French doors and opened the curtains. Paradise was just outside her back door. It was the perfect place for her to escape her worries.

"You know that all of us worry about you, especially now that you're over fourteen hundred miles away. You sure you don't want to come home?" Her brother had been asking the same question every day since she left New York.

She knew that her brothers loved her and she could always count on them to have her back. If only they understood she needed a little space right now.

"Katie, did you hear me? Is everything okay?" her brother asked.

"Sorry. I just got home from the office and my mind is kind of scattered," she said. After grabbing a bottle of water from the fridge, she unlocked the back door.

"How did it go? Did you get to see your friend Alex?" Mikey asked.

"No, he's still out of town on some type of family emergency. But I did get to go up today," she said. Stepping out onto the deck, she took a deep breath. The air was heavy with a humidity she didn't think she could ever get used to, but the soft breeze coming from the water made up for it.

"How was that?" he asked. "Any issues?"

If she told her little brother about almost losing her temper with the other emergency responders, he'd know something was wrong. McGees were known for their patience, and normally she was the most patient of the siblings. With four brothers, she had to be.

"No, it was great. I wish you could see this place. It's beautiful. The water is so blue and everywhere you look there's some tree or bush blooming. And the pace seems so much slower here."

Something moved in the short bushes that backed up to the deck. She eased back toward the French door even though her mind told her she was safe. A large yellow beak peaked out of a bush before it disappeared through the trees. A bird? She took the stairs down from the deck and followed the sandy path that Violet had used to get to the water.

"That's good, right? Not that I want you to get used to it. We still need you here in New York," her brother said. "What about that counselor from the precinct? You still talking with her?"

Hadn't she already dealt with this enough today? No one understood how hard it was to bare your soul to a stranger who clearly did not understand that all she needed was to work and put the shooting behind her. She wasn't going to let this one incident define her life.

She stopped on the path, not daring to even breathe. A large white bird stood a mere five feet in front of her. Its dark legs, long and spindly, made it over three feet tall. Was it dangerous? Would it follow her if she ran back into the house?

Before she could decide what to do, it unfolded a pair of impossibly large wings, making its size even more intimidating. With a couple flaps it soared into the sky, leaving her standing there with her mouth open. She stood and watched as its magnificent wings took it out of sight.

The sound of her brother's voice brought her back down to reality.

"Oh, my goodness, Mikey. There was this bird. This really big bird…like three-foot-tall big. It was beautiful. So beautiful. It was white and…" She stopped talking, suddenly hit with a need she hadn't felt since… since before her life had been shattered into a million meaningless pieces.

"I've got to go. I'll call you later," she said as she ended the call and raced up the path to the cottage as fast as she could. She tried to keep the image in her mind.

She found her sketch pad and pencils in an unpacked

box stuck in the back of the closet. Rushing back out-side, she sat on a wicker chair and pulled a small table in front her where she could arrange her supplies, and then she began. In minutes the image of a beautiful, but strong bird began to take shape. As the light began to fade with the setting sun in front of her, she filled in the background with the many different shrubs and flowering trees that she was just beginning to notice. She'd have to ask Dylan the names of all these plants. Maybe she could buy one of the smaller ones to bring back home with her.

Finally setting her sketch pad down, she realized how much she had enjoyed the last few hours. She couldn't remember the last time she'd truly relaxed for that long. It was like she had found her happy place, even if it would be for only a few weeks. She was right. All she needed was a little peace and quiet, and soon her life would be back to normal.

She headed inside and saw the folder she had meant to get back to Dylan. Before putting her art supplies away, she sat down and finished the paperwork. A peek in the mirror told her she needed to do something with her hair as the breeze had made a mess of it. She pulled it back into a careless knot then washed her face.

Checking her phone, she wasn't surprised to see that she'd missed a call from her brother. He must think she was crazy for hanging up on him like she had. She'd take a picture of her drawing and send it to him before she went to bed. He'd understand then. He'd always been the only one in the family that understood how much her art meant to her.

It was only after she rang the doorbell of Dylan's cottage that she realized it was probably too late for her to be visiting her neighbor. Why hadn't she thought to text him? He'd given her his number for things just like this. She started back down the stairs.

Dylan stood in the door staring down at something he'd never seen before: a smiling Katie. She waited on the bottom step of his home and something about that smile made his insides suddenly warm and weak.

"I'm so sorry. I wanted to get the paperwork back to you. I meant to get it to you earlier, but I got busy and I'm afraid I didn't realize how late it was." She held the folder out to him. "I guess I could blame it on the bird, but it really was all my fault."

"A bird? Why do I feel like there's a story there?" he asked. She really wasn't making much sense, but he wanted her to keep talking. There was something different about her tonight. Or maybe not different. Maybe this was the real Katie McGee. The one his friend Alex had told him about that was always smiling and fun. The intense woman he'd been with earlier that day had shown no sign of either of those two things.

"I was just in the backyard and there was this big white bird. It wasn't a stork. I've seen pictures of them before, they're stockier. But it was tall and it had these dark legs and big wings," Katie said.

"It sounds like a great white heron. We have them everywhere. There's a wildlife refuge set up for them here in the Keys. They're very common around here," he explained.

"A white heron? I knew there were blue herons, but not white ones. Aren't they beautiful?" she asked, another smile lighting her face.

"Very, beautiful," he said. Her eyes sparkled with

excitement that he saw every day when his eight-year-old made a new discovery. There were so many wonders on the island that he suddenly wanted to show her. So many things that he knew she would find enjoyment in.

Like a gust of wind, his daughter suddenly blew past him and down the steps to where Katie stood.

"Hey, Katie, what's that?" Violet asked.

His mind switched gears and he was reminded that his daughter was his priority. Not spending time with his new neighbor.

"I had a visitor today in the back of the house. Your father says it's a white heron," Katie said, passing Violet her drawing.

"Daddy took me to the park where there's a lot of these up in the trees in their nests. It's where they take care of their babies," Violet said, then handed back the sketch pad. "Maybe next time you can go with us. Can she, Daddy?"

Dylan looked down at the two of them, Violet with her hopeful eyes that had seen way too much for her eight years of life. And Katie, who just hours ago had been determined to prove to everyone that she was fine but anyone that looked at her could see the shadows under her eyes. While the first one held his heart, the latter brought out that old protective side of him that he knew he couldn't acknowledge. Not where Katie was concerned. He'd had enough of women coming into his life and wreaking havoc before leaving him to pick up the pieces.

"We'll see. How about you go jump in the tub? It's getting late. You did say you wanted to ride the bus tomorrow," he reminded her.

"Okay, but can I go over to Katie's when I get home tomorrow?" she asked with puppy dog eyes.

"We'll see," he said. He'd learned early that his daughter was a true negotiator with a talent that had gotten the best of him more than once. And once she got the answer she wanted, there was no way budging her no matter what might have come up. "Katie might have plans."

"Unless I'm working I don't have any plans," Katie said.

"Great. There's a big book in the library at school that has pictures of birds. I'll finish the book I checked out last week before I go to bed and check that one out if it's there. That way I can teach you about all the birds we have here," Violet said.

"There's not going to be any reading time tonight it you don't get in the tub. Now," he told his daughter.

"Night, Katie," Violet called as she rushed back up the stairs and disappeared into the house.

"Sorry. If she gets to be too much just let me know. We've had to have more than a few conversations concerning boundaries since she came to live with me." He smiled at the memory of that first conversation when he'd brought a date to dinner, and before the meal was over his daughter had somehow gotten the woman's whole life story out of her, including some things that had been more than enough to make him realize there wouldn't be a second date.

"I'm sure we'll be fine. I can't wait to see the book she's talking about," Katie said. "So, not married?"

"No. It's just me and Violet. Her mother and I were never married." He didn't see any reason to add that he hadn't even known he had a daughter until she and her mother had shown up on the houseboat he was living on at the time. "Lilly, that's Violet's mother, is a bit of a free spirit."

"Well, she seems to be a very happy little girl. I can tell you're doing a good job with her," Katie said. "And I've taken enough of your time. I'll check my email for my schedule."

"If you need to take some time to get settled just let me know. Alex leaves the scheduling up to me and with me filling in for him I've done some rearranging."

"I'm sure whenever you've scheduled me will be fine. Like I said, I don't have any plans right now." She started down the path before turning around and calling back, "Good night."

He didn't take his eyes off her until she had gotten to her front door and disappeared inside.

The woman was one big complication in his life. But there was something about Katie that made him want to peel back all those layers of armor that surrounded her to find out exactly who she was before her life had changed the night she'd been shot. But how deep would he have to go to find that woman? Did she even exist anymore? Or had the trauma she'd survived changed her forever?

And then there was that spark of attraction he'd felt from the first time they'd met, before he'd known who she was. Before he'd known she was just one more person passing through his life.

"I like her," his daughter said as she ducked under his arm where he stood in the doorway staring across at Katie's cottage.

"I think I do too," he said before turning and shutting the door behind them, wishing he could shut out the warning bells telling him this woman could be trouble. No matter how attracted he might be to his next-door neighbor, the last thing he needed was to find himself involved with another woman who was just passing through the islands. He'd had enough of those relationships even before he had learned that he had a daughter. A daughter that needed the stability she didn't get for the first seven years of her life.

But he couldn't deny how easy it would be to forget his past mistakes after seeing the wide-eyed beauty that had just shown up beaming with excitement over a common white bird.

# CHAPTER FOUR

KATIE FOLLOWED SUMMER into the hospital ambulance entrance as the other nurse explained the transfer process between the hospitals. They'd been dispatched to fly a patient from the local hospital to a hospital in Miami that could provide further cardiac diagnostic and treatment for his heart arrhythmia. With the man symptomatic as he continued going in and out of supraventricular tachycardia, the doctor in Miami had requested that he be transferred immediately by air.

"We're a small hospital, but you can't beat the care. It's just impossible for us to provide a lot of the specialties that our patients can get in the big-city hospitals," Summer said as they passed through another door that led to a hallway with an elevator.

"And the staff is always good to work with," the bubbly nurse continued, and not for the first time that day Katie wondered if Dylan had assigned her with Summer because he knew Katie had overheard Summer sticking up for her in his office.

Not that she was going to complain. If he'd put her with Max for her first shift things could have turned into a nightmare. She had enough of those at night. She didn't want to spend her days that way.

"A lot of the flight crew staff pick up days in the ER when they can," Summer continued as the bell on the elevator rang and she pressed the only button for an upper floor. "Does the crew in New York do that?"

"Several of us do. It's a good way to keep our hospital skills up. And it's a nice change, too, from the packup and deliver speed that we are used to on flights." And it had been Katie's backup plan if she'd had to give up flying after the shooting.

"I know. And it's nice to talk to your patients sometimes too. Most of our flights are spent with patients that are too sick to talk. And the flights are usually so short that we spend most of our time too busy to get to know them," Summer said.

So Summer was a people person. She could see that and even appreciate it.

Katie had been that way too. But then things had changed. It seemed her whole life had changed because of one night. It wasn't that she didn't like people. She did like most people on a one-to-one basis. But put her in a crowd, like the one she could see in the room they were about to enter, and the stress of being surrounded by so many strangers was just too much.

She had learned to work around her anxiety. No one thought there was something wrong with a nurse if she asked the family to step out for a moment.

Except for that first flight here, trauma scenes hadn't been a problem because everyone was so busy doing their jobs that they didn't get in each other's way.

Summer introduced her to the charge nurse on the cardiac floor before they entered the room where a fifty-ish male lay in the bed surrounded by family members.

"Hello, Mr. Marshall. My name is Summer and this

is my partner Katie. We're going to be your flight crew today."

After the information had been given to his family concerning the Miami hospital they would be flying to and their expected arrival time, they were soon back in the air and headed north.

Their pilot today was Jackie, and like Roy she had been military before retiring and taking a civilian job for Heli-Care. Katie relaxed into her old routine as she applied the monitors that would give them the cardiac tracing and vital sign information critical to their patient's care.

"Weather is looking good for us today. ETA in forty," Jackie said over the headset.

"Looks like this is going to be an easy one," Summer said as she pointed to the monitor where it showed the patient in a normal sinus rhythm.

"I'm glad the doctor agreed to order him some Ativan before we left. Fear of flying can send anyone's heart into tachycardia." Katie adjusted the fluids hanging as Summer recorded the vital signs.

"I love flying. Always have. You?" Summer asked.

"There's nothing like it. I mean look at that view," Katie said, looking down at the water that went from pale green in the shallows to a dark blue as the waters deepened. She could see several groups of people decked out in snorkel gear down below. She made a mental note to see about taking one of the boat tours to the reefs while she was there.

"You must have some great views in the city. Especially at night," Summer said.

"We do," Katie agreed, remembering the flight she'd been on the night she was shot. The lights of the city had been breathtaking. She remembered thinking that she'd sketch the scene out when she got back to their quarters. Then later at home, she'd pull out her paints and try to capture that perfect color of the dark night sky with the lights twinkling on and off from all the high-rise buildings, where some people were shutting down for the night, putting their children to bed and preparing for sleep while others still worked to hammer out a living in the local diner or one of the big corporations that made up the city.

But she'd never gotten the chance to record the beauty of that night. Instead she'd experienced the pain and violence that the darkness of the city had hidden from her until it was too late. Until a man had decided that taking her life was just collateral in his plan to kill someone else.

"Do you live in one of those high-rises? Those New York apartments always look so glamorous on television. It must be a big change living in Dylan's cottage. Not that I wouldn't love to live in that cottage. It's adorable."

"Believe me, my apartment is nothing like the ones you see on television. Most of them aren't. You could easily put two of my apartments into the cottage." And that wasn't even considering the space she had on the back deck.

"I bet you miss it, though. The city. I love it here on the island. I've always been a small-town girl. But sometimes I think about what it would be like to disappear into the crowds and live that fast-paced life," Summer mused.

"Well, if you decide you want to make a change, just let me know. I'd be glad to show you around the city and there's always an opening on our crew," Katie said. She checked their patient's vitals again and noted a small four beat of SVT before the man's heart rhythm returned back to the nineties.

"I don't know. I can't imagine the flights you get. I'm afraid I couldn't keep up with the pace. I don't know how you do it. Especially after what happened."

The monitor alarmed and they both saw the six-beat run of SVT, but once again the man's heart rhythm returned back to the nineties.

Katie checked his vital signs again and charted, glad to have something to keep her busy so she didn't have to continue her conversation with Summer. It seemed her new coworker was just as open about things as Katie was normally. But this was different. She didn't talk about what had happened with anyone except for her counselor and she only did that because she hadn't been given a choice.

"Going in for final landing," Jackie announced into the headsets while Summer was on a different radio station calling ahead with report that dispatch would forward to the receiving hospital.

They began preparations to unload their patient as soon as the skids touched down.

Later, Katie steered the conversation toward work as they made their way back to the Keys. Summer had only been a part of the flight crew for two years, but she had a wealth of information concerning the workings of the local hospital and the helicopter services Heli-Care provided for the community.

They were back in time to order a lunch delivery and after eating agreed that though the shift had been a cakewalk up to then, it could change at any time. It was best for them to get some rest then before the night calls began to come in. With a twenty-four-hour shift, you had to take it when you had a chance.

"How'd it go?" Dylan asked as he came out of the office and met them in the hall. "Good flight?"

"No problems," Summer said as she headed into her assigned room for the shift.

"Katie?" he asked. "Any problems?"

"Simple pack-up and deliver flight. Our patient was stable. He probably could have gone by ground." Was he going to question her every time she went out on a flight? "If you're asking if I behaved myself, I can assure you that I did."

"I wasn't worried about you behaving yourself. I was just making sure that you didn't need anything. It's only your second flight in a new location. I would check on anyone who had just arrived here. Unfortunately, until Alex gets back that's my job," Dylan added, his lips pulled down into a grim line that she hadn't seen on him before. It had to be stressful having to manage the crew by himself.

And here she was giving him grief because the only thing she had been concentrating on since she got here was herself. She hadn't thought about how much Alex's unexpected leave had burdened Dylan. As a single dad he had a lot of demands on him already, she didn't need to make things harder for him.

"I apologize. I know you're just doing your job. It's just hard feeling like I'm starting over with someone constantly checking on me after being a flight nurse for almost six years." She started opening the door to her room and his hand covered hers, its warmth calming and exciting at the same time. Her heart rate sped up, but it wasn't from fear or anxiety. No, this was even more frightening. This was a spine-tingling sexual attraction in its purest form. She wanted to pull her hand away. She wanted to stand there with him touching her forever.

"I'm sorry. I'm just starting to get worried about Alex. He's never been gone this long without checking in," he said, and then his eyes met hers and locked. "That's all it is."

Without waiting for her to say anything, he lifted his hand and walked past her, leaving her to wonder what exactly had just happened. Had he not felt that? Did she just imagine a spark between the two of them? Was it just her own mixed-up emotions that had tricked her into thinking something had passed between them when he'd touched her? It had to be.

Dylan shut the door of the office before running his hands through his hair. Why had he touched her? He'd decided he wouldn't let himself get caught up in his desire to protect Katie, but she brought out all of the old instincts he felt when someone he cared for needed to be comforted. Only, it wasn't just his protectiveness causing him problems. Ever since the other night, when she'd shown up on his doorstep with her eyes sparkling with excitement over a simple white bird, he could think of nothing but her.

He'd hoped it was merely one of those small attractions that would pass. He'd get to know her, spend some more time with her, and all the excitement he felt when she was around would fade. But after touching her hand, feeling her soft skin against his rough calluses, he was afraid that it could be more than the usual male and female sexual attraction.

And he didn't need more. He had all the stress he could handle with Violet and his job. He didn't need to get involved with any woman, especially not one that was only passing through. One like Lilly, who would only complicate his life with feelings and desires that he knew had no future.

Not that he'd known that about Lilly until the day she had explained to him what they had was just a passing fling and that it was time for her to move on to her next great adventure.

Pulling out his phone, he tried to get Alex, but the phone went to voice mail again. Whatever was going on with his friend, it was keeping him busy.

Which reminded Dylan of all the things he needed to get done himself before he left to pick up Violet from her after-school care.

Turning on his computer, he started work on the monthly reports that needed to be filed with the corporate office. But no matter how he tried to focus on the screen in front of him, his mind kept wandering back to Katie.

He picked up his phone.

Are you sleeping?

He only had to wait a few seconds for her response.

No, why?

He tried to think of an excuse for disturbing her,

then remembered his conversation with his daughter than morning.

Violet asked this morning if she could come over tomorrow after school.

Sure.

Okay, I'll let her know.

He forced himself to set the phone down on the desk then grabbed it up as soon as it dinged with a new message.

I'm sorry I gave you a hard time. It's just hard feeling as if there is someone hovering over you all the time.

What do you mean?

You can't deny that if it wasn't for me having been shot that you wouldn't be checking up on me. Everyone acts like I'm a different person after the shooting. My home crew, my family, everyone acts like I could have a breakdown at any point. I'm not made of glass. I worked hard to get back up in the air. I'm a good flight nurse.

He stared at the screen while he tried to figure out the best way to respond to her text. He could take her side. Agree that she should be treated as she had been before. Or he could play the devil's advocate and give her the opportunity to open up more.

But doesn't everything that happens to us change us in some way? Having Violet come into my life has changed me in ways I never imagined.

But that was a good change. You didn't mind changing because you love your daughter. It's not the same. No one acts like you can't handle yourself because you're a single father now? Not that it isn't hard. It has to be.

So you're saying you haven't changed at all? Or are you saying you don't like the changes?

When she didn't respond, he put his phone down. He hadn't meant to take their conversation into such murky waters. Hopefully he hadn't scared her away with his questions, because his instincts were telling him that she needed to talk to someone. And as a paramedic, he'd bet money on his instincts every time.

# CHAPTER FIVE

THE ONLY REASON Katie had agreed to come to the party was because she knew if she didn't show up, Dylan would want to know why, which would just lead to more questions she didn't want to deal with. Now looking at the crowd of people that were there, she considered disappearing back over to her own cottage and locking the doors.

Almost the whole Key West flight crew, along with other local emergency responders, had turned out. Dylan's deck, much bigger than the one at her cottage, was overflowing with men and women, some still dressed in uniforms from jobs they'd just left.

In the middle of the deck two large pots were being heated on top of open flames where she had just been told several pounds of shrimp and crabs would soon be boiling.

She'd managed to keep to the edge of the crowd so far, not daring to chance any reaction she might have if she suddenly felt penned by the large and rowdy group.

"It can be a bit much, can't it?" said Jo, a flight nurse from the Key West crew, who had joined Katie the moment she'd walked through the back gate. "I mean, the amount of testosterone at these cookouts can be over-the-top. Take that clown over there."

Jo pointed to a man who had rolled up his shirt-sleeves to show all the other men his "guns."

"He's one of the flight crew I met at shift change last week. Casey, right? Boyfriend?" Katie asked.

"Casey, also known as 'Casanova' Johnson. He's my best friend, not my boyfriend," Jo said.

But Katie noticed that the young woman's eyes lingered on her handsome friend a little more than she would have considered just friendly.

"I grew up with four brothers. That," Katie said, as they both looked on where a bunch of grown men were arguing over a game of cornhole, "was my life when I was growing up."

"You poor thing. And still you made it out alive." Jo shook her head at the scene where the men were now making wagers on what had been a friendly game.

"It wasn't so bad. I learned a lot from them. And I never had to worry about the bully at school." Katie counted herself lucky to have such supportive brothers, even though she hadn't leveled with them on how messed up her mind was before she'd left town.

"Hey, Katie. Hey, Jo," Violet greeted them.

It surprised Katie to see how Dylan's daughter seemed to gravitate to the adults at the party, though there were some other children playing in a side yard away from the hot boiling pots. She'd spent a lot of time with the little girl after school in the last week and Violet acted a bit more mature than what Katie would have expected from a child her age. And questions. The child was so full of them.

"What's new, Miss Violet?" Jo said.

"Not much. I checked out another book on birds from the library yesterday, but you weren't home, Katie. Want to come inside and see it?"

"Sure," Katie said. She gladly excused herself from the noisy crowd. Violet led her into a house whose layout was very much like her own rental. The rooms had been enlarged and the colors were much brighter, something she was sure could be attributed to Violet's influence, but it was basically the same layout.

"My room is this way," Violet said, leading her down the hallway and into a room of rose pink where the little girl climbed up on the bed and opened a large book. "See, there's more pictures in this book than the other one."

Sitting down beside the little girl, Katie studied the picture of a majestic white bird with long black legs and a bright yellow beak then read the name listed at the bottom of the page. "It's a lovely painting. I'm hoping to finish some of my own paintings before I go home."

Katie had shared some of her sketches and paintings with the little girl on her almost daily visits after school.

"Daddy says that there are a lot of birds here because they like the sun and the sand, just like him. He knows a lot of things about the islands. He says it's because he's lived here all his life," Violet said as she turned the pages of the book to another bird. "Have you lived in New York all your life?"

"All of my life. I even lived in the same house until I got out of college and started working in my first hospital," Katie told the little girl. "How about you?"

"We lived in all kinds of places before my momma brought me here to meet my daddy. Once we even lived in this school bus that a friend of hers had fixed up." The little girl jumped down off her bed and went into her closet, coming out seconds later with a large shoebox. "Momma left these with me so that I could remember all the places we went together."

As the little girl pulled out maps and brochures, postcards and pictures, it became obvious to Katie that during Violet's short life she had traveled all across the country. From the number of locations Violet said she had lived she couldn't have been in any one place for more than a few months. What had that been like for the little girl? Always moving. Never settling down long enough to make friends.

And now she was here in a different world without her mother.

Yet somehow, the little girl seemed to be taking all the changes in her life well. Wouldn't it be nice to be as adaptable as a child?

"I wondered where you two were. The food's ready." Dylan's voice came from the doorway.

Looking up from a picture Violet was showing her of a beach in California where the little girl spent her sixth birthday, Katie was struck once again by the fact that Dylan Maddox was the most striking man she had ever seen. Dressed in casual shorts and a button-up shirt, she couldn't look away if she wanted to.

How was it that some woman hadn't grabbed this man up by now? Or maybe they had. She didn't really know much about his past or what part Violet's mother had played in it.

"Violet has been showing me some memorabilia of her adventures," Katie said, sitting up on the bed where she and Violet had been lounging. "She's very well-traveled. I think she's been in more states than I have."

"I know. Everyone says that," Violet said, as she jumped off her bed and headed out the door.

Katie followed her and paused in the hall, where Dylan was waiting. "Nice party."

"Thanks. It's good to get the group together. We all work so closely and a lot of us grew up together," Dylan said as he followed her down the hallway.

"Violet says you've lived in the Keys all your life. Do your parents live close by?" she asked, then realized she sounded like his daughter. The little girl's inquisitiveness was rubbing off on her. Or was it just that she was curious about Dylan?

"I grew up in Islamorada on a houseboat in a marina my parents owned," Dylan said.

"A houseboat? You lived in the water?" She couldn't imagine it.

"It was a perfectly fine boat. I had a loft bedroom until I was in middle school when my mother insisted that my father build a house beside the marina. They still live there, though if my dad had his way they'd be back on the houseboat."

"You and Violet have lived such adventurous lives," she said as he started to open one of the French doors leading out onto the balcony.

"Violet had more than enough adventure by the time I found out about her," Dylan muttered as he stopped in front of the door.

"What do you mean, when you found out about her? You didn't know you had a daughter?"

"Not until her mother showed up with her. She never told me she was pregnant. I think she panicked when she found out she was having Violet. I think she thought I would hold her here if I knew about the baby. One night I came home and she was packed up and on her way out the door. I don't know if I would have ever heard from her again if it hadn't been for Violet."

She could see the pain in his eyes as he spoke about his past, but she didn't know if it was because of the time he'd lost with his daughter or the way he'd been treated by Violet's mother.

"Violet was getting too old to be dragged from school to school. She's a smart child and even at eight she knew that she needed to attend a school on a regular basis. That's hard to do when your mother can't seem to stay in the same place more than four months at a time."

She didn't hear the bitterness she would have expected toward his ex. Could it be that he still had feelings for Violet's mother? Or maybe he'd just accepted the past and moved on?

She found herself wanting to know the answer to those questions.

"Violet's very lucky that she made it back to you. You're doing a great job with her. I would never have known she'd been in and out of different schools from the way she was reading that book on birds to me."

"She's been the center of my world since she moved here. I wish I could have been there when she was born, but… I can't undo that," Dylan said as he went back to opening the door then stopped again. "What I've never understood is why Lilly thought that I would make her stay somewhere she didn't want to be. I'd never do that to a woman."

"Of course you wouldn't," Katie said as they stepped

out into the crowd, though it was the last thing she wanted to do. She had forgotten about all the other people being here while she'd been talking to Violet and then Dylan.

For the rest of the evening, she made excuses for going in and out of the house as she carried out drinks and gathered up trash. At other times, she'd wander off into the garden and pretend to be studying the bright blooms if someone came too close.

Since she didn't have the drive home that the other guests did, she offered to stay and help clean up. She'd learned several things as the night continued, besides all the ways to avoid a crowd of people. One, crab boils were messy and delicious, and two, the group of hardworking emergency responders were all loud and competitive, much like the men and women she was used to working with in NYC.

The quiet that descended after the last guest left was very welcomed. Violet had been put to bed earlier in the night, leaving Katie alone with Dylan.

"This is the last of it," she said as she walked into the house where they had been loading the dishwasher with utensils and serving plates.

"Thanks for staying to help," Dylan said.

"Just trying to make points with my boss," Katie teased, knowing that the man hated to be referred to as anyone's boss.

"I'm not your boss, I'm a fill-in. I think of myself more as your preceptor," Dylan said as he took the last dish from her.

"I don't need a preceptor. I've been the preceptor for more crew members than you have staff here." She tried to keep the bite out of her voice, but she was getting tired of being treated like a newbie. Her pride had taken enough of a hit after she'd been injured on the job. She didn't need someone making her feel even more of a failure. She thought he understood that.

"Okay, let's say I'm more of your mentor. Everyone needs a mentor at some point, right?" he said.

He turned around and was leaning against the black granite countertops. Why was he so determined to help her? And why did it infuriate her so?

But when she didn't say anything, he moved closer. His hand came up and pushed a lock of hair that had come loose from her ponytail behind her ear.

The room was quiet except for the hum of the air-conditioning unit. Her heart began to race and her breaths came more quickly. Her thoughts turned back to the first time they had met in the flight quarter's kitchen when his arms had come around her and her body had immediately reacted. They'd both been strangers then. In some ways, they still were.

"I didn't mean to make you feel inept. Your record shows that you're a good flight nurse."

She tried to concentrate on his words, on the anger she had felt earlier. But it was gone. All she could think about was his touch, his body so close to hers. What would he do if she moved closer? If she reached up with her lips and touched his?

Her hand went up and pressed against his chest before she could stop it. His heart beat a fast rhythm against her palm as hers did when he covered her hand with his own.

"Do you feel it?" she asked him.

What was she doing? This wasn't her. She didn't approach men. Not like this. Instead, she waited until they showed an interest in her before expressing her own.

"Katie, I…yes, if you mean do I want to take you in my arms and kiss you, and more, right now. Yes. There's an attraction between the two of us, but…" Dylan took a deep breath then stepped back from her, leaving her feeling empty and alone. "You're only here for a few weeks. I make it a rule not to get involved with anyone that's only here temporarily."

At first his words didn't make sense to her and then she thought of his daughter. "Because of Violet? Or because of Lilly?"

"I'm still trying to get this whole father thing down. But yes, it's best if we don't confuse Violet." Dylan took another step away from her.

Was that disappointment she saw? Or was that just her wounded pride being wishful? It didn't really matter, did it? She'd just come on to a man for the first time, only to be shot down. And he'd been her, sort of, boss. There wasn't anything that was going to make this any less awkward.

"If you think you can handle the rest of this, I'm going to head home." As she turned toward the entrance, she tried to leave with her chin up. How was she going to face this man the next day? Or the next? She'd made a really bad misstep here and she didn't know how to recover. She didn't want Dylan's pity. She'd had enough of that after being shot. It had made her feel weak and helpless, two things McGees never accepted.

"Katie—" Dylan caught her hand as she started to open the door "—don't leave. Not like this."

She made herself turn around. She made her lips curve in a smile, made her eyes hold back the embarrassing tears that she felt forming. She wouldn't let him know he had hurt her. Besides, it wasn't his fault that he didn't have the same feelings that she did.

"My daughter gets attached to people very easily and she's spent most of her life having to leave the people in her life behind as her mother dragged her from one city to the next. And then her own mother left her. I'm not likely to bring a woman into our home for a long while."

"I understand. It's not a big deal. I just…" What could she use as an excuse for that stupid confession of her attraction to him? "I'm sorry. I was out of line. I understand that things are more complicated for you now."

And with that admission she was out the door and halfway back to her rental before she could say anything else that would embarrass the two of them and make things even worse. Not that she thought they could. Not when she had to get up in the morning and face Dylan again with the both of them knowing that there was an attraction between them even though he couldn't act on it.

Dylan had finished cleaning up and was headed to bed when he glanced out his window and saw that Katie's light was still on.

He had so many mixed feelings where she was concerned. He was almost glad that she had forced him to admit his attraction to her, though he didn't know why. It certainly hadn't made it easier to let her walk away when all he'd wanted to do was take her into his arms and kiss her the way he had dreamed of since the night she'd shown up on his front porch with that smile that had awakened something inside him.

And now he'd hurt her, even though that had been the last of his intentions. And he'd ignored her suggestion that it was his feelings for Lilly that kept him from becoming involved with her.

He pulled his phone out of his pocket. At least that was something he could set straight.

It's not Lilly. At least not any feelings I have left for her.

It only took a second for her to respond.

Are you sure?

Yes. After she left I was pretty messed up. I didn't understand how she could just walk away like that. It was hard on my ego to accept that I had only been someone to pass the time with while Lilly planned her next big adventure. While I'd been making plans for the future, she'd been on her way out the door.

You were hurt. It's understandable.

I was young and innocent then.

You make yourself sound like an old man.

I feel old sometimes.

When she didn't text back, he went to bed. He was just turning off the lights when his phone dinged.

Thank you for telling me. I'm not like Lilly, but I do understand you wanting to protect your daughter. You're right. Things would never work between the two of us. I've only got six more weeks before I return to New York. I wouldn't want to hurt Violet when I left.

She didn't have to say that she wouldn't want to hurt him either. It was understood.

Good night, Katie.

Good night, Dylan.

The radio went off waking Katie up with a start from her nap in her quarters. She had her flight suit and shoes on and was rushing out the door before she could open her eyes enough to check the time, and she was surprised to see the sun coming up when she climbed into the helicopter. She was even more surprised to find Dylan occupying the seat beside her.

"Where's Max?" she asked as she buckled herself into her seat. There wasn't really time for idle conversation, but she couldn't help but be confused. When she'd gone to bed at 2 a.m. after a call for a scooter accident victim who needed to be flown to a Miami hospital where a plastic surgeon would try to fix the patient's many facial fractures, Max had been there.

"I came in early and found him in the lounge nursing a headache and upset stomach. I told him I'd cover till the next shift came on." As Dylan was going through their scene bag, she noticed that he was adding more bandages.

"I missed hearing the dispatch. What's the call?" she asked.

"Self-inflicted gunshot wound to the head. Fire and rescue on scene clearing a space in the parking lot of Zachary Taylor fort. EMS is on the scene with the patient," Roy said over the headset. "ETA eight minutes."

Her stomach clenched at the word *gunshot* and refused to relax. "Are we sure it was self-inflicted?"

"We'll let the police make that judgment," Dylan said. "Are you okay? You aren't coming down with what Max has, are you?"

"I'm fine," she said, determined not to let her mind get ahead of her. This would be fine. She just needed to keep her mind off the fact that someone had been shot. Instead, she would concentrate on their patient, who would need all of their attention if they were going to keep them alive long enough to get to a neurosurgeon, which was about all they could do for this type of head injury.

She spiked a bag of Lactated Ringer's. She considered also preparing a bag of the O negative blood that they had recently begun stocking for traumas such as this one, but she decided this would be a fast "drop, package and load" job so it would be best to wait until the patient was strapped in and headed to the hospital before starting a transfusion.

In what seemed like seconds, they were landing in a parking lot that had been blocked off by the other emergency responders. The second the skids touched down they were out and moving toward a firefighter who she recognized from the earlier scene that morning.

"He's this way," the man said as they followed him down a sandy path that led them out to a beach where she could see EMS working on their patient. Katie looked around the scene, anxiety sending a boost of adrenaline through her.

They were in the open, with only a small group of early-morning runners gathered around a young woman dressed in a tank top and runner shorts who was visibly upset. Was this the person who had found him? Or had she seen the man pull the trigger?

Or was this really a suicide? Could there be a shooter in the crowd? Her stomach churned at the thought.

She was being paranoid. There was no risk here. *I'm safe*, Katie told herself. *This is not New York. There is no place for a shooter to hide here.*

A police officer stood close to the EMS, snapping pictures of the crime scene. It only took one look at the sand beside the patient to notice a small revolver.

The sight of the gun and the smell of gunpowder set her stomach churning again. She could see the pool of blood under the man's head as it soaked into the wet sand.

For a moment she was back in New York as she watched her own blood as it flowed onto the asphalt, mixing with the rainwater that streamed across the parking lot. It was the sight of her own blood that she remembered the most about that night.

"We need to get an airway before he goes into respiratory arrest. Katie, you help them with that bandage and keep his head supported while I get this guy intubated," Dylan told her, breaking the hold of fear that had gripped her.

"Sure, okay," she said and moved to help support the man's injured head as a collar was secured around his neck. They were unable to see an exit wound, so it was possible the bullet had traveled into his cervical spine.

In the next few minutes it took to get the man packaged and loaded in the helicopter, Katie ignored everything that was going on around her except for what was happening with her patient.

Once they were back in the air and headed toward Miami, she quickly got a second IV line started as Dylan started the neurological assessment. The cabin was quiet while they worked together to stabilize their patient.

"He's going into shock. I'm going to increase the fluids and start some blood," she told Dylan as she took the first unit of O negative blood out of the cooler and began the task of prepping it. Once she had the tubing attached and primed, she hooked it into the second line she'd started and opened it up. After seeing the amount of blood at the scene, there'd been no doubt that this man had lain there and bled for a while before someone had come along and found him. If it had been another thirty minutes their services wouldn't have been needed. Even with their help in getting him to a trauma unit that could provide neurosurgery, his chances weren't very good.

"Pupils are fixed and dilated. Glasgow Coma Scale of five," Dylan said as he started his report to the Miami trauma unit.

In minutes they were landing and unloading their patient. As they entered the overcrowded emergency room, she took over manually ventilating the patient so that Dylan could give report to the trauma doc that had been waiting for them.

They both made quick work of transferring their

patient onto the trauma stretcher where he was immediately surrounded by qualified staff that would try to keep the man alive. After washing down the stretcher, they stopped in the lounge set up for the emergency responders and they each fueled up with a cup of coffee before heading back to the helipad with a cup of the thick, black liquid for Roy.

The flight back to base was quiet. Dylan didn't comment on her loss of concentration at the scene earlier and she was not going to be the one to bring it up. She'd made it through the flight and he couldn't find any fault with her patient care.

"What's the chance of that guy making it?" Roy asked them once they had landed.

"Better than the chances he had if we hadn't been there to transfer him," Dylan said.

"That's what you always say," Roy said.

"Because it's always true, though for this guy I don't know that there's much they're going to be able to do for him," Dylan said.

"It's a shame, isn't it?" Roy said. "That guy was so young."

"No one knows what demons drive someone to do the things they do. If he's lucky and survives this, the hospital will make sure he gets some help," Dylan said as he opened the door and they all walked in to find their relief enjoying a breakfast of eggs and bacon. "I hope you cooked enough for all of us."

"I'm not hungry. I think I'll just head home." Katie hurried toward her room to get her backpack. It had been a long twenty-four-hour shift and she wanted to get out of there before Dylan had a chance to corner her. She was sure they'd eventually talk about what had happened at the scene that morning, but she wasn't up to dealing with it now.

"Katie," she heard his voice call from behind her. They'd avoided each other the past week while at home. It seemed best after the awkward incident the night of the party. Unfortunately, avoiding him wasn't really an option here at work.

"Hey," Dylan said, catching up with her, "are you okay?"

"I'm fine. Just tired." She wasn't about to admit to him how much seeing that gunshot victim had triggered something inside her. She'd held it together. Maybe he hadn't noticed how she had become too absorbed in her own reactions to the scene this morning.

"Good, I won't hold you up, then. I hate to ask you this, but I was wondering if you could do me a favor."

Katie stopped where she stood, the doorknob of her assigned room in her hand, unable to imagine what Dylan could want from her. Was he going to ask her to keep away from him and Violet when she was home so he didn't have to worry about her attraction to him? It hadn't just been her avoiding him. She'd noticed there hadn't been any trips by Violet over to her house.

"Okay," she said as she prepared herself. No matter what it was, she would be professional. She had a room full of coworkers just outside that hallway. She still had some pride left.

"I just got a call from my babysitter who's been keeping Violet for me this week so I can work later and she can't make it today. Would it be okay if Violet came over this afternoon when she gets off the bus? It will only be for an hour. I've got a late online meeting that I don't want to miss."

Katie let go of the breath she was holding and for the first time that day she felt a smile tug at her lips. "Of course I can watch Violet. I'm going home to take a nap this morning, but I'll be up by the time she gets home. I've seen the bus out there so I know the time, though you might want to send a note to the school just so there's not a problem with me getting her."

"Thanks, Katie. I appreciate it. And Violet has been giving me fits about wanting to come visit you."

After assuring Dylan that she would enjoy her visit with Violet, she grabbed her things and quickly left the building.

But it was impossible for her to sleep. She worried about how the scene that morning had not only affected her but kept winding its way through her mind. She'd fought her way back to being physically capable of doing her job, and while she knew that the patient's care had not been compromised by her reaction, she had to admit that it had left her shaken.

Getting out of bed, she sent an email to the counselor she'd been avoiding. It was time she faced her own demons. As much as she tried, she had to accept that she couldn't just pretend everything was okay. She had tried to ignore all the signs, but the flight this morning had scared her. It had been a wake-up call.

# CHAPTER SIX

DYLAN HEARD THE laughter coming from Katie's back porch. He would recognize the giggles of his little girl anywhere. But there was another sound, one that he wasn't sure he'd ever heard before. The sound of Katie's laughter was as pleasant as Violet's and it warmed something inside of him.

Ever since the night he had admitted his attraction to Katie, he'd felt as if a part of himself had turned cold and distant. As if inside him was another man, one who wasn't happy with his decision to turn Katie away.

Which made absolutely no sense. It hadn't been the first time he'd explained his solid rule on not dating someone who was just passing through his life. It had never bothered him before. And now, with Violet, he had even more reasons uphold this rule. Unlike her mother, he knew that Violet needed a stable home, which didn't include people rotating in and out of her life.

Still, he knew something about the way he reacted to Katie was different or could be different if he let them have a chance.

A crash came from the deck and he picked up speed.

What were the two of them doing that would have furniture crashing to the floor?

The sight of Violet and Katie collapsed on the ground did nothing to ease his fears until he realized they were both rolling around in a fit of giggles instead of pain.

"What exactly are the two of you up to?" he asked. Standing over them, he couldn't help but join in the laughter.

"Katie is teaching me yoga. It's supposed to lighten us," his little girl said.

"Enlighten us," Katie corrected. "So far all it's gotten us is a couple of bruises. Violet is having some difficulty with the meditation part of the process."

"Katie says you can't talk during the meditation. It's supposed to help you relax. But how can you relax if you can't talk?" his daughter asked, genuine confusion reflected on her little pixie face.

"I can understand where that would be very stressful," he agreed with his daughter before looking over at Katie and giving her a wink.

"We decided it was best to move on to learning the yoga positions. Violet is a lot better at those." Katie gave his daughter a look of affection that completely warmed his heart. Could Katie see what a special little girl his daughter was? Violet was a beautiful and loving child, but sometimes she could be a bit much, at least for some adults.

"We've done the downward dog and now we're learning the cow pose. Only I told Katie that it looked more like a dog than the other one. And then—" Violet had to stop to giggle before she could talk again

"—Katie started mooing like a cow and it made me laugh so I fell over."

"I was not mooing. I was moaning from all the stretching my muscles were doing. They're not used to being mistreated," Katie said.

She was sitting with her back to the overturned chair, her hair plastered with sweat against her flushed face. He picked up two bottles of water sitting on the table and handed one to each of them. "It's a bit hot out here. Couldn't you do this in the house?"

"It said on the website that being outside was good for meditating." Katie took a gulp of water. "I should have waited till the sun went down. But we did have fun, didn't we, Violet?"

Violet agreed with a nod as she drank her water.

"So, you've never done yoga?" he asked. Looking down at the khaki dress pants he'd had to put on for the county commissioners meeting he had been required to attend on Alex's absence then looked at the deck. Deciding to take the chance of ruining his pants, he sat down on the floor between the two.

"No. My counselor recommended it, so I thought I would give it a try. If nothing else, I've learned that I need to get into better shape. And Violet definitely made it more fun than it could have been."

Her admission that she'd been in contact with her counselor surprised him. She'd seemed so set against getting counseling before. What had changed?

Was it her reaction to the gunshot scene this morning? He had intended to discuss it with her the next day when she reported to work. He'd seen her go pale when she saw the gun and blood. It made sense that something like that could trigger bad memories. It had troubled him all day, but he wanted her to have some time to recover before he brought it up.

"I had fun, too, Katie. Can I come practice with you another day?" his daughter asked. "I'll find a book in the library about doing yoga for us to study."

"Of course. How about I order us a CD to use?" Katie said.

As she moved to get up, he stood and offered her his hand. He couldn't help but notice the hesitation before she took it. Was he making things between them even more awkward with his presence?

"Is it okay if I go home and finish my homework? I forgot to bring my library book to school and I need to finish my report," Violet said.

"Actually, your nana is on her way to pick you up so you can spend the night with her."

"Really?" his daughter asked.

"She'll be here in just a few minutes so you better go get your clothes and books together. I've already opened the door. I'll be there to help in a minute."

"It's okay. I can get my stuff. Thanks, Katie," Violet called back as she dashed off.

"I'll have to go check her bag. She'll remember her favorite books, but she'll forget to pack her pajamas." He watched his daughter until she disappeared into the house. "I really appreciate you keeping her for me."

"Actually, it helped me a lot. After this morning, it was nice to have a distraction. You'e very lucky. Violet's a special little girl. She has an abundance of spirit and energy," Katie said, though he noticed she was looking down at her shoes instead of looking him in the eyes. "About this morning,"

"We can talk about this morning tomorrow." The

last thing he wanted was to create any more conflict between the two of them. He'd rather leave what happened at work, at work.

And why was that when he'd been the one to tell her that the two of them couldn't get any closer?

"No. I want to discuss it. Whilst the patient's care was not compromised, I need to talk about how the accident in New York affected me"

"Katie, you got caught up in your surroundings. Our patient wasn't affected. You need to realize that you're human like the rest of us. You should have seen me when Lilly showed up with Violet. I was a mess. Trying to figure out how I was going to take care of a seven-year-old daughter while keeping up with my job was too much some days."

"Really?" she asked, her eyes meeting his for the first time. "But you look so comfortable with her."

"Now? Yes, I've got a handle on things, though I know that could change at any time. I live in fear that Lilly will show up and want her back. And she's growing up so fast. In a few years I'll have a teenager to deal with." The thought of his little girl turning into a young woman was enough to send a shudder down his spine.

"You'll do fine. Violet has a good head on her shoulders," Katie said. She bit down on her bottom lip, drawing his eyes down to plump red lips that he had imagined kissing. He wanted to touch them, brush his fingers across their softness before he lost himself in a kiss he knew would shake the foundations of his closely held beliefs that getting involved with her would only be asking for heartache later for both him and his daughter when she returned to New York.

"Besides, if you have full custody the courts won't

let her take Violet," Katie said. "You do have custody, right?"

His stomach clenched into a tight ball as it always did when the question of Violet's custody came up. "That's the problem. Lilly was only here for a day before she was gone. There wasn't time for me to get anything but emergency temporary custody. If she came back and wanted to contest, I'm not sure what would happen."

"That doesn't make sense. Her mother left her. She apparently doesn't want to be responsible for Violet. Can't your lawyer just send the paperwork for her to sign?"

"Sounds simple, right? The only problem is that by the time we find out where Lilly is living, she moves again. We've even used private detectives, but she's always one step in front of us. If I didn't know better I'd think that she was trying to avoid us." And he was beginning to think that he was right which only made him more paranoid concerning his daughter's safety.

"I'm sorry. I didn't know. I'm sure that it will work out. You're doing such a good job with her I'm sure that the court would never think of taking custody away from you."

Katie's hand reached for his in what he knew was intended as a comforting gesture that shouldn't make his heart jump, but it did. And it wasn't only his heart that was reacting. His whole body seemed to buzz with excitement.

"I hope so. I'm lucky that I have a lot of support from our team and my family." He needed to leave. He needed to get away from those lips and her touch before the temptation had him throwing out all his remaining caution and taking a chance on what could be between the two of them—even if only for a few weeks.

"Daddy, Nana just drove up," Violet shouted from somewhere behind him, breaking him from the spell that Katie's tempting lips had cast over him.

"I'll be right there," he called back to her. "We'll talk tomorrow," he said, eager to make his escape. He'd almost forgotten what she wanted to talk to him about.

"Sure," Katie said, stepping back.

It wasn't until she backed away from him that he realized he had taken a step toward her. As he made his way across the yard to his home, he couldn't help but wonder what would have happened if Violet hadn't interrupted him? Would he have touched her? Kissed her? Or would he have stepped away as he knew he should?

Something told him there would come a time again when he would have to make that decision, when his daughter wouldn't be there to rescue him, and he had no idea how he would hand it. It seemed all his rules, no matter how important they had seemed to him just weeks ago, were crumbling around him.

After a long shower, Katie pulled on a pair of pajama shorts and a tank top before taking a glass of her favorite Moscato wine out to the deck. After sitting up the chair she and Violet had knocked over earlier in the afternoon, she took a seat and closed her eyes. A soft breeze from the beach ruffled her hair that she had left down to dry and the sweet scent of the hibiscus plants that edged the deck on both sides filled the air, relaxing her even more.

She'd been forced to accept some hard truths today,

but she felt better for it. Like her father had always told her, it was better to face a problem head-on than to sweep it under the table and ignore it. She'd done a lot of sweeping over the last few months. She'd been willing to do whatever physical work was required to get back to work as a flight nurse, but she'd ignored all the physiological signs her body had been giving her each time she found herself in a situation that reminded her of her own traumatic injury. She'd made excuses and pretended that all she needed was to run away to Florida and she would leave all her problems behind. If only it was that easy.

But it wasn't. There was nothing easy about her life right now. Her counselor said she had to accept what happened to her and voice it out loud, and Katie finally thought she understood the reason she'd hid it all behind her. Because it hadn't been just an injury as she had tried to pretend, it had been a violent attack with a gun. She'd been shot by an unknown assailant while trying to do her job and save the life of a young patient. And after living a life where she'd always felt safe, the admission of being vulnerable was hard to accept. It was time for her stop ignoring the pain and fear that she experienced that night. And it was time to stop pretending she was okay. She had to acknowledge that she was no superhero, she was simply one of many people who had gone through a trauma that would probably affect them the rest of their lives.

If she wanted to return to New York in better condition than when she'd left, she had to make a conscious effort to accept what she was going through and find a way to overcome the fear and anxiety that were controlling her. Before the shooting, she'd attended some of the most violent scenes imaginable as she tried to save patients who had been beaten, shot, stabbed and worse. Even when her heart was torn apart by the suffering of her patients, she was able to separate her feelings from her job to provide the best care. Now she had to find in herself the strength to separate from her own trauma, so she could go on with her life while still accepting that her life had changed forever. No, she wouldn't forget it, she'd come to realize that wasn't possible, but she could learn to live with it.

And she had to figure out what she wanted out of her life. She'd always put her job first, which was why instead of caring about her mental health she had concentrated more on her physical rehab after the shooting. Coming from a family committed to helping others, she'd lost sight of the fact that there could be more to her life. That was going to change too.

Watching Dylan and Violet and their relationship had affirmed for her the possibility of enjoying a life beyond work.

She opened her eyes and reached for the glass of wine on the side table and froze. A large green dragon looked up at her from the floor of the deck, its long, forked tongue shooting out toward her. She screamed.

Dylan just finished cleaning up the kitchen when a bloodcurdling scream tore through the silence of his home. Grabbing his keys and phone, he power-locked his front door before shooting across the yard to Katie.

Her cottage was quiet when he let himself in. Too quiet. He cleared each room before he got to the doors leading out to the deck. He could see by the outside string of lights that she sat straight up in the chair, her eyes fixed on something that was at her feet. Easing the door open, he made sure there was no one out of his field of sight before he took a step outside, only realizing then that he didn't have a weapon to defend her.

"Katie, what happened?" he asked calmly. Had she had a flashback? Fallen asleep and dreamed of the night she'd been shot?

"It's a dragon," Katie whispered, her voice quivering. "It's between my feet."

Her words confused him. A dragon? And then it hit him. New York City girls wouldn't have a lot of experience interacting with the kind of local wildlife they had here on the islands.

"Is this dragon green or brown?" He tried to keep the laughter out of his words.

"It's green and it's big. It's evil too. I can see it in its little beady black eyes. It tried to strike me with its tongue," Katie said, never moving her eyes off the creature that he could now see on the deck beside her feet.

"It's okay. It's just an iguana. They don't bite." He started toward her when what he saw stopped him.

"I've seen iguanas. This thing is too big to be an iguana. It's a monster. It looks like something that would fight Godzilla."

While he heard her words, he couldn't seem to find his voice to respond. He'd been prepared to see a three-foot iguana with a spikey row of spines on its back and its long thick tail. What he hadn't been prepared for was the sight of Katie in a pair of short shorts and a tank top that revealed everything it was supposed to be covering. He struggled to regain his voice. "Don't move. I'm going to get some oven mitts from the kitchen to pick it up."

"No, Dylan, wait. Don't leave me alone with this thing." Katie's voice was louder now. "Do something before it moves. What if it jumps on me? It's got claws."

Dylan headed back into the kitchen. "It's an herbivore. It won't bite you unless you make it mad, so don't make it mad."

"And how do I keep it from getting mad?" Katie asked, her voice getting higher and louder now.

"I don't know. Maybe you should talk to it?" Unable to find a pair of oven mitts he settled on a couple of pot holders and rushed back outside.

"And if you bite me I'll sic my brother John Jr. on you. He's one of NYPD's finest. He'll not only shoot you, he'll have you made into a belt to show all his friends. And if John is busy, my older brother Jacob will put a bullet between those evil eyes of yours and then…" Katie stopped her conversation with the iguana as soon as he stepped close to them.

"Sorry, I didn't mean to interrupt. I'm surprised the little fellow hasn't run off into the bushes shaking in fear from all those threats of violence." He stepped behind the iguana and with one quick movement had the three-foot-long creature caught between his hands. The green scaly creature gave him a disgruntled look, but made no move to attack.

Katie sank back into her chair. "What in the world was that thing doing out here? Where's its owner?"

"It doesn't have an owner. Haven't you seen them around the island? They're everywhere. If I'm not mistaken, this one here is named Pascal."

"Who…wait—" she held her hands up in surrender "—I know the answer to that one already. Violet named him, didn't she?"

"She did. Hold on a moment. I'm going to take him over to our back garden. He usually doesn't stray too far from there."

When he got back to the deck he found Katie hadn't moved, but her glass of wine was now empty and she held her phone in her hand. "Are you all right? I know iguanas look scary, but as long as you leave them alone they won't bite you."

"Oh, you don't have to worry. I will definitely leave them alone. Unfortunately, they're not the problem right now. It's the text I just got from my brother. It seems my father wants to hear from me." Katie started to take a drink from the glass before realizing it was empty and setting it down on the table.

"And that's a problem?" he asked. Wasn't it natural for a father to want to check in on his daughter?

But what did he really know about Katie's family life? Katie hadn't talk a lot about her life in New York. Had she been married before? Did she have someone waiting there for her? No, she wouldn't have responded to him the way she had if there was someone else. But why had it never occurred to him to ask?

*Because you told her there couldn't be anything between the two of you.*

"Let's just say that Captain John McGee Sr. of the NYPD is the man in charge of the McGee clan. If he wants to talk to me, there's something on his mind. He's probably checking up on me, making sure I'm doing a good job while I'm here."

"You haven't called him since you've been here?" he asked. Was this what he had to look forward to when Violet grew up?

"We've texted," Katie said.

"But you haven't called?" He could tell by the way her eyes shot down that there were some feelings of guilt there which made her admission even more surprising. "Because as a dad, I can tell you that receiving some texts would not be enough for me if Violet was away from home."

"I know it's hard on you. Thinking about the time Violet was out there in the world without you being there to protect her."

"If I'd only received one phone call telling me she existed, that she was out there, I would have found some way to get to her." Dylan's hands ran through his hair as he was filled with the familiar frustration that he couldn't go back and change things for Violet's first years.

"It's just…my father's a big teddy bear of a man as long as everything is going his way. When it's not, that's when things get a little intense. He's got a protective streak a mile long, especially for me since I'm the only girl, but he has high expectations for all his children. My brothers followed him into the NYPD. I became a flight nurse. He's proud of all of us, but he has a tendency to worry."

"So, call him. Put his mind to rest. Let him know you're good. I can understand his concern."

"But I'm not. Doing well that is. I didn't even tell him the truth about why I came down to Key West. He has no idea I was struggling at work after the shooting. I've never told him. I've never told anyone except for my counselor. And you."

And why was that? Maybe for the same reason that he felt so comfortable telling her about his fears for Violet's custody?

But he couldn't let himself dwell on the whys and what-ifs.

"The scene this morning was not a pleasant one. And I can see why it would have disturbed you. You're not superhuman. We all have something that digs into us on a scene. For me it's the kids. Seeing a child hurting just does something to me."

They sat in silence for a few moments. Having to treat a hurt child got to all of them.

"But let's get back to your father. What do you think your father expected after being shot? That you'd climb out of the hospital bed and head back to work. If he's been an officer long enough to be a captain, he's seen his fellow officers shot in the line of duty, which by the way is exactly what happened to you. You were on duty to take care of a patient and got shot at the scene. No one would have blamed you if you never returned to work. The fact that you fought to come back is a testament to your strength." His voice got louder as he thought about what Katie had been through, his protective nature reacting to the thought that she'd been carrying all this around alone. "I take it that's why you're not calling him. You're afraid he'll realize that there is something wrong?"

"I've never told him. About the dreams, the fear of crowds or the anxiety every time something reminds me of that night. I told him I was fine. And he told me he was proud of me. I want him to be proud of me. That's all I've ever wanted. He's been everything to me. My mom died of cancer not too long after my brother was born. I was only four. But he was a lot like you. He accepted that he was raising us alone and he made it work," Katie said as she wiped at his face. "But after this morning and after talking to my counselor, I know if I want to be the nurse that I was before the…shooting… I need to acknowledge the problem and find a way to overcome it."

"Can I ask you a question?" Dylan had pulled up on the chairs and taken a seat across from her while they'd been talking. Now he moved a little closer. "Why is it so hard to say that you were shot? I've noticed that you usually refer to it as 'the incident' or 'my injury.' Is it so hard to admit that you were shot?"

She bit down on her bottom lip and he was once more caught up in their spell. One day he would taste those lips even if he did have to break all his rules.

"I don't know. My counselor asked me the same question. She suggested it might be my way of refusing to accept that it happened. That I've been a victim of a shooting. Maybe she's right. I'm not supposed to be the victim. I'm supposed to care for the victim. I'm supposed to save the victim's life with all the special training I've received. That's my job. You know, they prepare us for the most violent scenes. The shootings and stabbings, the car accidents and the beatings, but never have I had someone explain what I'm supposed to do if *I* am the victim."

"What happened that night?" he asked. He needed to know. Not because of curiosity, but because he wanted to know what he was dealing with. He wanted to know how to help her. He ignored the warning his brain was sending him, reminding him of his vow not to get involved because that was how you ended up getting hurt. None of it mattered now. What he saw was a co-worker, a friend, someone he was quickly coming to care about who needed help. He might not be a counselor, but he could be there for her when she needed someone to talk to.

"It was just a regular call. A shooting victim had been left to die in an old run-down parking lot in Jersey. EMS had responded to the call, but this kid needed to get to an operating room fast if he was going to survive. It had been raining off and on all day, so we hadn't taken any flights until we were dispatched to this one. The lights in the parking lot had been shot out or had just died. But I had on this old yellow rain jacket, so there's no way someone couldn't see me." She stood as she talked and he followed her with his eyes. She looked defenseless as she paced back and forth with her arms wrapped around her body. "I was lead so I got to the patient first. He couldn't have been over eighteen. Just a kid, you know? After that, it's all kind of confused in my mind."

"Can you try to explain it to me?" He wanted to get up and go to her. He wanted to take her into his arms and tell her that she was safe now, but that wouldn't help her deal with all the emotions she had been apparently dealing with alone. Somehow he knew she needed to voice out loud what had happened. She admitted herself that he was the only one she felt comfortable talking to.

"I don't know if I can, but I'll try. They tell me that there had been someone hiding behind the building. They, the shooter, must have come back to make sure he finished the kid off. Maybe he saw that EMS had arrived and he was afraid they were going to save the guy and then there would have been retaliation. All I really remember was bending over the kid, EMS was trying to get an IV on the guy. The lights in the parking lot were all out and none of us could see very well. Then there was a popping sound, it sounded more like fireworks then gunshots. I felt something hit me in the chest. At first I didn't feel the pain. It was just a shock. I didn't realize what was happening." She continued to pace as she talked, still holding the empty wineglass in her hand.

"They tried to make it out that I was some kind of hero, saying that I tried to protect the patient, but I don't know if I was covering the kid or if the first bullet hit me and I fell over him. There were screams, I remember hearing them, but I don't know if they were mine or if they came from someone else at the scene. Sometimes I dream that it's me screaming and sometimes I dream it's the kid screaming, though that isn't possible since he was unresponsive when we arrived."

She passed in front of him and he caught the hand that held the empty glass in his and unpeeled her fingers from the thin stem. After setting it on the table, he pulled her down into his arms until she sat in his lap.

"What are you doing?" she asked.

Her misty eyes met his and he asked himself the same question. What *was* he doing?

But his heart told him this was what he needed. He couldn't sit there and watch her go through the hell of that night again without touching her. Without reassuring himself that she was safe. She was going through something that he couldn't imagine living through. How could he help her? By being honest with her?

"Can I comfort you?" he said, then waited. He wondered if she understood just how much hearing about her pain hurt him too. How could she when it didn't even make sense to him?

Her tense body suddenly relaxed into his. Her head came down to rest on his shoulders and the helplessness he was feeling eased as he wrapped his arms around her. They sat with him just holding her there for several minutes before he felt he could speak.

"I'm so sorry you went through that. I know you think that you're not satisfied with where you are in your recovery, but the fact that you've been able to get on a helicopter not knowing what kind of scene or what danger awaits you is a sign of your resiliency." But for how long could she continue before she pushed herself too far? He couldn't, wouldn't, let her do that. The look of horror on her face when she'd seen the gunshot victim had told him that she was still struggling. He would find some way to protect her.

"But it's not enough. Nothing is enough. I want to move on. I want to forget all about that night. I want my life back," Katie said, her voice muffled against his shirt.

She wanted her life in New York back. And if he had any sense he would get up right then and walk away from this woman. But it was too late. He had no defense against the feelings she brought out of him.

"Thank you for listening. I haven't been able to talk about it. About the night I was shot," Katie said, enunciating each word as if it were a pain in itself. "I know that trying to ignore what happened that night is making it harder for me to recover, but it's not something I've felt comfortable talking about with others. My brothers…they're so angry that they haven't been able to find the person who shot me. I can't put this on them."

"I'm glad you're comfortable talking to me," he said

as she raised her head from his shoulder. Her eyes had dried but they were still just as bright. Her lips, those red plump lips that had tempted him for days, were only inches from his.

When his gaze returned to hers, something passed between them. A need, a desire, like none he had ever felt before had him lowering his head as her mouth turned up toward his.

Her lips opened the second they touched his, surprising him with her own need as their tongues tangled. Desire for more shot through him. Even though he tried to tell himself that they were moving way too fast, he had to touch her. His hands were under her tank top and the feel of her bare breasts as he cupped them sent a dangerous desire through his body. The feel of her fingers as they curled into his back of his neck, her nails sharp against his skin, was almost too much. When she wiggled her shorts-clad bottom as she readjusted herself in his lap, he groaned. If they didn't stop that moment it would be too late. Was he ready to take this step?

He was torn in half, part of him wanting more while the other was determined this couldn't go any further.

Katie had been nothing but honest with him when she'd admitted her attraction to him. And he had been honest with her about the reasons that he couldn't become involved with anyone that would be temporary in his and Violet's life. Violet had to come first. His daughter had spent too much of her life without someone looking out for her. But that was his job now. He'd learned from Lilly that relationships had consequences. It wasn't a lesson he could quickly forget.

He lifted his lips, and his body protested with every

inch he put between the two of them, a deep ache settling in his groin.

"I want you, Katie. You know that, don't you?" he asked her as she blinked up at him, her eyes languorous and her lips swollen and even redder now from his kisses.

"Yes, I think that's pretty evident," she said as she rocked herself against the hard length of him, sending a jolt of desire through his body that was almost his undoing.

From the gleam in her eyes, he had no doubt that she knew she wasn't playing fair, but two could play that game.

He stroked her pebbled nipples and she arched into his hands. A sweet pain shot through him as he hardened even more. Only then did he realize his mistake. His control was slipping away from him again and he wasn't sure that he even cared.

"You're still not sure, are you?" Katie licked her lips before letting out an exaggerated sigh.

He didn't dare move. One more squirm of her tight bottom against him and no matter what his misgivings, there would be no going back.

"I should be angry, but I understand. We barely know each other and then I bare my soul to you. You have to worry that I'm dragging you into my life, which is absurdly complicated right now."

"Is that really what you think? That because you are struggling right now I don't want to become involved? That's BS and you have to know it."

"So it's not me, it's you?" she asked. She stood and stepped away from him.

He felt her withdrawal as if some part of him were

being ripped away. But much like the need to tear off a bandage and get the pain over with, this was for the best.

He stood and took a step toward her even though he knew he needed to walk away. This was madness. "I explained my reasons for us not getting involved. You have a life in New York that you will be going back to soon. Before Violet, we might have been able to make this work. A summer fling between two adults, yeah maybe. But I have more than my own needs to consider now."

He saw the moment she accepted his reasoning as all the defensiveness seemed to leave her body and she wrapped her arms around herself.

"I'm sorry. You've been nothing but kind to me. I don't know what's wrong with me. I'm not like this, you know. I don't go around throwing myself at men in New York."

Her words filled him with a surprising pleasure. He'd never believed that she reacted to other men the same way as to him, but it was good to hear it. But why was that? What made him different from all the men in New York?

Maybe that was the appeal. He wasn't the smart-dressed city boy that she was used to. He was just a simple beach bum, more comfortable in a pair of flip-flops than a pair of Gucci lace-ups.

Or was it the very thing that kept him holding her at arm's length? Was she just interested in him because she could walk away in a few weeks and never have to look back?

His heart told him that she was sincere in her interest in him, but his mind wasn't going to let him forget the way Lilly had walked away from him without ever looking back.

"It's late and you couldn't have gotten much sleep today before Violet came home from school. Maybe it's best if we discuss this later when our minds are clearer," he said.

A sadness had filled Katie's eyes when she turned toward him. Or was it acceptance? "Good night, Katie."

"Good night, Dylan. Sleep well," she said as she headed for the doors leading back into the house.

He had no doubt that she knew there would be very little sleep for him tonight, just like he was certain she would be the reason.

# CHAPTER SEVEN

"HI, DADDY," KATIE said when she heard the sound of her daddy's voice, gruff and comforting on her phone. She really should have called him earlier. She had no excuse to give him, but knowing her father there wouldn't be a need. Being a police officer in the NYPD had worn all the sensitivity out of him years ago.

"Katie dear, how are you? Have you gotten that Key West crew into shape yet?"

No, but they certainly were helping her get into shape. Or at least the experience there was helping her learn to deal with her problems. After all, she'd run as far south as she could. She'd given herself no option but to stop and deal with them.

Not that she could tell him that. That was the problem with a lie. You either had to continue the lie and live with the results, or you had to come clean about the lie you'd told which was always painful. She'd told her father that she was fine. How did she tell him now that she was struggling with anxiety and fear whenever something triggered memories of the shooting?

Her counselor advised her to be honest with her family so she could begin healing. But the thought of disappointing her father was more than she could handle now.

Baby steps. She needed to take baby steps right now. She only felt safe sharing those deepest memories haunting her with Dylan. And she hadn't even shared how empty she discovered her life was after the shooting. How could she, without him thinking that she wanted even more from him than their friendship?

"I'm actually learning a lot here. It's so much different from New York."

"How's that?" her father asked.

"Well, there's the weather. It's extremely humid and it rains a lot, but there are all these blooming trees and bushes. And there are these crazy iguanas. There was this huge one that came up on my back deck last night while I was sitting there. It was at least three feet long and it had these sharp teeth and these long spines on its back. It scared me to death."

"Did you shoot it?" her father asked.

"No, of course not. Dylan put it back in his garden." She knew her mistake the moment the words were out of her mouth. But it was too late. Her father had years of investigating under his belt. He never missed a thing.

"And who is this Dylan?" Her father's voice all business now. Captain John McGee Sr. alert and on duty.

"He's one of the flight crew members and he's my landlord." And the only man she'd ever met that could set her on fire with one touch. The night before had proven that. It also proved that Dylan was just as affected by her as she was by him.

She smiled, thinking of the way she had tortured him the night before. It was his own fault. Or was it?

Dylan had told her more than once now that he didn't get involved in short-term relationships.

Her smile turned into a frown. She needed to accept that there could be nothing between the two of them. It wasn't fair to him to expect more.

Still, he'd been the one to pull her into his lap. That showed he was interested in her, even if it was just for a short time, right? But that was something he would ever admit to. Violet's mother had hurt him too deeply for him to trust anyone.

"Katie?" her father asked, "You still there?"

"Oh, sorry. Did I lose you?" she asked, wondering if her phone service was the problem or simply her mind so caught up in her thoughts of Dylan that she hadn't heard her father. It felt like her mind did a lot of wandering lately. "What were you saying?"

"I was saying that you need to remember that you are in Key West to do a job. I've told you about the dangers of getting romantically involved with your coworkers. Never ends well, Katie dear."

"Never?" she asked, teasing her father, who had been seeing a woman, Ms. Elizabeth from dispatch, since Katie was a teenager.

"I'm not joking. You've had a hard year. The last thing you need is to come back here with some heartache over one of them beach boys down there."

Her father had no idea just how hard the last months had been on her, but he was right. She didn't need to lose her heart to Dylan.

"It's not like that, Daddy. Don't you have enough to worry about with my brothers right now? You know I can take care of myself," she said, hoping this wasn't just another lie she was telling the two of them.

"I don't doubt that a bit, Katie dear, but…"

Her hands tightened on her phone as her father hesitated. This was what she had feared. As always the man somehow knew there was something she was hiding. It was a gift that made him a good detective.

"I know it's been hard on you, not having a mother to talk to you while you were growing up. But you know I'm always here if you need me, right?"

Her big strong father sounded so vulnerable that tears flooded her eyes. She wiped them with her free hand. She'd cried more in the last few months than she'd cried her whole life. "I know, Daddy. It's been good for me here. Really good."

"I'm glad to hear that," her father said, sounding more like the man in charge that she was used to.

By the time she hung up with her father she'd somehow managed to reassure him that things were going to be okay and that soon she'd be on her way home to New York, ready to get back to her life in the big city, flying wherever she was needed and helping to save lives. Now all she had to do was to convince herself.

It had been a week of doing nothing but transfers that had Katie seeing red. Dylan had asked her to take some twelve-hour shifts working days and since she was the new person and only temporary she had agreed. She hadn't known the motive behind his request. She hadn't shared her experiences getting shot or the problems she was still learning to deal with just so Dylan could take her off the trauma calls. She'd assumed he understood what she needed was to get out there and function as a full-fledged flight nurse. Why couldn't he see that she needed to be treated like everyone else?

Or did he think, after hearing her story, that she couldn't do her job? There was only one way to handle this. She would have this out with him face-to-face as she'd been brought up to do.

A twinge of guilt hit her with the memory of the way she'd brushed off her father's concerns earlier in the week instead of facing her troubles. But this wasn't her father. This was business. This was her job. The one she was ready to fight for if it was necessary.

She knocked on the office door where she'd seen Dylan headed after the crew finished their last transfer from the Key West hospital to Miami. It had been an easy flight. They'd all been easy flights the last three shifts. She'd ended up the third wheel on the crew and been forced to take all the transfers. It wasn't that she minded helping out. It was the fact that she wasn't being trusted with the other calls.

Except for work, she and Dylan had rarely seen each other. She didn't need a flashing neon sign to tell her why he was keeping his distance. He'd been very plain that he wasn't interested in becoming involved with her. It hurt. She'd have to admit that, but she understood his reasons. She couldn't undo a past that had caused him to shy from short-term relationships and hurting Violet was the last thing she wanted. The little girl had quickly taken residence in Katie's heart and she knew that it wasn't going to be easy to leave her when the time came to return to New York. Confusing Dylan's daughter with a relationship that had no future wouldn't be fair.

She could hear that he was on a phone call and had turned to leave when the office door opened.

"Hey. Sorry I had a call I needed to take. What's

up?" Dylan said. His eyes looked tired and his hair was once more rumpled as if his hands had pulled at it too long.

"Is something wrong?" she asked, watching him closely. If he'd been speaking to the NYC office he would tell her, wouldn't he?

"Nothing for you to worry about," he said.

"What does that mean?" Had he told the New York office about the anxiety she was dealing with? The fact that she was suffering from what could only be PTSD? Had they decided to offer her another one of those desk jobs that she had already turned down after the shooting? Or were they working together to get her off the regular flight crew and only allow her to do transfers, just like he was doing here? Was that the plan? That once she returned to New York she'd be shuffled into some position where she'd transfer patients from one hospital to the other, never getting to see what was really going on in the city? Never getting to do the job of saving lives that she had been trained to do?

"It's nothing. Just some changes that are coming. I wish Alex was here to deal with it all," Dylan said. "Would you like something to drink? I really need a water."

Moving back, she watched as he walked down the hall to the kitchen. He came back with two bottles of water and handed her one of them. Sitting down at the desk, she glanced at the piece of paper in front of him where someone had been doodling stick figures. Was that a crown sitting on one of their heads?

It was plain to see that he wasn't going to tell her who he'd been talking to. She decided on the up-front method of interrogation that her father had taught her.

"Was it the New York office? Are they going to fire me? Is that why I haven't been on the trauma calls?"

There was no way to tell if the surprise in Dylan's eyes was due to her discovering the truth or her being way off the mark.

"Why would they fire you?" Dylan asked. He took a deep breath and then motioned to the chair.

"Because you told them I couldn't do my job. Isn't that why you only have me doing the transfers? Because you don't trust me?" she asked. She felt all the fight leave her as she voiced her greatest fear. By opening up to Dylan she had laid herself open for this, but she'd thought she could trust him to understand that she would never let her own problems affect her job or the safety of her patients. Had she been wrong?

"Maybe you should start from the beginning because nothing you've said since you walked into this room makes sense."

"Neither does anything you've said. You're holding something back and if it isn't that I'm going to get fired, what is it?" For a moment she thought he was going to tell her what had upset him so much, but then he shook his head.

"It's nothing to do with you. *That* I can tell you. And as far as you taking the transfers, that's a lot of what we do. As the fill-in you've ended up with a lot of those calls because the regular team has been busy during the night and I thought you could give them a break," he explained. "And if I have a problem with any of the staff that would require me to discipline or change their duties I would talk to them. You can trust me, Katie. I thought you knew that."

Their radios went off and they both stood. "Stat

STEMI transfer to Miami," Katie read as she headed out to the hall to join the rest of the crew. Doors opened up down the hall and they both met the crew.

"I've got this one," Dylan said to Max as he was zipping up his flight suit. She turned, surprised to see that Dylan had grabbed his own suit. They were buckled in their seats and in the air in less than four minutes.

"What brings you out of the office, boss? Getting bored?" Jackie asked.

"I just needed some flight time. You know how it is. And how many times do I need to tell you not to call me 'boss.' Alex is still the boss here," Dylan said, his voice over the headsets carried an edge she hadn't heard before.

They worked quietly together as she prepared the IV fluids and he readied the monitors they would need to transport someone who was having an acute heart attack.

"Don't they have a cath lab at the hospital?" she asked. She was pretty sure she had seen that they did some cardiac procedures.

"Only for diagnostic testing. The cardiologist in Miami must have determined that this guy needed immediate intervention," Dylan said.

Landing at the hospital, she was glad to see that the nurses on duty had their patient ready to go with an IV line running in each forearm.

"What's the story?" she asked as she switched the man's oxygen tubing over to their portable tank while Dylan transferred him over to their portable monitors.

"Here's the twelve lead," a nurse said as she handed Katie a copy of an EKG, which showed a textbook-perfect elevation of the man's ST segment.

"Mr. Singh, I'm Katie, a flight nurse with Heli-Care. We're going to take a fast trip up north to Miami where there's a cardiologist who can take care of your heart. Is that okay with you?"

The man nodded his head and they finished packing him up. They left the hospital with his family standing at the entrance waving their goodbyes. It was only when their headsets were on and the skids had left the grown that Katie exchanged a look with Dylan.

"I don't like the way this guy looks," she said, turning her head away from the patient. The dusky blue of the man's lips told her there was not a lot of time before he would be in trouble.

"I'm increasing his oxygen," Dylan said as he switched the oxygen tubing from the portable tank to the oxygen inside the cab. "I've got him up to fifteen liters. Do you see any change?"

"SaO2 is eighty-eight, respirations shallow at thirty. BP is falling too…eighty-eight over fifty-three," she responded. "I'm opening up the fluids to see if it will help with the hypotension. And I'm going to prepare for intubation."

"I'm radioing ahead. They need to be ready to take this guy straight into the cath lab." As Dylan started the process with dispatch to get in touch with the receiving hospital, she did a quick neuro check, noticing that the patient was harder to arouse. "Hey, Dylan. He's less responsive. It might be the morphine they gave him, but it's a definite change. I'm going to go ahead and intubate."

"Do it. This guy is going bad fast. I'm worried about that blood pressure too," Dylan said as he pushed the button on the monitor to recycle. The new reading wasn't any better than the earlier one.

"Interior wall ST elevation? Cardiogenic shock?" she asked as she pushed the medications she had drawn up for intubation. His head on the stretcher resting between her knees, she positioned the man's head and slid the laryngoscope in place, visualized the vocal cords and inserted the endotracheal tube. With the Ambu bag connected, she started ventilating the patient as Dylan leaned over and checked for placement.

"Good breath sounds. I'm waiting for an order from the doctor for a vasopressor. I wouldn't have this problem if Alex was here. I'd have an order by now," Dylan said.

She had so many questions concerning Alex's location and when he'd be returning. But they'd have to wait until they weren't fifteen hundred feet in the air.

"Going in for final approach," Jackie said through the headsets.

"Thank goodness," Katie said. "I want to hand over this guy before he deteriorates anymore."

"See, not all transfers are boring," Dylan said as the skids touched the ground. They hit the ground running as soon as the stretcher was unloaded.

Katie had thought that she would have a chance to talk to Dylan when they arrived back at the hangar, but she was quickly sent off on another flight with Max. And while her grumpy coworker was growing on her, she missed having Dylan by her side.

And that was a problem, wasn't it? She'd be leaving in a few weeks. There'd be no more flights with Dylan. No more crab boils or late-night talks. And no more kisses that set her body on fire with a longing that she had never felt before.

But she hadn't come here for a temporary hookup. She'd come here to heal and she knew that she was making progress.

She was just now accepting that some parts of her life had changed forever. Seeing that the changes could be dealt with, that she could learn ways to deal with the anxiety when it was triggered, was a good start.

She'd do her job and when her time was over here she would be ready to return to her real life, her life in New York where her family was waiting for her.

That was what she needed to concentrate on instead of some kisses that she'd shared with a man that could never be hers.

# CHAPTER EIGHT

DYLAN WASN'T SURE what drove him to Katie's door. Maybe it was the pacing he'd been doing back and forth in his bedroom while remembering the way Katie had felt in his arms, so soft and warm. Maybe it was his cold and lonely bed that made him question all his cautious rules meant to protect him and his daughter?

With Violet at a sleepover, he'd had the whole night to himself. But the light coming from Katie's cottage had kept him from settling down. Knowing she was awake, like him, was having the same effect as if he'd drank a whole pot of coffee by himself.

He'd opened a book, read a few words and shut it. He'd turned on the sports channel and turned it off.

What was she doing over there? Was she thinking of him like he was thinking of her? Was she reliving the kiss they'd shared like he was?

Or was it her worry for her job that was keeping her up tonight? Their conversation had been interrupted by dispatch earlier that day. It wouldn't be right to let her continue to question her place on the flight team without him reassuring her that she was wanted and needed there.

He needed to convince her that he had total faith in

her abilities. He couldn't understand why she worried about her future with Heli-Care. He'd worked with her enough now to know that she was much more than a capable flight nurse. And her employee file had been filled with excellent reviews.

He knocked on the door and waited. And waited. Had she fallen asleep with all the lights on? He started to leave.

"Dylan, what are you doing here?" Katie asked as she opened the door. While she wasn't in the tank top and shorts he'd been fantasizing about on his walk to her cottage, the long white T-shirt that barely covered the top of her thighs was enough to create new fantasies that would definitely be keeping him up again that night.

"You busy?" he asked. "We were interrupted this afternoon so I thought maybe we could talk."

His excuse for seeing her sounded weak even to his own ears. Their conversation could have waited until the next day. But his need to see her, to talk to her and, yes, the hope of more kisses like they'd shared before, wouldn't wait.

"Okay. Come on in. Is Violet asleep?" Katie said, though she didn't sound as if she was as excited about seeing him as he was to see her. Instead she appeared distracted.

"No, I'm on my own tonight. She's spending the night with a friend."

"I was just finishing up my paintings," she said as she led the way through the cottage to the small open living room where he could see an easel had been set on the dining room tabletop.

He walked around where he could see a canvas watercolor painting of a white heron. He recognized the setting as the one from her back deck. Picking up the canvas, he studied the details of the large bird. Its head was cocked up and its eyes, piercing, seemed to stare out at him. This wasn't the work of a hobbyist.

"You're good. Real good. Did you ever consider going into art in college?" he asked.

"And give my dad a heart attack? No, that was one profession I never considered." She said as she moved around the room putting her supplies away.

"So what were some of the professions you considered?" he asked, leaning back against the island that separated the room from the kitchen.

"Well, when I first got out of high school I considered following my other family members into the NYPD, but I've always liked the sciences. Especially my anatomy and physiology classes. They were my favorite. I thought about medical school, but I didn't feel that I had the patience I'd need to commit to that many years of school. A nursing degree gave me so many options. What about you? What made you decide to become a paramedic?"

"I'd had a lot of jobs since high school. Most were things I learned working with my dad growing up on the marina. A little construction work, some boat engine work, lots of general handyman jobs. But it was when I heard the community was in need of more first responders that I decided to look into becoming a paramedic. It was quite an adventure and I loved every minute of it. I wouldn't want to do anything else."

"That's why you get it. Get me. Isn't it? You understand how I feel about my job. It's my life," Katie said as she took a step closer to him.

"I can't pretend to understand what you've been going through. Being shot while just trying to do your job? That's a deep betrayal after everything you've done to help others. But yes, I understand the fear of not being able to do the job you feel you were born to do." He started to make a move toward her. He only needed to touch her.

She took a step back confusing him. Hadn't he just read that same need in her own eyes? Or was it just his imagination?

"Want something to eat?" Katie turned her back to him as she opened the refrigerator. "Or drink?"

He placed the canvas back on the table, then saw that there was another one that had been laid beside it.

There was no Florida sunshine or bright colored blooms in this one. Where the other painting had been light and cheerful, this one was dark and menacing with the only light coming from a few lit buildings in the dark background. A street of dark blues and browns was empty and lonely.

It was hard to believe the same artist could have painted them both.

Moving away from the table, he took a seat in a side chair as Katie shut the refrigerator door without taking anything out. Was his presence troubling her? If she needed space, he would give it to her. He'd say his piece and then leave.

He waited until she took a chair across from him. "I'm sorry about this. Interrupting you. I shouldn't have come over this late. I just saw your light on and thought…"

"That I was here worrying about if that phone call that upset you had something to do with my job?" Katie said, interrupting him. "I could have been. But no. I decided that I needed a little art therapy so I got my paints out."

"Art therapy?" That explained the picture so full of darkness. "Is that like the shopping therapy Jo and Summer are always talking about going to Miami for?"

"For me? Yeah. I guess painting has always been an escape for me. It's kind of like what some people get from reading. Or shopping, I guess. My counselor recommended it in New York, but I couldn't bring myself to pick up a pencil or brush then. Seeing that heron seemed to awaken that part of me again," Katie said as she moved to the edge of her seat.

"I'm glad. If you'd like, I can see about getting Pascal over here to pose for you?" he joked, trying to lighten the mood.

"I think I'll stick to birds, thank you," Katie said, a smile playing around the corners of her lips before disappearing.

"Why are you really here, Dylan?" she asked.

"I couldn't stay away," he said with an honesty that surprised himself. Unable to take his eyes from hers, he reached out a hand to her. She looked down at it then placed her hand in his. But there was a hesitation that hadn't been there before and he couldn't ignore it. "What's wrong, Katie?"

"Besides the fact that my whole life is a tangled mess and I'm wondering if I'm about to get myself even more tangled up in a relationship that we've both admitted has no future? Nothing has changed, Dylan. In a few weeks I'll be returning to New York."

Her words made him draw his hand back, but then her fingers tightened their grip on his, as if it was a lifeline, confusing him even more. He didn't want to complicate Katie's life.

"I'm as confused as you. I'm not into holiday flings or one-night stands. But this…whatever it is between us, I don't feel in control of where it's leading us," he said as he stood and pulled her into his arms. "Tell me to leave and I will."

"I don't want you to leave. I want you. But I know you have your own rules about who you get involved with. And I don't want you to regret this. We both have to understand that this need that keeps drawing us together, it's just a temporary thing." She bit down on her bottom lip. "Can we do this? Have this time together without any expectations? Go into this with the understanding that neither one of us will let this complicate things between us. People do that all the time, right?"

People might, but he didn't. He had never had a taste for one-night stands. It was why he had stipulations that he didn't get involved with someone who wasn't a local. And even that had been off the table since Violet had come into his life.

He'd been honest with Katie about everything, from her job to his history with Lilly and how that had affected him. But could he share his fear that it might be too late for him to keep things uncomplicated between them? Because the way he was beginning to feel about Katie was already complicated. Taking her as his lover would make their parting even more difficult. He was risking the pain he'd felt when Lilly left him.

But wasn't Katie worth the risk? Wasn't spending this time together worth it? As long as he could keep Violet protected, he could handle everything else.

He brushed his hand over her soft cheek and lifted

her chin up toward his face. Emerald-green eyes met his own with questions he wasn't capable of answering. They were both stepping into the unknown, but they were doing it together.

She was close enough that he could see a sprinkle of freckles across her nose he'd noticed for the first time. His lips brushed over them then grazed her mouth. He held his breath, waiting to see if she thought him worth the risk as well. When her lips parted, he rushed inside with an eagerness that he had never felt before. It was if she had thrown him an unexpected lifeline that was the only hope he had to survive. Their kiss was more passion than finesse as their need for each other took control.

How they made it to her bedroom he would never know.

Her arms wrapped around him and he lifted her off her feet. He walked them to the bed without breaking their kiss, unwilling to take a chance that one of them might come to their senses.

His shirt hit the bedroom floor minus most of its buttons. Her T-shirt quickly followed. He was finding it hard to remove the tiny polka-dot shorts she wore with her hand inside his shorts.

Her shorts and panties slid to the ground where they joined the rest of her clothes as her hand circled him. His gasp broke their kiss and they both came up for a breath of air.

"Do you have a condom?" Katie asked as she ran her hand up the length of his shaft.

Her words broke through the fog of desire that had taken over. How had he forgotten about needing a condom? It was his responsibility to keep her safe.

"I've got it." He stepped away from her and reached into his back pocket before discarding his shorts. Fumbling with his wallet, he pulled out the foil wrapper. He forced his lungs to take a deep breath and willed his body to relax. His control was slipping and he hadn't even touched her beautiful bare body.

One look at her lying on the bed and his body went right back into overdrive. He'd never been so affected by a woman. Not even Lilly, who he'd thought he loved. He forced thoughts of his ex and of love out of his mind. This was not the time or place for either.

He crawled onto the bed and covered her. "Katie, you are so beautiful."

The sensual feel of her breasts against his own skin set his pulse racing and he covered her perfect breast with his hand. Her heart beat against his palm in a fast rhythm that matched his own. Her nipple peaked against his hand.

"I want to know all of you. I want to kiss every intimate inch of you. But where do I start?" His lips trailed down her neck and she shivered against him. "Should I start here?"

"Or maybe here?" His lips replaced his hand on her breast. The feel of her tight nipple against his tongue set him on fire. His hand moved down her body and parted her curls. She was warm and wet against his fingers.

His lips followed a path down her abdomen, her stomach muscles quivering beneath his mouth. Her body arched up from the bed as his fingers found that sweet spot of her clit.

"Dylan, I can't…" Katie said, her breaths coming fast.

"Can't? But you're too strong of a woman to give

up when it's something you want. I know that. Do you want this, Katie?" His lips skimmed down her thighs.

"Oh, yes. I want it." Her breaths were ragged as she spoke. She moaned as she arched her body up to meet his mouth.

He pleasured her with his tongue and fingers. Her body tensed against his as her climax tore through her.

Katie came the way she did everything else: strong and fierce. Her scream cut through the room. It wasn't enough for him. He wanted to hear it again and again as she came for him. But his own breathing told him he couldn't take the torture of holding himself back much longer.

"Dylan, please. I want more," Katie gasped, her eyes bright with tears. Of course she would. She always fought for what she wanted. She'd always want more.

"I'll give you everything I have, sweet Katie," he murmured, brushing back strands of silky hair from her face.

With the condom safely in place, he entered her with one thrust. The warmth of her surrounded him, taking him inside her as her body opened up to him, stretched his control to a dangerous level. But still he held on. He'd promised her everything and he would give it to her.

The woman that thought she had lost a part of herself in New York was not the same woman in this bedroom. Wrapping her legs around him, she met each thrust with a demand that brought him deeper. Her body tensed and shuddered against him. He let himself follow her into the climax that took control of them both as they reached a summit higher than he'd ever climbed before.

Later, as he curled his body around hers, he knew what he had experienced with Katie was something more than he had ever experienced before.

With a response time that came from years of being awakened by emergency calls from dispatch, her phone only rang once before Katie was out of bed and grabbing it from the floor where it had landed the night before. Seeing her oldest brother's number on the display was surprising. She'd done her weekly required check-in with him only the day before. Why would he be calling her now? A familiar chill, one that came from being in a family of police officers, froze her in place.

As Dylan rolled over and sat up, she hit the button while she pulled her T-shirt over her head. "What's wrong?"

"Something wrong with me calling my baby sister? You still enjoying that hellish heat down there?" a deep voice asked on the other line.

"Wrong? No. Unexpected? Yes." She knew her brothers too well. There was a reason for this call. Her brother wasn't calling her to ask about the weather. "What's up, Junior?"

"We've got him, sis," her brother said.

She didn't have to ask who he was talking about. She'd known, even though they'd kept it from her as much as possible, that her father and two oldest brothers were on a mission to arrest the person responsible for hurting her.

For her part, she'd tried to forget that there was someone out there on the loose who'd almost ended her life. It wasn't like they'd picked her out specifically. She'd just been in the wrong place at the wrong time.

She had no reason to fear that he was going to come back to finish her off like he had her patient.

Or had that been her fear? Was that why she couldn't stand to have someone at her back? Was that the reason she was afraid in crowds? Her counselor had suggested this to her, but she'd always denied that she was still afraid of the shooter. Maybe she'd been wrong.

"You're sure it's him?" she asked as she looked over to where Dylan now sat up in her bed. He brushed back the sandy curls that had fallen into his eyes and a fire stirred inside her. How could just a look from this man affect her this way?

She didn't want to talk about the guy who'd shot her. She wanted to climb back in bed with Dylan and forget all about that night.

But that would be selfish and unappreciative. Her family had worked hard to make sure this guy got caught when her case could have joined the file room of cold cases.

"We found a good informant. It seems our shooter is a bragger. It's him." Which meant her brothers and probably her father had been laying out money to catch the guy.

"So what happens now?" she asked. A sheet was wrapped around her along with a pair of muscled arms. She hadn't even realized she was shivering.

"They picked him up last night after the warrant was issued. He's got a record, so hopefully the judge won't let him out on bond."

His words sent a rush of anger washing through her. After all the hard work her family as well as the other officers involved had done, the guy could still walk free? After all the pain he had caused in her life? After he'd taken the life of a young man?

"No," she said. "They can't do that. It's not right. He killed someone. He could have killed me."

*And he changed my life forever.* She was just beginning to accept that. Through her counseling sessions she'd been forced to face that she would never be the same Katie Lee McGee she had been before. Now she might have to live with the knowledge that the man responsible could be out there living his life like nothing ever happened.

"The district attorney is pushing to hold him without bail. He had a gun in his possession when they found him. If it matches the bullets we got from the deceased and… Well, if they match we'll have a more solid case." Her brother skipped over the words *the bullet that they dug out of you*, but she knew what he was trying not to say and she still felt the sting of the words. Acknowledging that she had been shot was hard for her and he knew it. "But, Katie, you know how these things work. There's no guarantee that the judge will agree with the DA."

Another shiver hit her and Dylan's arms tightened even more. Leaning back, she rested her head against him. She was suddenly so tired.

"I know," she said wearily as all the anger drained from her. She'd grown up with table talk of suspects that had been released as soon as they were brought in. "It's okay, Junior. I know it's not your fault. I appreciate everything you and the rest of the investigators have done. Make sure they know that, okay."

She hung up the phone not sure how she should feel.

Would it really be worse if the person responsible for shooting her got off than if he'd never been found?

The warmth of Dylan's body behind her was a comfort she hadn't known she needed. But she did need him. She needed him now. Turning in his arms, she proceeded to show him just how much.

# CHAPTER NINE

DYLAN WATCHED VIOLET and Katie talk colors and textures as they made their way through the art store. When Katie had mentioned she needed some supplies, Violet had been quick to volunteer to show her around the local hobby shops.

"Can I get some paints too?" Violet asked him. "I'll be careful with them."

He could see the carpet in her room covered in spilt containers of paint. His daughter had a love of color and art, which Katie had been encouraging over the last week.

They'd gotten into a routine of spending the warm evenings when neither was working on either his or her deck. While he grilled their supper, Katie taught Violet some of the basics of using watercolors. Though they were being careful of their interactions when Violet was present, they always managed a few clandestine kisses good-night. Still, he couldn't help but worry about his daughter as he saw the two of them become closer. He'd made a point of reminding Violet that Katie was only here temporarily like the other renters they'd had over the summer.

"She'll only use them with me on the deck," Katie said.

Two sets of eyes from the two most beautiful girls in the world stared up with him. It was official. He was outnumbered.

"Okay, as long as Violet understands the rules. She has a tendency to ignore the rules she doesn't agree with," he said, giving his daughter a look that had her giggling instead of chastised.

A part of him winced at his words. He felt like a hyprocrite. He had been breaking his most important rule since the night he'd slept with Katie.

But he had no regrets. Watching Katie and Violet with their heads bent together over a display of brushes, though, he felt his concern for his daughter intensify. He was an adult, and both he and Katie had gone into their new relationship knowing that it was only temporary.

But Violet was only eight. Providing stability had been his first and most important priority. He'd been careful to make sure that his daughter knew he wasn't going anywhere. He'd always be there for her.

But Katie wouldn't be. Hopefully his daughter would understand when her new friend had to leave.

"Can we walk down to that place with the funny art?" Violet asked after they'd paid for their purchases. "The place with the big statue of that bull dog?"

"Sure, but I don't think this is exactly what Katie is used to." There were a lot of artists that sold their work in the local shops. Pictures and paintings of everything from roosters to pirates hung in the gift shops and galleries. It was definitely not the same as the artwork available for viewing at the Metropolitan Museum of Art in New York City.

"It sounds like fun to me," Katie said. "This is a part of Key West I haven't seen."

They followed the sidewalk and turned onto Duval. A favorite with tourist for the local shops, it was more crowded than the other streets.

The crowd. He hadn't given a thought to how Katie might react to the tourist-packed streets.

"We don't want to get separated," he said as he took Violet's and Katie's hands.

"I'm not a baby," Violet grumbled, but she didn't pull away from him.

Katie squeezed his hand, but there wasn't any other sign that the people surrounding her were creating the anxiety he'd seen in her face before. Could it be that she was finally recovering?

They played tourists as they stopped in the brightly displayed shops. Katie bought an oil painting in a store that specialized in estate sails, before following Violet into an ice cream shop with fanciful creations.

As he and Katie ate their creamy dessert, Violet chased a small rooster around the table while eating a rainbow-colored ice cream cone.

"Having fun?" he asked, not knowing how to ask if the crowds were a problem for her. "We can leave if you need to."

"I'm fine. More than fine," she said. The smile on her face was genuine. "Thanks for inviting me."

"Thank you for helping Violet with the art lessons. She's always had an artistic flair but I hadn't thought she was old enough to take lessons."

"All I'm showing her is the basics. I'm sure you can find a professional to teach her when I leave," she said before looking away.

He glanced over to where Violet was talking to the rooster she'd cornered, to make sure they had some privacy, then placed his hand under her chin. Turning her face up to his, he stared down into troubled green eyes.

"It's okay, Katie. We both know our time together is short-lived. We probably should start getting Violet used to the idea, though. You're her new best friend and I'm not sure she understands that you are only here temporarily, though I've told her that your home is in New York."

His hand brushed over her cheek then trailed down her face. She had an expressive face with its bright eyes and big smile. He'd taken to storing memories of these times they shared.

He knew how her eyes sparkled when Violet told her a joke. How her lips turned up into the perfect smile every time she saw him. There was no shyness, no awkward moments between the two of them. And then there were the memories of their lovemaking. He'd never had a lover that was so responsive and passionate. He could see that she was returning to the happy, funny woman that Alex had once described to him.

Over half of her time in Key West had passed and she hadn't displayed any issues on a flight since the gunshot-wound patient they'd picked up on the beach the first week she'd arrived. Even Max had come to accept her place in their crew, something that seemed to surprise the staff as much as it had surprised her.

She was healing and he was thankful for that.

They toured a few more art galleries before calling it a day. It was a memorable day for all of them. While Violet exclaimed over her new paints, Katie clutched the framed portrait of one of Key West's famous roosters as if she had a priceless piece of art.

When Violet commented that he hadn't bought anything for himself, he didn't bother to tell her that he'd been given the best gift of all. He'd spent a perfect day with his two favorite people. What more could he ask for?

Katie couldn't say exactly when the change had taken place. One morning she had woken up feeling like she would never be the person she'd been before the shooting and the next morning she hadn't felt quite as broken. Slowly each day, she'd seen a change as she worked to fit in with the Key West crew. As she learned more about what it took for her to cope with the triggers to her anxiety, she grew in confidence. As she grew in confidence, her spirits lifted and the next day was a little bit better.

Now she woke up with a smile on her face, looking forward to the day. She refused to acknowledge that a big part of why she felt better was because of the nights she was spending with Dylan when Violet was away with a friend or a grandparent.

And it wasn't just the nights. They were spending every minute they could spare together now as her time in Key West ran out. There wasn't a night off that she didn't spend with Dylan and Violet. And if Dylan happened to work a shift when she was off, Katie had begun having Violet for sleepovers. On those nights, after Dylan had called to wish his daughter a good night, the two of them would spend hours talking. But she knew things couldn't go on like this. She needed to start making plans to return to New York.

She needed to start preparing Violet for her departure. She and Dylan had never let the little girl see that they were more than friends. But the amount of time they spent together could confuse Violet, even though the she and Dylan talked openly about her home in New York where she would be returning.

But like everything else that she couldn't deal with, she pushed her thoughts of leaving Dylan away. Her life was improving each day. She just needed a little more time here. She'd thought about asking for an extension on her contract in Key West, especially since Alex was still out, but she knew that wasn't the answer. No matter when she left Key West it was going to be hard. Staying longer would just make it worse.

And it wasn't just Dylan and Violet she was going to miss. She felt like one of the crew now. She'd worked with each one of them enough now that she thought they felt comfortable with her. She hoped they each felt as if they could count on her as a dependable partner.

She'd even learned how to deal with Max. When he'd given her crap on a flight to a car-bicycle accident, telling her not to run off all the first responders, she'd been ready. Telling him to make sure he didn't puke on their patient had gotten a rare laugh from the man. Since that day, he hadn't given her any trouble.

But her favorite partner was still Dylan. They worked together with a familiarity that would normally take years to perfect.

As they flew over the island together on their way to a possible drowning, her confidence was at an all-time high. She had a lot of experience in drowning calls in New York. Early resuscitation was always the key.

"Heli-Care Key West, be advised we have an update," the dispatcher called over their headsets.

"Go ahead," Dylan answered.

"The original call has been updated with two, not one, two drowning victims with one victim still not accounted for," the dispatcher said. "Key West Fire and Rescue is on site with your landing zone info."

Jackie signed off and changed their radio channel. Receiving their landing zone coordinates, she made a pass over the area of beach giving them a view of the EMTs who were working the scene.

"Two adults. It looked like one of them is doing okay," she said as she pointed to where a woman sat holding a small child with a rescuer applying an oxygen mask.

"Or there's another victim we're not seeing. Let's get down there where we can help, Jackie," Dylan said. "Maybe we'll be lucky and this will be just a trip to the beach."

The fire department had positioned their landing zone farther down the beach where they had cleared all the beachgoers from the area, which made the trip back to the scene a short hike.

The resistance of the sand as they fought their way to the scene had the two of them breathing heavily by the time they got to the first victim. She was a woman in her midthirties, not much older than Katie, who sat holding a little boy no more than four in her arms, rocking him between her bouts of coughing. The young child clung to his mother but he didn't cry.

Katie noted that though she had a cough, her lips were pink. She would need to be taken to the emergency room and watched for pulmonary complications such as pneumonia, but she wouldn't be taking a flight with them.

Leaving the woman with the EMT, she followed Dylan to where first responders performed CPR on a young man.

"What's the story?" she asked as she took over compressions from a young woman who was beginning to tire.

"It seems that this couple's little boy wandered off and the two of them panicked and hit the water looking for him. They both got caught in the undertow. An onlooker got the woman out, but the husband went down before he could go back for him."

"What's the estimated downtime?" Dylan asked as he started opening their scene bag and applying monitor pads.

"The guy who brought him in says it was less than a minute. He's a firefighter from North Florida and he started CPR immediately," said the EMT who was using an Ambu bag to ventilate the patient. "Total downtime is just at fifteen minutes."

"Time for a pulse check," the young EMT who she relieved said.

Katie placed her fingers against the man's neck and counted. The feel of blood pulsing through the man's carotid took her by surprise. "There's a pulse. We have a pulse."

She motioned to where the monitor that Dylan had just turned on showed a normal sinus rhythm.

"You sure?" asked the EMT who was preparing to continue chest compressions. "It could be a pulseless rate."

"Of course I'm sure." She wanted to take his challenge personally, but she remembered this was one of the crews she'd seen at her first MVC flight. She was going to have to live with the fallout from her loss of composure that day.

Checking behind her, the man placed his fingers where hers had been, then gave her a thumbs-up along with a big smile.

Maybe it wouldn't take as long as she thought to overcome that bad first impression she had given. Not that it really mattered. She'd be leaving soon and all those first responders that had seen her lose her cool that day wouldn't give her another thought.

"Katie, why don't you intubate this guy properly while I go talk to his wife," Dylan said before leaving them and walking over to where the woman continued to rock her little boy.

She bit her lip to keep from smiling. The EMT on scene had placed a temporary pre-hospital airway that could be inserted quickly, but most of the flight crew preferred to change over to an endotracheal tube before transporting if possible. Dylan was making a point to the EMT guy that he trusted his partner to intubate their patient.

She retrieved her supplies from the scene bag and replaced the temporary airway with the laryngoscope. She followed it with the endotracheal tube and quickly had the Ambu bag attached and began ventilating the patient.

The trip back to the helicopter where Jackie waited for them was a hard one. She was used to carrying people over hot asphalt, not hot sand where her feet sank down with every step. But she wasn't about to let the firefighters assisting them see her sweat. At least not figuratively. There was nothing she could do about the sweat that ran down her face into her flight suit.

As soon as they were buckled in and had lifted off, Katie got her Ambu bag changed over to the ventilator while Dylan called Miami for a consult with a trauma physician.

She did a neurological assessment and discovered that surprisingly the man's pupils were responsive. The percentage of people that survived a drowning was low, but it looked like this guy had a chance.

"Thanks for the vote of confidence back there," she told Dylan once their patient was settled.

"What vote? You don't need votes. There's nothing wrong with your confidence," Dylan replied.

"Thanks to you." She remembered that it wasn't just her and Dylan having a conversation, and added, "Working with this whole crew has been good for my confidence. You're all a great crew."

"Make sure you tell the big office guys in New York that when you get home," Jackie said over the headset. "They seem to think we play beach volleyball all day. Which reminds me, how are you at volleyball?"

"I haven't played since high school phys ed, why?" Katie asked as she did another neurological check on their patient.

"His pupils are still responsive. He might be one of the lucky few who survive. I wish he'd be a little more responsive, though," she said.

"He can be responsive after we land. The last thing we want is for him to wake up and start fighting us," Dylan said.

"I'm not a newbie. I've got my meds ready if he starts to come around. I'm not for fighting this guy either."

"Another few pounds and he would have been too heavy for us to fly. ETA in ten. Just make sure he stays out till then," Jackie said.

He was still unconscious when they left the emergency room, but the charge nurse promised she would let them know if he woke up on her shift.

They got a call from dispatch for transport from the hospital, but had to refuse it. A storm was moving in and the ceiling was too low for flying. They made it back to base as the storm broke, soaking them as they headed into their quarters.

The heavy rain was forecasted to last the night, but they made sure their scene bags and helicopter had been restocked while Jackie ran the necessary safety checks before they turned in for the night.

When her phone rang, she knew it would be Dylan. She kept her voice quiet so she wouldn't be overheard. "So what was that strange question of Jackie's about playing volleyball?"

"There's a volleyball tournament between all the first responders every year. There's an entrance fee for each player and the money goes to the winning team's charity. Jackie's our coach. Why, you want to play?"

"I've never played beach volleyball. I don't think I'd be much of an asset. Is your team any good?"

"We're awful. Besides, the firefighters have an unfair advantage. They have their tallest members on their team. Then there are the police. Most of those guys are in really good shape. We're a bunch of paramedics and nurses with a couple of retired military pilots. We haven't got a chance."

"Don't let Jackie hear you say that." She snuggled down into the sheets. Her eyes were getting heavy.

"Of course, we do have one defense that the others don't have." Dylan's voice was getting softer now. She knew that meant he was getting sleepy too. She only had to close her eyes to see that drowsy, sexy look he got right before he fell asleep. Not that they'd had many sleepovers. With Violet spending a couple nights a week away from home while he worked, he preferred to have her home with him at night.

"What's the defense?" she asked.

"Somehow every year the other team underestimates Jo and Summer. Then right when Jo is in the middle of charming them, Summer comes in for the kill. They never see it coming. At least not the first time," he said as he yawned.

"Sounds like fun. I'd like to come if I'm here." The finality of the words hit her. She only had three weeks before she would be leaving. Twenty-one days. After that life in Key West would go on without her.

"You know you're ready," Dylan said.

She didn't know how to take his words. Was he in a hurry for her to go? No. She wouldn't believe that he wanted to rush her into leaving. "I'm glad you have a lot of confidence in me, but neither of us knows that."

"It's the confidence you have in yourself. You've got it back, Katie. I don't know if it's the counseling or just being away from New York. Maybe Alex was right and you just needed a change for a few weeks. You're not the same woman who walked into this office five weeks ago."

She wasn't. She had changed in ways she'd never imagined. And it hadn't all been from her counseling or from having a change in scenery. The biggest change had resulted from Dylan coaching her along the way.

He'd called her out every time she'd tried to deny she had a problem. He'd told her what he expected of her and then told her that he knew she could do it. And that was even when he didn't know her.

What couldn't a woman do with a man like that backing her?

They said good-night with his words still echoing in her ears. Was she really ready to return to the tough streets of New York? Could she return home and still have this new confidence? How would she ever know if she didn't try?

# CHAPTER TEN

IT WAS A RARE DAY when all three of the women on their flight crew had the day off together, so they decided to celebrate with a trip to Miami. The fact that Jo and Summer had included Katie filled her with even more grief over the people she would be leaving behind soon. She didn't mention to any of her coworkers that there were just over two weeks until her time was up in Key West. She wanted to thank them all, but she felt it would be better if she waited until her last week to start saying her goodbyes. And today was for celebrating, not spending her time thinking about something she couldn't change. Dylan invited her out with him to downtown Key West for a night where the restaurants and shops stayed open late and the local artists displayed their art on the sidewalks and she hadn't brought anything that she felt would be suitable.

Katie hadn't left the islands by car since she'd arrived in Key West, so she had forgotten what a long trip it was when you weren't going by air.

"So, what's up with you and Dylan?" Summer asked as they sped up Highway 1 in Jo's Mustang convertible.

Katie had wondered how long it would take until the two women got around to questioning her about her and Dylan's relationship. They held out fifteen minutes more than she had bet Dylan they would that morning before they'd arrived to pick her up. Dylan believed the two women would start nosing their way into his and her relationship the minute the car door shut. He was wrong. They lasted almost thirty minutes.

Dylan had left it up to Katie to tell her friends whatever she felt comfortable with. The two of them had made no effort to keep things between them a secret from their coworkers the last couple of weeks.

"I like to think Dylan and I are really good friends," Katie answered.

"Friends, huh? That's not what Violet is telling everyone," Summer said. "She seems to think she's going to be getting a new mother soon."

Katie was stunned into silence. The only person that Dylan hadn't wanted to know they were involved, at least more than friends, was Violet. "I don't know why she would say something like that. We've been very careful not to give her any reason to believe that we're anything more than friends."

"She's an eight-year-old girl who watches princess movies. She sees romance as big fancy weddings where the prince and princess live happily ever after," Jo said with a bitterness that left no doubt there was a story there.

"But she's also an eight-year-old girl whose mother just dropped her off one day with a father who was a stranger. Not that it was Dylan's fault. He had no idea that he had a kid out there," Summer said. "That wasn't fair to either one of them."

"Dylan worships that little girl. Neither one of us want to hurt her." She'd have to let Dylan know what

Violet was saying so she could have a talk with his daughter and explain their friendship. Violet was the most important person in Dylan's life, as it should be. He didn't want his little girl confused by another person leaving her, especially if she'd had hopes that Katie would be staying forever. This wasn't good.

"So now that we know the two of you don't have plans to rush down the aisle of matrimony, what exactly is going on? I've seen the looks you two exchange when you don't think anyone's watching you. And by the way, you should know that everybody is watching you," Jo added. "Just like everybody is watching Summer and Alex."

"Alex? I don't see any Alex, do you?" Summer snapped before slouching down in her seat. "I've had one phone call and half a dozen texts in the last six weeks and none of them have explained where he is and when he's coming back. What could be so secretive that he can't answer a simple question about where he is? It's not like he's on some secret military mission. I know. I asked him."

"You asked him about a secret military mission? Did you really think he'd tell you the truth if he was? It's called a secret mission for a reason," Jo pointed out, laughing at her friend as they slowed down to drive through one of the many small keys between Key West and Miami.

"Have you asked Dylan? I think he's received a couple emails," Katie said.

"I have. He says he doesn't know any more than I do." Summer shrugged. "So back to you and Dylan, do you think you'll see each other when you return to New York?"

"We haven't discussed it." She didn't think that maintaining a relationship with that many miles between them would appeal to Dylan. What would they do, take turns flying out to see each other every month or two? She couldn't begin to imagine her beach-loving lover in the middle of New York surrounded by skyscrapers. Besides, there was Violet. She'd be more confused than she was now. They couldn't do that to the child.

"I can understand that. It's hard to maintain a long-distance relationship," Jo said.

"Especially, when you don't even know where the person you are supposed to be in a relationship with might be," Summer put in.

"How come nobody told me about you and Alex?" Katie asked. It seemed odd that everyone knew the two of them were involved but never mentioned it to her.

"Well, first, we weren't sure what your past relationship with Alex had been. Second, nobody but me, and now you, know that there is definitely something going on between the two of them," Jo said.

"The only thing between me and Alex is friendship. We worked together when he lived in New York. For full disclosure, I'll admit we did attend a Heli-Care corporate function together once, but that was all. I like Alex, but he kind of reminds me of my brothers," Katie said.

"Maybe you should introduce me to one of your brothers," Summer deadpanned.

"Hold on a minute. You have a man," Jo said.

"I don't see one. Do you?" Summer turned around to face Katie in the back seat.

"I have four brothers, but only two of them are single," Katie said.

They spent the rest of the trip with Katie telling them stories of growing up in a house full of men, and Jo teasing Summer about which brother would be the better catch. Jo insisted that Summer would be better off with a lawyer than a policeman. It was plain to see that Jo was trying to cheer up her friend.

By the time they hit the stores, they were all feeling the need to let off some steam, which apparently meant buying as much merchandise as could be squeezed into Jo's compact car.

They made the trip home surrounded by shoeboxes and bags of clothes and accessories. When Katie questioned their shopping habits, she was quickly informed that they only bought items on sale and they only went on a buying spree once every three months. It still seemed like more clothes than the two women could wear in a year, but what did she know? She hadn't had a mother to teach her how to shop. Her father had been a believer of having two pairs of shoes, and an outfit for each day of the week. She'd spent all her money on paints and canvases instead of fancy dresses and makeup.

The thought of her growing up without a mother reminded her of Violet. Either she or Dylan would have to speak with her. Her friend's explanations that Violet was just a little girl that read romance everywhere made sense. Katie and Dylan had spent a lot of time together the last few weeks. It could be that the child was just confused by what she saw between the two adults. Katie didn't want to think of Violet being hurt by something she misread that Katie had done.

It was late when she made her way to her front door carrying the few packages that she had bought. The lights at Dylan's place were out. She'd have to wait until the next day to speak with him about his daughter. She only hoped that he'd be able to explain his and Katie's relationship to Violet better than she'd been able to explain it to Jo and Summer. But then, maybe the problem was she didn't really have words for what was between the two of them herself.

Katie didn't know what she'd expected on Gallery Night, but this hadn't been it. Strings of tiny fairy lights ran the length of the art gallery shops staying open late for the night while other artists had set up stalls on the sidewalk, giving it a magical atmosphere with a French flair.

When Jo had talked her into buying the rose-colored maxi dress with its thin spaghetti straps for her night with Dylan, she'd thought her new friend was mistaken. She'd been to Duval Street just a few days ago where the average attire had been shorts and comfortable T's. Now as they joined the women dressed in cocktail dresses and men in dressed slacks and ties, she was glad she had listened. The attire would have fit into any New York five-star restaurant. The atmosphere was much more welcoming than any party she'd ever attended.

Just the walk from the parking lot had made her thankful that she had not listened to Jo when she tried to insist that Katie buy a pair of four-inch heels to go with the dress. Katie had gone with the two inch. It had been the smart choice.

She had slept in and missed seeing Dylan until he

arrived at her door that night. She knew she had to broach the subject of Violet and her misunderstanding about their future, but she didn't want the magic of the night to be interrupted. Violet was staying with her grandparents for the night. There would be no reason for Dylan to sleep at his house alone. As they walked the sidewalks admiring each artist's wares, a sexual anticipation was building between them…

Dylan's hand skimmed across her waist and she shuddered.

"You okay?" he asked. His eyes looked down at her with a protectiveness that touched her heart. "If the crowds are too much, we can go."

"It was just the breeze," Katie said. How did she tell the man that the mere touch of his hand was setting her body on fire?

She'd never felt anything like the need she felt for Dylan, both in and out of the bedroom. Would this ever fade? She was afraid that it wouldn't. And what would that mean for her? Would she be walking around New York like a zombie? Dead to all of life except for her job? Her only hope was that distance would make her see things more clearly.

A group of teenage tourists rushed past them and they were pushed into a small alley. Dylan's hands came around her waist and she leaned back into him as he wrapped his arms around her. Her head fell back against his shoulder and she breathed in the scent of him. Would she ever smell the breeze off the ocean and not think of him?

"We can leave whenever you're ready," Dylan murmured. The gold flecks in his green eyes reflected the light from the low-hanging string of lights over their heads. Wearing dress slacks and shirt, he could have adorned the advertisement billboards of Time Square.

And he only had eyes for her. She felt like one of Violet's princesses out for the night with her prince. Thank goodness the little girl wasn't there, because at that moment Katie knew anyone who saw them would think the two of them were in love. It was a good thing they had agreed to no complications in their relationship. Otherwise, she too might have thought Dylan had love in his eyes at that moment.

But they'd taken love off the table. Dylan had broken one rule by getting involved with her in the first place. She was sure he wouldn't break another one. They'd been upfront with their expectations in their relationship. When she returned to New York their relationship would be over no matter how much daydreaming she'd been doing.

"Katie?" he asked as he laid his forehead to hers. "Are you okay? We've seen most of the artists. We've can leave if you're ready."

No. She wasn't okay. She'd probably never be okay once she left this island and Dylan. She should pull back from him, start getting used to the distance that would soon separate the two of them, but she wasn't that strong. She wanted the time they had left together. She wanted this one night alone. She wanted it to never end.

"I'm fine," she said. Her lips brushed his. His teeth grazed her bottom lip as he gave it a little nip and pulled her tighter against him. His hard length pressed against her. Desire shot through her.

"We're almost to the end of the block, but I'm ready if you are." Her body was aching to take him in right there.

"We can see the rest of the artists another time," he said as he took her hand, all but hauling her out onto the street.

Did he even understand what he said? Didn't he realize that there wouldn't be another chance for her to see the other artists? She'd be back in New York before the next Gallery Night.

# CHAPTER ELEVEN

KATIE DIDN'T KNOW why she felt so nervous. She and Dylan had made love several times. It wasn't their first night together. But it could probably be the last time Dylan got to spend the night with her. She'd come to love those few mornings that she'd woken up to find Dylan asleep next to her. They even had a routine where she got up early to do her yoga and meditation, something that helped her tune into her mental health needs, and he'd later join her with her first cup of coffee for the day. They'd sit back on the porch and watch the trees come alive as the birds started their own day traveling from tree to tree.

She had begun to think of it as their time. That early morning time when it was just the two of them before they had to deal with disruptive phone calls and the other daily chores of living. She could see how dangerous that had been now. She'd been thinking of them as a couple. She'd let herself get caught up in emotions that she had no right having.

But the idea of distancing themselves as they transitioned into being separated held no appeal right then. What did it matter? The damage was done. Her memories of their time alone would be all she was taking when she left Key West.

She stepped out of the bathroom wearing a silky gown of white. It covered the top of her thighs and had thin straps and a dipped neck. It covered all of the important parts, but it clung to them too.

"I feel stupid," she said as she stood against the bathroom door while Dylan lay on his side of the bed staring at her. "It's Jo's fault. She's the one that talked me into buying it."

"I'll have to see about getting the woman a raise," Dylan said. "I loved the gown you were wearing tonight, but this? You look amazing."

"It's not something that I would normally wear. The gown I wore tonight, I mean. I'm not somebody that dresses up all the time." She walked over to the bed and sat down next to him.

"No, you're one of New York City's heroes who is more at home in a blue flight suit saving lives than dressing up for a dinner party," he said as he pulled her down to lay beside her.

How could someone who had only known her for a few weeks understand who she was better than some of the friends she had known a lifetime?

He'd taken off his dress shirt and removed his belt. Turning into his arms, she felt what could only be described as grief for what they could have had together if it weren't for the two of them being from different worlds.

His fingers tipped her chin up to meet his eyes. "I feel like you're already leaving me."

"I feel like I'm watching an hourglass as the sand

streams down faster and faster." She didn't want to ruin the night, but she had to share how she felt with him.

"We have the whole night. Give us this night. We have enough sand to last a lifetime right outside your door. Let's not worry about the ones that are falling tonight." Dylan brushed her hair back from her face.

What did he mean by enough sand for a lifetime? Was he saying that they could have more time together?

"Let's make some memories together tonight," he murmured.

He peeled down one strap of her gown and the other, exposing her breast to the cool breeze that flowed into the room from an open window. Her mouth was suddenly dry and she couldn't speak.

His hand cupped her left breast and stayed there for a moment. Her heart rate doubled then skipped a beat under his palm when his other hand began to move up her thighs.

She drew in a deep breath. Her body pressed up against his, waiting for the touch of his fingers on her most intimate parts. The touch that would drive her to madness.

His smile was one of satisfaction. He knew that she wanted him. But Katie had never been a passive woman. Not with her brothers, not with her job, and certainly not in the bedroom.

"Lose the pants," she ordered, then watched as he stripped for her.

Her fingers were around him before he could take his place beside her. He pulsed against her hand. She wasn't the only one who suffered from the madness that drove them into a feverish lovemaking.

She'd thought they would make slow and sweet love

tonight, but the need to have him inside her had taken away all her control. They had the rest of the night. She wanted him now.

His mouth was on her breast then, her nipples both hard and throbbing. His hand tortured her as it slid in then out of her wet folds.

She was so close to coming, but she needed more. She wanted to make their memory a spectacular one. One that would make sure he never forgot her.

When he started to cover her, she surprised him. Pushing him onto his back instead of pulling him down to her.

"My turn," she said as she straddled him.

"I'm all yours," he said, relaxing under her with a smile that took her breath away. Lying there, stretched out before her with those sexy curls falling around his face, her heart swelled with an emotion she wouldn't name. There was no future in it. No future at all for them. They had this moment. It was all she was assured and she wasn't going to waste it.

She bent over him, her hair a curtain that brushed against his chest before she placed a soft kiss against his lips. Three little words swirled through her mind, but she wouldn't let herself utter them.

His arms came around her, pulling her down against him as the kiss became more demanding, as seconds became minutes, as the kiss went from searching to passionate only ending when they were both too breathless to continue.

Pushing up with arms and legs that trembled with desire she stared down at him. This man brought out a passionate side of her that she hadn't known existed.

She lowered herself onto him, inch by inch, his arms

gripping her waist, and his gaze hot and fierce as he filled her. Removing his hands from her waist, she locked her fingers with his. She would let him see the woman that she was, strong and not afraid to take charge.

Rocking against him, she lost herself in the rhythm as he matched her every movement. His strong body arching up to meet her soft one, as they became one if only for this short time.

She'd lost her grip on his hands, but she wasn't sure how. All she knew was the feel of Dylan's fingers as he stroked between her legs.

Pleasure swelled inside her, intensifying until her breath caught in a climax that caught them both in its grip as they came together in a sensual satisfaction that she had never experienced before.

She collapsed on top of Dylan, her body boneless, her muscles failing to keep her upright. As Dylan held her, she wept.

When the phone rang the next morning, Katie did not answer it on the first ring or the second ring. Buried beneath a combination of covers and limbs, she didn't want to move. She wasn't on duty today.

She stretched her legs as best she could with one heavily muscled thigh thrown across her. She couldn't even work if she was needed. She and Dylan had spent most of the night in each other's arms. Their love-making had gone from fierce to soft and then back to demanding. When Dylan said he wanted to make memories of the night, he wasn't joking. The world outside her window started to lighten with the soft gray tones of dawn when they'd finally fallen asleep.

Her phone rang again.

Moaning, she lifted Dylan's arm and scooted out from under his thigh before grabbing her gown from the floor and picking up her phone. The number was from New York. Couldn't she have one night of sex without being bothered by one of her brothers?

She shut the bedroom door behind her before she answered.

"Good morning, Matt. I'm surprised to hear from you this time of morning. You just getting off shift?" she asked. Her night shift–loving brother was known to be grumpy in the early morning hours.

"Katie, it's…it's Junior," Matt said, his tone steady as only a man used to relaying bad news could be. She knew that tone. She lived in a world where conveying bad news was part of the job.

"Matt, what's wrong? What's happened to Junior?" Her voice quivered but she refused to break down. Not until she knew how bad things were.

"Another warrant went out for the guy that shot you. We've been putting the pressure on him and we got a tip he was involved in a drug deal that went down last night. We pulled the tape of the area and caught him making the exchange. Junior and I wanted to be there when they arrested him." The longer her brother talked the more his voice broke. There wasn't much that would make her street-tough brother break down.

"Is he alive?" Katie asked, unable to listen to any more information. She just needed to know that her brother was alive.

"He's in surgery. He took a shot to the gut. In and out the doctor said, but it did a lot of damage going through. He said they lost him once in the emergency

room. Blood loss. They were doing some rapid transfusion thing on him. Said it saved his life."

He would be okay. Her brother was in surgery now
and they'd do whatever repairs that were needed. They
had to. She couldn't lose her brother. Not like this.

"You need to come, Katie. You need to come home.
Dad's not looking so good. We need you here."

"I'll catch the next flight. Tell Daddy, I'll be home
as soon as I can. I'll call you when I get to the airport."
Katie hit the button to hang up. Then looked around
the room. She didn't know what to do first.

"What's happened?" Dylan asked from the bedroom
door. "Katie?"

Her mind tried to wrap around everything Matt had
just told her, but none of it was making sense.

"Junior went to arrest the guy who they arrested earlier for shooting me, and the guy shot my brother." She
wanted to blame the judge who'd let a dangerous killer
out on bail. She wanted to take the blame herself for
being the reason her brother had been shot. But none
of that would help John Jr. right then. She needed to
concentrate on getting to New York as fast as possible.

"I've got to get home," she said as she grabbed her
laptop off the kitchen island. She punched in her pass-
word. "I need a flight from here that I can take?"

"I think there's one flight a day that's directly to
New York. Go pack and I'll see what I can find out."
Dylan already had his phone out.

"Okay, thanks," she said and rushed back into the
bedroom.

She didn't know where to start. She'd brought so
much stuff with her. Her clothes, books, her paints.
She had no idea how long she would be gone.

But she didn't have to take everything now. She'd have to come back for the Jeep anyway. She could get everything she had to have in one bag and a carry-on.

She pulled her suitcase out of the closet and opened it on the bed. If she missed the one flight out to New York, she'd have Dylan drive her to Miami where there would be more available flights.

She dumped a drawer of underwear into the suitcase then followed it with one full of shirts and shorts.

"Your ticket is waiting at the airport," Dylan said as he bent to pick up a T-shirt she'd dropped.

"How long do I have?" she asked as she shut her suitcase then pulled out her carry-on bag.

He followed her into the kitchen where she grabbed her computer and vitamins. "You have an hour till boarding."

"I'll never make it." She looked down and saw that she still wore her nightgown.

"Go change and I'll load the bags. You forget that we're just a little island. I can have you there in fifteen minutes, ten if traffic isn't heavy."

"But I have to get my bags checked and go through security." She pulled a pair of jeans and a T- shirt out of the closet and rushed into the bathroom.

She stuck her brush and makeup into her carry-on. She could deal with that on the way. She picked the gown she'd worn the night before off the counter where she had laid it. She didn't have any need for it in New York, but she couldn't bring herself to leave it behind. Who knew what would happen in New York? She could be there for weeks.

She slid her feet into sandals and hefted her carry-on onto her shoulder. She wanted to take a last look at the cottage. She wanted to walk onto her deck and breathe in the air one more time. But time wasn't something she had right now.

When she stepped out into the sunshine to join Dylan, the rush of adrenaline that she'd been burning gave out. Was this goodbye? She locked the door to her little cottage with a finality that she wasn't prepared for. She had no idea how long she'd be needed in New York.

The ride to the airport was fast and it wasn't until they stood on the sidewalk outside that she realized Dylan had come to the same conclusion: this could be the goodbye they had known was coming. It wasn't fair that it was coming now, though. She wasn't ready to say goodbye yet.

They'd made plans for a trip to the beach after Violet came home from her sleepover. Violet. She had planned to tell Dylan about Violet's statements to Jo this morning.

"Oh, Dylan. I need to tell you something. I shouldn't have waited, but…it was just…and now I'm leaving…"

"Katie, there's no time. Your plane will be boarding in a few minutes. You need to go."

"But it's Violet. I was going to talk to you this morning about what Jo told me, but we didn't have the time." She knew she was just making excuses for not speaking about it earlier, when the truth was she'd been afraid that Dylan would want to end things between them after she told him. "But you need to know this, especially now."

"What about Violet?" he asked, his eyes, which had been avoiding her since they left the cottage, now locked with hers.

"Jo says she's gotten it into her mind that you and I, that the two of us, are a couple. She seems to think that I'm going to stay and that we're going to get married."

"And now I have to tell her you're leaving?" The shock on his face quickly turned to pain. She knew it had been his greatest fear that his daughter would be hurt.

He turned away to take her suitcase from the back seat of his car. It wasn't until they were at the airport doors that he spoke.

"I'll take care of getting the rest of your belongings packed and shipped," Dylan said as he handed the handle to her.

"I'm still on the schedule," she said. "And there's the Jeep."

"I'll take care of it. You don't need to worry about things here. Take care of your family," he said then pointed to the ticker board inside the entrance. "You better hurry or you'll miss your flight."

But still she stood there. Was this really how it ended? Was he not even going to kiss her goodbye?

He was angry. At her? At himself for not protecting his daughter? Did it really matter when she didn't even know if she would ever see him again.

She grabbed him by the shirt and pulled him to her. He might be ready to let things end between them as strangers, but she wasn't. He meant too much to her.

She pressed her lips to his and gave him a deep kiss that he was not going to forget easily before turning and running to make her plane.

# CHAPTER TWELVE

IT DIDN'T TAKE Katie but a moment to find her father and brothers in the surgical ICU waiting room that was crowded with NYPD officers, both uniformed and plainclothes.

"Katie, you're here," her youngest brother shouted, making his way to her. A sob escaped her lips as he caught her up in his arms.

"How is he?" she asked. Her brother had still been in surgery when she'd touched down in New York.

"He just got out of surgery. The bullet did a lot of damage, but the doctor says he stopped all the bleeding," Mikey said, as he led her over to the corner where her father stood waiting.

"Oh, Daddy," she choked, as she was once again wrapped inside strong arms.

"He's going to be okay," her father said, though she didn't know if he was talking to himself or her.

"Lisa just went back to see him," Mikey said as Katie took a seat beside him.

"How is she holding up?" Katie asked. His brother's fiancée, a district attorney, was as tough as they came.

Before anyone could answer, Katie saw the petite

blonde woman they'd been discussing enter the waiting room and head toward them.

"He's going to be okay. He's sleeping and they said they were going to leave him on the ventilator until tomorrow, but they say he's stable," Lisa said, breathless as she rushed toward them then suddenly broke into tears.

Katie gathered her into her arms while the other McGee men walked off using the excuse that they needed to tell the other officers the good news.

"They're all alike," Lisa laughed as she wiped her tears away. "They're ready to run into a burning building or fight their way through a hail of bullets to rescue someone, but as soon as a woman sheds a few tears they run the other way."

"I know," Katie said as the two of them moved apart.

"Thanks for understanding. It was just seeing him lying there. He was so still. You know Junior. He's never still. It just scared me." Lisa wiped at her eyes, then looked up at Katie. "They explained all the monitors to me and they say he's stable, but I told his nurse you were a flight nurse with Heli-Care. He promised to let you come in whenever you arrived. I thought maybe you could go check him out. You know. Just to be sure he's doing okay."

"Oh, okay." Katie stood, anxious to see her brother and reassure all of them that he truly was going to be okay.

It wasn't until a few minutes later, standing over her brother, that it hit her: only months ago she had lain in a similar room recovering from a gunshot wound much too similar to her brother's. The sight of her strong older brother pale and unmoving against the white hospital linen made her feel sick.

She waited for the anxiety that she dreaded to hit her, but it didn't come. If this had happened six weeks ago, she knew that she would not have been able to stand there. All the work she had done with her counselor and the confidence she'd rebuilt with Dylan's help made the difference.

After checking her brother's ventilator settings and reviewing his vital signs with his brother's nurse until she was satisfied that Junior was recovering as he should be, she made her way back to where her family waited for her.

Dylan sat on the steps to Katie's cottage and waited for his daughter's bus to arrive. No, not Katie's cottage. Katie was gone. And it had never really been Katie's cottage. She'd always been just a temporary renter. Just like, they had been temporary lovers.

Only it hadn't ever felt temporary. What they had together had grown when it shouldn't have. That was his mistake. Instead of keeping things light and friendly between the two of them, he'd crossed the line to caring about Katie as more than just a lover. Something that hadn't been in their agreement. There was a reason he had rules for his love life which included not getting involved with someone who was visiting the island. But he'd broken the rule and now he had to live with the consequences.

He had always known Katie's plan was to return to New York. Not only was her family and life there, he knew a part of Katie wanted to prove to herself that she'd made it back to being one of the best flight nurses in the biggest city in the country. Her confidence had been so low when she'd first arrived. He wasn't sure even Katie had believed she would recover enough to become the nurse she had been before. But something about the stubborn tilt of that chin of hers had told him that she wasn't a woman who was going to give up. Her determination was one of the things he loved about her.

He stood and swore. Love wasn't part of their agreement. Thank goodness he'd never let on to Katie about the way he felt. She had made it plain that she didn't want any complications any more than he did. Her goal was to get back to New York. His was to protect his daughter.

From what Katie had told him, he had failed.

The yellow bus came to a stop at the top of the drive. The pride he felt when his daughter ran up to him and hugged him eased some of the pain in his chest. He was so lucky to have Violet. Her mother could have kept her away from him forever. But Lilly had done the right thing for her daughter, bringing her to him. The little girl needed a stable home.

"Hey, Daddy, can we go inside and see Katie? I brought another book home from the library that I think she'll like." Violet stared up at him with the light blue eyes of her mother.

"She's not here, honey," he said.

"Did she go off with Jo and Summer shopping again?" Violet followed him as they made the walk from Katie's cottage. "Can I go next time? Jo promised to help me pick some new clothes."

"We'll see about you going with Jo, but Katie won't be able to go. A bad man hurt her brother and she had to go home." Dylan opened the door to the house and watched as his daughter hung her backpack in the small closet at their entrance without being told. She was taking Katie's leaving a lot better than he thought she would. Maybe Jo was mistaken about what Violet had said.

"That's okay. I can wait till she gets back," his daughter said as she shut the door. "My jeans are just a little short. It'll be okay."

"No, Violet, I don't think you understand. Katie isn't coming back. She would have told you goodbye but her brother is hurt really bad. She had to take the first flight she could get to take her home to New York." Dylan saw the moment his daughter understood his words. Once more he was left alone to pick up the pieces, only this time it wouldn't be just his heart, it would also be his daughter's.

Then she smiled and laughed. "Katie can't have left for good. She left her car. Besides, she can't stay in New York when you get married. She has to come back and live with us."

"Baby, what makes you think that Katie and I are getting married?" He'd searched his mind for some action or something he could have said that might have caused his daughter to come to this conclusion, but there wasn't anything.

"Nobody told me. But I saw you kissing her when you thought I was asleep. You were out on the deck. Don't you remember?" Violet asked.

He did remember being out on the deck one night when Violet had gotten up for a drink. Had his daughter been spying on him? But that still didn't explain why she thought they were getting married. She was much too young to understand his and Katie's friendship.

"Violet, come sit next to me on the couch." How was he supposed to do this? Was there a handbook out there for single dads with a chapter on how to keep your child from dreaming up romantic ideas concerning your love life? He took a deep breath.

"Honey, sometimes men and women kiss each other when they're just friends. It doesn't mean that they are going to get married. It can just be a way to show that you like someone." There. Simple and to the point. If only things between him and Katie could be that simple.

"I like Shawn Hart at school, sometimes. Does that mean I have to kiss him?" his daughter asked.

"No. Definitely not. There is not to be any kissing Shawn Hart or anybody else." He was messing this all up. He needed to take control of this talk before it ended up in places he was not ready to go.

"Look. The bottom line is that Katie and I aren't getting married. She has a life in New York that she had to get back to. My life is here with you. We'll both miss her, but we'll be okay."

"Don't worry, Daddy, Katie will be back soon. You'll see," Violet said before giving him a look which he knew meant her mind was made up and there was nothing he could say that was going to change it.

Katie scrolled through her texts, stopping at the only text she had received from Dylan since she'd left Key West and rereading it as she had every few hours for the last two days.

How is your brother?

He's doing better than expected. He's being extu-
bated this morning and should move out of the critical care unit this morning. How is Violet?

OK

She'd waited for him to expand on his answer, but
nothing else came. Those two little letters seemed to
have been all he had to say to her. And now she didn't
know what to do.

She'd typed message after message back to him,
then deleted each one before she sent them. His last
words of assurance that she didn't need to worry about
things in Key West, had seemed final.

Her door buzzed and she looked out to see that it
was her father.

"What's happened?" she asked as she flung the door
open. She'd just talked to her brother and he seemed
to be doing well.

"Everything's fine. I just wanted a few minutes
alone with my daughter away from that crowded waiting room," her father said as he walked past her into
her apartment. "Could I get a cup of coffee?"

There were dark circles under her father's eyes and
his usually perfectly pressed uniform looked as if he'd
been wearing it for days. She remembered him looking like this only once before. Then, it had been her
in the hospital that he'd been worrying over. "I think
you need a nap instead of more coffee."

"Coffee for now, if you don't mind. I can sleep later,"
he said, though he did take a seat in the nearest chair.

After starting the coffee, she returned to her father. "Really, Daddy, it's okay for you to take a break. Junior's doing fine now."

"I know. I'm headed home after I leave here. I just had to make a trip to the courthouse to make sure no judge was going to let that shooter out again. The man shot two of my kids. *Two*." Her father stood with those words and headed into her kitchen. She knew the coffee was only an excuse for him to leave the room. He'd been raised in a time when men didn't let others see any sign of weakness. She allowed him a few minutes of privacy before she joined him.

"So when are you headed back to Key West?" her father asked.

Startled, her first sip of coffee went down wrong causing a fit of coughing that took several seconds to recover from.

"I don't think I am," she said, setting her cup down and wiping the countertop for the umpteenth time that morning.

"Didn't your contract go until the first of the month? Shouldn't you be returning to finish it?" her father asked.

"Are you in a hurry to get rid of me?" she asked. Her father seldom made small talk. There was a reason he made the trip to see her but there would be no hurrying him to get to it.

"Of course not. I like having all my kids where I can get to them if they need me."

It was a very fatherly thing for him to say and she knew it was true. Dylan had expressed the same sentiment when he'd worried about not having the legal paperwork giving him full custody of Violet. Lilly could take their daughter at any time and he wouldn't be able to guarantee her safety.

"If you don't want to finish your contract, that's up to you. You've got to return anyway, don't you? That Jeep isn't going to drive itself back to New York."

Her father was right. While Dylan had offered to pack her things, a plane ticket to Key West would be much cheaper.

But returning to Key West would mean more good-byes.

"Besides, your brothers say you seemed happy there. More like the old Katie," her father said.

"You mean more like the way I was before I was shot?" she asked. Her father was as uncomfortable discussing that night as she had been. But that was before she'd gone to Key West. Before the work she'd done with her counselor. Before she'd had Dylan on her side encouraging her to do the work that was needed for her recovery.

"It's okay to say it. I won't break if we talk about it." Not now. Never again. No matter how hard it was to acknowledge, she would never hide from that night again. She'd given it power over her by keeping what happened that night in the dark. But now that she had brought it all out into the light, she knew that, though she would never be the same, she could be just as strong if not stronger.

"I should have talked to you sooner. It was just such a shock. With your brothers, I've always known there was a chance of them being injured. But you? This wasn't supposed to happen to you."

She stepped toward her father and wrapped her arms

around him. "It's okay, Daddy. I'm going to be okay. So is Junior."

Then for the first time since the shooting, she and her dad sat at her little kitchen table and talked openly about what happened the night she'd been hurt and the way it had affected her.

An hour later, after her father had promised that he would go straight home to rest and she had assured him that she would never let her fear of worrying him keep her from confiding in him, they said their tearful goodbyes and she returned to her phone where she saw she had received a new text from Jo.

Dylan told us what happened to you brother. How is he? Are you okay?

Katie didn't think twice before she returned the text. Her father was right.

He's doing great. See you soon.

Putting away her phone, she headed to her bedroom to pack.

# CHAPTER THIRTEEN

"KATIE!" VIOLET CRIED as she sprang out of the car and ran up the steps of the rental cottage.

Dylan had known Katie was returning to the island—Jo had spread the word to all the crew—but he still wasn't prepared to see her. He'd spent hours staring out his window at the cottage, knowing she would never return. But she had.

For just a moment, seeing her standing there, her hair blowing in the soft gulf breeze, her lips curved into a big smile for the two of them, he felt a momentary jolt of hope. And then he saw her suitcase and was reminded she'd only returned to finish out her contract. She'd be leaving again.

And he'd have to go through the same hell as he had when he'd watched her turn from him at the airport. His hand instinctively brushed against his lips as he remembered the kiss she'd given him before she'd run away. It wasn't one he would ever be able to forget.

Which was just more reason for him to stay away from her now. Memories that he'd thought would give him some relief from the pain of her leaving, now haunted him instead.

"Hello," Katie said, as she started down the stairs toward him.

"Your brother must be doing okay," he said as he made it to his daughter and put his arm around her shoulders.

"They're releasing him from the hospital tomorrow." She looked almost as uncomfortable as he felt.

"See, Daddy. I told you Katie was coming back," Violet said matter-of-factly.

"I see. Didn't you say you needed to start on your geography homework as soon as you got home?" He didn't need his daughter bringing up all her wildly romantic notions in front of Katie. Things were awkward enough between the two of them.

"I know. I just wanted to talk to Katie for a minute. Maybe she can come over for supper?" his daughter asked, her eyes pleading with him.

"We're eating at your grandparents' house tonight," he said quickly, knowing he'd have to make a quick call to his mother to warn her of their new plans.

He couldn't do anything that might encourage Violet's idea that he and Katie were a couple. Instead, he needed to remind his daughter that Katie was just here temporarily and the two of them were only friends.

"It sounds like you have a very busy evening ahead of you," Katie said to Violet before turning toward him. "I checked the schedule and saw I'm on for the four shifts next week."

"Jo and Casey took some time off and I figured you wouldn't mind since it's your last week," Dylan said, aware Violet was listening intently to every word. It was time his daughter accepted that Katie would not be staying.

"It's not a problem," Katie said before addressing Violet. "How about we get together next week for a painting day? If it's okay with your daddy, of course."

Dylan met Katie's eyes and knew he couldn't deny either one of them that one last day together.

"That would be fine. But right now, we both better go get ready before it's time for us to leave for my parents' home." He turned Violet toward their own home, making his escape as painless as possible.

As they reached the top of the steps, Violet turned to wave goodbye to Katie. Unable to help himself, he turned too, catching sight of Katie disappearing into the cottage.

It was Katie's last flight in Key West. In a couple more hours she would be clocking out for the last time. For now, though, she had no choice than to sit next to a somber Dylan, who had done a great job of pretending she didn't exist for the last week. As soon as the helicopter skids lifted off the ground, her stomach had begun to churn and it wasn't because of the speed at which they flew across the island.

"Hang on, guys," Roy said over their headphones. "This is going to be a quick trip."

As Dylan was lead, Katie prepared their scene bag, checking to make sure everything was in place.

"Miami General is accepting," Dylan said over the headphones. "They're notifying their neurosurgeon now."

"This place has a reputation for being rough so the county cops are securing the scene right now. They've got the suspect in custody, but it seems there was a drunken brawl in progress when they arrived," Roy said as he banked to the left.

The local fire department for the small lower key came over the radio with the coordinates of their landing zone and Roy had them landing only six minutes from takeoff.

"Where's our patient?" Dylan asked one of the officers who'd been designated to escort them. It seemed that though the fighting had stopped, the amount of inebriated customers had them all on alert.

"This way," the young officer said, leading them up to a large shack made up of large poles and what looked like palm limbs.

"They called this a bar?" Katie asked Dylan as they walked through the sand along the path through all the onlookers.

"It's a tiki bar. They're popular with the tourists," Dylan explained, speaking directly to her for the first time in days.

Following the officer, she was surprised to see that their patient now lay on top of the bar while an older woman, the only person besides the first responders who seemed to be sober, was wiping up blood with her bar towel. The scene was wrong in so many ways.

"Let's get this guy and get out of here," she told Dylan.

"It's okay. They're just drunk. The officers can handle them," Dylan said as he put a hand on her waist and gently urged her in front of him.

Startled by his touch, she jumped. Even through her thick flight suit, the one that had been made to strict specifications to protect her from the hottest of fires, couldn't protect her from the feel of his hand against her.

But as they took the last few steps up to the bar, she realized why Dylan had suddenly become so attentive. He thought she was reacting to the crowd that surrounded her. She wanted to laugh, but it hurt too much. Only when he thought she needed him to help her through her anxiety had he been ready to give her the attention she craved since she arrived back in the keys.

"It's not them," she said as she pulled away from him and pointed back to the crowd that was beginning to thin as the officers explained the bar was closed for the night. Or early morning as was the case.

"It's her," Katie said, pointing to the woman, who was now straightening the back of the bar, ignoring the unconscious man stretched across her bar being cared for by the local ambulance crew. "That's cold. Scary cold."

Dylan looked at the woman and nodded his head before moving in front of Katie and beginning his assessment of their patient. Maybe it would have been better if she had pretended the crowd was the trouble. At least then she wouldn't have to deal with the cold shoulder Dylan had been giving her.

Though she expected the patient's injuries were superficial except for what looked like an orbital fracture, she started an intravenous line in each arm and prepared to infuse a bag of fluid.

"Let's get him loaded," Dylan said after he finished bandaging a nasty-looking cut across the man's hand.

It wasn't until they were back on their way from Miami while she was staring out the window that it truly hit her: this would be the last time she flew across the beautiful body of water below her.

It was also the last time she'd sit next to Dylan, crammed into the two seats next to each other, something that she'd always enjoyed. Until now. The feel of his hand against her waist had brought back the deep need and desire that had once consumed her. Had it affected him the same way it had her? There was a time when she would have felt comfortable asking him, exploring those needs and desires. But that was before he froze her out.

It was a good thing that tomorrow would be her last day on the island before she packed up and left for New York, because she didn't think she could take any more of Dylan ignoring what they'd had such a short time ago. Had it just been a a couple months ago, that she'd been driven to seek some distance from her home in order to heal? And now she was running the opposite way.

Sometimes life just didn't make sense.

# CHAPTER FOURTEEN

DYLAN HAD LISTENED to the laughter coming from Katie's back deck all morning. Most of it had been his daughter's giggles, but occasionally he heard the sweet sound of Katie's own laughter above his daughter's.

He could have shut the door to his back deck, closed the windows he had opened to let the fresh air in, or gone into one of the other rooms where he couldn't hear the two of them. Instead, he'd chosen to let the music of their voices fill his home as he went through his weekend chores. It was a masochistic thing to do. He knew that. But he wasn't strong enough to pretend that he didn't enjoy the sound of the two of them as they painted and talked.

He knew it was only his threats of taking away her allotted television time that kept his daughter from making any comments about Kate's leaving. Trying to explain to his eight-year-old that real adult relationships didn't work like the animated movies she loved hadn't gone well.

The knock on the back door jarred him back into the present as his daughter raced by him to her room carrying several large pieces of paper.

"Hi," Katie said as she stepped into the house. She

carried a canvas but had it turned away from him. "I'm sorry. I was trying to explain to her that I had finished my contract and had to go home."

His daughter's door slammed behind her and the two of them were left alone. He'd known this was coming. At least he'dd prepared as much as any father could prepare for their daughter's heart to be broken.

"I know. I don't blame you." He blamed himself. He'd known no matter what, Katie leaving both of their lives would be hard. It was like Lilly leaving Violet all over again.

"I wanted to give you this. I know you said you liked it, though if you don't want to hang it I'll understand."

He took the canvas she held out to him and was surprised to see it was the painting of the white heron that she'd been so excited about. "Are you sure you don't want to take it with you?"

"I've got another one I'm taking with me. I've also got some supplies for Violet that I'm going to leave in the cottage." She looked down at her feet then back up to him. "I want to thank you for everything you've done. I mean…"

Her face flushed pink. "I mean I needed a friend when I got here. Thanks for being there. For being that friend."

What was he to say to that? How could she compare what they'd had to merely friendship?

"I've got to go. I'm meeting Jo and Summer downtown in a few hours."

Holding the canvas, he stood and watched as she rushed away. Had those been tears in her eyes?

"Why didn't you ask her to stay?" Violet demanded

from behind him. "She loves me and you. I know she does. Ask her. She'll tell you."

He should have known his daughter would be listening to their conversation. "That's not the kind of thing you ask someone, honey."

"How do you know if she would have stayed when you didn't ask her?" His daughter's voice was getting louder.

Why was she angry at him? He wasn't the one leaving.

"You didn't ask Katie to stay just like you didn't ask my mommy to stay." His daughter cried.

"Oh, baby," he said as he bent down and took his daughter into his arms. "Your mommy couldn't stay. She would be miserable here. We both knew it. But it wasn't because she didn't love you. She just can't be happy in one place for very long."

"But Katie can and you're too scared to ask her," Violet said as she pulled out of his arms, "Didn't you tell me that you never learn the answer if you don't ask the question?"

"I was talking about you asking your teacher questions if you didn't understand something. This is different." How did he explain that things weren't as simple as they appeared to an eight-year-old?

"Do you want me to ask her for you?" Violet said as she headed toward the back door.

"Violet Louise Maddox, you stop right there before I ground you for the rest of your life."

"Men," his daughter spat out at him as she stomped past him toward her room, looking nothing like the sweet little girl that had gotten up that morning.

His head was spinning. Where had he lost control of this conversation? Maybe where his daughter had thrown her mother's betrayal at him?

Violet had only been seven when her mother had left. There hadn't been a way to explain to her that before she'd even been born he had asked her mother to stay. And he would never share with his daughter how her mother had laughed at him before explaining that she'd had her fill of living on his little houseboat. There were bigger and better places to see out in the world. She needed more excitement than he and his little island could give her.

But Katie wasn't Lilly. Katie would never leave her child so she could roam the world looking for excitement. But could she ever be happy here? With just him and Lilly? Without the bright lights of New York City?

What if Violet was right? What if he let Katie walk away from them without him asking her to stay?

One thing his daughter was absolutely right about: if he didn't ask the question, he would never know the answer.

He found himself walking from room to room. Trying to work out what he needed to do until finally it hit him. Rushing down the hall, he opened his daughter's door only to find that she'd cried herself to sleep.

"Violet, wake up," he said, brushing his hand across his daughter's hair, "I have a plan, but I'm going to need your help."

Katie stood in the middle of Duval Street, dressed in a short emerald dress of lace and silk, and tried to balance on the three-inch heels Jo and Summer had insisted would be perfect for their last night out together.

"There you are" Dylan came up beside her. Dressed in a black three-piece suit, he looked more like a banker than a paramedic.

"Where're Jo and Summer?" she asked as she took the glass of champagne he held out to her. This was supposed to be a girls-only night. The two women had a lot of explaining to do. They could have at least warned her that Dylan would be here tonight.

"They're around here somewhere," he said. "They'll catch up with us later."

"Why are *you* here tonight?" she asked as they took a path down through the artist and galleries until they came to a stop in front of a small shop that she'd never noticed before. Jo and Summer were nowhere to be seen.

"I'll explain in a minute. There's something I want you to see," Dylan said as he opened a door that led into a room lit with crystal chandeliers.

The only furniture in the room was a glass case that ran across the back wall. As Katie approached the it an old man wrinkled with age stepped out of a back room.

"Dylan, I'm so glad to see you. Is this your Katie?" he asked.

"Katie, this is Peter," Dylan said.

"It's nice to meet you, Peter." She gazed down into the case that held as much sparkly jewelry as Tiffany's, forgetting for a moment that she was waiting for Dylan to explain what was going on. "You have some lovely pieces here."

"Peter was a master jeweler in Cuba before he

came to Key West," Dylan said then turned to Peter. "Is it ready?"

"Of course, it is ready," Peter replied. "Come see."

Katie watched as Peter pulled a small black velvet box from under the counter. A delicate ring of diamonds surrounding a round solitaire stone set into a white-gold frame lay in front of her.

"It's beautiful," she said. Her breath caught in her chest.

"A little girl told me today that if I didn't ask the question I would never learn the answer."

"She sounds like a smart girl," Katie said, her voice catching as she watched Dylan take the ring into his hand while her own hands began to shake.

"I think so," he said as he took her hand in his. She felt his hand tremble against hers. "Katherine Lee McGee, will you marry me?"

"I don't understand. You've been so distant. I thought you wanted me to leave." She wiped at the tear spilling down her cheek then pulled her hands up to where her heart was hammering inside her chest.

"Oh, yes, Dylan, there's nothing I want more."

She heard someone knocking on the shop window. Turning around she saw four faces pressed against the glass. Jo, Casey, Summer and Violet waved at them before they all spilled into the room.

Violet tugged on her daddy's jacket then whispered into his ear loud enough for everyone to hear her, "You have to kiss her now."

"I was about to," Dylan whispered back just as loud, "but you interrupted us."

After a very PG-rated kiss, Dylan took Katie into his arms.

She'd come to Key West broken and scared, but with the love and support of this man and these friends, she finally felt whole once more.

# EPILOGUE

KATIE STOOD ON the balcony looking out at the lights of the city. Inside the New York ballroom her family and friends were celebrating.

"There you are," her father said as he stepped outside to join her. "You look as pretty as your mother did the day I married her."

Stepping toward him, she did a twirl in the dress of lace and satin that her own mother had worn for her parents' wedding. "The dress was perfect."

When Violet asked to wear it one day, Katie's makeup had almost been ruined.

"Your mother would be so proud of you. As I am."

"Thank you, Daddy," she whispered before kissing his age-roughened cheek. "For this party and especially for not giving Dylan a hard time."

Her father had taken the news that she would be marrying a "beach bum" and moving to Key West better than she'd expected. She had to give some of the credit for that to Violet, who had quickly charmed all the McGee men, though her brothers' approval of Dylan hadn't been as quick to come. They'd all given her husband as hard a time as possible, especially Junior. Whenever Dylan was in sight, he could be heard muttering what a shame it was that his sister had picked a beach bum over one of New York's finest.

"I've got something else for you," her father said as he pulled an envelope out of his pocket. "It's the address you asked for along with the name of an old friend that can help if you need it."

She'd just taken the envelope when Dylan and Violet stepped outside to join them.

"Now if the two of you will excuse us, Violet and I are going to get us another piece of that cake?" her father asked Violet.

Katie waited until they left before handing the envelope to Dylan, who'd been eyeing it since he'd stepped out.

She waited anxiously while Dylan opened the envelope and studied the letter inside. "How did he get this?" Dylan asked.

"He pulled some favors and did some investigation on his own. Lilly has been in Chicago for the last two months. My father said there's a name of someone local that could help if you'd like your lawyer to contact them. If we call them tomorrow we could have it all settled by the time we return from our honeymoon."

"I don't know how to thank him," Dylan said as he wrapped his arms around her.

"He did it for us, for our family," Katie said as she leaned her head back against him and took in the New York skyline. "Isn't it beautiful?"

"Beautiful," Dylan murmured as he trailed kisses down her neck. "Regrets?"

She thought of the cottage that waited for them when they returned to Key West, the one where the three of them would make a home together. A home where they'd love and fight and she hoped they would welcome other children. It was more than she could ever have dreamed of.

Turning her back to the city, she whispered against his lips. "Never."

*****

# FALLING FOR HER
# OFF-LIMITS BOSS

LUANA DaROSA

MILLS & BOON

For Alex, my partner in crime in everything I do.
This is as much yours as it is mine.

# CHAPTER ONE

*ALEXANDER ATTANO MEMORIAL.* Emma's heart skipped a beat as she read the letters, pulling into the car park of the hospital that would be her new temporary home. With four boxes containing her belongings and a wounded heart, she had left San Francisco to flee from the chaos her ex-boyfriend Rob had brought to her.

Emma closed her eyes and shook away the dark clouds forming in her head. She had to remind herself that she had made it. She'd got out. Her life was her own again. And she would make the best out of her time spent as a locum tenens anaesthetist.

What better way of spending the summer than in Chicago, learning from the world-renowned Mark Henderson? Emma's heart skipped a beat when her thoughts drifted towards the famous surgeon who worked at the hospital.

When she entered the building the reception area was spread out right in front of her, with a middle-aged woman sitting behind the counter talking to a man wearing a white coat and dark green scrubs. The receptionist laughed at something the doctor said, waving her hand at him.

'I will page you as soon as they arrive,' Emma heard

her say as she approached the desk, her eyes running over this man who would be the first colleague she got to meet.

His dark brown hair was just long enough to be styled, but the way he wore it looked wild and untamed, matching the five o'clock shadow covering his cheeks. As he turned around she caught his glance, the friendly spark in his hazel eyes showing the friendship he shared with the receptionist.

A shiver trickled down her spine as his gaze locked onto hers. His face was familiar. She recognised him. But who was he? How could she forget the name belonging to such a handsome face? *Wait, was he…?*

Emma caught her thoughts before she let them go any further. In front of her stood her first co-worker. There were many words she could use to describe him, and handsome shouldn't be one of them. After Rob, she wasn't going to let herself regard her colleagues in any other way than with professional courtesy. The moment their personal lives had become at odds with their professional ones he had conveniently forgotten what a true partnership looked like. Even their slightest disagreements at work had become an issue of huge proportions once they got home.

It had taught Emma a valuable lesson. Work and private life should touch as little as possible.

'Thanks, Becky, you are a star,' the handsome doctor said, and walked off. But not without looking at Emma again, smiling as he passed her.

Her stomach lurched, and she held her breath for a moment. As he disappeared, Becky waved at her to step closer.

'Hello, dear, how can I help you?' she asked, the

friendly glow in her eyes remaining and setting Emma
at ease.

'My name is Emma Santos. I'm the new anaesthesiologist starting today in Oncology. HR told me to sign
in at the front desk.'

Becky's smile widened. 'Why, yes, I've been expecting you. Welcome to Attano Memorial! I have your
badge right here. Let me call someone from HR to sort
you out for today. Too bad Dr Henderson just left, or
he could have taken you with him.'

Emma snapped her head around, wanting to catch
a glimpse of the man mentioned, but he had already
disappeared.

'So it *was* Mark Henderson!' Her pulse quickened,
and Emma slipped a hand inside her tote bag, retriev-
ing the medical journal she'd brought from home. Mark
Henderson smiled up at her from its cover. The unmoving image didn't even begin to do him justice.

'Yes, Mark leads the oncology department. But his
focus lies within surgery.' Becky was looking at the
screen in front of her, oblivious to Emma's amazement.
She put a key card on the counter as she picked up the
phone, dialled a number.

Emma picked up the badge, examining it. The excitement bubbling up within her was subdued by a
nervous energy rearing its head from the pit of her
stomach. In her new role as locum anaesthetist she
would work side by side with Dr Henderson, a fact that
already made her stomach lurch.

She had read all his research on pain management
for different cancer treatments, and yearned for the
chance to contribute her own knowledge to it. The
devastation wrought by chemotherapy often required

a fresh approach to traditional pain medication, and Dr Henderson was one of the top surgeons in that area. He was the reason she was most excited to start her role here. His proximity had set her nerve-ends on fire. Now she understood why. She'd been inches away from the man she'd once thought might save her mother.

When her mother had first been diagnosed with Gardner Syndrome, a rare type of hereditary cancer, Emma had read every single piece of research around the disease. She'd wanted to understand the odds her mother was fighting against. Back then she had just started her second year of med school in San Francisco, which had made the different texts and studies a lot more accessible to her.

While not specifically focusing on Gardner Syndrome, Dr Henderson's research looked into types of aggressive colon cancer and how different treatments could be adapted to any specific case. His breakthroughs had given Emma hope that her mother might be able to get through the disease alive. A vain hope, as she now knew, but a few years ago she'd hung on to it with everything she had. To save her mother and also to save herself.

With a hereditary disease like Gardner Syndrome, chances were that her mother had passed the condition on to Emma. A potential diagnosis hung over her head every day, just waiting to drop. After her mother's diagnosis her father had urged her to get tested for the gene mutation, to determine whether she had the disease as well, but every time Emma had come close to taking the test she'd pulled out.

First she had told herself that she needed to focus on her mother. She didn't want to burden her with the thought that she might have passed this disease to her only child. But even after her death Emma hadn't found the heart to find out the truth. Her father, along with her aunts, uncles and cousins, regularly teamed up to inundate her with messages and phone calls about having the test. She knew that eventually she would have to find out. For the sake of her future children, she needed to know.

When things had started looking more serious with Rob she had been so close to getting the test, wanting to know how it would affect their future. A future that was no longer.

Emma's mouth went dry and she took those stray thoughts, stuffing them back into the box where they belonged. This was her fresh start, after having her heart and soul crushed by the man who had promised to love her. She yearned to learn and thrive. And put all that behind her.

Emma shook her head, straightened her shoulders, and found her smile again as the HR representative came to pick her up.

'Try to get a bit more sleep.'

Mark smiled at his patient as he approached the door, giving him a small wave before he left for the nurses' desk. He hadn't meant to wake him up, simply wanting to check up on him before his regular shift began. This was one of the happier cases Mark had worked on and a rare sight in the oncology department. The cancer had been at its early stages, but in a tricky position. Difficult enough that the oncologist had asked Mark to do the surgery.

Not that he minded the more complicated cases.

Everyone who needed his attention got it. From the moment he got a patient file up to the point when the patient walked out of this hospital, he considered them all his responsibility, and his colleagues were aware that he expected the same from everyone in his department.

He took down a few notes on the patient's condition and headed for the nurses' station. Theresa, the oncology department's head nurse, stood behind the desk, so engrossed in whatever was on her clipboard that she did not register his presence.

He cleared his throat, but it didn't grab her attention. 'Good morning, Theresa,' he said, with a slight smile that grew larger when she jumped, laying her hand over her heart and breathing a sigh of relief.

'Goodness! Stop sneaking up on me,' she said in a playful tone, rolling her eyes at him when he shrugged.

'I didn't mean to scare you. You were busy with your work, I swear.' Placing his arms on the counter, he leaned in. 'What are you working on?'

'I'm checking the schedule changes for today before I put it up on the board. With our new anaesthesiologist arriving yesterday, we can stop stealing them from other departments.'

Her words caught him by surprise. The new anaesthesiologist had started yesterday? The locum position was to cover the maternity leave of their own anaesthesiologist. She had only left last week, and he hadn't expected anyone to arrive so soon. Christine herself had only switched to the oncology department a couple of weeks ago. Now he needed to train a new doctor from scratch, when he knew exactly who would have been the perfect person for the job.

His left hand contracted into a fist and he glanced down. It had taken him a long time after the funeral to take off his ring. Even now, close to two years after Claire's passing, the weight of the wedding band sometimes still lingered on his finger.

She had been an incredible source of knowledge and comfort to him when they were working together on their cancer research projects. Then she'd been diagnosed with cancer herself. But her prognosis was looking good. Mark had thought they would spend the rest of their lives together. Until her oncologist had informed him that she was taking a turn for the worse.

Mark had already started his own work rotation at that point, since Claire had been headed towards remission. He wished he could say that no one in the department had seen it coming, that her demise had come overnight and blindsided them all. But the truth was far worse. He'd missed her last moments in life because he had been too busy trying to find the breakthrough in cancer treatment that they had both been working on for the last years. He'd been trying so hard to save himself the pain of losing her that he'd lost sight of what it meant to be an adequate husband to his dying wife.

Mark had promised he would be there for her when she died, but in the end he hadn't been.

The darkness that came with memories of his late wife was a familiar one, and the guilt of her death rested on his shoulders alone. It wrapped around him like a cocoon, blocking out any other emotion.

'What can you tell me about the new person?' he asked, to distract himself from his inner turmoil.

His question made Theresa lift her eyes from her clipboard. 'Why do you want to know? Don't think I haven't heard your complaints about having a locum anaesthesiologist hired. But you know we desperately need someone. Dr Anderson won't be back for another several weeks and you already scared away two replacements.'

Mark clasped his hands above his heart, feigning pain as he grunted, drawing a laugh from Theresa's lips. 'You think I'm the reason the new hires left? You wound me.'

'If the shoe fits…'

'I'm making sure they're committed to our service. With our patients, stability is one of the most important things. If they see a different doctor each time, how will they develop trust in us? I know it's not their fault, but that doesn't change the fact that our patients need consistency.'

'Her name is Emma Santos, and she came here from a private practice in San Francisco.' Theresa sighed. 'She has already arrived and is settling in for her first surgery this morning. You have one surgery with her later on—a tumour resection—so you can get used to each other then. I saw her pass by just moments ago. You should introduce yourself.'

Mark raised an eyebrow at Theresa's words. She had arrived early on her first day. That was an attitude he could appreciate. 'I'll do just that.'

Mark set high standards for the care of his patients. Those standards were responsible for his department dwarfing the national average recovery time. The last thing he needed was a stranger by his side, poking and prodding at those standards. Compromising patient care was unacceptable, and he expected his colleagues to be on top of their game.

Despite his own shortcomings, the team looking after Claire had been an invaluable resource to lean on. He'd become familiar with everyone on her team, drawing comfort from their experience. They knew everything there was to know when it came to consoling patients and their families alike. That wasn't something a doctor from a private practice could possibly know.

What was the chief of surgery thinking? Mark frowned. Locum doctors were no more than tourists, wanting to see the world while practising medicine. He had met enough of them to know he didn't like these kinds of mercenary physicians.

But, since he was stuck with this temporary colleague, he planned on ensuring she understood what kind of service he ran.

Emma had arrived early for her second day at Attano Memorial—the first day she would actually get to do surgery. After announcing her arrival at Reception yesterday, she had spent almost all her time sitting in the HR office, signing contracts and waivers about the hospital's safety procedures, code of conduct and other documents requiring her signature. After that, the HR assistant had given her the grand tour of the hospital, introducing her to some key figures.

It had disappointed her when Mark Henderson hadn't been one of the important people for her to meet. He was the reason she'd come here rather than going back to Brazil for a couple of weeks before starting her fellowship—a choice that hadn't come easy to her. Between med school, internship and residency, Emma hadn't had time to make the trip back to Brazil to see her family. Her cousins called her often, filling her in on the latest gossip in the Santos clan, but it made her long to see her family again.

When things had started looking serious with Rob, she had tried to convince him to take a trip with her and meet her family. But somehow it had never been the right moment. Business had been more important, and he'd refused to lose any appointments, guilting her into staying even when she had planned on taking a trip without him.

Because of that she hadn't been back to Brazil since her mother's funeral. But this opportunity had been too good to pass up, and when she'd called her father to tell him about it he had been beyond excited for her to learn from the best there was. He had always been her biggest supporter.

After stuffing her things into her locker, Emma found the whiteboard the HR assistant had mentioned would hold the surgery schedule, and when her eyes found her name on the board she couldn't help but smile. Her first surgery would be in ninety minutes with a Dr Shearer.

She typed the patient file number on the board into the tablet she had got at the nurses' station. The patient file soon loaded, including all the history and notes from the oncologist.

Nodding to herself, Emma glanced at the board again. Three surgeries were scheduled in OR One, her operating room for the day. One of them in the afternoon with Dr Henderson. The prospect of working with him both excited and terrified her in equal measure. His reputation was for being strict, but that that came from a deep care for his patients.

She entered the OR and glanced around, letting the

gravity of the moment sink in. The room was much larger than the operating theatres she had got used to during her residency.

Rob had convinced her to join him at his private practice rather than continue her residency at the hospital. She had believed him when he'd told her how much better it would be for her training. How *romantic* it would be for them to work together as a couple. When in truth he'd only wanted her close to him to exert control on everything she did, both at work and outside of it. Now she felt unprepared—deprived of the experience she could only have got in a hospital environment.

Emma swallowed to calm the insecurities bubbling up. She picked up the tablet and opened the checklist she'd written last night in preparation. She needed to be sure that everything was where it should be. Starting with the item at the top of the list, she circled the whole OR, checking every item, before a voice interrupted her.

'What are you doing in here?'

The voice was deep, with harsh concern tightly packed in those six words. Stunned at the sudden ferocity, she raised the hand holding the tablet, trying to defuse his tone with a smile. Her eyes scanned the person standing at the door and widened as she recognised who stood in front of her.

Mark Henderson. Dr Handsome.

His jaw was taut, but beneath his stand-offish stance she spotted the man who smiled with such kindness on the covers of magazines. And, going by what she saw as she let her eyes drift down, those magazines could be medical journals or a swimsuit special. He wouldn't look misplaced in either. His sheer masculinity commanded the room with no effort.

'You're Dr Henderson,' she said, omitting the nickname she had given him in her mind. To her eternal relief, her voice didn't crack. She'd only get one chance at making a good impression, and the way his eyes narrowed made her believe that chance hung by a thin thread. 'I'm Emma Santos—the new anaesthesiologist.'

He did not move. He crossed his arms in front of his chest, the sleeves of his scrubs tightening as his muscles contracted, offering her a sight she wanted to look at longer but knew she shouldn't. Especially not with this man. She knew he had so much more to offer than just looks.

Flames licked across her skin, spreading heat throughout her body. A reaction, she rationalised, brought on from meeting this important person and not from his sexy arms. And hair. And face.

Emma cleared her throat to push those thoughts away and lifted her tablet to show it to Mark. 'In my old practice I always went through a checklist to make sure everything was in place before surgery.'

'How far down the list do you go before you talk to the patient?' he asked, in a tone she couldn't quite identify. Not outright hostile, though she picked up on some apprehension.

This was not how she'd imagined meeting Mark Henderson would go. Instead of talking about the work they would do together, she found herself on the wrong side of unwarranted scrutiny over a surgery that didn't even involve one of his patients.

'I don't see how that is any of your concern, seeing as the patient is not on your roster.'

There was a more delicate way to handle his intrusion, Emma knew. But there was no way she would allow anyone to come into her OR questioning her when they hadn't even tried getting to know her before assuming she was terrible at her job.

'I'm the head of this department. Every patient is my patient.'

Emma flinched at the sharp barb in his voice. Her eyes drifted down to her hands and she turned the tablet around, showing Mark the list. 'Talking to the patient is actually at the very top of my list. But since I'm unfamiliar with her, and she doesn't know me either, I've examined her chart to make sure I can do what you hired me to do without disturbing her. After a formal introduction I will be able to do the proper preparation and aftercare.'

She held his stare, uncertain if she saw some remorse mixed in with his surprise, or if she just wanted him to feel that way.

His stance relaxed, his arms slowly dropping to his sides. He let out a deep breath, and with it Emma could see the tension drift away from him.

'That's good to hear. I want to make sure every patient in my ward is familiar with the entire team that is looking after them.' He paused for a moment, as if he was considering his next words. 'When Theresa told me you had arrived early, I was expecting you to be with the patient rather than already preparing the OR.'

'I thought, as a complete stranger to the patient, it would be rude to barge into her room this early in the morning.'

She met his eyes with a frown and straightened her shoulders as she prepared herself for an argument.

There had been no ill intent in her actions this morning, and she had made that clear in her explanation.

The silence between them seemed to stretch out, then Mark nodded, acknowledging her words. To her surprise, a smile appeared on his lips, creating a flutter in her chest that caught her off-guard.

'The residents assigned to oncology can introduce you to all the patients. They'll be able to fill in any blanks as well. I'll see you in surgery.'

Without giving her a chance to reply, he turned around and left through the scrub room, leaving her to contemplate her first encounter with the renowned Dr Mark Henderson.

Even if Emma had tried, it couldn't have gone any worse.

If their first meeting indicated how their professional relationship would be, she could take comfort in knowing that it was only temporary.

# CHAPTER TWO

THE ENCOUNTER WITH Emma had gone very differently from how Mark had expected it to earlier. He had approached the operating room expecting to have a frank conversation with her about his team and the bedside manners he expected from them. Experience had taught him that locum doctors didn't adjust well to new hospitals and held on to bad habits learned from other placements. If this was going to work, he needed to set his expectations right.

Only Emma had turned his plan on its head within the first minute of their meeting. The details on the checklist she'd shown him had contained everything he would have done himself. And instead of lecturing her about his standards of care within the oncology department, something else had happened.

Her presence in the OR had rendered him immobile for a few heartbeats, with all of his senses homing in on her as the soft scent of coconut had drifted towards him. The harsh light of the operating room hadn't affected her, and her dark, honey-toned skin had seemed to be begging to have its perceived softness verified with a brush of his fingers.

Something warm and very concerning had uncoiled

itself in Mark's chest. A sensation he'd believed himself incapable of feeling. A faint ray of light piercing through the darkness of the ever-present guilt that enveloped him.

It had taken him a moment to understand what it was.

Attraction.

He'd noticed Emma as a woman of stunning beauty. Something he hadn't done since Claire had passed away, his heart too consumed with guilt. The grief had faded, and he had made peace with the fact that he would never see her again when he'd taken his wedding ring off. But the guilt remained. She'd died alone because he'd chosen to distract himself from impending pain.

The hint of desire flaring in his chest had quickly turned to anger. At himself, but also at this woman who was trespassing in his OR—and in other parts of his being—unwelcome and unbidden. So he had lashed out at her, only for her to bounce everything straight back at him.

Emma Santos did not lack determination. Something he could appreciate despite the conflicting sensation rising within him.

Mark entered the scrub room and scrubbed his hands clean as he watched his staff getting ready to operate on Mr Norris, who was in for a tumour resection around his gallbladder. He spent extra time going over the chart and previous medical history as this was not a patient of his. Dr Andrew Fremo, one of his colleagues and Christine's husband, who had now gone on paternity leave to be with his wife, had performed the first surgery.

Mark hadn't needed to think before agreeing to take over Andrew's caseload. His own patient roster was quite full, but if extra work was what it took to ensure both his staff and patients were cared for he would take that bullet every single time.

He had broken his word once, and he worked hard to ensure it never happened again. He owed the memory of Claire that much. No matter how trivial it might seem, if he gave his word, Mark kept it.

As he stepped into the OR Mark scanned the room to see that everything was in place. The surgical nurses had set up the tray of instruments just as he liked, making him smile behind his mask. It was the little things that made the long hours worth it.

He glanced at the tablet showing the patient's chart and the surgical plan Mark had drafted earlier in the day. His eyes wandered around the present staff and locked onto Emma Santos's. Dark lashes surrounded her green eyes, creating an almost hypnotising glare.

He searched her gaze for apprehension, or any other sign of their earlier encounter. But all he found was a curious spark that spoke to him on a deeper level. His inappropriate outburst had not dampened her spirit.

'I've placed Mr Norris under anaesthesia and he's ready for you, Dr Henderson,' she said, breaking their eye contact and drawing Mark's attention back to the OR.

'Thank you, Dr Santos. All right, everyone. Let's make sure Mr Norris has the best conceivable chances at recovering. Ten blade, please.'

The second Mark set the scalpel to the patient's skin everything around him faded away. A life lay in his hands, and he reminded himself of that responsibility.

Except for his occasional request for a different instrument, the room stayed quiet as he focused on removing the tumour that grew between the gallbladder and the liver. As far as he could tell from the scans, the growth had penetrated neither of the two organs. If that was the case, they should be able to cut around the edges and remove the tumour entirely.

Only it wasn't that simple.

As Mark explored the area he could see that the walls of the gallbladder were compromised, and if he wanted to remove the whole tumour he would need to remove the organ itself. People lived a comfortable life without a gallbladder, but those people were not battling cancer on top of everything else.

Mark let out a sigh and looked up for a moment as he thought about his next steps. Emma's stare caught him off guard, and a warm sensation flared at the back of his neck. Had she been watching him the entire time? The thought broke through his focus and he caught himself looking at her. Neither of them seemed willing to break the eye contact first.

A sharp beep drew him back to reality and Emma's eyes darted to the monitor next to her. 'Blood pressure is dropping.' She rose to her feet as she said it.

Mark dropped his eyes back to the surgical field, looking for a reason for the sudden drop. He hadn't even started dissecting the tumour. There shouldn't be a rupture that led to this kind of pressure-loss.

'Where are you?' Mumbling to himself, he looked for the spontaneous bleeder. All the while he listened to Emma's voice as she kept him apprised on his vitals, helping him assess the situation as it went on.

'He's getting hypovolemic. We should hang another bag of A positive.'

Mark nodded at her suggestion, glad that she'd taken charge of her duties so he was free to focus on finding the issue at hand. 'Do it.'

He went back to work and after a few moments found a lesion on the liver and threw a suture there to stop the bleeding. Only a few more seconds and Mr Norris might have met with a different fate.

'How did this tear happen?'

Narrating his thoughts was a quirk of his in the OR, and the staff familiar with him understood he wasn't actually addressing anyone. He didn't expect an answer, so when he got one he lifted his head in surprise.

'I've seen this mentioned in a medical journal. Damage to the gallbladder can lead to weakness in the liver or liver failure, depending on the medical history of the patient. Maybe the tumour penetrating the gallbladder wall caused more strain on the liver.'

Emma was looking at him, her eyes alive with enthusiasm and something else that eluded Mark. But it was that something that vibrated inside his chest.

In one surgery she'd changed his mind about her placement in his team. If the presence of mind she had shown in the last couple of hours was an indicator of how private practice doctors trained, he would have to think twice before dismissing them the way he had before.

'Excellent call. Can you find the journal and let me know? I would like to include it in my patient notes.'

Emma nodded, the spark in her eye intensifying.

Mark had to force himself to look away. He needed to make sure Mr Norris got through this surgery with no more complications.

The skin on Emma's face tingled. The surgery had ended almost an hour ago, but adrenaline still pumped through her body and she struggled to focus on her notes. Different moments in the operating room kept replaying in her mind, and almost all of them involved Mark.

Of course they did—he was the leading surgeon on this case. Any other reason for him to stick out would be inappropriate. And Emma had had enough inappropriate work entanglements to last her the rest of her career.

Yet her heart fluttered inside her chest when she remembered those hazel eyes locking onto hers during surgery. Mark Henderson had shown her in that surgery why he was on the cover of magazines. And his stunning looks had nothing to do with it. What she had thought to be bravado turned out to be deep care and responsibility for his patients, who were going through the most challenging time of their lives. With that new understanding of him she could forgive the intensity of their first meeting, despite the memory still making her shiver with uncertainty.

Emma wanted to make the best out of her time here at Attano Memorial and learn as much as possible from the talented staff surrounding her before she started her fellowship in Rochester in two months.

As she jotted down the patient's notes she kept thinking back to the surgery, remembering all the essential details, so she could make sure they were up to the high standards Mark expected.

The standards she set for herself couldn't be any higher, so it shouldn't make a difference to how she approached them. And yet she wanted to impress him.

It was only natural, of course. He was a renowned doctor with a lot of influence. But it was more than that.

Rob was the only surgeon she'd worked with throughout her entire residency at his private practice—a move she now regretted as she witnessed her peers being so much more advanced in general medicine. It was one reason she spent so much time reading textbooks and journals in different fields. Love had made her choose poorly in her career, and she was paying the price for it.

This was Emma's chance to leave a lasting impression in the medical world. She had wasted enough time on things that brought her only pain. Her fellowship would be the last leg of her medical training and then she would have achieved everything she'd set out to do.

Once she got to her goal she would have to find the courage to get tested. But it could wait. At least that was what she told herself. Gardner Syndrome usually showed itself in adolescence. Emma had reached her early thirties without a single sign of a tumour.

She still needed to know, but there was no way she would let herself get distracted from her medical training again. One failed romance had already taken enough time from her studies.

Engrossed in her own thoughts, she didn't notice someone approaching. The chair they pulled out scraped over the floor, creating a loud sound that tore Emma's attention back to reality.

As if her thoughts had made him manifest in front of her, Mark turned the chair around and straddled it. He crossed his arms on top of the backrest and looked at her with those warm brown eyes that sent a searing spark through her. He folded his arms in front of him and rested his chin on top of them.

Emma became instantly aware of his proximity. Her eyes glided over him, taking in the enticing view. How did he have the time to stay in that kind of shape?

'Are you checking me out?' he asked in a low baritone voice, making her flinch at his bluntness.

As if she would ever go there with a superior of hers. Again.

'Of course not!' she said, cringing at how she came across as if she had very much been checking him out. Which she had. 'How can I help you, Dr Henderson?'

'Excellent work on Mr Norris' surgery. Theresa told me you transferred here from San Francisco. What made you come here?'

*You.* Though Emma couldn't tell him that. Especially not now.

At one point she'd believed he might be the one to cure her from the disease she might carry dormant within her. She had watched the oncologists follow his regime of pain management for her mother, easing her last days. Despite how hard it had been to watch, it had inspired Emma. She'd wanted to be a doctor who could help just the way her mother's doctors had.

When the opportunity to work at the same hospital as him had come up, she'd said yes with almost no hesitation. And it hadn't come a moment too soon.

After spending her residency years putting people to sleep for elective plastic surgery, she'd yearned for a change. Emma wanted to be challenged, and to add her own knowledge to the growing field of medicine.

And more recently there had been a quiet voice in the back of her mind, urging her not to settle for less than she wanted. What if her mother had passed her condition on to her? If she wasn't able to be a doctor any more, what would her legacy look like?

'I completed my residency, so my time in San Francisco was up, and I needed to move on.'

As Emma didn't want to tell him the truth, she went with a simplified version. She would never tell him how her manipulative ex-boyfriend had tried to force her to pass up the opportunity of a lifetime, because it didn't suit his own needs.

'I had a gap between completing my board exam and my fellowship position, so I came here.'

Mark shifted his head to the side, his eyes never leaving her as he contemplated her words. 'So, you're not from California.'

A statement, Emma observed, and her gaze shifted from him to the tablet in front of her. His eyes made her acutely aware of his presence, along with the faint scent of pine drifting from him. Even after a four-hour surgery, he still looked and smelled fresh. She felt as if she needed a shower before continuing this conversation.

The images of Mark and a shower combined themselves in her head, making the heat rise from her stomach to her cheeks.

'No, I'm not. I came to the States to study. My family still lives in Brazil. Is my accent still that bad after all the years I've spent here?'

'It's not bad, at all. I like it. There is a certain melody to the way you speak.'

A smirk appeared at the corners of his lips, and she wondered if he had noticed the tinge of rose on her face.

'It's rather unusual for an anaesthesiologist to do their residency in a private practice. Why did you choose that path?'

His eyes bored into her, and Emma almost squirmed under the probing look. He was asking about the dark corners of her mind, where she didn't want anyone to look. How could she tell a man like Mark that she had chosen to damage her career prospects because of love? Because she had been blind enough to fall for the fake promises of a man who was only looking out for himself?

'It seemed like a good choice at the time.'

She didn't trust herself to say anything else. The last thing she wanted was this man she admired judging her for the mistake she regretted most in her life.

He nodded, seeming content with her answer. 'What field are you specialising in for your fellowship?'

'Emergency medicine,' she replied with a sigh of relief, and saw a spark of curiosity ignite in his eyes.

'That's an interesting offshoot from anaesthesiology. Where are you headed?'

Despite anticipating the question, Emma's stomach still did a small turn, and she bit her lip, felt the blush in her cheeks intensifying.

'Rochester,' she said.

Mark's lips parted in surprise. 'You're joining the programme at Whitebridge?'

Emma nodded. An odd mix of pride and embarrassment overcame her every time she told someone about her fellowship. It was a competitive programme, and she was one of the few selected to work and learn at one of the most prestigious hospitals in the country.

The Whitebridge Institute was also the place where Mark had studied and worked for most of his career.

'It hasn't quite sunk in yet, even though I'm starting in a couple of weeks.'

'Not a lot of people get invited to that programme.'

His voice had adopted a strange quality Emma couldn't place. He sounded almost apprehensive. It made her heart stutter in her chest. Did he not have fond feelings about his time in Rochester? Was there something she didn't know about the institute?

'How long have you lived in the States? It must be a few years at this point,' he said, ripping her out of her contemplations.

'I haven't really left since med school. I was lucky to get a scholarship, or I might not have been able to study here.'

Her mother had received her diagnosis after Emma had left the country to study. Otherwise she might have never left Brazil, not wanting to put so much distance between her and her ailing parent.

'Luck is not usually a deciding factor in scholarships,' he said with a hint of humour.

She caught her breath. But she must have misread his tone—because there was no way Mark Henderson would flirt with her. What else could give his voice such a playful ring?

'Maybe the panel liked the melody accompanying my words,' she said with a laugh, as she tried to deflect the heat his probing gaze drew to the surface of her skin.

'There is a lot to like at first glance.'

Emma opened her lips to reply, but the words died in her throat. There it was again. A light vibration beneath his words that caused a warm spark to bounce down her spine, settling right behind her navel. This could not be happening. There was no reality in which it was acceptable for her to be flirting with her boss. Ever.

'I should go prepare for my next surgery,' she said, in an attempt to overcome the odd sensations battling inside her.

As she got up, Mark reached out and placed a hand on her forearm, halting her. The warmth prickling in her cheeks cascaded into a wave that swept through her body, leaving a hot sensation where he had touched her.

'I meant what I said about surgery. It's a tough specialty we're in, so while your quick thinking won't save a lot of lives, it will give our patients an edge. And in their situation they need every advantage that we can give them.' He paused and looked at her with an intense expression. Then he lifted his hand to let her go. 'If you are serious about your work here, then I welcome you to the team and I look forward to teaching you.'

Emma's stomach tied itself into a knot, and she swallowed to ease away the lump in her throat so she could answer him with composure. 'Thank you, Dr Henderson.'

'Please, call me Mark.'

'I will see you in our next surgery, Mark.'

His name had dropped so fast off her lips that she almost repeated it, just to hear it again.

# CHAPTER THREE

MARK SAT BEHIND the desk in his office, sipping his coffee and looking through his patient files for the day. There was only one patient on his surgical schedule: Georgina Williams.

The last week had been interesting in many ways, with Emma Santos being at the centre of his contemplations. She had integrated herself into his team, and his attending surgeons were already gushing about her competency and hard-working attitude.

What he hadn't expected was the effect she had on him after just one week of working together. He treated all his staff with the same amount of attention and respect. A pleasant working environment where everyone could work well and be honest with each other was a point of pride for him. But something beyond that drove him to seek Emma out. The warm tendrils of attraction he felt drew him in each time he let his guard down.

It was a feeling Mark could not reconcile within himself. The flutter he was experiencing in his chest, the heat igniting the blood in his veins whenever he let his thoughts stray towards her—those were things for available people. He was the furthest he could be from that.

He'd never even entertained the thought of another woman. When Claire had needed him the most, he had failed to be a proper husband to her. Though it pained him, Mark had admitted to himself a long time ago that he wasn't strong enough for what life had thrown at him. All he had left to do now was to be the best kind of doctor he could be. That was where his strength lay.

Downing the last bit of coffee from his mug, Mark got up. He grabbed the tablet off his desk and made his way to Georgina's room for the pre-op check before her surgery in the afternoon. He'd opened up her patient chart on the tablet in his hand and was scrolling through the pages, looking for her latest lab results, when he noticed the file was being edited.

With furrowed brows, he watched as notes appeared, giving him all the information he needed and doing all the pre-op checks he'd planned on doing himself. His residents knew he liked to do it himself.

But the notes he was looking at right now were almost exactly how he'd make them. Could it be Emma?

Mark cleared his throat as an unexpected dryness spread through his mouth. And as he entered the patient's room, his suspicion was confirmed.

Emma stood next to the patient's bed, talking to Georgina and updating the chart. Between the chatter and the noises from the monitor connected to her, neither of them had heard his knock or him entering the room.

Emma stood tall in her heels—much taller than he remembered from their surgeries in the past week. Her white lab coat covered most of her body, but underneath she wore a deep blue woollen dress with a dipping neckline that left just enough to the imagination. Her dark curls flowed over her shoulders in tantalising waves.

Diligent and beautiful. A combination that would force many men to their knees.

Not him, though.

The tempting sense of attraction that stirred in his chest when he looked at her consumed his mind whenever he let his thoughts drift. The warmth emanating from her sought him out, finding the cracks in his armour and awakening a dormant part of him. But it only took a second for that feeling to be gripped by the guilt living in his heart. How could he look at another woman and feel the faint whisper of desire?

Unnoticed, he looked from Georgina to Emma and then his eyes landed on Harald, Georgina's husband, who sat on a chair and shrugged with a small smile as the two women shared a laugh.

Mark remembered a time when he had been the spouse sitting in one of these chairs, trying his best to project an aura of confidence. As a husband, your role was to support your sick wife. You needed to be strong, so your partner could lean on them.

The toll of that had been greater than Mark had expected. Until Claire's diagnosis he had only ever experienced the disease from a physician's point of view. A viewpoint he'd slipped into when her condition had got worse. As a doctor, he could get away with being emotionally distant. Only she hadn't needed another doctor. She had needed her husband.

Emma's laughter pulled him out of his contemplation of past regrets and Mark swallowed the lump building in his throat as his gaze drifted over her once more. No one ever looked good under the fluorescent lights of a hospital room. But somehow all Mark could focus on was her wavy dark brown hair and how it would feel if he ran his fingers through it. Silky, smooth, smelling of coconut and filling his head with fantasies…

As he stepped forward Georgina spotted him first, before Emma turned around to face him, a small smile on her lips. 'Perfect timing! Mrs Williams has just asked about the upcoming procedure. Do you have time to walk her through it step by step?'

'Please call me Georgina. I figure someone who wants to know so much about me gets to call me by my first name.' Georgina waved her hand at Emma, who chuckled again.

'She still makes me call her Mrs Williams, mind you,' her husband said from his seat, turning her chuckle into a full laugh.

'I see you're in great spirits today,' said Mark. 'Good. Keeping a positive attitude is important for a quick recovery.'

Mark made another step forward, positioning himself next to Emma. His shoulder brushed hers when he passed her, sending a spark down his arm. He tried his best to ignore the sensation while focusing on his patient.

'I'm sure Dr Santos has already introduced herself. She's joining us for a couple of weeks as our staff anaesthesiologist. I want to give her as many opportunities as possible to hone her skills while she's here with us. So I'm going to ask her to present your case,

Georgina. If there is anything unclear just let me know and we will go back a step.'

Emma's lips parted as Mark nodded at her, clearly expecting her to walk Georgina through all the steps of her surgery. Even though she wasn't a surgeon, and hadn't received any surgical training, she had studied the procedure for her own preparations. So she caught herself and cleared her throat, looking at the tablet in her hands to find the notes she'd made last night.

'Georgina Williams, age thirty-two, diagnosed with a tumour on her left ovary. Scheduled for an oophorectomy this afternoon...' She presented the patient's history to Mark, who nodded at her with a hint of a smile before turning back to Georgina.

'What that means is that this afternoon we will remove your left ovary to get the potentially malignant tissue at its origin. We'll send some samples to the lab to confirm whether it's malignant.'

Emma focused her attention on their patient, and it helped her banish the tingling heat that spread through her stomach. From the notes in the chart, Emma could tell that the tumour had been discovered quite recently. But despite that Georgina always smiled and didn't seem to fear her diagnosis.

It was a quality Emma envied. She wanted to be just as brave with her own diagnosis, but she couldn't even talk herself into having a test. Only two more years and then her training would be done. She would worry about her next steps then.

Mark stepped up to her, drawing her attention. All her senses homed in on him as she registered his proximity to her. This was a more immediate concern she needed to deal with. The pangs of heat cascading through her body whenever she was close to him were inappropriate for more reasons that she could count.

'Why are we performing a partial oophorectomy rather than a full hysterectomy?' He looked at her as he asked the question.

'The scans suggest the tumour is isolated in one ovary. To preserve the patient's reproductive organs, an oophorectomy is less invasive.'

Emma hadn't expected to be questioned the same way interns were, but it made sense. He had told her he looked forward to teaching her.

Mark nodded with a smile that caused a wave of warm sparks to ignite behind her navel.

'After the surgery, Georgina, you will need to recover from the stress we'll be putting your body under before we transfer you to an oncologist if you need chemotherapy.'

Emma continued her explanation and saw a spark of fear enter Georgina's eyes—a look she was familiar with. Emma's chest tightened.

She stepped closer to her and rested her hand on hers, giving it a reassuring squeeze. 'I know it sounds scary, but if you do need chemotherapy I'm familiar with some remedies for a few of the side effects. Make sure a nurse pages me, and I can tell you what helped in my case.'

Georgina raised her eyebrows.

It was only then Emma realised what she had said. 'Oh, no, not me. My mother had cancer.'

Georgina breathed out a sigh of relief and Emma took a step back, daring to look at Mark again. Any composure she had built up melted away in an instant as she saw the warm glow of sympathy in his eyes. He'd clearly caught the piece of personal information she'd revealed by accident.

'We also have you scheduled for a visit from the gynaecologist to harvest some of your eggs, if necessary, as well as talk to you about any questions on fertility that you might have,' Mark said, looking at both Harald and Georgina as he spoke. 'If you need chemotherapy it will impact your healthy eggs, which is why we like to harvest them before you move on with your treatment. Ideally, we'll also fertilise the eggs before we freeze them, but that's something the two of you can discuss with Dr Clark when she comes to see you.'

Emma's heart went out to the couple. Georgina's tumour had thrown all their plans into disarray—to the point where they now had to discuss their future children on a clinical level.

It was a concern that crept into her own mind every now and again. While Emma didn't have any siblings, she'd grown up on the same street as her cousins, so she hadn't lacked friends her own age to bond with. Whenever she'd got into fights with her parents she'd found shelter in her cousin Livia's room, where they would contemplate the hardship of being a teenager in the Santos clan.

Even now her big family was a source of comfort, even though they lived on a different continent. She couldn't imagine her life any other way, and yearned to have her own family one day. Though if she did have Gardner's how she made that family would differ from how she'd imagined.

It was another reason to get an answer to that open question. And one more reason she didn't want to

know. How was she supposed to make all these decisions on her own?

Emma cleared her throat, forcing those intrusive
thoughts away. She needed to focus on the task ahead
of her. 'And I think that is the gist of it. Are there any
questions left on your side?'

Georgina looked at her husband for a moment before shaking her head, and that slight gesture caused
Emma's heart to twinge in her chest. That was what
she wanted. A person to help her through the tough
times she might be facing. Someone who understood
what she needed with a mere look.

In a different life, she'd thought Rob to be that person for her. She'd been too wrapped up in his manipula-
tions and her own insecurities to see their relationship
for what it had been—nothing more than a means to
further his private practice at the cost of her career.

'No, all good here. Let's kick this tumour's butt.'

Harald laughed at his wife's choice of words.

'Good. Keep your spirits up, and we'll see you this
afternoon.'

Mark smiled at Georgina before turning around and
nodded at Harald on his way out. He paused at the
door, holding it open for Emma. They walked to the
nurses' station, where they both deposited their tablets.
The hair on her nape rose as his brown eyes met hers.

A week had passed since she'd arrived in Chicago,
and the very thing she'd sworn wouldn't happen was
happening. In front of her eyes, her respect for Mark
and his work had been transformed into a subtle pull
of attraction. Whenever she let her mind wander she
ended up thinking about him.

They'd recovered their relationship after a rocky

start, and were making an excellent team inside the OR. More than once she'd thought she had seen his gaze wander over to her. Had he been checking her out or judging her work? The thought that he might look at her as a woman almost made her laugh in derision. He was Mark Henderson, award-winning surgeon and researcher. He was her boss. She was just a doctor from the poorer part of Brazil, who couldn't even take a simple test to save her life.

'It's good to see her so enthusiastic about her treatment,' Emma said, and Mark nodded.

He leaned his hip against the counter of the nurses' station as he turned to face her, his arms crossed in front of his chest, enticing her to let her gaze roam for a bit.

'It's a rare sight to see such an upbeat patient. A good sign for the course of her potential treatment. Patients with a positive outlook have a much higher rate of recovery.'

'I imagine it's not always easy to inspire that kind of mood.'

Mark's hands dropped to his sides at that comment, his eyes drifting away for a moment. 'No, not really. Most people in our care are looking at a worse battle. We get a lot of patients from out of state, looking at us for their third and fourth opinions.'

He said it so casually, as if it had never occurred to him what it meant that people sought him out when they had no other hope left.

'They want to be treated by the best. They want you. I can understand that,' she said.

His dark eyes came back to her, a strange expression fluttering over his face. He seemed confused. But there was no way he didn't know why people were travelling here to be treated by his team of doctors. Or was he just not used to hearing it in such plain words?

Her train of thought came to an abrupt stop when his lips parted in a smile, sending her heart slamming against her chest.

A faint blush sneaked onto Emma's cheeks, making Mark wonder what thoughts were rattling around in her head that were intrusive enough to make her flush all on her own. He didn't want to admit how much he enjoyed watching it happen. Was she thinking of him? Or was he projecting his own inner turmoil back at her?

Despite his desire to keep things professional, he wanted to learn more about her. The compassion she'd shown Georgina was the energy he wanted in the oncology department. The road to recovery for all patients was a difficult one, and Emma would soon learn that they didn't earn as many victories as they wanted.

Before Claire had got sick herself, they had both poured a lot of their professional lives into researching cancer and developing new treatments. She'd focused on different ways of relieving pain while he looked for overall treatment options. It was Claire who had made a connection between the different patients they'd observed and their overall personalities. She had got sick before she could finish her research paper on it, but he remembered how much of it she'd applied to herself. No matter how tired the radiation therapy had made her feel, she had tried to smile—for herself as much as for him.

Knowing that Emma had a loved one suffering from cancer explained a lot about her compassion. It added another layer to her, making her more than she seemed. She intrigued Mark—something that was even worse than the attraction he felt stirring in his chest. Curiosity wasn't something he could indulge with his colleagues. Emma was here to learn from him, not to be a target of his misguided attraction.

'Is your mother a cancer survivor?' he asked, to distract himself from his thoughts.

Regret turned his stomach as profound pain contorted her face.

'No, unfortunately not' was all she said, her eyes dropping so he couldn't see her full face any more.

The expression his question had summoned to her face was one he was familiar with himself. For a split second the urge to confide his own loss to her grew inside his chest. He had put her in a situation where she'd had to reveal her past pain to him. What surprised him was how much he wanted to share his with her.

Most of his days Mark spent shrouded in the oppressive darkness that was the memory of his final days with Claire. Despite the guilt of missing her last moments still clinging to his heart, he had transformed his feelings into something to serve him. A drive to hold himself and his staff to the highest standards possible, so that no spouse would have to feel the same way he did. So that no one would need to bear the weight of everything all by themselves, like Harald was doing for his wife right now. As Mark had failed to do for Claire.

That kind of drive was another thing that he and Emma had in common. The woman was getting more intriguing by the minute, and he felt his surrounding darkness ease as he got to know her better. It was an odd sensation, that was unbidden but not unpleasant.

He wanted to know more about her, despite knowing that it was best if he didn't. Attachment to anyone was something he tried to avoid.

'Have you seen anything of Chicago yet?' he asked, to distract himself from the urge to reveal his darker thoughts to her.

'No, I only arrived the night before yesterday.' She pressed her lips together before chuckling. 'No rest for the wicked.'

'I'll show you when we have a day off together. You shouldn't leave for Rochester before you've eaten rib tips from one of the barbecue stalls at the waterfront.'

'Rib tips? I thought you Chicagoans were all about your deep-dish pizza?'

Her lips parted in a smile, and the urge to reach out to feel her skin underneath his fingertips resurfaced.

'We can eat deep-dish pizza, but you would be missing out. Don't let the clever marketing of the pizza industry deceive you. Trust me, you will thank me later.'

His quip drew another laugh from her lips, a sound vibrating through his body and igniting a gentle heat across his skin.

Why had he invited her out? He hadn't had time to contemplate his suggestion before his mouth had formed the words, uttering an invitation he hadn't meant to extend. The tension arching through his body should be something he buried and ignored. Not acted on by inviting her out on a date.

No, it was a professional courtesy—not a date. Emma would head to the Whitebridge Institute after her short stint here, and Mark knew that the chief of surgery would want him to make her experience a good one. He wanted her to leave thinking of all the great things she had learned at Attano Memorial.

'One of the surgical residents is running pre-op procedures today. So I will see you in the OR,' he said, his mouth a thin line as he gave her only a curt nod before leaving.

Mark needed to watch himself. To enjoy the warmth coming from Emma was one thing. Another thing was to act on it.

Taking a deep breath, he forced himself to walk away and to focus on the fact that they made an excellent team. In surgery, as well as when she was walking a patient through each step of their upcoming procedure, Emma showed him the depth of her compassion and skill. Their interactions with each other were flowing and seamless, even without them having worked together before.

This kind of quality was much more significant in Mark's world than something as fleeting as attraction.

Georgina's surgery would be the first test for that.

# CHAPTER FOUR

EMMA GRABBED HER phone out of the pocket of her lab coat to check the time. Her conversation with Mark had gone on much longer than she'd thought it had. They would be in surgery two hours from now. With all the pre-op check-ups done, she didn't need to do much more to prepare for the procedure. Only her pre-surgery checklist remained, and Emma needed to be in the operating room for that.

As she walked down the corridor she caught a glimpse of herself. Having worked at a private clinic, Emma had got used to dressing up every morning, only changing into scrubs when it was time for surgery. Rob had insisted that the patients only saw her in nice clothes, wanting to sell them an experience on top of their procedure. He'd criticised her on several occasions for looking too casual, and asked her to change before leaving the house.

In the corridors of Attano Memorial, it surprised her to see no one in anything else other than scrubs or a lab coat. She even saw some of the staff arriving in scrubs in the car park.

Painful humiliation stabbed Emma in the chest as she looked down on herself again. She had left, regained control of her own life, and yet she still hung on to the habits she'd cultivated to please Rob. Not only had she lost out on the level of training an anaesthetist would have received in a hospital environment, she'd also forgotten how to be comfortable in her own skin.

With her family being so far away, the people she worked with were the closest thing she had to a support system here in the States. As a doctor, she didn't exactly have oodles of free time, so the only people she could rely on were her co-workers. Emma wanted to blend in with her new colleagues—wanted to belong and feel comfortable.

Not too comfortable, though. With the friendliness of the staff surrounding her, it was way too easy to forget that this was only a temporary assignment and that before long she would pack her car again and be on her way to Rochester.

Her first on-call shift started today—a prospect that made her insides lurch with both excitement and dread alike. During her day shifts at the hospital, they always assigned her to the oncology department, working on cases with the surgeons there. That changed for the on-call shifts. To ensure the strain on the anaesthetist was as minimal as possible, the chief of surgery there had put them all into one large rotation, so that each of them only had to work one on-call shift every couple of weeks.

This would be her only on-call shift in her time at Attano Memorial. A prospect that wouldn't seem as daunting if she had worked in such an environment before. But thanks to Rob, and his web of lies, Emma's unpreparedness stood out like a sore thumb. Which, at the end of the day, she had only herself to blame for.

While she had been tricked and lied to, each decision she'd made had been her own. The knowledge of how willingly blind she had been stung as much as the lies he had enveloped her in.

She tried not to be too hard on herself, but it was difficult. Back in Brazil she would have had her cousins to advise her. They butted into her affairs more often than she wanted, giving her guidance without her asking for it. It was something that had annoyed her back then. Now she missed them. They would have warned her about Rob even if she hadn't wanted to hear it. But being all alone, in a place that had felt very different from Brazil, Emma had leaned on the person who had extended to her some comfort. Even if he had done so for his own goals.

Looking back at their relationship now filled Emma with a sense of horror and sadness beyond words. She couldn't grasp how much she had let herself tolerate when the writing had been on the wall all the time. But instead of seeing him for what he was, she'd kept finding ways to make excuses for him, giving him the benefit of the doubt over and over again. She had tried to discuss her mother's death with him, and to tell him about what she might be carrying within her. She had tried to turn to him for support, to see if together they might find out the truth.

Rob had told her their surgical schedule was too busy and that he wasn't sure they could afford to take time off at a pivotal moment for his practice. Maybe later, he had suggested. After that, she had felt too self-conscious and exposed to bring it up again, thinking she was selfish to want him to take so much time away from his work.

With a sigh, Emma pushed those thoughts away and opened the door of her locker in the residents' changing room, taking the stethoscope from around her neck and hanging it on the open door before removing her lab coat. She grabbed the folded scrubs from inside and paused when she spotted the object lying beneath them: an old Polaroid picture of her with her parents, on the day she'd got accepted into med school.

The photo had travelled with her wherever she went, as a reminder to keep going. Her mother had been so proud when she'd got the acceptance letter that she had planned a *churrasco* for the same evening, inviting the entire street to celebrate the fact that her daughter was going to be a doctor.

It was the last time she remembered seeing her mother full of life. The next time she'd made it back home during a break at medical school was the time when she had been confronted with her mother's diagnosis and rapidly deteriorating health.

She had flown back to Brazil to see her mother as much as she could, but a visit during her second year had turned out to be the last one. The pain of her mother's death had been so raw and all-consuming that she hadn't wanted to go back to med school. Her father had had to physically remove her from his house to get her to go back to the States.

The memory now made her smile to herself, but back then tears had stained her cheeks.

The possibility that she might suffer from the same disease her mother had died of infused her with a naked fear that took possession of her entire body when she thought about it. But the terror demanded space she couldn't afford at the moment. She had to make up for time lost. Her peers were all ahead of her in clinical hours and research, so getting back on track was Emma's key priority.

This also meant that she avoided talking about her mother in front of anyone, as it invited more questions than she wanted. Until she'd found herself in that room with Mark and their patient and the words had tumbled out of her mouth. Without trying, he had slipped past her defences and uncovered a piece of information she didn't usually volunteer to anyone.

What had made Emma's breath hitch in her throat had been the warm glow of sympathy in his eyes when he'd learned of her mother's death. He'd seemed to understand her pain without needing to ask any more questions than the one he had. Had he spent enough time surrounded by cancer patients that he felt their pain as if it was his own? Or had he, too, lost someone dear to him to cancer?

Either way, she had glimpsed the kind soul that lay behind the unyielding and devastatingly handsome exterior.

No, she couldn't think about Mark in such terms, Emma reminded herself, pulling the scrub top over her head and slipping into the trousers. Kind, smart, talented. Those were acceptable words with which to describe her boss. Handsome? No, not allowed.

Her interest in him was professional, and she couldn't afford to miss this opportunity to work with him because she found herself distracted by his alluring eyes. Or his handsome face. Or the fine lines of muscle she'd spotted beneath the loose fabric of his shirt. If she could only run her hand over one of those lines... maybe that would be enough to satisfy her curiosity.

A hot sensation licked over her cheeks and Emma caught her breath. *Absolutely no more daydreaming*, she told herself. That path only led to more heartbreak, and she shouldn't even be contemplating anything like that. What made her think a successful surgeon like Mark would be interested in her, anyway?

With a sigh, she raked her fingers through her hair, pulling it into a tight bun that sat at her nape. She had surgery preparations to make. Rather than focus on Dr Handsome, and the scrubs that revealed as much as they obscured, she vowed to concentrate on their work as a team and what she could learn in the precious few weeks that they had. He'd let her present Georgina's case, and that showed her he was keen on teaching her. They were an excellent team—in the strictest of professional senses.

She straightened herself as she wrapped the stethoscope around her neck again and left for the operating room.

Done with her pre-op checklist, and having checked all items off, Emma retreated into the scrub room to re-scrub. As she washed her hands, the doors on the far side of the operating room opened. Two interns pushed Georgina in, with Mark walking next to her. The surgery was not due to begin for another thirty minutes, so they were a bit early.

Emma peered through the window into the OR, her eyes fixated on Mark. Despite her standing at the lit window he didn't see her, his full attention on his patient. His hand grasped Georgina's as they shared a laugh, which made his entire face light up. The fine lines around his eyes told a story of many smiles, and Emma wanted to reach through the glass to touch them, to feel the captivating curve of his lips under her fingertips.

The flutter originating in her stomach radiated through her body, and to drive those intrusive thoughts away Emma splashed some of the cold water on her face. What had happened to no daydreaming about the boss? If she lost focus that fast, she'd never get through a whole surgery with him in such close proximity.

The soft expression on his face as he spoke to their patient betrayed the stern nature he projected when talking to his staff. Emma glimpsed a profound vulnerability hiding beneath the gruff exterior, and for a moment an uncomfortable pinch settled in her chest. He and his patient were having a personal moment that she shouldn't be watching. But Georgina needed to be started on her first round of medication in a couple of minutes, so she would be ready for surgery.

Emma dried her hands with a fresh towel and took a face mask, tying it behind her head and pressing the button to open the door. It slid open without a sound and she walked in, freezing in her step when the conversation between Mark and Georgina didn't stop. It seemed neither of them was aware of her.

'Of course. The second we finish here I will update your husband on the surgery.' Mark smiled at Georgina and took her hand when she reached out to him.

'Thank you, Dr Henderson. You know, Dr Fremo warned me about your charm, but he forgot to mention the good looks. I should have put on my nice hospital gown for you,' she said, drawing a soft chuckle from his lips that mingled with her laugh.

'Georgina, I enjoy being your doctor, so don't let my wife hear any of this or I won't be your doctor for long.'

'Oh, you and Dr Santos are married and you work together every day? I don't know if I could be around Harry all day.'

Mark laughed again, shaking his head. 'No, Dr Santos is not my wife. How did you get that idea?'

'I'm a matchmaker by trade. I know desire when I see it.' Georgina smiled, looking at him with a spark in her eyes.

'We make a good team. I think that is what you may have glimpsed.'

Emma stood still in the doorframe, wishing she had made them aware of her earlier. In her mind, the noise of the door should have been enough, but she realised now that they hadn't heard her enter, and she'd intruded in a very private conversation. She didn't know how to move now without seeming as if she had been eavesdropping. An impression she wanted to avoid.

One of the OR nurses came to her rescue, opening the door on the far side of the operating room to wheel in a monitor. The surrounding commotion ended their conversation and allowed Emma to step up to her spot. She glanced at Mark as he stood up, hoping the mask obscured her expression enough so that he wouldn't notice she had heard everything he'd said to Georgina.

Her mind was still processing what she had overheard. He was married.

Emma's chest tightened, and a stabbing pain left her paralysed for a few breaths. Why did she care? Mark had been off-limits before she had even met him. Finding out that he was married just cemented her 'absolutely no daydreaming of any kind' rule.

'All right, Georgina. This medication will make you sleepy.'

She got up from her chair and headed over to the instrument tray, popping the syringe out of the vacuum-sealed packaging and double-checking the numbers on her tablet before filling the needle with the medication and injecting it through a small port in the crook of the patient's arm.

'Will you count down from ten for me?'

She tried to smile at Georgina, to reassure her, thankful that the mask hid most of her face as the woman started counting down. Her voice trailed off when she got to eight, and the number seven didn't make it past her lips.

The OR around her burst into life as everyone prepared to start the surgery. Emma picked up the curved laryngoscope from her tray of instruments, intubating Georgina and connecting the valve of the tube to the aspirator.

'We're good to start, Dr Henderson,' Emma said, and it took more effort than she'd thought it would to keep her voice from cracking. Her mind was racing.

Biting back a sigh, Emma settled down on her chair and took a few deep breaths. Right now she had a job to do. And at least she now knew that the attraction she'd sensed was not mutual.

The entire team in the OR had followed the surgical plan without a single hitch, leaving Mark pleased as they wheeled the still unconscious Georgina out and back to her room, where her husband would be waiting.

He'd caught himself looking over to Emma from time to time, seen her dark eyes narrowed and fixated on the monitor sitting next to her. She had been quiet throughout the procedure and hadn't shown any interest when he'd started walking the interns through the steps of the oophorectomy as he performed the surgery. He'd sensed something was off, and the urge to investigate had grown stronger as the surgery had gone on.

As the nurses transported Georgina back to her room, Mark turned to the interns. 'Grab the sample that we biopsied and bring it down to the lab. Once we have the results you can update Mrs Williams' chart and page me so we can review it together.'

Mark turned around, wanting to catch Emma before she left, but her assigned seat was already empty. He had not turned his back for more than five minutes. She must have left in a hurry.

'Did you see Emma leave?' he asked Theresa, who was preparing the room for the next surgery.

'Emma?' She raised an eyebrow at him. 'Dr Santos left a few seconds ago. She's probably finishing her notes on the surgery somewhere.'

Mark nodded and went on pursuit. Something wasn't right, and he wanted to understand it straight away.

He poked his head through the door of the break room, but she wasn't there. She wasn't at the nurses' station either, and when he asked the nurse there about her, she indicated that she had seen her come by just a couple of minutes ago.

His options running low, Mark started checking the on-call rooms, and found her in the second one he checked on his floor.

He would have searched every single room in the hospital just to find her.

That thought lingered at the edge of his mind—something he couldn't admit to himself. Would he have done it for anyone else, or would he have just let them cool off and then catch up with them the following day?

'I was looking for you,' he said as he spotted Emma sitting on the top bunk with her tablet on her lap.

Her eyes narrowed as she looked at him, sending an icy shiver down his spine. Now he was sure there was something not right between them.

'You found me. How can I help you?'

'You left so fast after the surgery. I just wanted to check in on you.'

He stepped closer to the bunk she sat on, her elevated position putting them at the same height. The dark waves of hair were contained in a tight knot, which granted him a view of her neck and shoulders, and for a moment he wondered how her skin would feel underneath his fingers. Would she be as soft as she looked?

'I did my part and I didn't need to stick around. I administered the drug to take her out of anaesthesia, so now I only need to check in on her after she's woken up to see how to manage her pain.'

Why was he chasing after her? While he would admit that he liked his doctors to work in harmony with one another, he knew disagreements happened to the best of them. That someone should choose to step away so as to not escalate conflict was a good thing. Instead of pressing her, Mark should take her words at face value and leave. It would be the professional thing to do.

After all, what other reason did he have for his presence here?

He didn't have any interest in Emma that went beyond their working relationship, so he should say nothing more and leave.

'Did I do something I'm not aware of?' The words left his lips before he could stop them.

Emma released a breath. 'No, I came here to write up my notes before getting some rest. I'm working an on-call shift today.'

Her words were short. He sensed there was something she wasn't telling him. A strange need inside him pushed him to probe further. He felt an almost irresistible draw from her. His hand seemed to demand he reach out to smooth the frown from her lips with a gentle touch. To untangle her hair so he could find out how her locks felt between his fingers.

Control almost slipped from his grasp and Mark took a step back, aware of every inch of air between them. As much as his insides protested, he needed to let go of this conversation and move on.

'I find the bed over there the most comfortable. It's close to the door, so people avoid it,' he said to change the subject. He pointed at the bed opposite. 'Trust me. You'll sleep better.'

Emma eyed him for a moment, and he could tell she was weighing her words. In the end she gave him a faint smile, and Mark caught his breath at the sight. It was like a sunrise after a frosty night, dispersing the dark fog gathered around him.

'Thanks for the tip. I'll try it out.' As she braced herself to jump off the top bunk the seam of her scrub top caught the metal rod of the bedpost, causing her to lose her footing.

Mark reacted instantly, closing the gap between them with one step and wrapping his arms around her waist to prevent her from falling to the ground. Her eyes widened in surprise, and she looked at him as a gasp escaped her lips. He met her gaze, felt her scent filling his nose and clouding his thoughts, enticing him to close the last few inches between them and steal a taste of her lips. He just needed to lean in a bit…

'Mark, I…'

Her breath fluttered, grazing his cheeks, and her eyes narrowed. She relaxed against his arms, giving in to his pull—and then the shrill alarm of her beeper cut through the moment between them.

Despite his better judgement, he hesitated to let go of her. He was enjoying the closeness a lot more than he should.

'There's a trauma case incoming. I have to go,' Emma said as she looked at the pager.

For a moment their eyes locked again. The moment they'd almost shared was reflected in her expression. Grabbing her tablet from the top bunk, she squeezed by him and left without another word.

Mark sat down on the lower bunk behind him, burying his face in his hands. How had he let it get so far, so fast?

Emma had something incredible about her that he struggled to put into words. Whenever he was around her the clouds around him lifted, making way for the warm light emanating from her. By her side, the pain of his past seemed less. But could he let himself feel attracted to someone when the guilt of Claire's death still clung to his heart?

Memory came rushing back into his consciousness. This entire time he hadn't thought of her, and the realisation thundered through his body. His draw towards

Emma had made him forget everything except for the fire a mere glance of her ignited beneath his skin.

Mark had thought he'd moved on when he'd taken off his wedding ring. Yet now, confronted with his obvious attraction to Emma, he couldn't help but feel the weight of his past mistakes with Claire. She served as his beacon, as well as a warning. Her memory drove him to be a better doctor, but he doubted he could be a better man.

The fact that he could still feel this kind of attraction was a new discovery. He didn't know what to think of it. Or what to do. One thing was certain: Mark could not act on the desire uncoiling itself inside his chest.

The noise of his own beeper interrupted his thoughts and he jerked up, looking at the message appearing on the screen.

911 in OR Two

He forced himself to push all thoughts of Emma aside. His obligation to his patients would always come first.

Her heart pounded against her chest with such urgency that Emma thought if she opened her mouth it would leap right out of her body. The nurse preparing the operating room had informed her they were expecting the victim of a car crash. Her first case on her on-call shift.

Emma took a few deep breaths, calming the turmoil in her chest. Images of Mark flashed through her head, his lips so close to hers she had almost been able to taste them.

Heat spread through her entire body and Emma

shoved those thoughts away, focusing on the work in front of her. There was no time to contemplate how she had almost jeopardised her place at this hospital by kissing her boss. Her *married* boss.

'Then page another general surgeon. She's being prepped as we speak,' the nurse behind her said to the person on the other end of the phone.

The nurses wheeled the patient in and Emma began her preparations, getting the age and the weight of her to get the anaesthetic right. A lump appeared in her throat when she inspected the young woman lying on the table. As the nurses around her set up the surgical field, she spotted her belly, protruding in a gentle slope.

'Is she pregnant?' Emma asked no one in particular, even as she opened the patient's file on her tablet.

The ER team had sent her bloodwork to the lab, but the results hadn't come through yet. There were no notes about any examination or ultrasound of her abdomen. Her medication would be different if she were pregnant.

The door swung open and the surgeon walked in, receiving his gloves and gown from the nurse who had been on the phone a few minutes ago. Only when Emma looked up to ask the nurse a question did she notice that they'd paged Mark to perform the surgery.

The scene in the on-call room came back to her mind, and she pushed it away.

'Can I get the ultrasound machine set up?' Emma asked.

The nurse hesitated, looking at Mark. 'What do you need an ultrasound for?'

Emma lifted her tablet, showing the patient's chart. 'The blood panel hasn't come back from the lab yet and I think she might be pregnant. I need to know so I can give her the right type of anaesthesia. We'll also need to set up a foetal monitor to check on the baby during surgery.'

She feared she would have to explain herself further, wasting precious time they didn't have. But to her relief Mark nodded and indicated that the nurse should set it up for her.

'All right, Dr Santos says she needs an ultrasound, so let's turn it around. Time's wasting.'

As the nurses brought in the ultrasound machine, Mark worked on exposing the lower half of her body. The nurse handed her the transducer and Emma took a deep breath as she squeezed some gel onto the patient's abdomen and placed the transducer on it.

The last time she'd performed an ultrasound on her own had been many years ago, and though she remembered each step, and the principle of it, she suddenly doubted her skill. What if she did it wrong? This wasn't her speciality.

If she had worked at a hospital for her residency, working with pregnant patients would have been a more frequent occurrence. Not for the first time since starting her temporary placement at Attano Memorial, Emma cursed herself for compromising her medical training for the empty promises of Rob. Thanks to her own naivety, she was now riddled with insecurities about something as simple as an ultrasound.

'Maybe we should page OBGYN,' Emma said, and was about to put the transducer down when Mark stepped forward, looking at her with a reassuring spark in his eyes.

'You can do this, Emma. Take a deep breath,' he

said, in a voice intended for her ears only. 'Place the transducer beneath her navel and locate the uterus. What do you see?'

Emma swallowed her insecurity and followed the steps. She remembered them from her internship years. Her eyes focused on the screen display of the ultrasound, looking for a foetus. The operating room fell silent around her as she moved the transducer over the patient's abdomen. After a few seconds of intense focus, Emma pressed the button to freeze the picture and pointed at it.

'There it is.' She put down the handle and wiped the excess gel off the young woman's belly.

Mark nodded, the corners of his eyes crinkling in a half-obscured smile that made her knees weak.

The nurse wheeled the ultrasound machine to the edge of the operating room, and Emma resumed her position at the head of the patient. She prepared the anaesthetic drug and everyone around her kicked into action.

'All right, everyone. There are two lives we're saving today,' Mark said, just as Emma completed the last steps of putting the patient under anaesthetic. She looked over at the monitor showing the patient's vitals, and then she nodded at Mark to begin the surgery.

They worked in unison, with Mark repairing the damage left by the accident while Emma monitored both the mother and child, ensuring they remained low on stress as Mark worked through everything that came up.

The hours passed them by, and only as Mark placed the last stitch did she notice how many had passed. Her tongue clung to the roof of her mouth. She was yearning for a sip of water but she had denied herself, too lost in the procedure. She sighed, the tiredness of the long surgery washing over her.

'Nice work, everybody. Beth, please page OBGYN to make sure they check on the baby,' Mark said beside her. He laid a hand on her shoulder as the people around them shuffled things around. 'That was an excellent call. You saved both their lives today. I know how hectic it can get in the emergency room. It's more efficient to wait for a blood test rather than to do an ultrasound on every single woman who comes through the doors. It's up to us to pay attention.'

Emma smiled as she grabbed her tablet and watched Mark discard his gown and gloves in the bin next to the exit. She pushed the door open with her elbow, and they stepped outside together.

The moment they came out of the OR, Emma felt tension return to her insides as she remembered their encounter in the on-call room. She dared to glance at Mark, wanting to gauge his reaction. Was he flustered, like her? But his face showed nothing of their almost-kiss, and his calm stance as he walked beside her in silence did not betray a single thought.

This was not just her imagination, was it? They had almost kissed. And, more than that, didn't he have a wife? Her eyes darted to his hand, but she didn't spot a ring. Most surgeons decided not to wear jewellery, as they always had to remove it to perform surgery. So his bare finger meant nothing.

Mark didn't look one bit perturbed. Maybe this was him telling her how to deal with the situation. Pretend it had never happened.

'Should I expect to see you join emergency surgeries more often? Not that I'm complaining,' she said, thinking this would be just the thing colleagues would say to each other if they hadn't just almost kissed just a few hours ago.

Mark chuckled. 'I help wherever I can.'

Their eyes locked onto each other's for a second, before his gaze wandered to the wall clock behind her.

'It's longer than I planned on staying, but with one of the general surgeons not being able to come in, I'll probably get paged again.'

They walked into the empty break room and the smell of fresh coffee filled Emma's nose, drawing an awareness of how tired she was.

'Would you rather stay here?' she asked. 'I'll let you have the good bed.'

The memories of their encounter earlier mingled with the snippets of conversation she'd overheard before Georgina's surgery. What was she doing, almost kissing a married man? His proximity had made her forget that important bit of information for a moment. But there was no way of bringing it up. It wasn't any of her business if he had a wife.

Except that he had almost kissed her, too.

'It would shock you to know how often I've chosen to sleep here rather than go home.'

Emma blushed. 'This is my first on-call shift since completing my internship.'

'Your residency must have been mostly nine-to-five, then.' He walked over to the counter and poured himself a coffee, turning around and raising the mug in silent question.

Tempted by the scent, she hesitated a moment before shaking her head. She wouldn't be able to grab any sleep for the rest of her shift. 'Most of the time. Unless a patient needed to be observed overnight— in that case, I would stay. But most of the procedures didn't have long recovery times, and our clients could heal at home.'

Mark plopped down on one of the chairs around the table and she followed suit, sitting down next to him. Her proximity to him made the fine hair along her arms stand on end.

'Clients?' He looked at her with a raised eyebrow, the mug obscuring half of his face.

'Bad habit from working in private practice.'

'Your quick thinking today shows you have lost none of the intuition needed to work at a hospital.'

He lowered the mug, a small smile curling his lips. Emma's stomach lurched under his gaze, and she regretted passing on the coffee. Drinking it would have given her an excuse to break the stare.

'With your talent, I'm curious to know how you ended up at a private practice. Didn't your hospital want you to stay on?'

Emma stared at Mark for a few heartbeats, dreading the turn this conversation had taken. The last thing she wanted to discuss with him was her poor judgement of Rob and her career. Embarrassment flooded every corner of her mind whenever she thought about how ready she had been to give up on her dream for the promise of love. A promise that had crumbled right in front of her when she'd demanded more.

When she had told him that she was going to accept the fellowship offer from Whitebridge, with or without him, he had shown his true colours, trying every tactic to make her feel guilty about choosing her career over him.

But Rob had only ever strung her along, conveniently forgetting about all the times he had put his career first, or the times she had tried to speak to him about their future. And now she was on her own, trying to overcome the insecurities he had foisted on her with his deceit.

'An attending surgeon I'd worked with a lot asked me to join him at the practice he'd started a couple of weeks before my internship finished. He held all the required licences to teach for the board exam and convinced me to join him.'

She chose her words with care, not wanting anything to show through. Emma would prefer it if Mark thought her choice odd rather than have him knowing the full extent of her naivety.

His hazel eyes darkened as he looked at her, his gaze leaving her face to look at her lips—a small flicker that wasn't lost on her.

Then the low grumble of her stomach cut through the quiet, making her wince. The surgery had gone on for half the night, and the last time she'd had a bite to eat had been before Georgina's surgery. Heat shot into her cheeks, colouring them a soft rouge. That was one of the last sounds she'd wanted Mark to hear.

To add to her embarrassment, his lips parted in a wide grin. 'You're right. It's almost breakfast time.' With one long gulp, he drained the liquid from his mug, putting it back on the table. 'There's a good diner just around the corner. Close enough for us to dash back in case we need to. Let me treat you to some food.'

Breakfast with Mark? Her pulse quickened. She

should refuse. Sure, it wasn't unusual for colleagues to have breakfast together, but those colleagues hadn't have an almost-moment in an on-call room a few hours before. Although if what had happened had affected Mark as much as it had her, he wasn't letting on to the fact. Or was this his way of gauging her interest? No, that couldn't be it. He was married, and a man of integrity. He would never betray his spouse like that.

Her attraction to him was one-sided, and it would be better for her if she kept her distance. She should definitely say no. It was the sensible thing to do.

'Yes, I'd like that.'

# CHAPTER FIVE

THE ONLY PEOPLE visiting the diner at this hour were people after a night out, looking for a quick breakfast before finding their way home, or people working the night shift at Attano Memorial like themselves.

Mark walked through the door and straight to his regular booth, waving at the waitress as he sat down. He smiled when Emma plopped down opposite him, looking around in curiosity. Despite them having just spent half the night saving a young woman's life, she still looked fresh-faced, her sharp eyes darting around and scrutinising the people in scrubs she saw in the seats.

Even in an unusual setting like that, her eagerness to learn had been the predominant characteristic he'd noticed in her. A trait that the pressure of working with terminally ill patients every day had taken from a lot of his colleagues. A rueful smile curled his lips when he thought of Emma losing that spark.

With a shake of his head, Mark tried to wave the thoughts intruding upon him away. This time was meant to be about getting to understand his colleague better. His drop-dead gorgeous and intelligent colleague, who was chewing at her lower lip as she studied the menu the waitress had just handed her.

Already familiar with Mark, she didn't bother to hand him one. Instead she just looked at him with her usual sunny demeanour. 'Late-night pancakes?'

'You know me well, Pam,' he said with a chuckle, and looked at Emma as she lifted her eyes from the laminated paper.

'Oh, pancakes! I think I'll go with the same.'

She paused for a moment and then handed the menu back to Pam, who took it from her and vanished through some doors to the kitchen, to get their order sorted out.

'You weren't kidding when you said you spend more time at the hospital than at home. They know what you like to eat here.'

'It gets better.' He chuckled when she raised her eyebrows at him. 'They also know what I like to eat at what specific time. Between midnight and dawn, it's always pancakes.'

Emma laughed at that, as he'd hoped she would, her green eyes full of sparkling amusement. His eyes trailed down from her face for a moment. He dared to appreciate the view, despite knowing that this was as far as anything would ever go between them. The scrubs made all the staff appear rather uniform, yet somehow she made herself look distinguished.

The vision of her standing in Georgina's room, wearing that dress with the dipping neckline, came back into his mind, tightening his chest and along with it some other parts of his body he hadn't felt in ages.

'Tell me more about your private practice experience,' he said, in a voice he hoped she would think sounded tired rather than thick with the misplaced desire his own thoughts had evoked within him.

When he'd asked her about why she'd done her residency in a private practice rather than in a hospital, Mark had sensed her selecting her words with care about how she might sound. There was something about her experience at her last job that pained her. He could see it written on her face.

'It was a lot different from what my peers experienced in their hospital rotation. I didn't get exposed to a lot of different cases or departments. The patient profiles were quite similar to each other as they were elective cosmetic procedures.' She looked down for a moment, her long lashes obscuring her eyes from view. 'It made studying for the board exam a lot harder, as the questions are varied.'

'Why did you choose that path, then? Seems you understood you were making things harder for you than they needed to be.'

That question had burned in his mind, and he knew the answer would give him some understanding of the intriguing puzzle that was Emma Santos. A part of him urged him to let matters be. But he ignored the small voice. The fire of his own curiosity was demanding to be sated.

Emma hesitated, her eyes dropping from his face for a moment as she took a deep breath. 'I was in love with the man who convinced me to leave the hospital and join him in private practice. When he promised me that the experience would be superior to working at the hospital, I believed him. But it turns out I was wrong.'

Mark raised his eyebrows at the confession, a twinging pain stabbing into his chest. The sudden intimacy as she'd bared her heart to him had caught him off guard, and his pulse quickened. This wasn't the direction he'd wanted the conversation to go, and yet he didn't mind as much as he should. He wanted to know more.

But the pain darkening her face gave him pause, awakening an almost primal protectiveness.

'You're still sharp. Noticing a pregnancy that early on, that attention to detail, that's something that will get you far in your medical career.'

His words seemed to wipe away her pain, and a faint rose colour on her cheeks replaced it, along with an embarrassed smile that drove a searing urge through his body. After his wife's death he'd withdrawn from any kind of female attention, as even the thought of looking at another woman had brought guilt and betrayal to his chest, thickening the darkness he'd woven around himself.

He didn't know what was different about Emma, but something was. Like a breath of fresh air, she was reminding him of the things he denied himself. She was a reminder of what it was like to be attracted to someone again.

*Lust.*

Desire stirred in his insides from a deep slumber, exciting him more than it should. Concerning him a lot less than he thought appropriate. What had possessed him to invite her to breakfast in the first place?

Mark knew the answer to that question. It was her aura, the warmth she spread through his body just by being near him. She granted him a brief respite from the fog surrounding him.

'I appreciate the compliment,' she said in a quiet

voice after Pam had laid the pancakes out in front of them and whisked away at the call of a different patron. 'At the private practice some people were desperate to get their surgeries, despite having factors that might make the procedures riskier. I had to become exceptional at reading people's non-verbal cues so that if they weren't being upfront I would get a sense about it. It's a useful skill for advocating for patients who are already unconscious.'

She paused, grabbing cutlery, and sliced into the first pancake. Mark, holding a fork himself, paused to watch her reaction as the first bite landed in her mouth. Emma's eyes went wide, as if she was surprised at the taste, before she closed them with an appreciative soft moan that vibrated through Mark, shaking up the already growing sensation within him.

'*Meu Deus*, this is delicious,' she said under her breath as she ate another forkful of the fluffy goodness on her plate.

Amused at the way she'd reverted to Portuguese out of pure pleasure, Mark started digging into his own pancakes. His mind wandered, imagining other ways he could bring her so much pleasure she wouldn't be able to help but fall back to her native language.

The thought manifested itself inside him so casually, so non-intrusively. He stopped with his fork halfway to his mouth, wondering what had come over him. He was lusting over his new subordinate like some love-crazed teenager who'd just discovered the opposite sex.

'Are you okay?' she asked, her soft accent mingling with her words, giving them a melody that sounded smooth and distinct.

'Yes, of course,' he lied, and he shook off his contemplations by clearing his throat, desperate to change the topic to something else.

'I'm just feeling tired. I was about to leave before I got paged to the OR,' he said, to bring the topic back to something they could both talk about. Medicine.

'I have to admit I'm excited about my week of on-call shifts at the hospital. I know I can learn a lot,' she said, stopping his thoughts straying from their designated safe space again.

It only took seconds of being within her range for his thoughts to wander, his senses to be filled with awareness for the Brazilian doctor across him.

'That's a helpful attitude to have—especially in a teaching hospital like Attano Memorial. You're going to have an incredible experience if that's how you think.'

Her smile widened, and his own lips curled upwards in reciprocity. His self-restraint was rendered meaningless when faced with that kind of magnetism. Emma had sidestepped some of his walls, reaching a place within him that had been locked away until meeting her. Getting lost in the attraction, even for one moment, was alluring—and dangerous. It was the place where the lines got blurry…something Mark never permitted.

Was he really ready to move on? What would that even look like? How could he think of someone else when he hadn't been a good enough partner for his late wife?

Mark tried to remind himself of that, of the reasons he had withdrawn from any sort of female attention. But Emma made recalling all his reasons difficult. All he could think of in her presence was the consistent tug of something within his chest.

\* \* \*

Emma's heart thudded against her chest in an erratic dance. After their almost-kiss in the on-call room, she'd promised to distance herself from Mark. Instead of doing that, though, she had just opened up about Rob and how he'd tricked her into following him into his practice. She had ended up oversharing, driving an embarrassed heat to her cheeks that had only intensified when she'd noticed his gaze gliding down her body.

He'd made all the fine hair on her nape stand on end as she noticed him checking her out—a picture of pure masculinity and power. Though instead of stopping at some point, and coming back to her face, his eyes had kept going and eventually come to rest on his own hands, lying on the table. His left hand had contracted into a tight fist for a second, before he'd let go of the tension with a slight shake of his head.

It had been a subtle gesture that had reminded her of the conversation she had overheard in the operating room.

'Did you forget to put your wedding band back on?'

The words flew out of her mouth before she could decide whether asking the personal question was a good idea.

Mark's eyes shot up to hers, the glimpse of vulnerability she'd noticed in them just a moment ago vanishing as thick walls appeared around him. Emma knew she had crossed some invisible boundary she shouldn't have touched.

'What makes you think I'm married?' he asked, with caution lacing his words.

Was this where honesty would be the best policy? She hesitated for a moment, before deciding that she had nothing to lose. Despite the resistance she sensed within her, warning her not to get attached to anyone here, she wanted to know Mark better. For years she had read his research papers and publications, admiring his work and hoping, in the quiet corners of her mind, that he might be the one to discover a cure for the disease that had taken her mother. That might lie dormant in her, too.

'I overheard the conversation between you and Georgina when she was being prepped for her surgery. You must not have noticed me, but I was already there.' This version was close enough to the truth that she didn't feel as if she was deceiving him.

The lines around Mark's jaw tightened for a moment, and she braced herself for a reprimand. His conversation with Georgina hadn't been meant for her ears. Though instead of telling her off he relaxed against the padded back of the booth's bench he sat on and looked at his left hand again before letting out a tired sigh.

'I was married,' he said after a momentary silence, his voice strained with something that could only be fury at her intrusion. 'I'm widowed now.'

Emma's chest tightened at the profound sadness that wove itself through the edges of his words, exposing his wound for her to see.

Her breath caught at the sudden intimacy they shared.

His initial reaction told her he didn't enjoy sharing this part of himself with people, and she remembered the gentle tone he'd used with their patient when comforting her. And now she had prised it out of him to satisfy her own curiosity and nothing else.

Insecurity and regret wrapped themselves around

her, creating a tight ball of chaos that wedged itself into the pit of her stomach. 'I'm sorry for bringing it up. I'm sure you don't need me prodding at your wounds.'

The problem was that she wanted to probe further. She wanted to *know* him, to engulf herself in the tantalising aura that came from him. Every time he looked at her, her core contracted, begging her to do something stupid. To reach out and touch him. To pick things up where they'd left off in the on-call room.

His warm breath grazed her cheeks as his scent filled her nostrils—a smell reminding her of pine and clean laundry. Of pleasures untold.

Emma shook her head and got up, unable to deal with his narrowed brown eyes shooting daggers at her. 'I should get going. There could be a surgical case coming in at any moment,' she said.

She was reaching into her pocket to grab her wallet when his hand wrapped around her wrist and pulled her back down onto her seat. A spark travelled down her arm from the spot where Mark touched her, creating fires across her skin as it bounced around before settling in her core.

'Stay,' he said, his dark eyes veiled in an expression she couldn't read.

Her body was no longer her own to command. She sat back down.

'Mentioning Claire helps me bond with patients, so this is probably not the last time you'll hear me talk about her. It's easy for us doctors to appear larger than life to our patients when we talk to them about treatment plans and their options. They need to think of us as capable. But it's scary to put your life into the hands of someone you feel is so different from you. A sur-

geon talking about his wife is a much more approach-
able person. It helps to humanise me.'

He stopped for a moment and took a deep breath.

Emma hadn't expected this explanation from him.
In the quiet corners of her mind she had wondered why
he'd presented himself as married to Georgina when
he was widowed. But she had known that wasn't something she could ask her boss. Along with the hundreds
of other questions that burned on her tongue.

'I'm sorry for your loss,' she said, remembering that
she hadn't expressed her sympathy earlier.

Mark smiled at her. 'Thank you. It's almost two
years since she passed away, but she still helps me look
after my patients.'

While his tone was serious, she couldn't detect any
kind of pain in his words.

'Please—you don't have to explain yourself to me,'
she said, with what she hoped looked like a self-as-
sured smile.

Heat coursed through her cheeks. She couldn't believe she had asked these kinds of personal questions
of her superior. Nor that he had shared his experience
with her without hesitation. Having lost her mother,
Emma knew how much it hurt.

Mark leaned back while still looking at her, crossing his arms behind his head, giving her a view of the
sculpture that was his upper body. Emma was thankful that she was sitting down, feeling her core ignite
as she looked at the man in front of her. Her boss, she
reminded herself. Someone who was off-limits.

After everything Rob had put her through, the only
thing she would entangle herself in was a no-strings-

attached fling before she left this city on her way to a brighter future.

Although she still dreamed of love and romance, of someone to complete her, who wanted to have a family just like her. Despite her chances of bearing her own children being potentially compromised, she hadn't written off building her own family altogether. She knew from the depths of her heart that she and her partner would make it work somehow.

Rob had shown no patience or interest in discussing the topic when she'd approached him about it. Something she now realised was one of the many red flags she had missed, making her wonder what was wrong with her that she hadn't seen the writing on the wall. He couldn't have made it much clearer to her, yet she'd found excuses after excuses for his behaviour. It made her hesitant even to think about her future spouse, or relationships in general. What if she couldn't spot the red flags again?

Maybe a casual encounter would help her with that. Flings were not family material, but neither was her being in Chicago. They were both temporary—a means to an end. She'd come to this place to put her career back on track, as well as to mend her broken heart. Maybe a first step in that was to let go of control. She had never been with anyone outside an actual relationship. This was the first time since med school that she'd been single and not having to work eighty hours a week. Now would be as good a time as any if she wanted to try.

But not with Mark.

He was still her boss, and nothing about him made

her think he was a person to indulge in casual affairs. Not when he spoke of his late wife the way he did.

If only he didn't make every inch of her skin tingle with not much more than a fleeting look...

A soft notification tone from her phone interrupted the quiet atmosphere between them, and with an apologetic look she grabbed it from her pocket to look at it. 'One of the interns is asking about local anaesthesia for some stitches in the emergency room.'

Mark raised an eyebrow at that. 'Why are the interns texting you?'

Heat shot up her cheeks under his probing gaze, making her aware of his proximity despite their having an entire table between them. 'I may have given them my number for emergencies.'

Her voice faltered when his eyes scrutinised her with the same precision he used in the operating room. For a moment she was certain that he could look through her skin and right into her mind.

'I gave the ER head nurse my number, so she could contact me in case she needed my help without making it a 911 page.'

While on call, she knew her primary responsibility was to administer general anaesthetic in emergency surgeries coming in through the ER, but Emma wanted to be more useful to her colleagues than that. There weren't usually many trauma cases throughout the night, and since she was in the hospital anyway, she wanted to contribute.

Mark remained quiet for a moment, and then his lips parted in a smile that turned her insides into molten lava.

'That is silly of you, because now they won't stop texting you for every small thing. Admirable, but silly.'

A laugh that sounded a lot more nervous than she'd wanted it to be escaped her lips as the lava reached her cheeks. 'At least it will only be for two months, and then I can ghost them.'

Her comment made him laugh, and he reached for his wallet, putting a couple of notes down on the table before standing up. 'Let me walk you back to the hospital so you can teach the interns which way to hold the stethoscope.'

Emma's blood hummed with her awareness of Mark with each step as they strolled back to the hospital, her heart beating against the base of her throat. The man next to her, making butterflies dance up and down her stomach, was award-winning Mark Henderson. A man who regularly graced the covers of different medical journals. Someone who had lost his wife almost two years ago, and who still spoke about her with a gentle fondness in front of their patients.

No matter what kind of pull she felt coming from him, there was no way a man of this calibre would ever be interested in her—casually or otherwise.

'Thanks for the pancakes,' she said when they got to the door of the hospital. 'Now I know where to go when I get hungry.'

They looked at each other for a moment, both of them silent, feeling the pull coming from one another. His eyes narrowed as they wandered down her face, stopping at her mouth. She licked her lips as she noticed their dryness. Her breath caught when Mark leaned in and reached his hand out to her face. A stray strand of hair had fought its way out of the bun, and his fingers brushed over her skin as he pushed it behind her ear.

Her skin was alight with the sparks of his touch. She looked at him. Watched his face come closer to hers again. The moment only lasted a fraction of a heart-beat before he pulled back, his expression shuttered and unreadable...

Mark's chest tightened as he took a step back from Emma, giving himself some room to breathe. That was the second time he had come close to doing something he could never take back. His barriers were up. Yet whenever he got too close to her the resolve within him melted, giving way to the urgent, blazing hot need that he'd denied himself ever since Claire had passed away.

Was that the reason he reacted to her with such strength?

No, something about Emma was different. Unique.

Maybe it was because she would only ever be a tem-porary addition to his team and his life. Less than two months from now he would have his old anaesthetist back, and whatever traces Emma had left here would soon leave with her. At least that was something he could appreciate.

Was that the reason he'd found himself willing to share so much of his past with her? Mark had not planned on sharing even those few details that had slipped out. His memories of Claire had dropped from his lips before he'd been able to stop them. Something about Emma had been so disarming that his usual de-fences had failed to kick in.

Mark knew he needed to watch himself as he felt

something grow within his chest. It would be best to distance himself. He had shared too much already. There was only one thing he needed to do before he could establish some space between them.

'Since you're working the on-call shift this week, you must be off for a couple of days next week?' he asked, remembering that he'd approved the shift rotation for the oncology department.

Emma nodded after a slight hesitation. 'Yes, that's right.'

'Then let me make good on my promise to show you around Chicago. You shouldn't leave the city before you've had the authentic experience only a Chicagoan can give you.' He smirked. 'And after what you said about deep-dish pizza, I know you need my help.'

He had extended the invitation many hours earlier, but now he was determined to make good on it. Mark was a man of his word.

'I don't want to impose on you,' she said, bringing his thoughts back to reality. 'I appreciate you caring so much.'

'It's no imposition at all.' He paused for a moment, a smile curling his lips. 'I'd ask you to show me around Rochester, should I ever come to visit, but I'm sort of familiar with the place—as you may know.'

She laughed, as he'd hoped she would. A small part of him wanted her to refuse, so he could bow out with no promises broken. But an even larger part wanted to remain close to her, to enjoy the sparks her proximity created within his chest.

It wouldn't lead to anything. Not physical, and definitely not emotional. But it had been a long time since that kind of heat had coursed through his veins, and for a moment he just wanted to enjoy it.

'I guess it would be a shame to leave the city without a proper tour,' she said with a smile, her gaze shifting down his face and stopping at his lips for a moment before coming back up.

A soft scarlet coated her cheeks, and imagining where her thoughts had strayed sent hot blood coursing through his body.

'Great—give me your phone. I'll type in my number so you can text me where to pick you up.'

Emma handed him her phone and he typed in his number before returning it to her. His chest tightened once more when his fingers grazed over her soft skin as he handed the device back to her.

He waved at her as she turned and walked through the door, smiling when she looked back as if to have just one more look at him before she vanished around the corner.

With his heart beating against his chest at an unsteady pace Mark walked to his car, his mind reeling from the last couple of hours. Something had shifted inside him. He knew the wise thing would be to turn away. He would never be available on an emotional level, and she didn't strike him as someone who liked things casual.

With a drawn-out sigh, he closed the car door and started driving. He would show her around Chicago, and they would have a decent time talking about the city and the work they had in common. He'd said he would show Emma around, and that was what he was going to do. After that, he would distance himself.

Desire made his pulse quicken, but he couldn't go

there with anyone—even if he kept emotion out of it. But at the very least he'd learned that this part of him was not lost completely.

# CHAPTER SIX

EXHAUSTION CREPT INTO every corner of her body when Emma came out of her last on-call shift, and only with a supreme effort did she get to her flat before passing out on her bed, too tired to shower or have a bit of food.

Despite being there only for emergency surgeries, she'd found herself busier than she'd thought, assisting the more inexperienced doctors with general tasks. As wiped out as this left her, the sleep that enveloped her was an excellent one, her feelings of accomplishment letting her drift off into a relaxed slumber.

Until a certain Dr Handsome sneaked his way into the adventures she was dreaming of.

Emma woke up several hours later with her sense of accomplishment gone, replaced by a more heated, pinching feeling in her core as the visions of her dreams faded away. With an annoyed grunt, Emma threw her covers off and opened the curtains to look outside for a moment.

The sun was shining high in the sky without a single cloud in sight. Of course it would be the nicest day Chicago has seen in ages, when she wanted it to rain and thunder. A storm would be a more appropriate representation of what was going on within herself when she thought about who she was going to spend the afternoon with.

Dr Mark Henderson—famous surgeon, and the reason she'd come to Chicago—had asked her out on a date. No, Emma reminded herself as her stomach lurched. There had been no mention that this was a date of any sort. This was nothing more than a professional courtesy extended from the department head to his newest employee. Anything else would be inappropriate.

Although it was the 'anything else' part that made Emma's pulse quicken. Could there be more behind his invitation, or was she constructing something in her mind that didn't exist? There had been that moment in the diner last week, when an unexpected closeness had enveloped them as they'd shared things with each other they both didn't talk about under normal circumstances.

Her heart squeezed tight within her chest when she remembered the hurt in his eyes as he'd revealed his wife's death to her. It had only been visible for a second before he'd regained control of his expression, his eyes shuttering right in front of her before she could reach out.

I'm leaving soon. Should be at your place in thirty minutes.

Emma stared at his text, her stomach turning itself into a knot as she read the words, hearing them in his voice. Her fingers hovered above her phone, and she contemplated whether she should cancel. She couldn't deny how drawn to Mark she was, on more than just a professional level, and it was that magnetism that gave her pause. Along with the way he had looked at her when they'd almost kissed, turning her insides to liquid fire.

After their conversation in the diner Emma had called her cousin Livia to talk through some of her thoughts, careful not to reveal too much or the entire family would be on her case about it. It was Livia who kept encouraging her to 'let loose'. She had also been the one to help her through her break-up with Rob.

What Emma hadn't mentioned was that the man who'd caught her attention was her superior. She knew she should know better than to get involved with her boss.

See you soon.

*He isn't married.*

Emma's heart skipped a beat when that intrusive voice echoed through her mind. Why should she care? His not being married didn't make him less off-limits. In fact, his having lost his wife made him even more off-limits. He hadn't specified how she'd died, and Emma hadn't wanted to ask after he had just shared so much with her. But she had her own shadows of mortality chasing her. She could be sick herself, and live not much longer than her mother had.

The hurt written on Mark's face had been the same hurt she had seen so many times in her father's face. She refused to put anyone through that. Emma would get the genetic test before she started to date again. And, since she had convinced herself to get the test after her fellowship was over, she had a timeline to work with. Nothing serious until her time in Rochester was up.

She looked at the time on her phone screen and jumped, cursing at how much time she had just wasted daydreaming when she needed to get ready.

Most of her belongings were still in the boxes she had used to bring them from San Francisco. With her locum tenens gig only lasting two months, she hadn't bothered to unpack anything or to get too comfortable in the apartment. She would be out of here before she knew it, and would rather spend the energy of home decoration on her flat in Rochester.

The sole exception was the two large potted plants standing on a windowsill. They were exotic plants, native to her home in Brazil. Caring for them helped with the occasional pang of homesickness Emma experienced whenever too much time passed without seeing her family.

She dug through a box with clothes in it, finding a knee-length summer dress with a high neck and a blue floral print. Nice and appropriate. She threw it on, slipped into her heels, and by the time she'd tamed her curls the doorbell rang, making her jump.

Her heart beat against the base of her throat with such erratic ferocity that she was certain that if Mark looked at her collarbone, he would see her pulse. Why was she reacting to him with such yearning when she knew that there wasn't anything between them? Was she that starved for attention? There were more than enough reasons for her to be cautious rather than excited.

Shutting those thoughts away, Emma took a deep breath and opened the door. Her breath caught in her throat when she saw Mark leaning against her door-frame with a small smile on his soft-looking lips.

*'Olá,'* he said, oblivious to the flames licking across her skin.

*'Você fala português?'* Upon hearing the familiar greeting, she reverted to her native language, raising her eyebrows in surprise.

Mark chuckled and raised his hands with a shake of his head. 'I assume you asked if I speak Portuguese, and I regret to say no. But I used to work closely with a Brazilian physician a few years back, and picked up a few bits and pieces along the way.'

'Oh, so I'm not your first Brazilian doctor?' she said, unsure what had driven her to verbalise that thought.

An amused spark entered Mark's eyes as he looked at her. 'Would you believe me if I told you she meant nothing to me?'

Emma looked at him in surprise, feeling the blood rush to her cheeks at his tone. Of all the things he could have said, she hadn't expected him to be flirtatious.

'Oh, so I'm just one in a series of many?' She tried her best to sound outraged, but couldn't keep the play-ful edge out of her voice.

Mark clasped his hands over his chest, as if struck by her words. 'She was part of the team looking after Claire when she got sick.'

Her illness had required an entire team to look after her? Emma made a note of that as she tried to uncover more about his past without the risk of things getting too personal. For a moment she wondered if it had been cancer. It would make sense, given his obvious dedica-tion to the oncology department at Attano Memorial.

He hesitated a moment, and Emma could see him considering his next words.

'You look lovely,' he said eventually, and those three words created a cascade of fireworks across her entire body, exploding everywhere and leaving a pulsating warmth behind.

'Thank you,' she said, cringing as her voice faltered for a moment. 'I've never seen you in street clothes before. I was half expecting you to wear dark green scrubs.'

He laughed at her quip and led her down the stairs, opening the car door for her as they reached the vehicle, leaving her to glance around for only a second before he took the driver's seat.

'So where are we headed?' she asked, desperate for him to drive so he would take his eyes off her. His glances, along with his scent, were filling her head with pictures of her steamy dream, and fire was engulfing her core.

'There are some food stalls along the waterfront at Millennium Park. It's quite a popular place for both locals and tourists, with a magnificent view of the harbour and a curious structure people like to call The Bean.'

Fifteen minutes later, Emma understood what he meant. Rising tall in front of her was a sculpture in the shape of a bean, its two ends standing on the floor, forming a gate large enough that people could walk underneath it. The Cloud Gate—which was the actual name of the sculpture—was made of a mirror-like material, reflecting everything around it.

Emma circled it with wide eyes, watching as the reflection of the surrounding city changed as she walked farther. Mark stepped up to her, pointing her towards the harbour, where she could already spot a few food stalls and a large group of tables and benches where people were enjoying their meals.

To her relief—and it *was* relief, not regret, Emma told herself—Mark kept a respectful distance between them. Although despite the several feet separating them, she could still feel the electric current of their tension skipping between their bodies as they walked together. Mark's entire demeanour was calm and unyielding…only the spark in his eyes betraying his thoughts.

'Is it time for some rib tips?' she asked as they walked close to one stall.

The veiled expression on his face made a shiver crawl down her spine and heat reach for her cheeks.

'I would recommend that—and I would hope you'd trust me over some strangers on the internet,' he said, with a chuckle following his words that made her shake at her centre.

After the intense moment they'd shared in the on-call room, a little more than a week ago, Emma had thought she'd made it clear to herself that this attraction she was giving in to was unacceptable and downright irresponsible. He was her boss. She couldn't let her primal needs override what was the career opportunity of a lifetime.

'You were right about the pancakes, so I trust your recommendations.'

She pushed the intrusive thoughts away and focused on what was important—making a lasting impression on Mark that was based on her competencies as a doctor and not the fluttering of desire within her centre.

Her attraction to him would only make things more complicated, and difficult things were at the bottom of the list of things Emma wanted.

Now that she knew about his late wife, keeping distant had become even more important. She brought her own baggage in a potential cancer diagnosis. Something that she couldn't put on anyone—especially not someone like Mark, who had already seen enough suffering to last him a lifetime.

After ordering their food, Mark led her away from the stalls and tables surrounding them, settling down on a bench overlooking the harbour. Lake Michigan sparkled in the afternoon sun as if covered with a million tiny diamonds.

'I didn't think a place here could remind me so much of Rio de Janeiro,' she said as she looked out on the water, remembering the white beaches and the glistening waters of her home.

Mark looked at her with a smile. 'Do you miss home?'

Emma poked around in her food as she considered his question. It was more personal than she wanted it to be. After sharing so much of her pain around Rob with him last week, she wanted to be careful not to breach their professional boundaries again. If only he didn't make it so easy to open up.

'Home is such an abstract concept,' she said after a few moments of silence. 'I've always considered home to be wherever I am. But I miss Brazil sometimes. When I was growing up, it seemed almost impossible to leave. And I'm used to having my family surround me. Going from that to being all by myself is still strange sometimes.'

'I wonder what that must be like.'

Emma looked up from her food, quickly enough to catch a glimmer of longing in his eyes before it faded. 'Do you not have a family here?' she asked.

He shook his head. 'My parents are making their best out of their retirement years. Every couple of months they're in a different country, so we don't see each other much. Claire's sisters used to visit her a lot at our place in Rochester…' He paused for a moment, as if thinking about his next words. 'It was nice to have them around. I guess I understand what you mean.'

They looked at each other, and the fine hair on her arms stood on end as she recognised the glimmer of unexpected closeness in his eyes. She got the sense that he wasn't used to sharing these kinds of thoughts with the people around him. That he had shared some of his memories surrounding Claire with her sent a warmth cascading through her.

'But you grew up here in Chicago?' She wasn't sure, but the way he spoke about the city made it sound as if he'd spent a lot of time here.

He nodded, his eyes drifting back to the lake with a fond smile. 'My parents had a family practice in one of the suburbs. They were thrilled when I started med school. Less so when they realised I wasn't going to take over the practice.'

Eyes wide in surprise, Emma tilted her head. 'You don't have any siblings to share the spotlight?'

Mark shook his head. 'I had an older brother, but I never met him. He died only a few weeks after he was born. I was a bit of a surprise baby to my parents when they had given up.'

'Oh, no, I'm so sorry.' Emma's thoughts went to

her cousins, and how each one of them played an important part in her life. She couldn't imagine losing any of them.

'Don't be. I was born many years later, with extra-large shoulders to carry the expectations my parents had for me. Maybe that's something I learned to appreciate with Claire and all her sisters. They had each other to lean on when they were growing up.' He paused, a wistful smile on his lips. 'That closeness didn't stop as they grew older, and they were there to support us when she got sick.' Stillness settled between them as his voice trailed off, and eventually he cleared his throat. 'What about you?'

Emma was also an only child, though she wasn't sure if it was by choice or not. She knew there had been complications during her birth, but she'd never asked for more details. By the time she'd been old enough to care, her mother had been diagnosed with Gardner Syndrome and it hadn't seemed to matter any more.

'No siblings either—though my cousins filled that gap for me. We all lived on the same street and we could walk into each other's houses whenever we wanted. It's something I'd like my own kids to have as well.'

'You want your children to grow up in Brazil?'

Mark raised an eyebrow at her, with a curious spark in his eyes that caused a flutter in her chest. How had they got onto such a personal topic? This was the exact opposite of the detached conversation she'd wanted to have.

'I guess I do… I haven't thought much about it. Children are very much only a concept at the moment.' She paused, heat climbing up to her face. 'What about you? Would you be happy to have a family here in Chicago?'

The question left her lips before she could think about what she was saying, her curiosity getting the better of her. What a stupid thing to ask a widower—as if he hadn't had plans and watched them all fall apart when his wife died.

Mark remained quiet for a moment, his hand going up to his face to tap against his chin. 'Not something I've thought about since Claire died. When she fell ill, we had to have a serious discussion about it…with the chemotherapy and all.'

'Oh, she had cancer?' The confirmation of her suspicion didn't make the information any easier to swallow. Although it explained a lot about his work ethic, and how much he cared for each patient. 'It mustn't be easy to watch your patients struggle through the same steps.'

Mark sighed, shook his head, and let his eyes drift back to her. 'It rarely is, but it comes with the job.'

His gaze still lingered on her, and awareness of his proximity flooded her senses as she tilted her head to look back out on the water.

'If you're close to your family, why did you come to the States?' he asked.

'I always wanted to be a doctor. My family had little means, so I needed to have the grades and some kind of scholarship to get me to my goal. I threw everything I had at it, and landed myself a place at med school in San Francisco.' She paused for a moment and laughed. 'When my mother passed away I was almost ready to quit and stay in Brazil. But my father wouldn't let me. He said he wouldn't let me make decisions I would later regret because of the grief we were going through together.'

A flutter of an expression moved over Mark's face, the moment too short for her to recognise it. 'You remain close with your father?' he asked.

Emma nodded with a big smile. 'Very much. I had just turned twenty when my mother passed away, but even before that my dad and I were supporting each other through the procedures and the hospital visits. You've seen it yourself how people band together in crisis. Even though he had lost his wife, he made sure that I came through the other side.'

'I'm glad he did,' Mark said after a pause, in a low voice that made her insides hum with awareness of him.

The gentleness of his tone took her by surprise. He was genuine, clearly meaning what he said. But what did that mean?

She looked at him for a moment, her eyes wide, before dropping her gaze to her hands, the tension it created too intense. She was afraid she was reading too much into his intentions. He was a talented surgeon who liked to surround himself with passionate people. There was no reason for her to believe his interest in her went beyond any professional boundaries.

Before Emma could contemplate his words any further, he stood up and extended his hand towards her. 'Care for some more walking? I'd like to show you the flower gardens surrounding the fountain at the centre of the park.'

She took his hand and got up from the bench, her skin tingling where they touched. Their gazes meshed for a moment. Her body reacted to his proximity, her senses humming with an awareness of how close they were. His expression softened, his thumb brushing over her fingers as she stepped closer to him.

Emma lifted her chin as he stood firm in place, a curious spark lighting up his dark brown eyes. Her breath caught in her throat when he leaned in. Was he going to kiss her?

'I like…flowers.'

Those were the only words manifesting in her mind that were okay to say in such proximity to her boss. A myriad of other things rolled around in her head, but none of them were professional or even appropriate.

Her words seemed to snap Mark out of his strange trance. He blinked, and the next moment the strange curiosity in his gaze faded, replaced by the impenetrable barriers she was used to seeing.

He stepped away from her and they started walking down the sunny paths of the park. Heat was blooming inside her chest, despite her mind telling her that this had already gone too far.

When they entered the gardens she almost immediately forgot all her reservations as she marvelled at the beautiful flowerbeds that were laid out around an impressive rococo fountain. Lush green rose bushes lined the twisted pathways, weaving themselves through the pristine grass. Every single leaf looked as if it had received special attention from the gardener, carefully manicured so the flowers could present their best side to the visitors admiring them.

Emma had grown up in Rio de Janeiro, far away from the rainforest, but it had always held a special place in her heart. When she was younger, she had convinced her parents to take a trip to Manaus, so she could see the Amazonian forest with her own eyes.

That trip had sparked an appreciation for plants. While she wasn't a talented gardener herself, she still kept plants around her that reminded her of the tropical forest of her home country.

'*Que lindo!*' she said under her breath as they kept on walking, occasionally stopping for her to take some pictures. 'My cousins are going to love these.'

Mark smiled at that. 'I noticed your apartment was mostly plants and boxes. Do you already have a place to stay in Rochester?'

Emma blushed at the thought that he'd seen her dishevelled flat. 'No, I haven't—though it would be a good idea to start looking soon. Any recommendations?'

Mark watched Emma's expression as they strolled through the park, an intense feeling of longing growing within his chest as a faint rose-pink coloured her dark honey-toned cheeks. His hands twitched, wanting to reach out and feel the warmth that her flesh promised. But he knew he couldn't go there.

Her family dynamic sounded unfamiliar and intriguing to him. Unlike her, he'd grown up by himself. Although through Claire and her sisters he had witnessed a similar dynamic to the one Emma had described. Her family had never been far away when they'd needed them.

Growing up had been very different for him. His parents were doctors, too, and had prioritised their careers over a big family. Not that he hadn't been loved or cared for. They had been amazing and inspiring parents to him. But the closest Mark had ever got to having an extended family was the staff at his parents' clinic. His parents had always encouraged him, but would they have pushed him out of the darkness the way Emma's father had done for her?

Her father's words had reached him in a strange way he couldn't quite explain. After her mother's death, he hadn't let Emma follow a destructive path out of sheer grief. Was that what Mark had done? He had moved on, forgotten about the life he and Claire had planned before she fell ill. But fragments of the past followed him around, always reminding him of his failure. As a doctor he hadn't been able to find the path towards a cure, and as a husband he hadn't been present enough to be there when she'd needed him in her last moments.

Those shadows still chased him, though he had noticed their relentless pursuit fading, giving way to other things. Such as the desire and attraction that had set his blood ablaze the moment Emma had opened the door to her apartment.

Mark had readied himself that morning with cool detachment, not wanting to let Emma glimpse any more of his past than she already had. But right now his body and mind were in a constant battle for dominance. And the warmth from her touch when she'd grasped his hand, held out to help her off the bench, had trickled into his arm, disturbing his already uneven balance with a rush of desire.

He'd been close to crossing his self-imposed line at that moment, and as he watched her marvel at the fountain he was edging towards it again. The soft curve of her lips filled him with desire, and all he could think of was to steal a taste of them.

Mark forced himself to look away. His thoughts turned to her question, and then memories of his time in Rochester surfaced in his mind. Memories he guarded close.

He and Claire had lived near the Whitebridge Institute as they'd been working there before Claire had got her life-altering diagnosis. Back then, he'd still believed they were going to survive the disease, putting all his effort into the research that would save her and millions of other people's lives. Something that remained his mission to this day.

'We stayed close to the clinic. Claire wanted to live in a house with a garden, so she could grow vegetables. I don't know where she found the time with the schedule we were keeping,' he said, remembering the many jars of pickled vegetables filling their cupboards. 'Our proximity to the hospital allowed her to escape her room more often than other patients.'

Emma stared out onto the water of the fountain before looking back at him with a small smile. 'Do you miss the research opportunities at Whitebridge? I notice your name hasn't appeared as much as it used to in the journals I read.'

'I'm proud of what I've built here in Chicago,' he said. And then he contemplated his answer. 'After everything that happened I couldn't stick around. I miss the research, and the people I worked with, but I didn't have the heart to stay.'

With her question, she had found a weak spot without even trying. Not being able to do as much research as he'd used to was the price he'd paid when he left Rochester. It hurt to admit it, but he hadn't been strong enough to stay there. Wherever he went, his surroundings had reminded him of his broken promise and his crushed heart.

What caught Mark by surprise was how easy it was for him to admit all this now. Not only that, but it was also freeing to unburden himself in front of someone who understood where he came from. While he had worked with his staff at Attano Memorial for the better part of two years now, he had never found himself in a situation where he could speak about Claire in such detail.

They moved away from the fountain, their feet choosing their own path as they focused on their conversation. Eventually, they stood near the waterfront again.

'Which research papers have you read?' he asked.

Emma chuckled. 'All of them. When my mother was diagnosed, her oncologist recommended I read up on your work when she realised I was attending med school.' She blushed as she looked away. 'Your papers on pain management in cancer patients were inspiring.'

'You found the papers inspiring?'

Mark knew his words were bordering on teasing, but he couldn't help himself. Despite being content with his move, he enjoyed hearing that his research still held relevance for people. Or was it the fact that it was Emma who'd enjoyed his work that sparked the warm feeling in his chest?

The blush blooming on her cheek was exquisite, and Mark fought the urge to reach out to her. He already knew how soft her skin was to his touch, and he craved more. Much more.

'And now that I know why you worked so hard on your research I'm even more impressed. You wanted to save your wife.'

A noble but misguided notion. He'd wanted to save

Claire and their future together. But when he'd realised he couldn't, he'd wanted to spare himself the pain of her death. Though he couldn't bring himself to admit that in front of Emma. He had already shared so much of his past with her. The details had escaped his lips before he'd been able to think of a reason not to share them. Most concerning of all was how much lighter he'd felt after it. Almost free to appreciate the yearning feelings developing in his chest.

What was it about Emma that made him unable to keep things professional? Her admiration flattered him, but other women had approached him with similar words and hadn't caught his interest. It couldn't just be the fact that she would leave soon. Or was it the only way he dared to feel like a red-blooded man again? Because he knew it would lead nowhere?

He stared out at the water of the lake again and sensed her eyes drifting away, joining his in looking straight ahead.

'It's a lot warmer than I expected it to be so close to the border,' she said, and he could almost hear the smile accompanying her words before tilting his head to see it. The melody of her accent was tinting her every word.

'Is this the first time living this far north for you?' he asked.

She nodded. 'I'm glad I made it up here in summer, though. I wonder what it would have been like later in the year.' Emma paused for a moment, hesitating before speaking her next words. 'I've never had a cold winter.'

Mark smiled at the confession and tried to recall the winters he had spent studying in Minnesota. 'You'll be in for a surprise. Just make sure you get some UV lights to combat seasonal affective disorder. I would also recommend chocolate, but for overall nutrition, light would be better.'

Emma laughed at that, her lips parting in a sensual smile that drove all his blood to the lower half of his body. How had they turned a discussion about the weather into sexy banter?

'If you write me a prescription for chocolate, do you think my health insurance will cover my grocery bill?'

Mark shrugged, desire coiling itself around his chest in a tight knot that took his breath away. If the weather wasn't a safe topic, he needed to talk about something else.

'What made you choose anaesthetics as a speciality?' They had spoken about her career before, but he'd never asked her why she had chosen that path. Or why she wanted to deviate from it now.

Emma swallowed, her lashes fluttering as she cast her eyes down for a moment before she looked at him again. 'When I started med school I thought I was going into surgery the second I could get my hands on a surgical internship. But then, halfway through, my mother's condition got a lot worse.'

In an instinct to comfort her, he reached out, grabbing her hand and squeezing it for support as her voice trembled at the memory. She smiled, but the pain was still visible in her deep green eyes.

'The team that took care of my mother was so dedicated to her care, and to making sure her last moments were as peaceful as they could be. That's when I decided I wanted to work around pain management, so when anaesthetics came up in our studies, it seemed like the perfect fit.'

Emma paused for a moment as if to compose herself—or maybe to relive the moment in her memories. Mark couldn't tell, nor could he explain the ache blossoming in his chest, but the display of such delicate vulnerability gave way to something inside him. His mouth went dry at the familiarity of the pain she was so openly showing him, and his heart stuttered in his chest.

'So why move into emergency medicine now?'

'I wasted my time on someone who wasn't serious about me, who compromised my career.' She paused for a moment to shake her head in disbelief. 'Instead of learning from the surgeons at a hospital, I got stuck witnessing the same procedures over and over again, with nothing to challenge my mind. I needed a change, and now I find myself in a situation where I have no more time to waste. I'm not getting back the time that I lost, but at least now I can focus on doing what I want...'

Her voice trailed off and Mark looked at her. She had opened up about the man she'd been in a relationship with before coming to Chicago before. A fact that gave rise to different emotions inside his chest—none of which were appropriate for him to indulge.

Mark was furious at the mistreatment Emma had suffered at his hands. The hurt shone through her voice each time she mentioned him. That she'd had her trust abused like that speared white-hot anger coupled with an irrational protectiveness into his body. But what affected him even more was the vulnerability with which she'd laid her heart bare. To him. A virtual stranger. Unlike Mark, she possessed the courage to let him see her hurt, because it was a part of her story.

Something inside him shifted at that thought.

Emma chuckled into the silence. 'I thought I was shooting for the stars when I applied to the programme at the Whitebridge Institute, and it still hasn't sunk in yet.'

'From what I've seen of you so far, I know you'll be an invaluable asset to the programme. Being surrounded by so many passionate medical professionals was the experience of a lifetime for me, and I still lean on the relationships I built there to this day.'

'I want to be part of a bigger thing, and I hope this choice will help me accomplish that.'

Even before Claire's death Mark had declared cancer the enemy of his life, vowing to work hard to find a cure and to help people survive. Emma—just like him—had experienced loss and transformed it into something noble. Into a new purpose to dedicate themselves to. They were cut from the same cloth.

He reached out, unable to stay his hand any longer, brushing his fingers against her cheek, relishing the exquisite feel of silken skin beneath them.

This road would not lead Mark anywhere he should go, but he wanted to go there regardless. Emma reached a place in him that had lain dormant and obscured for the last two years. He wasn't sure what it was, or how she had managed it.

When had he let his guard down long enough for her to slip through?

It didn't matter. His soul felt weightless for the first time, and he wanted to enjoy it for as long as it would last.

He looked at her, at the dark green eyes wide in a puzzled expression, her lips slightly open as if inviting him to follow the thoughts forming in his hungry mind. The voice in his mind cautioning him faded away as he closed the remaining gap between them. His fingers wandered down underneath her chin, angling her face towards his as he captured her mouth with his, enrapturing them both in a kiss.

Emma watched as Mark came closer, her insides turning into liquid fire as the tension became unbearable. Then their lips touched and fireworks ricocheted across her skin, setting fire to every nerve in her body.

Unable to resist—or to even to recall a reason why she shouldn't surrender to Mark with her entire being—Emma leaned in as her longing for him took over. His mouth brushed against hers with a gentleness that was at odds with the fire roaring within her. Yet the softness of the moment was exactly the way she had imagined it since their almost-kiss in the on-call room. It was a kiss filled with promise and suppressed desire, ready to break through the restraints she had been bound with.

Her hands came to rest on his chest, and she melted against him as he pulled her closer into his embrace. As he deepened their kiss her senses were overloaded, and when his hands wandered down her back the fire across her body roared with an intensity Emma hadn't known she could feel.

Sense tried its best to pierce the thick cloud of need as she gave herself to Mark. He pulled back for a moment, his dark eyes peering into hers. His hand rested on her face, and he stroked her cheek with his thumb before he pulled her into another kiss that left her catching her breath. What was she doing? This wasn't some nameless surgeon to fulfil her need for a fling. No, she was kissing Mark Henderson himself. The man whose research she had spent countless hours reading. Her boss.

Emma didn't know if he could sense her thoughts, or if his own mind had caught up with what they were doing, but Mark broke away from her with a moan that gave her an idea of how hot the desire was running in his veins.

He looked at her for a moment, his expression veiled, not letting her see what was going through his head. His hands let go of her and he stepped away, creating some space between them.

'I'm sorry. I shouldn't have done that,' he said, rubbing the light stubble on his cheek with his hand. His chest was heaving, the connection they had just a couple of seconds ago still visible.

Emma opened her mouth, searching her mind for an appropriate response, but no words manifested themselves. She shouldn't have done it either, for so many reasons that she needed both her hands to count them. Mark was her superior. This was something that could disrupt her job. The career that she had just saved from the ashes of her last relationship. But even more than that were their personal circumstances, which ruled out any kind of emotional attachment.

He had lost his wife to cancer, and now dedicated his life to fighting the disease. It was a fight she wanted to join him in, with her own looming condition a constant shadow at the back of her mind. For that reason alone she could not let herself get attached to Mark.

What if she got ill? He wouldn't want to burden himself with another sick person in his life. Something she didn't want either.

This was only ever going to end in a calamitous disaster. Emma knew that. Yet she felt the space Mark had put between them in the pit of her stomach, and her entire body was yearning to get back to the kiss they'd shared. To take it even further. Every nerve in her body sent the same signal, wanting to get lost in the luscious feeling of his body pressed against hers.

'I—' she began, but was interrupted by an urgent beeping coming from Mark's phone.

He pulled it out of his pocket and looked at the screen. A frown appeared on his face. 'I'm being paged for an emergency,' he said with a sigh.

'Go. I can find my way back home,' she said when she saw his hesitant look.

'No, I should take you home first.' Mark's eyes wandered to the message on his phone again, his fingers hovering over the screen to send a reply.

'You'll lose too much time.'

Mark looked at her for a moment, his expression a mixture of longing and regret, but he nodded as he put his phone away. 'You're right. Thank you for understanding.'

Emma shrugged. 'It's a doctor's life—nothing I'm not familiar with.' She tried to lighten the mood, though the smile on her face felt almost frozen in place.

He looked at her for a moment, his hands hovering by his sides, as if he was deciding what to do next. Eventually he gave her a small wave as he left in the direction they had come from only a couple of hours ago.

With an enormous sigh, Emma let herself fall onto a bench nearby, burying her face in her hands. What had just happened? Had she really kissed Mark, the head of the oncology department at the hospital? Of all the things she'd expected to happen on her brief stint in Chicago, this hadn't been one of them. How could she have let her impulses get the better of her?

A casual fling was one thing—but not with this man. The memory of the kiss came back to her...the softness of his touch raising the hair on her arms into tiny goosebumps. Their connection was undeniable, despite her having so many reasons to forget this day had ever happened.

'Why couldn't it have rained today?' she mumbled into her hands, before letting out another sigh.

By the time she looked up the park already seemed a lot darker. She didn't know how much time she had spent lamenting her poor decision-making, but it was time to get home. A warm shower and loads of ice cream would help her make sense of the turmoil brewing within her chest.

## CHAPTER SEVEN

MARK'S NIGHTS WERE filled with pictures of Emma. Her soft lips trailing over his collarbone. Her hands exploring every inch of his body. His taut length finding sweet release within her.

He woke up each morning, banishing the thoughts of something that hadn't even happened. Wouldn't happen ever.

Mark could not believe he had let it get as far as it had. Staring at his bedroom ceiling, he waited for the heavy blanket of guilt and obligation to descend on him like it always did. But it never came, leaving him instead with heat spreading from his chest to his groin.

Was this the last step he had been waiting for? All the support groups and the literature around grieving told him that the pain would fade away. That fond memories would replace it instead. His failings as a husband were still present, though.

He and Emma had spent the last two weeks avoiding each other after what had happened in the park, and while he knew their distance was for the best, he couldn't get her out of his head.

How could that be? The allure coming from Emma was unlike any attraction he had experienced with any woman ever since he'd met his late wife. The intensity of their connection was exhilarating. And deeply concerning. It was as if she saw through the surgeon persona he had constructed and stared right at the man he'd used to be. The man he might even become again one day.

And, as much as the desire wanted to wreak havoc throughout his body, he couldn't give himself permission to give in to anything emotional. The one chance he'd had at a happily-ever-after had died with Claire. But what if this wasn't emotional? What if this was a purely physical attraction between two consenting adults?

The thought kept rolling around in his head without any apparent purpose or destination.

Was that really something he wanted to consider? He'd only ever been with one woman, having met Claire right after high school. Mark wouldn't even know how to start that conversation.

Giving up on falling back to sleep, Mark rolled out of bed and went about his morning routine before getting into the car and driving to the hospital. He had already helped with several emergency surgeries this week, and reached the maximum amount of hours the hospital's policy permitted him to work.

Luckily for him, he had found a loophole in that policy. While he wasn't allowed to work at the hospital, he was permitted to spend time at the free clinic that the Alexander Attano Foundation ran. The clinic was always understaffed, with the hospital often being unable to free up more than one or two physicians to help, so he relished the thought of spending his time in such a meaningful way.

The nurse managing the front desk sighed with relief when he walked in. 'I was praying we would see you today. We only have one other physician here. They said they were going to send someone else in a bit, as one of the surgery boards is light today, but she might need some training—so who knows what kind of intern they're sending us?'

Mark took the tablet she was offering him with a raised eyebrow, looking through the patients who were waiting to be seen. The nurses had already asked their first diagnostic questions, triaging the patients by severity. The first five all needed stitches.

He walked up to the first patient. 'Good morning, Ms Scott. My name is Dr Henderson. The nurses tell me you've come in with a cut on your arm. Would you mind if I had a look?'

The older woman nodded and Mark put on his gloves and lifted her arm so he had a better view of the wound.

'I slipped while trimming my hedges,' the woman explained as he continued his inspection. 'My grandson tells me he'll do it for me when he gets home from school, but I don't want to trouble him.'

Mark looked up, a soft smile curling his lips. 'I think your grandson just worries about you, Ms Scott.'

She shook her head. 'Please, call me Lucy.'

'All right, Lucy. This is superficial, but we'll need to apply some stitches before we bandage you up.' He got up from the stool he'd sat on. 'I'm going to grab the supplies we need and then we'll get started.'

As he walked to the supply cupboard to grab a suture kit, the figure standing at the front desk with the admissions nurse caught his attention. His chest tightened when he recognised Emma—all soft curves and beauty, even in the uniform scrubs she wore—talking to the nurse sitting behind the screen.

The nurse made eye contact with Mark and waved him over. Emma turned to see who she was waving at, and he noticed the slight blush spreading through her cheeks. Memories from that day two weeks ago came rushing back into his conscious mind, the lust she evoked in him clawing at him again the moment their eyes met.

His reaction to her was visceral, eluding any kind of self-control he tried to exert on himself. Two weeks had not been enough to cool anything between them.

'Theresa has sent Dr Santos down here to help. Could you show her around and split up the current patients? Once you get through them, I'll admit more for the day,' she said when Mark stepped closer to the desk.

Steeling himself, he turned to Emma. The last thing he needed was any of the staff to pick up on the tension thrumming between them. He asked her to follow him with a nod, not wanting to say anything until they were out of earshot. He didn't plan on having any kind of confrontation. What had happened the other day had been nothing more than a lapse of judgement as he rediscovered what it was like to be attracted to a woman again.

The silence between them grew, and unspoken words hung between them.

'What's your experience with general medicine?' he asked to break the silence as he walked them to the supply closet. Best not voice what had happened between them, or he might find himself in a similar situation again.

'I did a lot of patient care in my intern years. Less so in residency. I'm confident in my diagnostic skills, though,' she replied.

Mark believed her, but he was hearing a slight edge in her voice. The tension between them picked up the second he was near enough to touch her, as his body remembered what she'd felt like pressed against him. Was she thinking about their kiss as well?

'Most cases here tend to not be too severe, though today we have a couple of wounds that need to be stitched. How comfortable are you with those?'

He grabbed a suture kit and turned around to look at her. Emma bit on her lower lip and looked down, her long lashes obscuring her eyes for a moment. The curve of her mouth drew his gaze, and remembering the softness of them against his own drove the blood to his groin.

'I haven't done any stitches since my time in med school,' she admitted, and swallowed.

The tension within him softened at her worried look, and he was filled with a different urge. He remembered the hurt in her voice when she'd told him about her time at the private practice she'd worked at. How she believed she'd compromised her career because of love.

A strange protectiveness wrapped itself around his chest. And, despite knowing that those feelings had no place within him, he wanted to be there for her. A foolish thought that he tried to brush aside.

'Doing stitches is like riding a bike. Once you start doing them again it will come back to you. Come,' he commanded, and he shook off the dark clouds gathering in his mind.

They left the supply cupboard and walked to the bed where Ms Scott was waiting.

'Lucy, this is my colleague, Dr Santos. Would you mind if she watched me do the sutures on your arm? We're a teaching hospital, and we want to give our doctors every opportunity to learn.'

Ms Scott nodded, and Mark took a seat on the stool next to the bed, indicating to Emma with the pointing of his finger to grab a chair from next to an empty bed and join him. As she sat down next to him the scent of coconut drifted up to his nose, and again he had to push the memories away. This patient deserved his undivided attention and, while his attraction to her made working with Emma a lot more complicated than he'd expected, she should still be able to learn from her senior surgeon. He'd told her he would teach her, and he meant to keep his promise.

Even though keeping his last promise of showing her Chicago had got him into hot water...

'Okay, this cut is clean and was inflicted by a sharp blade. That makes it a lot easier to stitch together. What is the challenge with uneven edges to a wound?'

Emma leaned in to look over his arm, a slight movement that brought an awareness of her to all his senses.

'Lining up the edges of the wound to close them is a lot less straightforward,' she said. 'If the edges are even, it will heal cleaner, leaving less scar tissue, and therefore is less likely to get inflamed.'

Mark nodded, wrestling his focus back to the patient in front of him. 'Exactly. So, first we'll put some local anaesthetic on, to make sure you'll be comfortable and still, as we do the stitches, Lucy.' He smiled at the patient to reassure her, and handed the anaesthetic cream that came with the suture kit to Emma. 'I don't need to explain that step to you,' he said, and she laughed at that, rolling her eyes before putting the cream on the patient's skin.

'What do you grow in your garden, Lucy?' Mark asked as they waited for the anaesthetic to numb the skin. If he could take her mind off the procedure for a moment, he would decrease her overall stress.

'All kinds of vegetables, but I'm most proud of my tomatoes this summer. Each year they're my worry child, with none of the plants coming in the way I want them to. But this year they did...' Her voice trailed off as she smiled, relaxing.

'They must be very popular in your neighbourhood. My late wife used to occupy herself with growing cucumbers. Everyone would get at least one jar of pickles from us.'

The memory had tumbled out of his mouth before he could stop himself. Talking about Claire had always been something he leaned on when connecting with a patient. The patient's needs always exceeded any discomfort he might feel at reawakening memories of her.

He didn't allow himself that kind of sentimentality around his staff, though. He wanted to be the rock they leaned on. But with Emma around, he found he didn't mind sharing those thoughts. Maybe they had become fond memories and he just hadn't realised it until he met her.

'Oh, no, you seem far too young to be a widower,' Ms Scott said.

Mark tried his best not to flinch at that. He never

usually referred to Claire as his *late* wife, wanting to keep that detail to himself. How had that slipped out?

He turned his attention back to Emma. 'Since this cut is the best-case scenario, we can do simple sutures. Here, let me show you how to start.' He took the needle in between forceps and threaded it with the string from the kit. 'Lucy, you might want to look away for a moment,' he advised his patient, who raised her eyes to look at a TV at the far end of the room.

Mark aligned the edges of the wound and pulled the needle through one edge and then the other before pulling the string together and tying a precise but simple knot. He clipped the string close to the knot before threading the needle again and continuing in this fashion until only two stitches were left.

'I'm almost done here, Lucy. You're doing great. I will ask Dr Santos to do the last stitches under my supervision now, and then we'll bandage you up.'

Emma's head whipped around to him, her eyes wide in surprise. She opened her mouth, but he shook his head before she could protest.

'Take the forceps and the needle,' he said, passing her the tray of instruments before getting up to give her space to do the stitches.

He elected to stand, needing the extra space between them to keep his mind focused. The soft scent of sweet coconut wrapped his head into a luscious fog of untold desire that he knew he must not get lost in.

He watched Emma pick up the instruments and follow his instructions. She placed two perfect stitches, and left no doubt in his mind that she remembered everything from her training. She didn't need any supervision from him, and it relieved him to see that. The less time he needed to spend with her in the free clinic, the better.

'All right, Lucy. Dr Santos will explain all the aftercare to you and send you on your way. Give your grandson a call so he can help,' he said, and took off his gloves, disposing of them in a bin nearby and then walking over to the counter to fill out some notes on the patient's chart.

He moved on to the next patient and saw from the corner of his eye that Emma had done the same. With both of them working on the stitches while the nurses kept on triaging the incoming patients, they had soon put a considerable dent in the number of people waiting to be treated.

As he finished up his latest set of notes Emma joined him at the admissions desk, a big smile gracing her face and lighting up the surrounding air.

'Thank you for taking the time to teach me,' she said as she reached him, leaving a deliberate few handspans of space between them. 'I was worried when Theresa asked me to come down here.'

Worried about what? How could she have known he'd be here?

'You came here to learn, and I promised I would teach you. That hasn't changed.' The words both of them left unspoken hung between them, recreating the tension sparking from her body to his and back. A spark that could cause a whole forest fire in mere seconds.

'I didn't see you on the OR board today. Are you not doing any surgery?' Emma asked, forcing his thoughts through the fog that was his awareness of her.

'It's my rest day today. I've exceeded the maximum hours I'm allowed to work in a week so the chief benched me.'

'Wait—you're here as a volunteer?'

'The chief doesn't like me spending my paid hours here, but there's more than enough work to go around so I come here whenever I can to help.'

Emma looked at him with such softness that his chest tightened and new sparks danced over his skin in a tantalising lure.

'That's so generous of you,' she said.

Her voice was only a whisper, and a lightning bolt of desire struck his body as she smiled at him, robbing him of the ability to form any other thought than how to possess her.

A soft vibration interrupted him before he could reply, and Emma looked at her pager with a sigh. 'I have to check on some post-operative medication. I won't be long, if you still need my help.'

Mark lifted his hands to sweep them around him. 'We always need help down here, and we won't reject anyone willing to spend their time at the clinic.'

Emma nodded and then looked at him for a moment, as if expecting something, before turning around and running off to check up on her patient.

Mark let out a long sigh and took a few deep breaths, willing the fire coursing through his veins to ease so the heat within him would calm. There were patients waiting right at this moment while he was lusting after one of his subordinate physicians.

He shook his head to rid himself of any thought of Emma and grabbed the tablet, ready to work on the patients already admitted to the clinic. If he worked fast, and with no kind of distraction, he might be able to see everyone who'd come here for help today.

Emma's having to check up on one patient in the oncology department turned into several, along with answering a bunch of questions the interns had for her. By the time she got through all her tasks, her shift was over.

The sun had already set, and after grabbing her tote bag from her locker she made for the exit. Then she changed her mind at the last minute. Before leaving, she wanted to check on the free clinic. They must have closed by now, but if there were any patients still left to see, she wanted to ease the load.

Her heart stuttered inside her chest when her thoughts turned to Mark. There were at least five things she could list off the top of her head that she wanted to do on her days off. None of them involved leaving her house, and most of them were some form of sleeping. The long hours she worked at the hospital were tiring, leaving her like an empty husk most of the days.

Yet Mark went there on his day off, because he realised that the people who came needed help only a trained physician like himself could give.

The sheer kindness and generosity of such an act weakened Emma's knees. Something she was trying to avoid at all costs. Because that would add another layer to her attraction. Another layer that made things so much more complicated.

She didn't want complicated. She wanted simple. Her move to Rochester was less than a month away now, and she was just learning to be by herself.

Her work in the oncology department was teaching her so much about the different conditions her patients presented, and how they coped with their diagnoses. It was strengthening her own resolve over her potential diagnosis. She wasn't ready to know yet, but she was determined to stick to her plan.

The way Mark spoke about his late wife had made her realise she couldn't let anyone get close to her until she'd figured her condition out for herself. By the sound of it, he and Claire had had their whole life planned out, only for her to be snatched away in an instant. Though while he now shared his memories of Claire more freely, Emma detected no hidden hurt underneath his words. After losing her mother, she'd thought the pain would never go away. It still hurt sometimes, often in the most innocent of moments, but those times became rarer as life went on.

The lights were still on when she approached the door of the free clinic, but as she entered she didn't see anyone at the admissions desk or in the patients' area. Had someone forgotten to turn off the lights?

As Emma walked around, looking for the light switch, she spotted Mark sitting at a table at the far end of the clinic, engrossed in whatever was in front of him. For a moment she hesitated, unsure whether she should approach him. Seeing him here had suddenly filled her with dread, and she was worried about what he might have to say about their kiss.

The kiss that had been lingering at the edge of her mind manifested itself fully, and for a brief moment his scent enveloped her once more. The memory caused a small spark in her stomach to reignite, sending warm showers in every direction of her body.

When agreeing to a tour of Chicago, Emma had not expected to kiss her boss. Or to have him reject her the way he had, with the sort of cool detachment she was used to seeing in other male surgeons.

The instant regret that had contorted his face still speared a sharp pain into her chest. His rejection had hurt more than she wanted to admit, even though the rational side of her brain should be rejoicing at the thought that she had extracted herself from a sticky situation with her senior surgeon. But Mark had set a chain of events in motion within her that he didn't even notice.

The more time she spent with him, the more she understood the diagnosis she had been avoiding since her mother passed away, and what kind of impact it might have on the people around her. She had convinced herself that she could wait until her training as a doctor was done. But what if she was wrong?

'Not even the free clinic lets you escape the paperwork,' she said, when she realised the patient charts were occupying his attention.

Mark looked up, clearly not having noticed her approach, and sighed. 'The clinic's is a lot harder. Since we treat a lot of uninsured people here, the board of directors at Alexander Attano wants to see where every single dollar goes.'

She took the seat next to him. 'So you're doing inventory more than patient notes?'

'Basically. Everything I use needs to be accounted for. You should see how much of a hassle it is when I need to account for my time.' He sighed and leaned back for a moment, scrubbing his hands over his face in a tired gesture. 'It's easier for me to come here on my days off rather than try to justify in front of the chief of surgery why I'm down here rather than in one of his ORs.'

Emma's chest tightened at the frustration visible in his stance. The free clinic obviously didn't get as much priority as he thought it should.

'Now that I know I can do that, I'll spend some time here,' she said, and her breath caught in her throat when Mark's gaze snapped to hers, his eyes darkening.

'You don't have to do that to please me,' he said.

She shook her head, sensing where his thoughts were headed. 'I'm not doing it to please anyone. I just want to help where I'm needed.' She shrugged when Mark raised an eyebrow at her. 'I'm only here for another month. I have nothing else going on, so I might as well do something meaningful with the time I have left.'

The way his eyes wandered down her entire body caused a shiver to trickle down her spine. All her senses were aware of his proximity.

'There's nothing else you would rather do for fun?' he asked after a brief period of quiet, his voice so low and full of gravel that it made her hair stand on end.

Was he flirting with her? After expressing regret about kissing her and before they had even found a moment to talk about their kiss?

'What I do for fun at the moment involves a lot of heavy medical textbooks,' she said, hoping the heat in her cheeks wasn't as visible as it felt. It was true. When she wasn't at the hospital, Emma put most of her time into studying for her fellowship. 'Though I've discovered that there's a greenhouse on the rooftop, which makes a pleasant change of scenery during my shifts.

I don't have the greenest of thumbs, though I do find caring for plants soothing.'

'I'm in no position to reject any help that the free clinic gets offered, as long as you do it on your days off. Chief Singer would kill me if I started scheduling a very expensive locum tenens doctor into the clinic.'

Mark gave her a one-sided smile and for a moment they sat there in silence. Was each one of them trying to guess what the other was thinking? Should she say something? There wasn't that much to talk about on the surface. They'd kissed, he'd apologised for over-stepping, and he'd left. Except that moment in the park hung between them, creating an air of strange closeness mixed with a significant amount of hesitation.

The sigh dropping from Mark's lips pulled her out of her contemplations. 'I'm not sorry I kissed you,' he said as he looked at her.

His smile had faded, leaving a veiled expression that Emma struggled to see through.

'It was inappropriate, as I'm the head of the department you work in. But I don't regret doing it.'

A surge of heat seized her body as she made sense of his words, her heart speeding up to a point where she could hear her blood rushing in her ears. Why was he saying that? His dark brown eyes were narrowed, intensifying the goosebumps already covering her flesh, and the spark in his gaze was reminiscent of what she had seen in the park right before he'd kissed her.

'I appreciate you saying that,' Emma said when she found her voice again, struggling to form the words with the big lump sitting in her throat.

She watched as he drew closer to her, her breath catching when his eyes flicked to her lips for a moment before coming back to her. Just like the last time when they had kissed. The ends of her nerves caught fire as she imagined kissing him again, and her entire body was aware of the minimal distance between them.

But Mark stopped with a wistful smile on his lips. He reached out with his hand, placing it on her cheek with unending gentleness. His thumb grazed over her cheekbone, with each sweep creating sparks that trickled down her body, raising the heat within her to new heights.

'I haven't been intimate with anyone since Claire passed away.'

The confession took Emma by surprise and she leaned back, her eyes wide. Even though he had shared some of his memories about Claire with her, it had never even occurred to her that he might not have been with anyone since her death. So the last person Mark had kissed before Emma had been his late wife...

Her mouth went dry as the thought manifested itself in her head, making it that much harder to swallow the still growing lump in her throat.

'Do you feel guilty about kissing another woman?' Emma asked.

She lacked any kind of reference point. The only person she knew who came close was her father, and he'd had no interest in dating after her mother passed away. Though she'd never asked him if it was because of guilt or other reasons. Did she want to hear that Mark felt he was betraying his late wife when he touched her?

But he shook his head. 'No, that's not what I feel guilty about.'

Then, ever so slowly, he leaned in. His nose touched

hers first, grazing over the skin, and that minuscule touch was already enough to make her shiver with anticipation and need. She drew in a shaky breath and a firework exploded in the pit of her stomach, drowning out any thought when his lips touched hers.

She gave in to the sensation almost immediately, closing the tiny gap remaining between them. Infused by the fire his kiss sent licking across her skin, she opened her mouth to his, deepening their connection so she could feel it at her core, which contracted with each of his touches that elicited a response of untold desire.

He didn't feel guilty about being with another woman.

The meaning of those words was drowned out by the need surging through her. All she could focus on was where his hands were roaming over her body, making her writhe at every turn. Could she really be the first woman he'd been with after all these years? The moment seemed so monumental, so significant. How could she keep the emotional distance she needed to maintain?

Emma put her hands on his chest, forcing herself to break the intimate embrace. 'Wait…' She sighed, not sure what she wanted to say next.

Did she want to take things slowly? Despite her passionate reaction to his touch, she wasn't looking for another relationship. Mark fanned the flames of desire within her, making her react on impulse rather than following the plan she had set out. She couldn't afford to lose control or things would just end up like last time—for both of them.

Or was this the moment where she established the boundaries of what would be a casual affair? She had thought about the idea since arriving in Chicago, but had rejected it being with Mark. If she dared to engage in something with no strings attached it couldn't be with her superior. Or did those things not matter in affairs?

Mark let go of her, and the space he created between them felt like an insurmountable chasm that filled her with instant regret. The longing for his touch rushed to the forefront of her mind, tempting her to disregard her caution. She tried reading his expression, wondering if his blood was running just as hot as hers. The fire in his eyes caused her breath to catch in her throat, but behind that she spotted something else mingling with the desire written on his face.

Was he not sure if he was ready for something, either?

'I think we should talk about this first,' she said, with a slight shake in her voice.

Mark cleared his throat before he nodded and started to respond. Yet the words he meant to speak never crossed his lips. A shrill beeping coming from Emma's bag interrupted him.

'Are you *serious* right now?' she said under her breath, digging through her bag to find her pager just as Mark's pager beeped with the same urgency. Was there no moment when they could talk without being interrupted by some kind of emergency?

He grabbed his pager with a frown and jumped to his feet as he read the message. '911 page for Georgina,' he said, and Emma's pulse quickened.

They hurried to the oncology department where Georgina had begun chemotherapy after her tumour had been found to be malignant. They found two interns in the room, doing chest compressions to resuscitate their patient. Emma went over to her monitor, checking her vitals. Mark barked orders as a nurse wheeled the crash cart into the room to administer the medicine he'd ordered.

'Her blood pressure is coming back up,' Emma said as the epinephrine kicked in, and she let out a sigh of relief when Georgina's pulse evened out and steadied itself. 'How did this happen? I know she's struggled with the side effects of her chemo, but it shouldn't cause heart failure. Apparently earlier this morning she was sitting up gossiping with the nurses.'

Mark walked out of the patient's room to the nurses' station, where he took a tablet to check out the latest scans. A different tension built around them now as Emma stood next to him, watching as he scrutinised the images on the tablet.

After a long stretch of silence he pointed at the part of the scan that showed Georgina's thyroid. Emma stared at it before lifting her eyebrows. 'It looks clean to me. And the biopsy of the lymph node came back inconclusive.'

'I don't think it is. Call it a hunch.'

He waved an intern over, instructing him to do more scans once Georgina was stable enough, and asking if Harald was still here. When the intern nodded, Mark sighed. The toll this day was taking on him was visible in the deep lines on his face.

'I can talk to him,' Emma offered, wanting to lessen his burden in any way she could.

But he shook his head. 'I'll update him and then head out. Georgina will need to recover before she can be moved to the CT. We'll be able to go over the scans tomorrow morning.'

Emma nodded, feeling her stomach tying itself into a knot as she watched him walk away. It was as if a gloomy presence had taken hold of him as he'd looked at Georgina's scans, and it was filling Emma's chest with worry. The urge to look after him pulsed through her, and she caught up with the intern Mark had just spoken to.

'Page me when the scans are up,' she said, thinking the chances were that Mark would wait around to gain some clarity about their patient.

'We'll do more tests once she's stable.'

Mark placed his hand on Harald's shoulder as the man digested all the information he had just given him about his wife's condition.

'This is not all bad news. She's alive, and we'll have a deeper look at the cause of her heart failure.'

Harald looked like a husk of a man, his eyes unfocused. The sight wrenched at his heart, reminding him of when he had been in Harald's place. Georgina's case reminded him so much of Claire and his own experience that he felt the wounds of his past tearing open under the pressure.

Mark knew he should distance himself...not get too attached to the fate of a patient. But each time he looked at Harald he saw himself in his shoes, and he was fighting hard to prevent him from having to deal with the pain of losing his wife.

He walked to his office rather than to his car to go home. It would take a couple of hours for Georgina's condition to be stable enough to move her. Enough time for him to stretch out on the couch in his office to see if he could fall asleep.

He dropped down on the soft cushions, closing his eyes for just a moment before a faint knock drifted to his ear. 'Enter,' he said, too consumed by his own thoughts to get off his seat.

To his surprise, Emma came in, balancing two take-away coffee cups on top of one another while closing the door with her other hand.

She hesitated before she smiled. 'I came here to convince you to go home for the evening, but in case that didn't work I brought some coffee to keep you going.' She looked around for a moment. 'You don't actually have an apartment, you live here—am I right?'

Her quip pierced through the fog enveloping him and a genuine chuckle crossed his lips. 'Don't tell anyone. They'll revoke my privileges.'

Emma touched her lips in a gesture as if she was zipping them closed before stepping towards him and handing him a cup. 'I'm heading home. See you tomorrow.'

'Wait.' Mark looked out of the window, noticing how much time had passed since they'd left the clinic. 'Let me walk you to your car. It's dark outside, and I know how far away they make the temporary staff park.'

'That's unnecessary,' Emma said with a deflecting smile, but he was already on his feet and opening the door for her to escort her through the car park.

He had to admit that he was doing it for himself as much as for her. When he was near her, the shadows surrounding him didn't feel as oppressive, and at this moment he needed that. He couldn't let her go just yet.

When she'd come to find him in the clinic, he'd had

no intention of sharing so much of his feelings, despite them being true. The thought of being close to another woman frightened him to some extent, but Emma evoked something within him he hadn't felt in ages, and before he'd been able to stop himself his lips had already been moving, sharing his thoughts with her.

His mind struggled to grapple with what that meant, and he didn't want to think about it. For once he just wanted to feel as if things might be okay one day.

'Are you kidding me?'

Emma sighed when they got closer to her car, and he watched her kneel behind one of her rear tyres. It was flat.

He reached out his hand to help her up and a hot spark travelled down his arm when her delicate fingers wrapped themselves around his hand. Their hands remained intertwined for a moment before she withdrew, leaving him aware of the space between them.

'Come on, I'll drive you home,' he said, but she shook her head.

'Thank you, but that's unnecessary. I'll take a cab and call a tow truck in the morning.'

She started when he grabbed her hand again and walked her to his parking spot.

'Don't be silly. I'll drive you home now and you can take a cab in the morning, as a compromise. How does that sound?'

He refused to heed any more protests, and surprised himself when he found the way to her flat without having to consult the navigation system. Somehow once had been enough for him to remember.

Mark pulled up in front of her building and turned to her to say something, but the words died in his throat when his gaze met hers. There was an intensity brimming in the dark green eyes that drew him to her like tiny insects to a roaring flame.

'Do you want to come up?' she said, and Mark narrowed his eyes for a moment.

'What?'

'I mean to talk about the case. I found some takeout menus in a drawer, so we could order some food while we strategize. You've had a long day—maybe a second set of eyes might be helpful.'

Of course that was it. How could his mind have even thought of anything else? And the answer was no. He didn't want to go up. Except he did. Desperately. The darkness closing in on him lifted the moment Emma came close, and today the fog was more suffocating than usual.

Even though he knew that at some point he would have to surrender himself to the encroaching darkness again, just for a few hours he wanted to escape.

'Sure, let's work out how we can help Georgina,' he said with a nod, and followed her up the stairs.

# CHAPTER EIGHT

EMMA'S HAND SHOOK as she put the key into her apartment door, opening it up and inviting Mark in. Why had she done that? The second the invitation had left her lips she'd wanted to snatch it back and swallow it whole.

Ever since her second day at Attano Memorial, when she had almost kissed him in the on-call room, Emma had failed at keeping her distance. To invite him up to her apartment now was the cherry on top of the sundae that was her awful decision-making.

It was about food and helping Georgina, Emma told herself. The way he'd looked at her when she'd entered his office had made her heart ache with sympathy. The defeat in his eyes had been palpable.

Mark looked around him and wandered over to her living room, leaving her alone with the takeout menus. A few medical journals and textbooks were stacked on top of the coffee table. He plopped down on the couch, browsing through the journals and then grabbing one, flipping it open at random. To keep herself from staring at him, she took out the paper pamphlets from the drawer.

'Do we want late-night burgers, or just a gigantic pizza?' she asked.

There was no reply. Then, 'I haven't seen this one in ages.'

His voice trailed off and Emma looked up from the stack of menus. What had fascinated him so much that he couldn't answer the important question of food?

The second she heard him laugh she understood which journal he had found and rushed over, throwing herself on the couch to take it away from him. 'You were not supposed to see that!'

Mark moved the hand holding the magazine above his head and out of her reach and she climbed on top of him to pull the journal out of his grip. She stretched her arm, her fingertips unable to reach their goal.

'Dr Handsome?' he asked, with amusement shining in his eyes.

Her habit of writing her thoughts and feelings in the margins of the magazine was coming back to haunt her. The man who'd written the article had just read her thoughts about *him*.

Her hand was resting on his broad chest, their faces only inches apart. It was then that she realised how close she had got to him to take the medical journal away from him. Fire rose to her cheeks, leaving a burning trail throughout her body as she commanded her brain to put some distance between them. But her body did not heed her. All she could focus on was his warm breath grazing the already hot skin of her face.

Her entire being trembled when Mark dropped the journal on the floor so his fingers could touch her cheek. He cocked his head, his dark eyes entrancing her as a snake charmer would enthral his pet reptile to do his bidding.

A small smile appeared on his lips. 'I didn't know you liked me *that* much,' he said teasingly, driving a spear of hot lava into her centre.

'I don't,' she lied. But her voice failed her on those important two words. If there ever was a time to sound sure of herself it was now, and yet her lower lip quivered as she drew in a shaky breath.

'Then how come you kissed me twice?'

'Me? You were the one kissing me—both times.' The words sounded a lot more defensive than she'd meant them to be.

'I don't know… That doesn't sound like something I'd do. Let me try to jog my memory.'

His playful tone quickened her pulse. She watched as his face closed in on hers, and a moment later he'd captured her mouth in an earth-shattering kiss.

Everything around Emma faded away as she lost herself in Mark's touch. More demanding this time around, he pulled her against him, his hands finding the seams of her clothing and pushing the top over her head in an almost frantic motion.

This moment had been a long time coming, and neither wanted to wait another second. Her thoughts went to their kiss in the clinic. She had stopped him then, wanting to talk about this attraction between them. Emma liked clear rules and boundaries within which she could operate. But how had the rules helped her in her last relationship? Even when she had done everything the way she was supposed to, supporting Rob and putting his needs ahead of hers?

Emma was done with letting her past experience

dictate to her. She had left and it was time to be brave, to embrace the moment. They were both here, both willing. What else was there to know?

This kiss was nothing like the tender moments they'd shared earlier. Their desire and need was setting both of them alight to the point where the fulfilment of their passion for each other was the only thing dominating their thoughts. This was what she wanted in this moment. They'd have plenty of time to talk about it later.

Throwing the piece of fabric on the floor, Mark dipped his head, trailing kisses along her collarbone. His tongue licked around the hollow of her neck before finding his way down her sternum.

She shivered when he pushed her bra aside, releasing the stiff peaks of her nipples that had already been straining against the silk of her underwear. A moan dropped from her lips when his warm breath grazed her breast before he took her dark nipple into his mouth, lavishing her sensitive skin with the untold pleasure she had seen written in his eyes since their encounter in the park.

What did she have to lose? Neither of them was looking for something serious. This was her moment to relinquish control and to learn how to go with the flow. To 'let loose', as she'd been told.

Her hands wandered down his back, feeling the hardness of his broad shoulders as she looked for something to hold on to. To anchor her in this world as the fire of passion within her immolated everything in its wake. She tore at his clothes with unprecedented urgency. A growl left his throat when she pushed him away from her to yank the scrub top off his body.

The wetness of her core caused a shiver to cascade through her body as she drank in the view of his bare chest. Her eyes wandered down, following the line of hair as it vanished below his waistband. Her gaze drifted further, and her breath caught in her throat when she saw his erect manhood straining against the fabric of his trousers.

She reached out, biting her lower lip as she did so, but his hand closed around her wrist. He stopped her before she got to fulfil all her fantasies of the past couple of weeks. And then he smiled at her, and all her walls and insecurities came tumbling down at that pure expression of affection. It stoked the fire within her into a frenzy she'd never experienced before in her life.

'Bedroom?' he asked, and Emma pointed down the corridor to the single door standing ajar.

As she tried to get up, he wrapped his hands around her waist and picked her up. She yelped at her sudden loss of footing and wrapped her legs around his hips to help her balance while her arms encircled his neck.

He nuzzled his face into her neck, making fire lick over her skin as he walked them to the bedroom. He dropped her on her bed with surprising gentleness. As he straightened himself he hooked his fingers into her trousers, dragging them down and throwing them behind him before pouncing back on top of her.

Emma writhed under the look Mark gave her as his eyes drank her in, passing over her ample curves with unveiled hunger and longing. Then his mouth found hers again and fireworks exploded all around Emma's body as their bare skin touched, the sensation overwhelming her. And just as she thought she couldn't feel any more bliss than he'd already given her, his hand slipped past the silken fabric of her underwear and his deft fingers found her sensitive spot.

A bolt of lightning shook her entire body, meeting the waves of pleasure crashing through her and creating a perfect storm at her core, blurring the fine line between pleasure and pain. She gasped, a part of her wanting to retreat from this exquisiteness. But the part within her that had hungered for Mark the second she'd laid eyes on him was much stronger.

She was ready to get lost in this moment. With this man.

Emma moaned against his lips as his talented fingers coaxed her over the cliff, shattering her into a million pieces. Her head tilted backwards, and all of her instincts were occupied with keeping her mind intact enough to kiss him back.

For a longing moment Emma thought this must be the end. There could be nothing else to give. Yet Mark was determined to prove her wrong. His mouth trailed along her neck while his hand let go of her to relieve her of her underwear, tossing it aside. The feral look in his eyes caused a shiver to claw through her body as she prepared for what was about to happen.

Mark laughed when he caught her gaze trailing downwards, to where his manhood was still contained by his trousers. 'You *do* like me,' he said with a grin.

'No, I don't,' she replied in defiance, though her hands betrayed her words as they wandered over his broad chest and down his abdomen, appreciating the hard ridges of his muscles for a moment before slipping under his trousers. Her heart beat against her chest as she wrapped her hand around him and heard a muf-

fled groan escape his lips. 'In fact, I think you're the
one who likes me.'

Mark chuckled again, a playful gleam in his eyes as
he stood up to peel himself out of his remaining clothes,
standing in front of her in all his glory. 'Preposterous!
You have no evidence to support such a claim.'

Instead of saying anything Emma grinned, her eyes
moving to his erection before coming back to his face.
She raised an eyebrow in a silent question.

'We're both doctors. You should know that this results from external stimuli and not emotion,' he said.

And before she could say anything else he was on
her again, his mouth capturing hers, pulling her into
the sheets with a kiss charged with the sexual tension
that had been building up since they'd first met.

'Speaking of being responsible doctors…' His voice
trailed off for a moment, as if he was looking for the
right words.

'I have an IUD,' she said, understanding what he
was about to ask.

'That doesn't help with all the other risky things.'

Emma paused for a moment as the heat from her
core shot up to her cheeks. 'I've rarely done this kind
of thing. And definitely not recently.'

The smile that appeared on his lips took the breath
out of her lungs. He lowered his face to kiss along
her neck again, coming to a brief stop next to her ear.
'Good. Neither do I,' he whispered, before his mouth
found hers again.

Emma opened her lips to him, felt their tongues
creating an erotic dance that threatened to undo her
all over again. She would be his first woman since the
death of his wife. The thought got through the luscious

fog enveloping them. But did it even matter? He was a willing participant, just as she was. It didn't need to mean anything—and who was she to decide that this needed to be an important moment for him?

Her body trembled, aching for his touch, and Emma let go of the last remaining shreds of control she was hanging on to. Her legs fell open as he positioned himself between them, and the desire to have him controlled every single thought in her mind. She held her breath as his length pressed against the apex of her thighs, and a moment later she felt whole.

Emma wrapped her arms around his neck as he rocked against her, their lips connecting again as he thrust into her with a certainty that sent sparks flying all over her skin. The primal groans coming from his throat with every thrust filled her belly with wild butterflies. Knowing that she'd brought a man this kind of intense pleasure threatened to undo her both body and mind.

He wanted her just as much as she wanted him.

She hung on to his back, her hands digging into his flesh as the sweet fingers of her next climax clawed at her, and as if reading her mind Mark slipped his hand between them to caress her, sending lightning bolts through all her extremities.

Emma sobbed his name as she fell apart in his arms, letting herself get lost in the pleasure of their lovemaking. She pulled his face to her lips in a last kiss as Mark shuddered above her with a guttural growl before collapsing on top of her.

The smell of food broke through the heavy blanket of sleep surrounding Emma, and with a start she sat up. The space next to her was empty. Her mouth went dry as memories of last night came rushing back into her consciousness, reigniting the fire that had kept her going for the last hours.

Had he left?

The tension in her chest only lasted a second, dispersing as she walked out of the bedroom and caught a glance of Mark standing in front of the stove, wearing nothing but his underwear.

The sight of his lithe and muscular body, of him standing in her kitchen, made her knees weak as a myriad of different emotions started a fight for dominance within her. The wetness that the sight of him brought to her core showed her that their night together had done precious little to satiate her growing hunger for the man in front of her.

Her boss.

The thought dropped a heavy boulder into the pit of her stomach. Last time she'd let herself fall for her boss the relationship had turned into a toxic mess that she'd only just untangled herself from.

Except this wasn't a relationship. They'd had sex one time. She didn't want a relationship anyway, she reminded herself. Not with her leaving Chicago soon.

Despite their brief acquaintance with each other, Emma felt she had got to know Mark over the last couple of weeks. He'd shared so much about his life in Rochester with her, letting her know about the good and the bad things surrounding his previous marriage. How much it shaped him to this day.

Another reason not to get attached.

What if Emma fell ill with the same disease that had taken her mother? The chances were there, however unlikely, and she had yet to get tested for it. Mark would never want to involve himself with a cancer diagnosis waiting to happen.

'I don't know why it surprises me to see you cooking, but it's not something I ever imagined for you,' Emma said as she approached the counter, trying to quell the storm brewing inside her. Every fibre of her begged to jump back into his arms. Every inch of distance between their bodies sizzled on her skin like a hot iron, intensifying the ache in her core.

'As a physician, you should understand how important a balanced diet is,' he said with a smirk, as he opened a few cupboards until he found the plates. 'I used to do most of the cooking even before Claire got too sick to do it. We worked the same hours at the clinic, but she was way more driven than I was.'

*Claire.* The name suddenly rang with a familiarity that she hadn't sensed before. She and Mark had worked together at the Whitebridge Institute before she'd got sick. How come Emma had never heard of her if she'd been so closely linked to his work?

Then she remembered where she'd read the name before, and her jaw fell open. 'Wait—your wife was Dr Claire Dubois? Your co-author?'

Emma's gaze moved over her shoulder to look at the stack of medical journals on her coffee table.

Mark looked up from the pan, a slight smile softening the lines around his mouth. 'That's her. She was an anaesthesiologist as well—though when we worked together she only focused on our research around pain management.' He paused for a moment and chuckled. 'She did most of the writing—she was much better at putting our findings into words.'

Emma raised her eyebrows in surprise. Unfamiliar feelings bubbled up inside her stomach as she considered his words. The last thing she'd expected to hear this morning were more fond memories of his wife. It didn't bother her, but it intrigued her. Had he reached the point where he was ready to move on from his marriage?

Though another part of his sentence also stood out to Emma. 'Claire wrote all the papers?'

Mark nodded with a one-sided smile. 'I don't think people understood my ramblings and tangents.'

The realisation stunned Emma. 'I can't believe it. All this time I thought it was you, when in actuality I fell in love with the words of your wife.'

The dreaded word had crossed her lips before she could stop herself. Emma cringed, instant regret wiping out all other emotions dancing in her chest. Why had she said the L-word when any other word would have done?

'She was an excellent writer,' Mark said, and nothing in his face betrayed whether he'd taken exception to her words or if he even cared. Instead, he focused on the task in front of him, finishing up their breakfast as he spoke. 'Maybe that was one reason why I stepped away from research. I love the discovery and the progress, but I never enjoyed writing. That task belonged to her, and I guess I wasn't ready to let someone else take over a part of the research that was so important to her.'

'Do you feel ready for it now?'

Emboldened by his previous words, she asked the question. Mark had just shared a side of him she hadn't known about. Despite her putting her foot in her mouth a mere few seconds ago, she decided to push on. They had just spent a night of toe-curling passion with each other, and while Emma still guarded herself, she wanted to peep behind the curtains.

He looked at her, his expression letting her know he hadn't missed the subtext in her words. Being ready to let someone else step into his life applied to more aspects than just his research work.

Mark sat down on the barstool next to her, his eyes glued to the plate in front of him for a moment. 'I don't know. I've never had time to think about it.' He stopped for a moment, contemplating. 'The head of research at the institute has been courting me ever since I left. They seem to miss me there.'

'Would you ever go back?' Emma tried to sound casual, as if the answer didn't matter to her. It shouldn't, anyway, because entertaining any thoughts of both of them living in the same city long term was ridiculous. It implied an emotional connection where there couldn't be one.

Her heart twinged inside her chest when Mark shook her head with a resolute finality. 'I can't go back to that place—not for anything. It's where I lost everything that's ever been important to me.'

His voice came out in a strange monotone, and an instant later she saw those walls come up in front of his eyes. He looked at her, but his expression was guarded, not letting her see the exact effect those memories were having on him.

Strange thoughts were chasing each other in Emma's mind—thoughts she tried to stop. His answer shouldn't mean anything to her. She didn't want him to come to Rochester with her because she didn't want a relationship with him. So his answer shouldn't hurt the way it did.

'Even for someone on the go, four cardboard boxes seem like very little to fit your entire life into,' he said, changing the subject as they finished their breakfast. He was looking around the bare apartment with a strange expression.

An embarrassed heat shot into her cheeks as she followed his eyes. 'I left the city in somewhat of a hurry and only took the things that were important to me.' She stopped for a moment, considering her next words. 'I wanted a fresh start.'

His gaze narrowed on her. 'What did he do to you?' he asked, and Emma wasn't sure how to answer the question.

The hurt caused by Rob was something that still haunted her, even though he was miles away and had no more power over her now than she was willing to give him. The comparison between her failed relationship and her current entanglement was easy to make, but did it mean it was true? Mark was so different from her ex-boyfriend and he had shown her that ten times over. Maybe trusting him would be okay—as long as they remained clear that this was only a casual affair.

It wouldn't hurt her. She would make sure she wouldn't fall. She would not let anyone get close to her until she'd answered the question about her potential Gardner's diagnosis. No matter how different Mark was.

'He convinced me to give up my spot at the hospital to work under him at his private practice. I was worried that my training wouldn't be as well-rounded as I needed it to be. But he brushed these concerns aside, insisting on his need to develop his career as a plastic surgeon. He promised me that once he'd made a name for himself it would be my turn. When I told him they'd accepted me into a programme at the Whitebridge Institute that promise meant precious little. He refused to leave, trying to convince me that I would be better off as his staff anaesthesiologist and to give up my fellowship. When I wouldn't, he tried to discredit me in front of our contacts in the medical community. He couldn't cope with the fact that he had lost control over me.'

She paused for a moment, the memory of many abusive messages and late-night knocks on her door flooding back into her consciousness. Despite her best efforts to forget everything about Rob and his treatment of her, tears stung her eyes, and she blinked them away.

This wasn't a part of her life Emma had planned on sharing with anyone, and yet here she was, baring her soul to Mark right after they'd spent the night together. For a fleeting moment, she wondered what he would think if she told her that she might be sick, too. She had tried to reveal her secret to Rob, but her attempts had fallen on deaf ears. His main concern over her condition was whether or not it would impact on her work.

Would Mark feel deceived and lied to if she told him? Was she even obligated to talk to him about it?

The shame of her own shortcomings as a doctor burned in her chest and she hardly dared to look at him, too scared to see judgement in his expression. But his eyes were not chastising or demeaning. They shone with kindness. And something else hiding beneath. An unbridled fury.

In one fluid motion he got to his feet and pulled

her from her seat to crush her against his chest. He dipped his head to capture her mouth with his, wiping all thought from her brain.

'You are a powerful woman of amazing calibre. He is the villain in this story. You aren't to blame for believing his words were sincere when they weren't.'

He held her close, his low voice vibrating through her as she wrapped her arms around him, feeling again the sting of tears in her eyes.

'Believing the person you love is as natural as breathing. Don't blame yourself.'

Emma had been terrified of being judged. Yet Mark cradled her with affection, his hands stroking her back as she worked through the pain.

They remained like that for a moment, with her head lying against her chest. Then Mark's hands drifted from her back up to her neck, cupping each side of her face as he drew her into a gentle kiss.

'Look, I don't want things to be awkward between us,' he said when their lips had parted, his voice a low growl that vibrated all the way to her bones. 'You are an amazing woman of stunning beauty and I admire your skill as a doctor. I've told you how I haven't been in any kind of relationship outside of marriage, and I don't think I'm ready for anything serious. I don't know if I ever will be.'

'It doesn't have to be serious,' she replied in a whisper, convincing herself that this was the truth. The fact that she had just shared her past hurt with him didn't change the fact that she wasn't looking for love. It didn't matter that her heart beat against her chest, longing for the gentle kindness she had just seen in his eyes. 'I'm leaving in a matter of weeks. We can leave it at that. A clean cut.'

Emma knew they couldn't have more. Not when she might slip away at any moment, tumbling down the same path as her mother. The threat of her own condition dangled over her head, ever-present.

His firm hand became more demanding. He slipped it under her shirt as he pressed her against him, first caressing her back, before slipping to her front, cupping her breast in his palm as his thumb brushed over her reaching nipple. Her mind and body wrapped in the sensual cloud produced by Mark's touch and proximity, Emma took a deep breath in a futile effort to calm the storm raging within her.

All her thoughts were drawn to the present moment when Mark's hand slipped to her back again, crushing her against him as he deepened the kiss. His full length pressed against the apex of her thighs, his hunger as ravenous as it had been last night. Her hands wandered down his spine, and nimble fingers found the edge of his underwear. It fell to the floor with a single tug, drawing a growl from Mark's throat.

Emma gasped when he grabbed her by the waist and picked her up. She wrapped her legs around his midsection, and as she found her balance his tip found her entrance.

'Bedroom?' she asked between mewls, as his head dipped down to her breasts to lick and suck at her dark nipples.

'Right here,' he replied, with an imposing certainty that brought a shiver down to her core.

'Right here is good,' she said.

And she gasped again when Mark took two steps so

that her back leaned against the cold wall behind her. His hands cupped her buttocks as he angled himself, and a skipped heartbeat later her thighs trembled as he plunged into her.

# CHAPTER NINE

THE FOG AROUND Mark had lifted, and for the first time in ages he could breathe again. Not only could he live again, he could enjoy the company of a woman without having the soul-crushing weight of guilt sitting on his chest every step of the way. For that, he was grateful, and it was that feeling that made him want to spend himself with Emma over and over again.

Each night of the last week they'd ended up in Emma's apartment, arms and legs and hair intertwined until exhaustion took them. But he was worried about things getting messy.

Her confession of what had driven her to leave San Francisco left him in a state of perpetual fury each time he remembered how she'd been mistreated and discarded. To think someone had been cruel enough to waste her affection in such a manner brought Mark's blood to a boil.

So much so, he had to remind himself to stay grounded. The physical passion they shared ran so hot he needed to rein himself in. Despite how brilliant she was, he needed to be careful not to let his emotions stray. He was not at liberty to promise his heart to anyone, and he needed to stay within the boundaries they'd agreed on.

His broken self would never be enough for her.

Mark's gaze wandered over her now, and hunger was stirring in his chest when the soft buzz of his phone interrupted his lustful plans. Peeling his eyes away from her, he checked his messages and frowned.

'The oncologist has cleared Georgina for further treatment.'

Emma, curled up in his arms on the couch beside him, looked up with a furrowed brow. 'It took her a long time to stabilise after the strain of chemotherapy,' she said, giving voice to his thoughts. 'Can you ask them to send over the updated scans? We can look at them once they arrive.'

Georgina's recovery from her heart failure a week ago had been a slow and arduous process that troubled Mark more than he wanted to admit. So much about her case revived the memories he had buried alongside his wife.

Emma interrupted his contemplations when she wound herself out of his grasp to look through the journals and textbooks piled onto the coffee table.

'I remember reading about a case just like that…' she said.

'I don't think this is a medical mystery. I see it all the time in oncology. There was only a hint of metastasis on the scan before, too small for the naked eye. It will probably be visible on the scans now.'

He watched her with a small smile on his lips as she leafed through a journal. As he traced her voluptuous curves with his hands a fire ignited in his groin when she glanced over her shoulder with a suggestive wink, before putting her attention back on the journal in her hands.

Even a slight gesture like that was enough to re-awaken the searing passion within him. Emma had found a way around the daunting defences he'd built and nestled herself into a warm spot. She'd even got him to talk about his late wife without the oppressive darkness consuming him. In her presence he found himself free to appreciate his memories for what they were.

There was no way Mark would ever let himself love again. But he could be happy with a temporary affair. Emma was leaving in a matter of days, which would end their dalliance as painlessly as possible. There would be no misunderstandings about emotional attachment or love.

His eyes drifted away from the deliciousness that was her body to the different books lying around. Quite a few of them were textbooks specifically around oncology, with bookmarks sticking out of them to mark specific passages.

He opened the first book at a marker and inspected the passage. It was in-depth diagnostical research around Gardner Syndrome. Mark closed his eyes for a moment, recalling what he knew about the disease. His search for a cure, or even just an edge to help Claire survive longer, had put him in front of a lot of different types of cancer. He wasn't an expert in genealogy, but looking at what made certain conditions hereditary helped him understand the disease on a more fundamental level.

To his surprise, the next book had passages concerning genetic cancer diseases like Gardner Syndrome marked as well. 'What's your interest in Gardner's?' he asked, and watched as she paled. His chest constricted as a harrowing thought entered his mind. She wouldn't have kept that kind of information from him, right? 'Do you…?' His voice trailed off, and he sighed with relief when she shook her head.

But the silence enveloping them now was deafening as he watched a myriad of different expressions flutter over her face. Her chest rose and fell, becoming more pronounced as she put the journal down. She hesitated for a moment, licking her lips, and took a deep breath before she spoke.

'No, I don't think so.'

The relief washing over him was warped again as he interpreted her words. 'You don't *think* so? Do you have any family history?'

Emma swallowed visibly, her eyes darting around for a moment before looking at him again. There was another pregnant pause, as if she had to think about her answer. Was there some obscure relative who had once shown signs of the disease?

'My mother had Gardner Syndrome.'

Her *mother*? Gardner Syndrome could be passed on from parent to child. If a child had the genetic marker for the disease, part of the early prevention system was to get regular cancer screenings, so any potential tumours could be caught early. Why had she not mentioned it?

'When was your last scan?' he asked.

She squirmed under his knowing look.

A foreboding sense of dread settled in Mark's chest when Emma remained quiet, avoiding his probing gaze. Tension wound itself into a coil in his abdomen as he awaited her answer. He suddenly found himself in a situation so familiar that he felt the same naked fear creep out of the corners of his memories.

'I've had a prophylactic scan before my internship ended. But no official diagnosis.'

Mark swore under his breath and got up from the couch as hot fury replaced the chilling dread in his veins. 'Get dressed. We're going to the hospital right now,' he said, and picked up his clothing from where he had dropped it the night before.

'Mark, this isn't your problem,' Emma said, pushing her chin out with a defiant gaze.

'You are a doctor, Emma. Someone who works with cancer patients day in and day out. You know better than anyone what this disease can do to people, and yet you have not tried to ensure your own health is cared for when you know you might have a genetic condition.' He balled his hands into fists at her dismissive look. 'Have you even done the genetic test?'

Emma shook her head. 'My father urged me to get tested, but I don't want to. At least not yet...' She left the rest of the sentence unspoken.

Mark stared at her. He felt an icy hand gripping his insides as he came to understand the full gravity of the situation. Despite working with cancer patients every day, Emma hadn't looked after her own health and had ignored the potential diagnosis of a disease that could change her life in the worst possible way. How could she not have acted on this information? Did the people in her life mean so little to her? Did he?

'Why not? You have first-hand knowledge of what kind of situation this can be. Why would you not prepare yourself?'

'It's because of *this*, right here, that I didn't want to know. Now to you I'm Emma, potential Gardner Syndrome patient, rather than your…' Her voice choked and fear entered her eyes.

The tension within him dissolved when he caught that frightened look. Relaxing his hands and taking a deep breath, he forced himself to remain calm. The terror in her eyes had struck at his heart, and the twinging inside his chest was great concern for her.

Though that concern was almost overwritten by immediate detachment as his mind shifted into doctor mode and sought to create some distance between him and the situation. It was the same pattern of behaviour that had made him miss those last days with Claire. That wasn't the man he wanted to be.

He forced a couple of breaths into his lungs, reminding himself of the fear Claire's sudden revelation had struck in his heart. The same was true for Emma—only amplified by several magnitudes. And if he was scared in this moment, she must be terrified.

Could he be there for her the way he hadn't been able to be present for Claire? It wouldn't make up for his past failings, but maybe he would be able to reclaim something of the person he'd used to be.

Mark sat back down, putting his hand under her chin and lifting it so she would look at him.

'I never took the test because I've never felt ready to know,' she said. 'If I know I have the gene mutation I'll have to plan. I'll have to…make peace.'

Her voice faltered and tears fell down her cheeks. He wiped them away with his thumbs before pulling Emma into his arms.

'You don't have to get tested if you aren't ready.

But we should get you a scan at the very least. You know how much early intervention can help with a prognosis.'

Emma buried her face in his shoulder for a moment, before nodding.

'We'll get you in for some blood work, a CT and an MRI scan, so dress accordingly,' he said, before releasing her and putting on his own clothes.

It had been a few years since Emma had seen the inside of a CT machine. The last time had been just before her internship had ended. After learning about her mother's diagnosis, Gardner Syndrome had become a constant companion in her life. A source of chaos when she wanted control. Especially as Emma had got used to driving her destiny forward, pursuing her goals in her own way.

A terminal illness did not fit in with that plan, and she hadn't known how to control the chaos it had brought into her life. So she'd done what she knew best: she'd made a plan. It hadn't ben a good plan, she had to admit. But it had given her something to hang on to. Her life would move along the path she had planned until her fellowship ended, and then she would have time to cope with anything else.

Now, Mark's words kept replaying in her head—but, more than that, his experience as a surviving spouse of a cancer victim struck a terrifying chord within her.

Had she let things go too far? Their connection was explosive, their passion for each other infusing her mind and body alike. But the hurt in his face when she'd told him about her family history with Gardner's had taken her breath away. He'd seemed genuinely concerned about her wellbeing. And what that meant terrified her. Such concern didn't mix well with the casual nature of their affair. Was this another part of her life where she had lost control?

He had shared his struggles with her, let her see the uncensored pain that he kept hidden from anyone else. He'd trusted her, and that solidified her resolve. She couldn't permit herself to feel this surge of emotion bubbling beneath the surface of their casual entanglement. For her sake as much as his.

'We're almost done. Hang in there for a couple more moments.'

As if her thoughts had summoned him, Mark's voice came through the speakers of the machine, mixing the dread dwelling within her with something else that she wanted to focus on even less.

Emma pushed thoughts of him away as a shiver brought on by memories of his unreserved concern for her threatened to rock her body. His anger had scared her almost as much as her potential diagnosis. But behind it she'd glimpsed the true nature of his fury—a deep affection for her. It was a thought that scared her all over again. What if he wanted something from her that she couldn't give him?

The machine rattled and hummed around her and she closed her eyes to block out all thought. A moment later the noise stopped, and she was pulled out of the machine.

Mark waved her into a booth where her scans were already on a screen. Her gait was unsteady as nervousness flooded her system, and as much as she willed her head to turn, to inspect the scans, her eyes remained on Mark, watching his face for some kind of sign.

Relief washed away the dreadful uncertainty coiling in the pit of her stomach when he gave her a small smile accompanied by a nod. 'We're still going to do some blood work, but the scans look clean.'

Emma released her breath, only just noticing that she had been holding it all this time. 'That's good news.' With a sigh, she turned to the scans, running her eyes over them herself. 'No sign of any abnormalities.'

'This time,' Mark said, with a pointed note to his voice that made her flinch.

'Mark—' Emma started, but he raised his hands in defence before she could continue.

'I'm sorry. I said I was going to drop it and I will.' He got up from his chair and stepped closer to her, so she had to tilt her head to keep looking at him. 'I just worry about you.'

*Don't*, she wanted to say, but the word refused to cross the boundaries of her lips. Worry wasn't something that worked in the confinements of this affair they'd created. Concern implied something more substantial than she could permit in her life. Besides, he had been clear that he wasn't ready for anything beyond a physical relationship. She'd be foolish to believe otherwise.

His head dipped, his mouth brushing over her lips in the soft suggestion of a kiss. 'Let's go and get your blood drawn.'

Mark stepped away from her, and the void he left between them rushed into her awareness as a yearning unlike the one she'd experienced over the last week swept through her body. Its roots lay in comfort rather than desire, and it filled her with a gentle, cosy warmth.

She pushed those emotions away and followed him

through the door into an exam room, where he sat her down on the table as he put on gloves.

'You good?' He looked at her, his dark brown eyes still sparkling with the same concern that had driven him to demand to take her to the hospital straight away.

Emma watched as Mark drew her blood, all too familiar with the sight. 'Can you file this under Jane Doe? I don't want it to cause any trouble, should anyone hear about my blood being tested.'

'Sure. I was thinking the same thing—for the sake of your own privacy as well.'

He shook the vial, to make sure the blood mixed with the anti-coagulant, and pressed a piece of cotton wool against the injection wound. They sat there for a moment, his thumb pressing against the crook of her elbow while his other hand grazed over the inside of her hand in a reassuring motion.

'This will take a while, so we might want to think of something to do.' He looked at her, a mischievous grin curling his lips.

Emma laughed and rolled her eyes at him. 'We are in the hospital, Dr Henderson. Get your mind out of the gutter. I can list ten reasons why that is a terrible idea.'

He placed a plaster on the injection site and released her arm. 'Is that so?'

'One: while it's not specified in the employee handbook, it's implied that staff need to be clothed at all times. Two: I'm only here on a short-term contract, which can be dissolved at any moment. Three: have I mentioned this is a hospital?'

Mark interrupted her by standing up from his stool and towering over her, forcing her to tilt her head all the way back. His hands wove through her hair, pulling her face closer to his as he wrapped her in an indulgent kiss full of promise and potential.

Emma sighed, melting against him and forgetting every word she had just said. The spark of desire and the longing to give in to his suggestion cascaded through her and mingled with something else—an unbidden sprouting of deep affection for the man standing in front of her.

That affection would prove her undoing, something within Emma whispered, loudly enough for the meaning of the words to pierce her consciousness.

What if she got sick? How would that affect them? She could not let this kind of misguided affection take root in her heart. He'd been clear about his expectations of their fling…had even shown her the damage his wife's fate had left within him. Not only that, but Emma was headed to a place he refused to go.

With greater effort than she wanted to admit, she moved back out of reach of his lips and took a deep breath. 'You are trying to get me into trouble at this point.' Her voice sounded a lot more playful than she felt, and to her relief Mark stepped back, so she didn't have to rely on her sense of self-preservation alone. Because she knew if that was what it came to she would be in deep trouble.

'You're right, of course,' he admitted with a one-sided smile. He grabbed the vial and placed it in a transparent bag which he labelled 'Jane Doe'. 'Care to walk me to the lab?'

They walked in comfortable silence, and her thoughts wandered enough that she didn't notice they'd arrived at the lab until an intern approached her.

'I didn't realise you were already here. I've got the

scans from Mrs Williams ready, if you want to have a look.'

Emma furrowed her brow as her brain found its way back to reality, but Mark turned around beside her, looking at the intern. 'Let's see what we're working with here. Can you bring me a tablet loaded with the scans? We'll take it from there.'

The intern nodded, and only then did Emma catch up. 'Oh, Georgina's scans.' She frowned as she noted the time. 'It took her longer than I would have expected to be stable enough for a scan.'

Mark nodded, his grim expression a reflection of her own thoughts on the prognosis of this patient.

The intern brought the tablet, and Mark motioned Emma to follow him to his office, where he sat down behind his desk to look at the scans.

Emma moved around the desk so she could watch over his shoulder, the hair on her arms rising at her proximity to him. She squeezed her eyes shut for a moment, willing her thoughts away as she reminded herself that bigger things were at stake right now.

'There's nothing there,' he said, and sighed. They stared at the scans, each of them following their own diagnostic thoughts. 'I wonder if the chemotherapy shrank any metastasis before it became visible. Though that doesn't explain her heart failure, or her deteriorating health. She seemed fine last week.'

He swore under his breath, and for a moment Emma thought he might throw the tablet across the room. But he laid it down on the desk instead, burying his face in his hands. He was more tense than usual. She could see the strain this case had put on him was higher than with other cases they'd collaborated on. She thought of Georgina and Harald and their circumstances. Did the case remind him of his own struggles as a spouse?

'What can we do?' Emma picked up the tablet to look at the pictures again.

Mark sat up at the question, his eyes veiled with deep thoughts. 'We could go for another lymph node dissection. The first one didn't come back negative— it was inconclusive. The surgery itself is not as taxing if we go through a keyhole, although her body has already been through a lot at this point. I'm worried about what another surgery might do to her.' He sighed again, with a frown. 'I don't think she can stand any more radiation. Her condition is a lot more critical than I expected.'

A shadow flickered across his face. A well of pain was clearly springing to life within him. Emma got a glimpse of it for the duration of a heartbeat before his expression shuttered.

'Are you okay?' she asked. She wanted to understand the pain he was hiding from her, despite knowing it would be better if she didn't.

'I'm fine.'

The shortness of his answer hurt more than Emma cared to admit. He clearly wasn't fine, and while it was better for their entanglement if he didn't lean on her for emotional support, she found she wanted him to anyway. And she knew just what to do.

'Her oncologist won't be here until later. Let me take you somewhere before we plan Georgina's surgery.'

'Somewhere' wasn't far from his office. They didn't have to go very far before they reached their destination.

Emma twirled around in the greenhouse on the roof

of the hospital. The founder of the hospital had enjoyed the cultivation of medicinal herbs so much that he'd made it a permanent fixture. Mark had never been up here—his department needed a lot stronger medication than plants could yield—though he knew Emma had enjoyed some time up here among the plants for her own leisure.

Unsurprising, he thought, as he remembered how fond she had been of the flower garden in the park. However, Mark wasn't sure why she had brought him here now. Georgina's vitals were steady at the moment, but they weren't within a range that made him confident about performing surgery on her.

A strange desperation gripped him whenever he thought of her case, and a feeling of inadequacy clung to his heart with her every turn for the worse. Many patients had died before, and he knew he couldn't save everyone. But this had become a lot more personal than it should have, unearthing old insecurities that he'd thought he had left behind.

He hadn't been able to save Claire, and in trying he had made her suffer so much more than if he had admitted that he couldn't. Mark had been absent, driven by the wrong motivation. He hadn't wanted to lose her, but they had reached the point of no return. He had ignored that, instead focusing on forestalling the inevitable so he wouldn't feel the pain he'd seen barrelling towards him.

Georgina and her struggles had brought those memories back, confronting him with a time of his life when he'd been at his lowest.

And then there was Emma.

She led him by the hand through the greenhouse,

stopping now and then to show him an interesting plant before moving on. Her presence calmed him, but now he felt something else. She might be sick, too.

Mark had no right to feel deceived, yet that was one of the emotions battling for prominence inside his chest. They weren't a couple. He had established that firm boundary himself. She was under no obligation to tell him something that personal. Yet it still disappointed him that Emma hadn't. He had shared so much with her—much more than he had with any other person. It hurt to think she didn't have the same trust in him.

They'd arrived at the far end of the greenhouse. To Mark's surprise, he was staring at a cushioned swing bench.

'I'm not the only one who likes to seek refuge in here. It's very calming to be around plants,' Emma said, and sat down on the bench. 'I figured you needed some time away from your office to clear your head. Is Georgina's case getting the better of you?'

'Among other things,' he mumbled without thinking, and he scrubbed his hands over his face, feeling the strain of the last couple of hours draining all his remaining energy.

'Ah…' Emma breathed, noticing the subtext in his short answer. 'You think I should have told you about my potential diagnosis earlier?'

Mark looked up, searching his mind for an answer that wouldn't come. He opened his mouth, only to be interrupted by Emma waving her hand.

'Let's try something before we continue this conversation. We have a hard day ahead of us, so we need to feel fresh.' She moved to the far side of the bench and patted her thighs. 'Lie down here for a couple of moments.'

'On your lap?' Mark raised an eyebrow, unable to remove the scepticism from his voice.

'Just try it. If you don't like it I will release you.'

Emma indicated her lap again with an encouraging smile until Mark relented, lying down on his side until his head came to a rest on her thighs.

The sweet scent of coconut drifted up his nose, mingling with the fresh aroma of the herbs being cultivated in the greenhouse. He closed his eyes for a moment as he stretched out on the bench, his thoughts coming to a rest for the first time in hours.

Emma laid one hand on his shoulder while the other one ran through his hair, her fingers playing with the strands as she caressed his scalp. A deep sigh left his chest as each muscle in his body relaxed, one after the other. He didn't know how long they lay like that, with her fingers gently scratching his head, until Emma spoke again.

'Georgina's condition must hit close to home.' Her fingers didn't stop their caress, easing some of his stress. 'Do you feel you should be doing more?'

'No, I've done everything I should.' His voice sounded hollow. Those were words he had said to himself before.

'Does she remind you of Claire?'

Emma's words came out with a hint of hesitation. Was she uncertain whether she wanted to know? Did he even want to talk about this? Her hands felt so reassuring and calming. He didn't want to leave the warm bubble behind. But he sensed a disconnect within him—a myriad of emotions clashing with each other and brewing up a storm inside of him.

Georgina did remind him of Claire, of his loss and his failings. But, even more, Emma reminded him of how pain had almost destroyed him.

'She does,' he said. 'But so do you. A lot more than Georgina.' He paused for a moment, releasing a deep breath.

'I didn't know how to tell you,' she said. 'Not after hearing what you went through with Claire. I was afraid of how you would react to my wilful ignorance.'

She spoke from somewhere above him. He shifted around so he could look up at her. The fear in her eyes was something he was too familiar with. He had lived with the same terror for a long time.

His heart had almost fallen out of his chest as he'd waited for the results of Emma's scans to load up. An enormous sigh of relief had fallen from his lips when they'd come back clean. Mark had become a lot more attached to Emma than he should have allowed himself to. But the ghosts of the past still lived in his heart. He had failed to fulfil one of the most important promises he had made in his life.

*In sickness and in health.*

'This place has become important to me.'

The wistful tone of her voice drew his attention back to her, and he looked up to find her eyes with his. The emotion shining in them made his heart slam against his chest.

'This greenhouse?'

It was an obtuse question, but Mark needed something to deflect the truth he saw written in her face. She must not admit to feelings for him. They just couldn't go there.

'Yes, the greenhouse as well. It's been a haven when things are overwhelming. The scent of earth and petrichor reminds me of the time we went on holiday to the rainforest. I wanted to see a jaguar, but all we ever spotted were some bush rats.' Emma laughed at the memories, before falling quiet again with a contemplating look. 'But I meant Chicago. I didn't plan on getting attached to this place. But things changed. You changed them for me. We became something I never expected, and I…'

Her voice trembled, and Mark watched her swallow, as if there was a heavy lump in her throat. His pulse quickened, feelings of both warm affection and icy dread welling up in him. They weren't allowed to go there. Emma was leaving for the Whitebridge Institute, where she would do extraordinary things. It was the place where he had laid all his demons to rest, before turning his back on it for ever.

She might want to give it up for him, knowing he wouldn't set foot in this place again. But Mark didn't want to create a situation where she would feel compelled to choose one thing over another. He wasn't a person worthy enough to warrant such a sacrifice. Just as he couldn't put himself in a situation where he had to be a doctor and the spouse of a sick person at the same time.

The last time had broken him irrevocably. He couldn't let Emma go on with that sentence.

'Nothing has changed. This isn't more than two people enjoying each other's company.' The words he'd spoken turned to ash in his mouth and he swallowed the bitterness, not wanting it reflected in his expression.

Emma's hands stopped moving, and he felt her body stiffen under his head. 'What? A moment ago you were upset at me for not telling you about my condition sooner, and now you're telling me you don't care about me?'

The intimacy of the moment broken, Mark sat up to look at her. 'We're doctors. We should know these things about ourselves—which is why I pushed you to get scanned. How are you going to advocate for your patients when you can't face the truth yourself?'

Emma looked as if he'd struck her, her eyes wide in disbelief at his words. He'd regretted them the moment he said them, knowing that they did not convey everything he wanted to tell her. That she too had become important to him over the last couple of weeks.

He stood as if at the edge of a cliff, ready to fall for her but too terrified of what he saw beyond the cliff to move. It might be blissful happiness. Or another wave of unending heartbreak.

Mark couldn't tell her. The likely chance was that they were looking at the latter of those two things.

Emma stood, taking a few steps away from him towards a winding plant that was climbing its way up a trellis. Her hands were balled into tight fists hanging by her sides.

'I guess I was wrong about you,' she said eventually as she turned to face him again, her expression shuttered and unreadable.

Mark got to his feet with a sigh, feeling a pain stab through his chest that made it hard to breathe. He hesitated for a moment, unsure if he should explain himself any further or if the decision had been made for him. His hand hovered in the air as he thought about wrapping her in his arms. If this was to be the last time, he wanted to remember it. But he knew he would only make things worse by giving in to his selfish need for one last touch.

'I should check on Georgina,' he said, with a last look at Emma.

She had her back turned towards him, stiff as she processed what had happened between them. Her hand was touching a large, waxy leaf on the plant she stood in front of.

If there was such a thing as a good place to have this conversation, it was this one, Mark thought with a rueful smile. She would soon realise that he wasn't worth the heartache and live her best life away from him.

Those were the thoughts Mark leaned on as he left her in the greenhouse, struggling to cope with his own broken heart.

# CHAPTER TEN

THE NEXT COUPLE of days went by agonisingly slowly, but at the same time the hours seemed to be just flying by for Emma. The end of her contract was fast approaching. Soon she would have to pack up her life again and move to Rochester, finally starting her fellowship at the Whitebridge Institute. The moment she had been looking forward to since reading her acceptance letter.

Only now a heavy sense of regret had mixed itself into her excitement, bringing a bitter taste to her mouth. She was due to leave soon, and the connection between her and Mark had already all but fallen apart.

How had she ended up in the situation she'd told herself to avoid the second she'd laid eyes on him? The rules had been clear from the start. She wasn't to fall for her boss again.

Now that was the only thing occupying her mind.

She wanted Mark.

The rules, boundaries and walls she had drawn around her had done next to nothing to protect her heart from this incredible man. The moment they'd met, Emma hadn't been able to resist him. She'd let her guard down, and now she was paying for it.

The meetings between them since that day in the greenhouse had been tense, neither of them willing to mention what had happened.

How could she have been so close to confessing her love to him, only for him to pull away from her? It had just been about sex for him. The thought crushed her almost as much as his rejection, and she couldn't believe that her brain had misled her.

Words were one thing, but the concern he had shown when he'd learned she might be sick had convinced her that there might be more. That he might feel the same way. A silly, misguided notion, Emma now knew. He had been worried about one of his doctors being sick, not about her. He wasn't worried about losing her, because she meant nothing to him.

Emma shook those thoughts away as she wrapped up in the OR. This was her last surgery with this particular team, so she made her farewells to everyone on staff. Christine, the department's anaesthetist, had already returned to work, so Emma had handed over most of her active cases. The only one left was Georgina.

She had grown so close to the woman that she wanted to see her case through until her very last day. Even though that meant having Mark in her space.

A hot spear of hurt pierced her chest every time she saw him in the corridors, along with a sense of deep longing and affection. The feelings remained no matter how much she told herself that this was for the best. She should never have fallen for him in the first place.

With a sigh, Emma approached the nurses' desk and grabbed a tablet to check on Georgina's notes before she went into surgery in a couple of hours. They'd scheduled a full lymphadenectomy as her scans had once again come back inconclusive. Despite her fragile state, an exploratory surgical procedure remained their best option.

'You look glum,' Theresa said from behind the counter, catching Emma's attention.

'This is going to be my last surgery here. After this I'll hand over Georgina's case to your permanent anaesthesiologist.'

That wasn't the true reason for her gloomy mood, but it was plausible enough not to raise any suspicion. Though Emma hadn't counted on the well-connected head nurse.

'What? No, you can't leave yet. Not before you patch things up with Mark.'

Theresa's words made her feel as if someone had poured a pitcher of iced water into her veins, spreading a chilly shiver throughout her body.

'What? We didn't—'

Theresa waved her hand in front of her, dismissing any further objections. 'Please don't insult me by lying to me. I know everything that goes on in my department.'

'How could you possibly know?' Emma was in shock. If Theresa knew about their affair, how far had it spread in the hospital?

As if reading her thoughts, the head nurse shook her head. 'You weren't exactly subtle, with the way you were tiptoeing around each other, but don't be too worried. It's just us nurses who pay enough attention to notice something like that. You doctors are way too self-absorbed.'

Emma breathed a sigh of relief, though the sensation didn't last long when she looked at Theresa. 'Well, whatever it was, it's over now. He's made that clear.'

'I struggle to believe that. He was so reserved when he first started, but that changed after you arrived. There's no way he doesn't have feelings for you.'

A confusing heat ignited under her skin, mingling with the chill she had felt just moments ago. Mark had feelings for her? No, that wasn't possible. He had stopped her confessing her affection for him. Why would he have done that if not because he didn't love her? Or had she misread the situation?

Her thoughts were interrupted when the target of her contemplations arrived at the nurses' station. He glanced at Theresa for a moment, before turning to her.

'I've updated Georgina's surgical plan after consulting with the oncologist. You can find it in her file.'

Emma nodded, not daring to open her mouth. She searched his face for the same stabbing pain she felt in her chest, but his expression remained flat. Unyielding.

'I think you're wrong,' Emma said as she looked at Theresa before letting her gaze go back to Mark. 'I'll see you in the OR, Dr Henderson.'

Mark stood over Georgina, looking down at the incision site with his fingers wrapped around his scalpel. The way he'd planned the surgery, he'd put the scalpel on her skin and make a small incision right on her armpit, not much larger than the span between his fingertip and the second knuckle. Through the small opening, the resident surgeon assisting him would feed a small tube-shaped camera that would be their guide.

Mark himself inserted a long, staff-like instrument with a sharp claw at its end into the keyhole. His eyes left the patient and fixed on the monitor at his eye level to find their way to the lymph nodes. They were located close to the surface, so neither of the two instruments had to go far before they got to their goal and started extracting the lymph nodes.

They were just finishing up the first half of the lymph node extraction when a sharp beep demanded their attention.

Mark looked at Emma.

'Blood pressure is dropping,' she said, standing up from her stool, her creased eyebrows the only thing visible on her otherwise masked face. 'It's not a reaction to her anaesthesia.'

'Get me the portable ultrasound right now,' he barked at the resident standing next to him. He hurried to retrieve the small machine from one of the storage cases on the far side of the OR.

A drop in blood pressure could only mean blood loss somewhere. Scanning the screen in front of him, Mark could see that there was no bleeding where they had been working, so the cause must be located somewhere else.

The intern handed him the ultrasound, and Mark moved the gown from the patient's neck, rubbing some gel on her skin before placing the transducer on her shoulder.

The machine came alive with a whirring noise as he moved it around the other side of the armpit and down her ribs, finding no free-flowing liquid. Mark listened to the updates on her vital signs while he moved over to her chest. That was where he found the source of the loss of blood, and he swore.

'There must be a tear somewhere along her aortic

artery.' He looked up at one of the assisting nurses. 'Page someone from Cardio—we need to have an expert in here. You.' He looked at the resident, who was still holding the camera in place. 'Prep her chest. We're going to open her up to look at the aorta.'

While the resident worked fast to change the surgical field, Mark removed the camera and instruments they were working with before stepping up with a fresh scalpel.

'Heart-rate's dropping.'

Emma's distant voice altered him. If he could get to the heart fast enough, he could keep her alive until the cardiac surgeon arrived.

But Mark was not prepared for the devastation that he encountered there, and his years of training as a surgeon told him that there was nothing he could do to fix that kind of damage. The walls of the aorta had ruptured, weakened from the ongoing stress her entire body was under. Georgina had fought, but in the end they were going to lose her.

Emma picked up on his hesitation, stepping forward to look at the surgical field. 'What do you want to do?' she asked as he stood there, looking defeat in the eye.

'There's nothing we can do. The damage is too big.'

His voice sounded hollow, and the edge to it surprised him. He had been in this place many times before. People came to this hospital from all over the country after they had exhausted their first and second opinions. But with his stellar reputation came the drawback: the saw the hardest cases, so he lost as many patients as he saved.

This case had been different from the very start. Despite his experience as a doctor, he'd got attached

to Georgina and Harald. Their situation was so haunt-
ingly familiar to his own with Claire. Right down to
this moment now, where he couldn't save her.

By the time the cardiac surgeon arrived Mark had
already declared the time of death. One look at the
scene before her made the heart surgeon come to the
same conclusion.

'She was in danger before she got on your table, Dr
Henderson,' she said to reassure him, as he instructed
the residents to close the patient up.

Now he had to go and talk to Georgina's husband
about what had happened. A conversation he'd had so
many times in the past.

In his specialty Mark had learned early on to untangle himself from his patients so he could cope with
the emotion. Plenty of doctors ended up choosing different specialties for that precise reason, yet for him it
had always been a point of strength to comfort people
in their time of need. But at this moment, as he walked
out of the operating room, he felt a paralysing fear grip
him as the darkness came rushing back at him.

No matter how hard he fought to save his patients,
redemption for his past failings seemed out of his
grasp. He would always be the man defined by the
mistake he'd made with the person who had depended
on him the most.

'Mark, wait.'

Emma's voice made him stop mid-stride.

'Let me come with you.'

'I don't need your help to talk to a patient's husband.'

The hurt flickering over her expression for a mere
second pulled a tight string around his chest, making
him regret the lack of control over his tone.

'I'm sorry.'

'It was a rough surgery.'

She closed the distance between them, grabbing his hand and squeezing it for a moment before letting it go. The warmth of her touch lingered on his skin, shining a faint light into the dark fog inside him. He could sense relief for a moment, a yearning for the short reprieve to be permanent. But he didn't dare to get used to it or it would prove his undoing.

She had awoken something in him he'd believed long dead, and the thought of examining that something more closely sent pangs of terror through his chest. He'd let their affair go too far, and now he was fighting an internal battle on how to take it back.

Emma had been brilliant, filling his plagued soul with life and laughter. She'd shown him there was still hope for him when he'd believed it all gone. But was he strong enough to go through all this again?

Doubt clawed at his heart, reaffirming the decision he'd made several days ago to distance himself from her. The thought of losing her down the line, of having to bear the weight of the entire world on his shoulders again, filled him with a cold anxiety that kept him up at night.

Mark hated to admit it, but if he hadn't been strong enough back then, how could he be strong enough now? Emma deserved someone who could carry her all the way, no matter what the ending looked like.

'I'll go and inform Harald about the surgery.'

The same news that Mark himself had heard two years back. Words he had delivered to patients countless times without his own chest feeling tight with the pressure of anxiety. Nothing should be different this time around. But something inside him had shifted, making announcing the outcome of this surgery almost unbearable.

Gritting his teeth, Mark swallowed the anxiety spreading through his chest as he approached Harald, who was waiting in Georgina's room for news about his wife.

Georgina's death shook the entire oncology department when news of the surgery spread.

Emma stood at the nurses' station, filling out the paperwork both Mark and Harald would need to sign.

Emma's heart went out to both men. Mark liked to seem detached with his patients, hiding behind the professional distance he put between himself and his cases. But she knew the bad outcome of this one had impacted him. Everyone had fought so hard to keep Georgina alive.

Emma sighed, picking up the piece of paper and starting the walk to Mark's office. She wanted to drop the paper by his desk and then leave this place behind.

A small voice within her urged her to check in on Mark, to make sure he was okay, even though she wasn't sure he even wanted to see her. His nerves must have been shot after the surgery. But he had never snapped at her like that. Could it be that he really didn't care for her at all?

Emma pushed those thoughts away as she knocked on his door before opening it.

Mark sat on the couch, his face briefly lifting to see who entered. When he saw her, his expression softened, and he let himself slump backwards with a heavy sigh on his lips.

Emma put the paper on his desk before sitting down

next to him, leaving a hand span of space between them. They sat there in sombre silence for a few heart-beats, each one chasing their own thoughts about to-day's events.

Emma grew more tense, the uncertainty between them wrapping itself around her shoulders and chest, making each breath harder than the last. Would he re-ject her offer of comfort and ask her to leave?

She knew they weren't on good terms, but they had both lost a patient they'd been working with since she'd first started there. Despite their very painful relation-ship, she couldn't leave him without another word when Georgina's death had impacted him so much.

As if sensing her tension, Mark reached out and pulled her into his arms without a single word. Her head came to rest on his shoulder and she felt his warmth seeping through her skin, reminding her of a time when things had been simpler.

His chin rested on the top of her head as his fingers trailed up and down her spine, leaving tiny goosebumps as they went. She wanted nothing more than to enjoy being in his arms once more, to let herself be carried away by his touch the way she had in the last couple of weeks. But she couldn't trust his intentions. Hadn't he rejected her just a couple of days ago?

'Mark…' she whispered, and felt his arms around her tighten.

'I broke an important promise,' he said in a quiet voice.

She twisted out of his arms to look at him. 'What? You didn't promise Harald and Georgina a good out-come.'

She tried to catch his eye, but Mark kept on staring ahead, deep in thought.

'No, I broke my promise to Claire. I promised to be there for her, but when the time came I couldn't do it.'

He moved away from her, burying his face in his hands. Emma laid her hand on his back. She'd come here to comfort him—one last act of affection before she left him and this city behind for ever. Only she didn't want to walk away if there was a chance for them. In all her life she had never felt so connected to another person that it had changed her life in a profound and meaningful way. She knew she was in love with Mark.

Maybe Theresa was right, and he felt something, too. He had been the one to break things off, but in this moment, when he was vulnerable, he leaned on her.

'What happened?' she asked when he remained silent.

'Claire... She was getting better. But her oncologist was still cautious, warning us that it might just be a second wind. I knew that, of course, and I'd seen it myself in so many patients. After seeing her scans, as a doctor I should have told myself to prepare for the worst. I knew that—and yet I didn't. Instead of being there for her as she deteriorated I was in the lab, chasing an impossible cure, when I knew full well I was decades away from any results.'

Mark's voice was calm, but Emma felt his muscles tense under her touch. He still carried so much guilt around when he had reacted little differently from any other spouse—clinging to hope, however unlikely it was.

'You tried to fight it your own way,' she told him. 'Some family members do little more than sit there and pray while the doctors do their best to make a good outcome happen. You were different, having an entire research department at hand. It's only natural that you'd seek an answer there.'

Mark lifted his head to look at her, a haunting expression in his brown eyes. 'Maybe that's true. But my mad dash to the finish line was no more than a distraction. The woman I married was fading away in front of my eyes, and I couldn't be there for her. I got distracted, wanting to save myself the pain of losing her rather than paying her attention in her last days.'

It was something Emma understood well. It had been one of the hardest things to watch her mother grow weaker every day. Some days it had been too much to sit by and watch her suffer. In those times she'd had to look no further than her family. They'd made sure her mother was never alone while she and her father got some space to mend themselves.

'You were all by yourself?' Emma asked, to confirm her suspicion.

Mark looked puzzled for a moment, as if he didn't understand the relevance of the question. 'It was just me and her.'

'No wonder you struggled. The death of a spouse is one of the toughest times in many people's lives—especially when you have to deal with it all alone. Haven't you noticed how many people our patients surround themselves with?'

Emma paused for a moment. She wanted to reach out to him, pull him back into her arms. She had never realised the extent of the hurt he still carried around with him, how much he blamed himself for what had happened.

'My father and I shared the burden with my aunts

and uncles, each of us staying with her while the rest looked after ourselves.'

'But I grew distant, anticipating the pain and looking for a way to minimise it,' he said. 'I chose to be selfish.'

His voice sounded brittle, as if he was going to break at any moment. Emma's chest constricted. She was feeling his pain in her own body.

'No, you did what anyone would have done under mounting and unrelenting pressure. You reached the end of your rope. There was no choice but to let go.'

'I…want to believe that's true…' Mark hesitated before looking at her again.

The expression on his face was a mixture of gratitude and the mental anguish he had been putting himself through over the years. And Emma knew he understood everything she'd said to be true. She had heard himself say those things to patients when they were struggling. Harald had been one of those cases where the next of kin didn't have any immediate family for support. But Mark ran a team of compassionate doctors and nurses, who were all willing to step in when any of the over-extended spouses needed a break.

'Is that why you won't admit what I know we're both feeling? Because you want to keep punishing yourself for being human?'

'Emma…' His voice trailed off as he searched for the right words.

'I love you,' she said. 'I tried hard not to fall for you, but that turned out to be harder than I expected. You are a good and kind man, who deserves to be happy.'

She had to say it or she would regret it for ever. If there was even the whisper of a chance that what she sensed between them was true, she needed to know she'd tried.

Her life was complicated, and the addition of a potential Gardner Syndrome diagnosis made it so much harder. The last thing she wanted was to inflict the same anguish on him again. But it wouldn't be the same. Her family would surround him—*their* family—and they would help him get through it. Wouldn't that be worth the happiness they could find with each other?

The burdens of his past which he had been carrying around for the last two years were lifted from his shoulders. He had never thought to confide in anyone until this moment, too troubled by his failings. But to his own surprise he felt lighter, more at peace with his memories.

Emma's hands were still on his chest, keeping him grounded as her sparkling green eyes encouraged him to bare his soul to her. And Mark noticed that he wanted to. For years he had been the bearer of his own memories, fighting off anyone who stepped too close to him. Thinking that he didn't deserve kindness or love ever again—not after breaking the most important promise he had ever made. He wasn't trustworthy, and as penance he had thought he must carry the guilt of it around for the rest of his life.

Until Emma had appeared in his life just a few weeks ago.

But when she'd said those words—the ones he'd imagined her saying in the dead of night as he'd watched her drift off to sleep—a thrill of terror entered his chest.

He got up from the couch abruptly, crossing the room in long strides to put some distance between them. Raking his hands through his hair, he looked up to the ceiling as he tried to find his composure. Deep down in his heart he wanted to say it back. He loved her too. But fear struck hard, much harder than he'd imagined, drowning out everything else in him.

'I can't do this again,' he said with a lump in his throat, and he looked at Emma.

A torrent of hurt engulfed her eyes. 'Because I could be sick? That's the reason you're going to deny everything that's gone on between us?'

Mark shook his head, trying to make sense of the onslaught of different feelings rising within him. Her words from earlier rang in the air, and he searched their meaning for truth. Despite hearing about all his demons, and knowing how he had failed Claire, Emma was ready to forgive him.

But was she ready to put the same kind of trust in him? How long would she have kept that secret to herself? He couldn't help but wonder, and the small voice in the back of his head whispered those words in his ear.

'You didn't tell me you were sick until I stumbled upon the information myself.' His eyes snapped back to her as he crossed his arms in front of his chest. 'Would you even have told me if I hadn't confronted you about it?'

Emma swallowed, pale under her usually tanned skin as she took his words in. 'You must know that's an impossible question to answer. I didn't think I would fall for you, so I didn't think it would be necessary to talk about it. The plan was for me to leave without you.'

His jaw felt tight, and Mark took a few breaths to relax, though the exercise did precious little to calm his inner turmoil. 'After everything you knew about me, you kept it from me. How did you see that playing out?'

'Why are you acting like you're entitled to know every detail of my medical history?' Emma got to her feet as well, her hands balled into fists by her sides. Her eyes narrowed to a glare. 'You were the one who told me this was only a physical relationship. I don't tend to share that kind of information with men I don't mean anything to.'

Her words hit harder than Mark had anticipated, stabbing a searing pain into his chest. She wasn't wrong. He *had* been the one to insist on a purely physical affair, because he'd wanted to avoid exactly this kind of moment.

'Would you get a genetic test if I asked you to?'

He didn't know why he'd asked that question, but he wanted to know. There wasn't anything she could tell him that would convince him that not knowing was better than knowing. He couldn't live in that kind of vacuum—just waiting for the sword above their heads to drop. Though he wasn't sure if he would give them a chance even if she said yes. What if he wasn't strong enough again?

Emma hesitated, a deep frown on her face. She clearly hadn't expected that question.

'I haven't thought that far ahead. Would that change your answer? You need to know whether I'm sick or not to decide if you want to be with me?'

She paused, looking at him with expectant eyes, waiting for him to deny it. Mark stayed silent. Only their breaths were audible.

'That can't be true. That's not the man you are, Mark.'

'Then you don't know me as well as you thought you did.' He had to force the words out of his mouth, and the taste of them turned bitter when her face contorted in pain.

'Mark, I don't do ultimatums. Not any more.'

Her voice sounded hollow, without any of the warmth and affection he had heard just a few moments ago.

'I was stuck for too long, wasting time I didn't have. You either want to be with me or you don't. Whatever a genetic test says shouldn't matter.'

'It's not just your life that hangs in the balance in this situation. You picture it as a black and white question…a yes or no answer. But it goes far beyond that.' He rubbed his hands over his face, his chest constricting with the pain of the words.

'But it is. It's *my* life, and I'm the only one who gets to decide what I'm comfortable with. That's the deal you're buying into if you want to be with me.'

Mark dropped his head for a moment, scrubbing over his hair with his fingers. Terror constricted his chest, pushing the air out of his lungs to the point where it became hard to breathe as history repeated itself in front of his eyes. As much as he regretted it, he knew he wasn't strong enough to withstand another storm.

He shook his head, unable to utter another word.

'You're right. I really don't know you at all.'

Her voice trembled when she said that, and a shaky smile pulled at the corners of her lips as she turned to leave.

The urge to stop her leaving, to wrap her in his arms and never let her go, burned through him, and it took every ounce of self-restraint for Mark to keep his distance.

Emma looked at him for one last glance, a silent plea in her eyes. He dropped his eyes to the floor, releasing the sigh he had been holding in when he heard the door open and close.

# CHAPTER ELEVEN

WEEKS HAD PASSED since Emma had left Attano Memorial, and Mark was still waiting for things to go back to the way they were. Each day he woke up thinking things might be easier today, and each day brought a new disappointment.

He missed Emma in the corridors of the oncology department, spreading cheer and compassion among staff and patients alike. He missed her in the OR, where her calm voice had helped him navigate the most difficult surgeries. Most of all he missed her in the part of his heart that had been an open wound since the day she'd left.

His grief over the life he couldn't give her, the life he couldn't permit himself to have, clung to his soul like black tar, making it hard to breathe.

He'd done the right thing, hadn't he?

The nagging question at the back of his mind was the worst part about trying to move on. It struck at him in the quiet moments, when he was trying his best not to think about Emma and how she was doing.

'Mark?'

Theresa's voice jerked him out of his gloomy contemplations. 'Sorry, what were you saying?'

The head nurse raised her eyebrow at him. 'I said hello. Are you okay?'

He looked at her for a couple of breaths. Mark was almost certain that Theresa knew about his feelings for Emma, even though she had never outright said anything.

'One day I hope to be,' he said. He didn't want to lie to her, but the conversation she was trying to start was not one he wanted to have right now. All he wanted was a few quiet moments to grieve for the future he had denied himself. 'I have to go.'

A thought entered his mind as he analysed the inner turmoil he was going through. Grief. That was what he'd felt for the last couple of weeks. Grief over Emma, over their relationship and their future together. It was an emotion he was intimately familiar with.

Mark glanced at his watch. Just a couple of minutes past noon. If they hadn't changed the schedule since he'd last visited, they would start in a couple of minutes. His next surgery wasn't until later in the afternoon, so he had the time.

In a snap decision he went to the psychiatric floor, to see if the support group for surviving spouses was still meeting at the same time and place where he had first attended meetings on his arrival in Chicago.

A familiar sight unfolded in front of him when he pushed the door open. A bunch of chairs stood in the centre of the room, making a circle so the people sitting down could all face each other. With no empty chairs remaining, Mark moved to one side of the room where they had laid out refreshments, pouring himself a coffee as the meeting started.

When he had first arrived in Chicago he hadn't

wanted to hear anything about 'processing' his grief, or the different stages he would go through as he came to terms with his wife's death. But when Theresa had learned that he'd lost his wife she'd asked him to attend, telling him that he might be able to recommend the group to the surviving spouses of patients who were going through a similar experience.

The counsellor there, along with the members of the group, had made him reflect on his actions and his emotions, helping him to unpack most of the issues he'd been dealing with. Despite his initial resistance, he'd ended up attending the meetings for several weeks before stopping.

He'd listened to different people speak, discussing their thoughts and feelings. He'd recognised a lot of their thought patterns in himself when he'd first dealt with the loss of Claire. He'd felt as if he himself hadn't moved on that far, still struggling some days, but on hearing other people discuss their pain he'd realised how far he had come in dealing with his own inner demons. They still lurked in the shadows of his mind, but he had learned to deal with them, their darkness no longer consuming his mind.

After an hour, the group dispersed, some of them moving to his side of the room to grab refreshments. Mark was about to leave when a familiar voice stopped him.

'Dr Henderson. I didn't expect to see you here.'

Harald Williams approached him, stretching out his hand in greeting. The shadows under his eyes were familiar ones. The nights were one of the worst things to deal with. The empty spot in bed a constant reminder of what was missing.

'Mr Williams, what a pleasant surprise.'

Harald showed a weak smile. 'One of your staff members suggested this group to me when I came to pick up Gina's things.'

Mark raised an eyebrow. 'After everything that's happened, I didn't think you would want to set another foot in this place.'

'Why not? I know you did everything you could to save Gina.' Harald seemed surprised by Mark's suggestion.

'Don't you find it overwhelming to be in the space where she died? Reliving those terrible memories every time you come here?' Mark looked around at the faces of other people, to see if he recognised any of them, wondering if they had all lost someone here at Attano Memorial.

'I prefer to think of the good times we spent here. Like when I gave her a bunch of crazy haircuts as she lost her hair. Or the time I spent reading to her when she was getting her treatment. Gina loved to read, but the chemo left her so drained. I took over, reading aloud to her.' He stopped for a moment as he relieved his memories, a small smile on his face. 'But what are you doing here? Is everything okay with Dr Santos?'

Mark looked at him, his eyes wide in surprise. 'Dr Santos? Oh, no, my wife died two years ago.'

Harald sighed. 'Gina was sure you two were going to make it. She thought you would be happy together.'

'I don't know if I can ever be happy again. Feels like I had my one chance at that and it didn't work out.'

The words left his mouth before could stop them. Something about Harald was strangely disarming, when Mark had never been talkative during the support sessions, preferring to listen to others rather than speak himself.

To his surprise, Harald chuckled. 'You're not going to find happiness if you fight it so hard. Do you think that's what your wife wanted? Gina would have my hide if I let her death bind me to the past. She'd want me to be happy when I'm ready for it.'

When he was ready for it? Was that the struggle he'd been feeling all this time? Was his heart telling him he was ready to take the final step? But how could he know that was what it was?

Harald's words reached him at his very core, with Mark almost gasping as things fell into place within him. He had made a mistake, letting the ghosts of his past prevent him from remembering the good times he had in his marriage.

Despite her illness, he and Claire had spent so much time laughing with each other, cherishing the moments, knowing they were going to be their last ones together. Claire had made him say goodbye every time he left the room—made him swear he wouldn't make her an anchor. She had tried to save him from living a solitary life where he denied himself love in her name because he had promised to be with for ever.

Hadn't he done just that?

They walked out of the room, and Harald waved at him as he left. Mark went back to the oncology department, his thoughts racing as a decision formed in his head.

He'd made a mistake in letting Emma go. Gardner Syndrome, working in Rochester—none of it mattered. They were all just excuses to keep up the self-destructive cycle he had been going through the last two years of his life. His demons weren't attached to a place or a specific memory. He'd let them remain within him.

No more. That pattern ended today. He wanted Emma, and he would fight for her.

He arrived at the nurses' station, where Theresa was still sitting behind the computer. 'Can you page Dr Fremo? He needs to take over the surgery for a while.'

Theresa furrowed her brow. 'What's going on?'

'I need to leave. Page him. I have to know he can take over my patients before I head out.'

Everything within him urged him to get to Rochester as soon as possible. If he left now, he could be there by the evening.

'Okay.' Theresa lifted the phone and dialled Dr Fremo's pager number before hanging up. 'Where are you going?'

Mark hesitated for a moment, not sure how much he wanted to share. The gleam in the nurse's eyes, however, told him she had guessed. 'You know where I'm going.'

A big grin parted her lips. 'You're going to Rochester!'

Theresa reached into the drawer under the table, grabbing something. She tossed it at him, and something heavy and metallic landed in his hands. His car keys.

'Wait—why do you have keys to my car?'

'Just go. I can move things around so our patients are cared for.'

Mark grinned, holding up the keys. 'We're going to have a conversation about this, Theresa,' he said, before he turned around and hurried to his car, praying that he hadn't wasted too much time.

\* \* \*

Emma sighed when she looked out of the window. The sun had set a couple of hours ago, but she was nowhere near ready to leave. Her apartment contained little comfort outside of the plants she had brought with her. She'd rather distract herself with work.

The few weeks she had spent at the Whitebridge Institute so far had been an eye-opening experience. The brightest medical minds of the country were at her disposal, teaching her everything she needed to know about emergency medicine.

Her switch in specialties was a jarring one that kept Emma on her toes. Her patient care was a lot more hands-on now, requiring her to work more with patients and general medicine. It was a challenge she relished. But it came with its own unique set of stumbling blocks. The most painful one being her broken heart.

When she'd left Attano Memorial that evening, nothing had prepared her for the devastating heartbreak. It had left her numb, and she'd barely managed to put her life together once more and move up here.

But, despite her sadness over how things had ended between her and Mark, she wasn't sad that it had happened. She wanted to be with him. Her entire body ached with the longing for his warm embrace. But deep down within her she understood his hesitance. It hurt, but she knew she came with a lot of baggage. And, as much as her heart was bleeding inside her chest, the affair with Mark had helped her realise a lot of things about herself.

One of them being that she needed to know her diagnosis. Today.

Life was short, even without the possibility of a

terminal disease hanging over her head. She wanted to have fun, to travel the world, to fall in love. To do that she needed to know what was going on inside her body, no matter how much it might scared her. Whatever the result might be, she wanted to be in charge of her future.

So now Emma sat in one of the exam rooms in the ER. On the table in front of her spread out were a couple of cotton swabs, some vials containing different liquids, and a syringe to draw her blood. Despite the pain his memory caused her, she knew she had to thank Mark for her newfound courage.

Emma had picked up the first cotton swab, rolling it over her arm to prepare herself for the blood draw, when a knock on the door interrupted her.

'What is it?' she asked, irritation colouring her voice. She had waited until she was sure she was alone to do this.

An intern poked her head into the exam room. 'There's someone here to see you.'

Emma raised her brows. 'Who is it?'

The intern shrugged. 'Don't know him, but it looks like a new doctor's starting here.'

A new hire? Making the rounds this late at night?

'Tell him to come back tomorrow. I'm done with my shift for today.'

The intern vanished and Emma tied the band around her arm, rolling up her sleeve as she balled her hand into a fist to help her find a suitable vein.

'Oh, don't worry about it. She won't mind. She's going to marry me, though she doesn't know that yet.'

The familiar voice sent hot and cold showers down her spine.

'Sir, I really can't…' she heard the intern say.

But a moment later Mark stood in the exam room, all tall and handsome just like she remembered. He smiled at her, a smile full of affection and care, and then his eyes darted downwards, looking at her arm.

'What's happening? Are you okay?'

But before Emma could say anything, still stunned by his sudden appearance, Mark nodded knowingly and was soon sitting down and pulling gloves over his hands. He took the syringe out of her hand. When he'd finished drawing her blood, disposing of the used needle and gloves, she finally found her voice again.

'What are you doing here?' she said, her voice only a whisper. She was still in shock over his sudden appearance.

'I'm here to apologise for how much of a complete idiot I was,' he said as he grabbed the cotton swabs, popping them out of their sterile packaging.

He took one swab and placed his hand on her cheek. His thumb grazed over her lip for a moment before he poked it with his index finger, prompting her to open her mouth. He swished over the inside of her cheeks twice, each time rolling the wooden end of the stick in his fingers. Once done, he unscrewed the plastic vial with the liquid in it, dropping the swab in with the cotton end first. He placed the lid back on top, then put it on the table.

'I was scared of how important you had become to me…how impossible it would be to lose you.'

Mark had lowered his voice. His hand grasped hers, easing her fingers apart so he could weave his through them.

'No, I was wrong to—' Emma stopped when he shook his head, his hand squeezing hers.

'I've realised that this kind of fear has been ruling my life for the last two years, and it took watching you walk away for me to understand how much I was denying myself my true feelings out of fear of pain.' He paused and lifted her hand to his mouth, breathing an airy kiss onto her skin. 'I love you, Emma. I want to be with you. And I don't care what might happen. I know we'll brave anything that comes our way.'

Emma's heart beat against her chest in a near frantic motion, fast enough for her to hear her blood rushing through her ears. He was here. Of all the days he could have picked, he'd come today. When she'd decided to find out the truth once and for all.

Although one thing was burning a hole in her chest. 'But I can't leave here—not now.'

Mark shook his head. 'I came here knowing full well what it meant. It's true that this place holds a lot of my past pain, but that isn't strong enough to hold me back. I'm yours, and if you'll have me I'll move anywhere to be with you.'

Tears stung her eyes, and she blinked a few times. Unable to find the right words to say, instead she stood up from her chair, pulling him from his and wrapping her arms around his neck. He hid his face in her curls, kissing her neck before letting her go long enough so that his mouth could find hers in an indulgent kiss full of all the longing and affection they'd been nurturing for each other.

'I'm so glad you came today,' Emma said when she took a moment to wipe a stray tear off her cheek.

'Are you having another scan?' he asked.

Emma nodded, pressing her head against his chest, finding comfort in the familiar scent of pine that surrounded her. 'Scans to make sure I'm still cancer-free…' She hesitated for a moment. 'And a genetic test to find out whether I have Gardner Syndrome.'

Mark pushed her away from him, his eyes wide in surprise. 'Are you sure? I don't care what the test says, and I would never ask you to do this for me.'

Emma nodded, her resolve strengthened. 'I'm doing it for me. For us.'

Mark pulled her into another kiss, and Emma melted against his powerful frame. All the worry and the anguish she'd been carrying around fell away from her. Her stomach had turned when she had first recognised his voice as he'd spoken to the intern, but now she felt lighter than she had in weeks.

'Wait—my intern said you're the new doctor working here… And what was that about marrying you?'

Mark chuckled, a wide grin on his face. 'I think we have a few things to talk about.'

Emma's heart sighed as relief washed over her. They both understood the risk. Despite that, he wanted to stand by her. Whatever the result of the test might be, Emma knew she would be okay. Mark would make sure she was.

# EPILOGUE

'PAULO, *QUIDADO*!' EMMA flinched as her son came tumbling down the lawn. His cousin sprinted over, pulling the boy back on his feet as they continued their game of *futebol*.

'You worry too much—he's fine. I've heard his mother is a doctor of incredible talent,' said a voice behind her, and Emma looked up.

Mark sat down next to her on the warm stone porch overlooking the back yard of their house on the outskirts of Rio de Janeiro.

They had become Paulo's parents a month ago, after spending the better part of the last year going through the adoption process. Emma's genetic test had come back clean, clearing her of any further prophylactic treatments or scans for Gardner's Syndrome. But despite her clean bill of health they decided to go down the adoption route when they'd met Paulo on their most recent trip to Brazil—a journey they'd taken to get married.

Together they had planned their wedding, opting for a small beach ceremony so the entire Santos clan could attend. One of their guests had told them about the small non-profit clinic he ran in the *favelas*, piquing their interest. Emma's fellowship had been about to end, and they'd started to discussing what to do next. They'd both wanted to do something where they would make a difference.

When they'd gone to see the clinic, a young boy had come in on his own, with a large cut on his upper arm. Emma had spent some time talking to him while she patched him up, and through that conversation she'd learned that he had lost his parents months ago and had since then been living on his own.

That was when they'd both known they wanted to live in Brazil permanently. Their skills were needed, and they had just met their son. Both had known the instant they spoke to him that it was meant to be. Just as *they* were meant to be.

When they'd returned to the States after their wedding they'd wasted no time before arranging their permanent move to Brazil, so they could make their plans for a family a reality.

Emma leaned against Mark with a small smile on her face as she watched the children kick the football around with an abundance of energy and vigour. When she'd taken the test and it had come back negative, a whole new world of possibilities had unfolded in front of her. Things she hadn't dared to dream about had suddenly become a reality because she had known she would be around to see it all through.

And it was thanks to Mark that she'd found the courage to take that step. She'd gone to Chicago to escape the heartbreak of her previous life, not knowing that she was taking the first step in her new life. A life with Mark by her side. He was her rock when she needed him most, pushing her beyond her comfort zone and daring her to grow.

Emma knew that with him by her side nothing bad could ever happen.

* * * * *

# COMING SOON!

We really hope you enjoyed reading this book. If you're looking for more romance, be sure to head to the shops when new books are available on

## Thursday 31st March

To see which titles are coming soon, please visit
**millsandboon.co.uk/nextmonth**

# MILLS & BOON®

## Coming next month

### FORBIDDEN FLING WITH DR RIGHT
JC Harroway

At Darcy's front door, she fumbled with her key in the lock, her heart pitter-pattering in anticipation and fear of them being alone in her empty house.

Darcy breathed through the panic of her ill-judged invitation. Already she had a head full of erotic visions involving Joe, except now that they'd worked as a team to save Holly, that he'd needed her in moment of alarm... that meant something more to her than the physical attraction there since that first day they'd met.

Did he see her as an equal...?

In the kitchen Darcy dropped her bag, flicked on the lights and then the kettle. She reached overhead for two mugs with jittery fingers, the hair at the nape of her neck rising with awareness of Joe in her kitchen, filling her personal space with his magnetic aura. When she turned to face him, prepared to fake a bright smile and make small talk or resurrect the personal conversation they'd begun in the car, he'd stepped closer.

Face to face, a mere pace apart.

Darcy fell into the depths of Joe's stare and all thoughts of conversation dispersed.

Heartbeats pulsed through her like lightning strikes, marking the seconds they stood in tense silence.

He raised his arm, slow and steady to brush back that stubborn lock of her hair determined to reside on her cheek.

As if conditioned to his touch, Darcy turned her face into his palm, part of her craving more, craving it all. 'Joe…' His name passed her lips all breathy and pleading. For what? She wanted him physically, of course, but they had complication written all over them, the space between them an emotional and professional minefield.

He was still grieving the death of his daughter and perhaps even the demise of his marriage, and before meeting him, she'd sworn to focus on her career, a career she stood to jeopardise if they started something personal. Even sex would be a far from straightforward exchange between two people who shared insatiable chemistry, for good or bad. Come Monday morning she'd have to face him, he'd still be her boss. She needed his reference for her consultant position applications.

Could she risk clouding their work dynamic just for sex?

'I want you,' he said, his expression starkly open and honest.

Overwhelming need built inside Darcy, its pressure centred between her legs.

'I've tried to resist,' he said, his voice full of gravel, 'but I'm failing badly.'

Darcy wavered. Joe's eyes brimmed with repressed emotion. He was clearly experiencing the same conflict tugging Darcy in two different directions.

*Continue reading*
**FORBIDDEN FLING WITH DR RIGHT**
by JC Harroway

*Available next month*
www.millsandboon.co.uk

# MILLS & BOON

## THE HEART OF ROMANCE

## A ROMANCE FOR EVERY READER

**MODERN**

Prepare to be swept off your feet by sophisticated, sexy and seductive heroes, in some of the world's most glamourous and romantic locations, where power and passion collide.

**HISTORICAL**

Escape with historical heroes from time gone by. Whether your passion is for wicked Regency Rakes, muscled Vikings or rugged Highlanders, awaken the romance of the past.

**MEDICAL**

Set your pulse racing with dedicated, delectable doctors in the high-pressure world of medicine, where emotions run high and passion, comfort and love are the best medicine.

**True Love**

Celebrate true love with tender stories of heartfelt romance, from the rush of falling in love to the joy a new baby can bring, and a focus on the emotional heart of a relationship.

**Desire**

Indulge in secrets and scandal, intense drama and plenty of sizzling hot action with powerful and passionate heroes who have it all: wealth, status, good looks…everything but the right woman.

**HEROES**

Experience all the excitement of a gripping thriller, with an intense romance at its heart. Resourceful, true-to-life women and strong, fearless men face danger and desire - a killer combination!

To see which titles are coming soon, please visit
**millsandboon.co.uk/nextmonth**

# JOIN US ON SOCIAL MEDIA!

Stay up to date with our latest releases, author
news and gossip, special offers and discounts, and
all the behind-the-scenes action
from Mills & Boon...

 millsandboon

 millsandboonuk

 millsandboon

*It might just be true love...*